Also by the same author:

SF
Worlds Beyond Ours
The Wizard of Kálar

Historical
Murder in Hattusas
Madduwatta's Rebellion
Mittani Kidnapping

Humans were spreading, as they once did on earth, into every niche that would sustain them. There were human colonists on the rim of the Milky Way looking longingly across the empty chasm of intergalactic space at our neighbouring galaxies, hoping a way would be found to bridge the chasm. The way to the next galaxy was through a stabilised wormhole. Yet this last piece of the technological puzzle was being sabotaged.

Out there, an entity was undermining humanity's one way of reaching the other galaxies. The scientists were on the verge of succeeding in stabilising the wormhole yet all the information on wormholes was under threat. Any enterprise trying to stabilise wormholes was being attacked. The culprits had to be found. Humanities interstellar dream demanded it.

The Praut Investigation Agency is hired to uncover the guilty party. This begins a chain of events leading to murder, war, and mayhem. The reader is taken across the galaxy, following Praut's ingenious sniffers, to various planets in pursuit of the culprits.

On one occasion, they follow a sniffer to a bizarre hippy planet, yet on another planet, they are rescued by Sámi reindeer herders from a crash landing in the tundra. Praut and his people are forced to suffer hardships, trek through snow, fight their way through numerous adventures. All in a search of the mysterious guilty perpetrator who is out to destroy the technology with which humankind hopes to reach out into the universe.

The final outcome shocks Praut and his companions, and threatens the very existence of humanity for some time to come.

# GALACTIC SNIFFERS

**Sasha Garrydeb**

**Science Fiction**

**London**
**2013**

Published in Britain in 2013
by ABC Publishers
24 Treadgold Street London W11 4BP

e-mail: abcpublishers@ntlworld.com



A CIP catalogue record for this book is available from the British Library.

ISBN 978-0954814496

Printed by
ABC Publishers,
Notting Dale,
London W11 4BP.

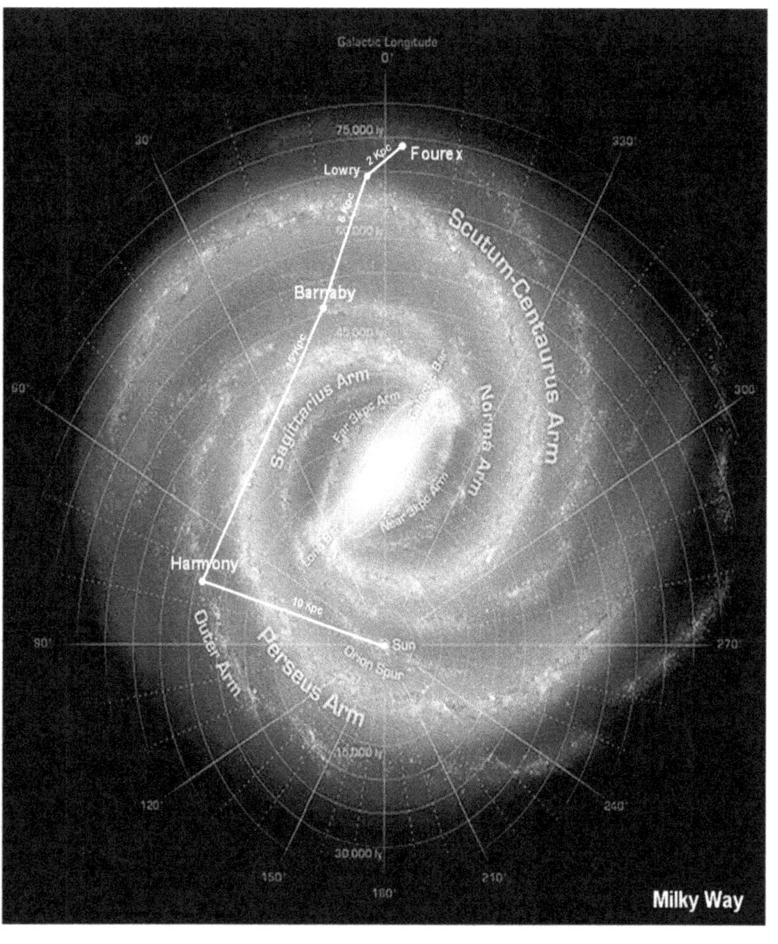

Galactic Longitude
0°
30°
330°
60°
300°
90°
270°
120°
240°
150°
210°
180°
75,000 ly
30,000 ly
Fourex
Lowry
2 Kpc
6 Kpc
Barnaby
15 Kpc
Harmony
10 Kpc
Sun
Scutum-Centaurus Arm
Sagittarius Arm
Norma Arm
Perseus Arm
Outer Arm
Orion Spur
Far 3kpc Arm
Near 3kpc Arm
Milky Way

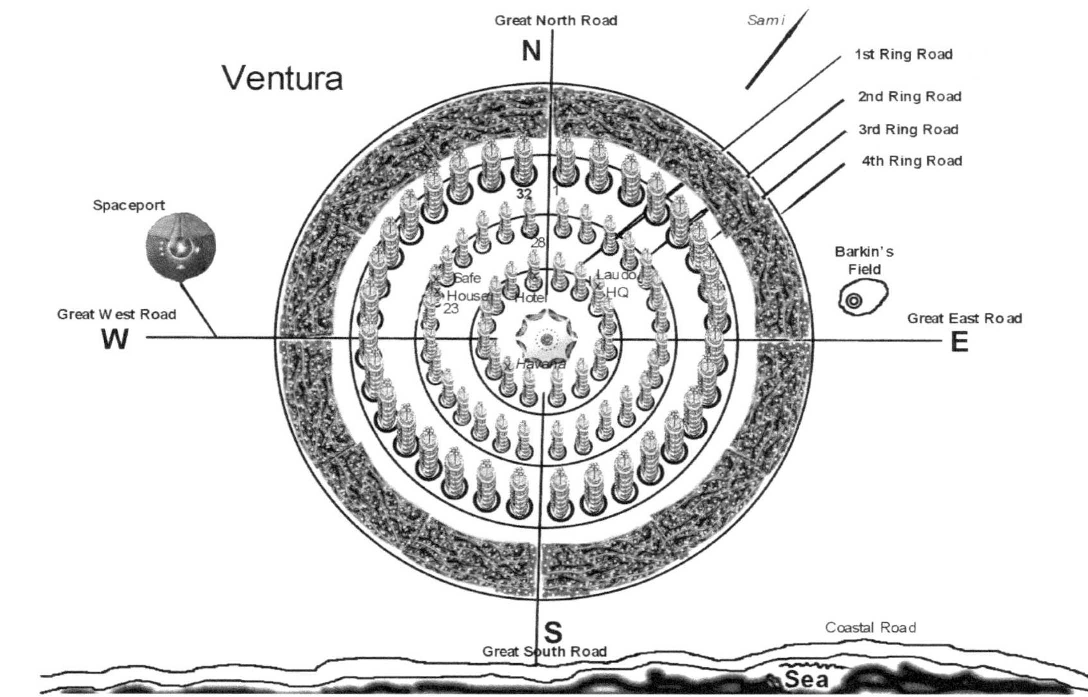
Ventura
Great North Road
N
Sami
1st Ring Road
2nd Ring Road
3rd Ring Road
4th Ring Road
Spaceport
32
1
28
Safe House
23
Hotel
HQ
Havana
Barkin's Field
Great West Road
W
Great East Road
E
S
Great South Road
Coastal Road
Sea

# 1
# THE VISITOR

Reclining in his birthday suit on his hover-loafer, squinting at the midday sun through piercing blue eyes, Praut felt his skin baking beyond wellbeing. His left hand searched for the control panel to turn the sun's penetration down a couple of notches to a more comfortable level. In the corner of his vision, he watched the underbelly of his gondola lightly kissing the water as the airship bobbed gently in the southerly breeze.

The South Seas holo-deck image was carefully constructed. The sea was calmly lapping at the underbody of the oversized airship and his auto chef was laying out his favourite meal in the gondola diner. His stomach rumbled in anticipation.

'*Sir*, you have a visitor,' declared a rift in the sky.

'You're kidding? Are you *sure*?' Praut asked his auto-sec in irritation.

'In person, in the reception area. The Chief Con-Exec of Darhlburg sir. Insists on a face-to-face.'

'Damn! Face-to-face, eh? Must be something serious. Suppose I'd better see him. Get me everything you've got on Darhlburg Industries, put it in a meme-cap. I'll interface with it while the holo-controls switch over.'

The meme-capsule materialised in his hand. The loafer vanished, as did the sun, sea, and airship. The drab black and yellow holo-grid replaced the idyllic scene and Praut stood fiddling with the meme-capsule trying to pop it into the neuro-pad. It should have slid in with a satisfying click, but for some reason he was having trouble integrating it. It finally clicked in, and he held the neuro-pad to the back of his brain against Wernicke's area at the left cerebral hemisphere. It fed his neurals with the info, making him an up-to-date expert on the Martian conglomerate.

The building's holo-grid q-computer reshaped the grid so his normal office reappeared, and he parked himself at his desk in his contour-seat, his powerfully built body now fully dressed.

'Van Rag Yang,' announced his auto-sec. 'Chief Con-Exec of Darhlburg sir.'

An oversized male appeared through the wall, walking confidently on a gravity support girdle, hand outstretched. A door after-imaged into the wall as he stepped into the middle of the room, eyes fleeting around, looking for Praut. Mars tall and muscular, with an aura of power preceding him, Rag Yang looked like a man with problems. Blonde hair and piercing blue eyes sat uncomfortably on a furrowed brow, merging incongruously within dark skin.

*More genetic fiddling*, thought Praut. 'Welcome to the agency, Herr Rag Yang.' Praut shook the outstretched hand. 'Do have a seat.' Praut waved his hand at a contour-couch. 'Are you comfortable in this gravity?' Praut was looking at the slim-line gravity girdle, essential for this Martian from a lower gravity planet.

Rag Yang ignored the last question. 'Herr Dilmore Praut?' He faced Praut with his piercing eyes.

'Yes, that's me. What can I do for the Chief Exec of Darhlburg Industries? What's so important it required a face-to-face?'

'Is the place clean?' asked Rag Yang, searching around for nanomorphs, as if he could see the tiny objects.

'Swept every hour on the hour. Not a bug in the place. You can talk freely.'

‘I’m parked in orbit, Station 5; came down here by space elevator. I…we…have a problem. You’ve been recommended to me by Liddlebock. Speaks highly of you. Says you have the most advanced sniffers anywhere.’ Rag Yang finally sat himself down on the contour couch, the gravity girdle almost imperceptible.

‘Ah yes, the sniffers. Specially designed for me by… well, you don’t need to know, do you?’

‘No, suppose not. Anyway, Liddlebock gave me your address: Europa Trade Centre, Floor 999. Look here, I can spare you an hour, then I must get back to Mars. So, in a nutshell; we’ve been robbed. I have my firm’s security chasing whoever did this, but we’re getting nowhere. I’m at my wit’s end. I’ve got to get the data-cube back or we’re sunk. Don’t even know how they got the plans. I understood those quantum computers were theft proof.’

‘Where there’s a will, there’s a way,’ spouted Praut smoothly. ‘What plans are these?’

‘We’re working on new wormhole technology. All hush-hush. Three times the range and far more stable. We’ve got a large lab half way up Olympus Mountain. We thought that mountain would be a good barrier…seems not. We’ve got a force-field round the lab, we’ve got anti-cloak scanners, DNA locks on all input and output to the q-computers…still they’ve bypassed them. Worse, they’ve erased the plans from the system.’

‘You must have a backup, surely,’ Praut smiled at such a simple quandary.

‘They got at the backup as well. Whoever did this was thorough. They used a grabworm.’

Praut asked the obvious question, ‘Do you know who did it?’

‘The person, who’s supposed to have done it, was on his hover-boat on the Hellas Sea in the Southern Hemisphere at the time, half way round the other side of Mars. Everything points to him; yet he’s got a solid alibi.

We've used drugs *and* neural scanners, but we can't break the alibi. My security people have ruled him out. The plans have been downloaded onto a data-cube *and erased* from our system, and the booster is missing.'

'Booster? What booster?'

'It's a mock-up prototype booster which increases the wormhole range. We had that in an underground facility… two kilometres deep. The booster slots into the Monk-ranger and is controlled by the Glaffy gyrator…' Rang Yang broke off, seeing the glaze appear on Praut's face.

Praut came awake again when he heard the Con-Exec stop talking. 'Your people check for nanobots, nanomorphs, and teleports?'

'A teleport needs computing power, and they always leave a trace. No sign of any trace. No trace of any nanobots or nanomorphs either. We've swept the place from top to bottom. The problem is, we can't figure out how it's been done. We know where the info was accessed, but not by whom.'

'If they've got the plans, why bother with the prototype. They could've simply replicated it, or 3D printed the booster from the plans when they got home...wherever that is.'

'That's another puzzle…worse than Boolos. Again, my people have drawn a blank…which is why I'm sitting here. I thought it best not to advertise we've lost the plans. That's why we didn't use the normal com-lines with you. Had to be face-to-face. This leaks out, and the firm's stock will crash. We'll be ruined. Everything I've told you is in the strictest confidence.'

'You have my word.' It wasn't in Praut's interests to advertise his clients secrets.

Rag Yang didn't look convinced.

'Mein liebe Herr, the Praut Agency motto is *Galactic sniffers to the well heeled,* and we'd hardly survive if we leaked our clients business problems, would we?'

Rag Yang shrugged his large frame as if he was still in pain, his dark face winced. He'd been forced to bring this problem to *this* Agency…forced by the Board. He'd been threatened with the sack. Him, the head of the founding dynasty of the company. If the plans were not retrieved, and the thief dealt with…the whole conglomerate would go under.

Darhlburg Industries was the biggest employer on Mars…hell, it *was* Mars. The financial survival of Mars was at stake. It had taken four hundred years to terraform Mars, and throughout that time, Darhlburg had been the lead contractor. Now…?

'Sir, Fanny's here to see you,' intoned the auto-sec.

'Send her in,' commanded Praut.

Rag Yang looked alarmed. 'Who's this Fanny?'

'Relax, she's a colleague of mine. Fanny Fester, she works with me. One of my best agents. If I take this on, you'll be liaising with her.'

Fanny appeared through the door, 'Hi Dil, what's up?'

'Hi! Let me introduce you to Herr Van Rag Yang, Chief Con-Exec of Darhlburg Industries.' Praut pointed his palm at the seated Martian. 'He's brought us a problem… needs our help. As usual, you're going to act as our go-between.'

Fanny nodded at the Chief Exec, and he nodded back at her, while having an unashamed ogle at her physique. Fanny was what people called, *a looker*. She was well built and dressed with style. Tall, slim, red haired with ice-cold green eyes. She was used to these looks and didn't mind them. Fanny could take care of herself. She parked herself in another contour chair opposite the Martian Con-Exec.

'Herr Rag Yang was telling me,' continued Praut, 'he's lost some valuable info from his system back on Mars. He wants us to find it. I want you, Olga and Claymore, to go to Mars with Herr Rag Yang.' Praut turned to Rag Yang and said, ‘You don’t mind taking three of my people back with you, do you?’

‘If I must. They’ll have to be ready to go in half an hour…I can’t wait any longer.’ Rag Yang looked uncomfortable, but had been given little choice.

‘They’ll be ready. Fanny, make sure Olga takes the sniffers, and get Claymore to find out how the system failed. It has to be something to do with the DNA access. Then report back to me as usual. That’s it. Good luck.’

‘Is that it?’ asked Rag Yang.

‘That’s it. You’ve just hired the Praut Agency. I’ll give you our standard contract to sign right now, and we’re done.’ Praut had his auto-sec pop a cube on the desk. ‘Stick you e-sig on that and then it’s legal.’

Rag Yang climbed from the contour-couch and came to the desk. He used his e-sig-ring and pocketed the cube. The cube e-zipped the e-signature into Praut’s system as his copy.

‘As an initial payment, two million credits have been transferred to your account with my sig-ring. I hope your Agency is worth it Herr Praut,’ griped Rag Yang.

‘At the end of a case, most clients would double their payments if I allowed it,’ Praut threw back at him.

‘Herr Praut, this matter is *urgent*, I mean you know that.’ This Con-Exec really didn’t want to be here…asking for help.

‘Yes Mein liebe Herr, I’m aware of the urgency. I mean you’re here on a face-to-face; it speaks for itself. Don’t worry, I’ll keep you posted. One last question…you must have a suspect? Someone who wants your technology, or wants to destroy your company. Who is it?’

‘That’s our main problem…we don’t have a rival… Then he cut off mid-sentence. There’s someone doing something similar, but we’re *not* rivals. Everybody’s concentrating on warpdrive. The wormhole technology was fabricated last century and hasn’t moved forward since then.

The big breakthrough is, we've stabilised the hole. We're the only ones toying with it…apart from this other lot. We're not a threat to anyone. The warp people laugh at us. They think we're nuts for messing about with this. Our breakthrough has been kept quiet.'

'Not quiet enough, obviously.'

Rag Yang scowled. 'Obviously.'

'So who's this *other lot*?' Praut insisted.

'Singularity Inc.,' Rag Yang said almost inaudibly.

'Who?' Praut had to ask again.

'*Singularity Inc.*' Yang said loudly. 'They're on Callisto…but we're not in competition, I promise you.'

'Then whoever bust your system, must be someone either working on warp…or someone who you're putting in danger by stabilising the wormhole. Someone out of range of Central Government as of now. Someone who doesn't want to be scrutinised too closely by the bureaucrats. Anyone spring to mind?'

'So it's someone close-by, or someone on the other side of the galaxy, is that what you're saying? I can't think of anyone. I've turned this over and over in my mind…and come up with zilch. So have my security people. Which is where you come in.' Rang Yang looked uncomfortable again as he said the last.

'Oh well, we'll get to the bottom of this. You have my word. Have a nice trip. *Au revoir*!' Praut frowned at his client's dilemma. *Apparently, he's about to be sick. Doesn't want to be here...pushed into coming, eh? I can name a few members of the Board who did the pushing. Well, he'll thank us when we're through. I'll make sure of that.*

Rag Yang straightened up and walked haughtily through the door without looking back, followed by Fanny.

Two people were waiting for them in the reception area. The Agency had a vast holo reception area for its client's visual enchantment, containing a small lake in the middle, with water fowl swimming around. Olga Oblomov's dark eyes matched her short dark hair, both parked on a medium build body, which was decorated by a silicone-nanofilament-cherry-red one-piece. She waited with Claymore Snout, brown hair, hazel eyes, small build covered by a blue jump-suit. Both waved at Fanny from the side of the lake. Spotting them, Fanny motioned them to follow. A c-fibre luggage box hovered behind in the duo's wake.

'There's a teleport interface over there,' Fanny told Rag Yang, pointing to the left.

'Don't use them,' he retorted dismissively. 'Don't trust them. We'll take the shuttle to the Space Elevator and ride it to my ship.' The decision wasn't up for discussion.

Fanny looked at Olga, who smiled at the foible. Claymore kept stum. None of his business.

'Could take the shuttle all the way to your ship,' Fanny switched tack.

'I don't get to come to earth too often. The elevator ride gives a great view, don't you think. Earth is so cool… blue…soothing. Be patient, we'll get there soon enough.' Rag Yang was opening up.

Fanny needed to establish a working relationship with this huge man, which is why she was probing him. She needed to get him to talk to her as a collaborator; not just in monosyllables. 'But Mars looks just like another earth, now you've terraformed it all,' Fanny reminded him as they walked through the lobby.

'With one difference,' he swept his hand at the building's reinforced glass-composite. 'This is humanity's home. No matter how far we spread through the galaxy, there's only one home.'

The four reached the shuttle gate. A few moments later, the barrier opened and they boarded the shuttle. The shuttle left the almost four kilometre skyscraper and wended its way towards Ecuador on the equator, where the Space Elevator was rooted earthside. Rag Yang looked wistfully out of the shuttle window at the Atlantic Ocean spread far below.

The shuttle docked at Level 100, twenty kilometres up. The air-lock vestibule was empty but the duel-disk elevator arrived a short while later and the gates *hissed* open. They all stepped into Gondola 2 and the doors *whooshed* closed.

The breathtaking scene outside was projected onto the walls around them as they were seamlessly propelled by laser beams up the graphene ribbons into space at 200 kph. The sky changed from deep blue to black, as the shielded elevator sped through the torus plasma of the Van Allen radiation belts. Then abruptly, a new holo image appeared near Rang Yang.

'Good day Councillor Rang Yang,' said a smooth ingratiating voice from the new holo-image hanging near him. 'We on the Luna Council would like to invite you…'

'*Off*,' shouted Rang Yang to the image, '*off*,' he repeated.

'…to visit the Moon for trade negotiations…'

'***Off***,' screamed Rang Yang, '***off***.'

The holo-image hesitated, then put a notice up, 'If you would prefer a different Ad, please scroll through to your favoured Ad.'

'*Off, you stupid machine*,' shouted Rang Yang, getting really angry.

Fanny said to Olga, 'There's a ad-nanomorph in the gondola. Find it and squash it.'

Olga retrieved a terahertz scanner from her waist-belt pouch, and began sweeping the gondola from floor to ceiling. She located the ad-nanomorph disguised as a light in the centre of the ceiling. She unholstered her zapper and kilojouled it. The morphing light fell limply to the floor. Rang Yang quickly stamped on it with determined venom, although by then it had morphed again and was too small to see. The holo-image vanished into a dot, leaving a tiny afterglow.

'Damned thing latched onto my DNA,' lamented Rang Yang. 'Bloody things ought to be outlawed. We don't allow them on Mars.'

'In that case I might move to Mars permanently,' quipped Olga smiling at the Con-Exec.

Rang Yang smiled back, down into her dark eyes and said, 'Thanks for zapping it.'

'My pleasure, I assure you.' Olga especially hated the holo-ads.

The space elevator arrived at geostationary transfer Base Station 5, parked at 35,786 km GSO, sixty thousand kilometres below counterweight Spaceport Alpha at its pinnacle.

Offloading into the terminal, the little group waited for their leader to summon his transport.

'Bring the ship down, we're leaving,' commanded Rang Yang into his throat mike, still a little nonplussed at being ambushed by the holo-ad.

Station 5 had a number of space ships parked around its perimeter, waiting for their owner occupants to arrive or depart. The Darhlburg Mars Cruiser docked at port seven, and the group of four boarded. Auto-customs scanners checked their implants, clearing them to leave earth's geostationary orbit.

People strapped in, while the navcomp plotted a route to Mars, then the impulse engines kicked in to near light speed following the Type 1 conjunction transfer orbit, after they cleared Station 5. It took thirty-five minutes to cover the fifty million kilometres at three quarters impulse, or a hundred million kph. They were in near Mars orbit before they could settle in properly. No time for chitchat or any other getting-to-know-you stuff. They'd docked at the Martian equivalent of the Space Elevator, areosynchronous orbit (ASO) at an elevation of 16,600 km above the planet.

Rag Yang gave a sigh of relief as he discarded his gravity girdle. 'Good to be home.'

Fanny stretched languidly, Claymore yawned and scratched his stomach, and Olga was busy at the back with the c-fibre luggage box. She didn't want anyone tampering with her sniffers.

'This high up, doesn't the elevator tether hit Phobos or Deimos?' Fanny asked Rag Yang, trying to get a conversation going.

'No my dear. The tether's over ten degrees above the equator. The moons never go that far north; they don't travel much away from the equator. All been worked out.' Then he raised his voice so both his earth companion could hear, 'Be careful, the gravity here is one-third of Earth's and you both need to readjust your walking style.'

*Condescending bastard*, thought Fanny. *Who's he calling a dear*. 'Oh!' she said aloud. She had a dig at his phobia, 'Shuttle again?'

Rag Yang nodded, not looking at her.

They took the elevator down to Level 7 above Tharsis Dome where the space elevator was tethered. The base station was thirteen degrees above the equator for the tether to avoid both Martian moons.

'Damn, look at the size of that mountain,' exclaimed Olga, as they were descending the graphene ribbon. She was indicating west at the biggest mountain in the solar system. She was having a bit of trouble with her balance.

'That's one big rock,' agreed Claymore, hanging on to the rail.

'It's where we're heading,' Rang Yang interrupted. 'Our Olympus Mountain lab faces west so you can't see it from here…it's half way up the mountain.'

'How high up is the lab?' asked Fanny.

'The mountain's twenty six klicks high; the lab's at fifteen klicks,' Rang Yang informed her.

'I never realised how much of the planet was water,' Olga commented.

'Up to the north there, you can see the Borealis Ocean. To the north-east there's the Gulf of Chryse which feeds into the Mariner Valley. The valley floor is flooded to a depth of two kilometres. It's been a massive piece of work liberating the water from the regolith, but well worth it when I look at the results.'

From Level 7, they transferred to a shuttle for the ride to the Olympus Mountain lab.

'To the left, just below the clouds, is Ascraeus Mountain, one of the three Tharsis shield volcanoes,' explained Rang Yang, feeling more relaxed now he was on home turf. 'Olympus Mountain is another shield volcano, just in case you didn't know. The volcano's been thrown up by lava flows. It's an accretion of broad sheets of lava, built up and spread-out over each eruption. At its base, Olympus Mountain spreads six hundred klicks.'

'How interesting,' sucked up Olga impishly.

'Fancy that!' added Claymore. 'Ye live and learn, hey?'

The sarcasm seemed to go right over Rang Yang's head. He took himself far too seriously to notice such witticisms.

'Over there is the city of Perungrad, the one with the tall skyscrapers,' enthused Rang Yang further.

'Beautiful…with that nice bridge running over the nearby river?' asked Clay trying to get in on the game.

'Yes, that's the one. It's got a population of three million,' Rang Yang continued, oblivious of their wit. 'Just over to the other side of those mountains is the bigger city of Huosingjing.'

Fanny gave them a sharp glance, telling them to behave.

Olga winked at Fanny, and Claymore sniggered into his hand. Fanny thought, and not for the first time, computer whiz-kids were still in their nappies when it came to humour.

'I seem to have lost weight,' Olga announced proudly.

'Nah, that's the grav,' Claymore earnestly reminded her.

To distract Rag Yang, Fanny asked, 'Is the volcano still active?'

'Last time it blew was two million years ago, but geologically it's deemed active. Don't worry, we'll let you know if it's about to blow,' Rag Yang smiled condescendingly at her.'

Fanny ignored the patronising gumpf and gave him her best alluring smile. She needed to get him to talk.

That encouraged the Con-Exec. 'Our biggest problem when we started, was shielding Mars from the GCRs. Mars has a weak magnetic field, so the GCRs could be a problem for any life out in the open here if we didn't deal with them. No use starting to terraform if we couldn't shield the planet from cosmic radiation.'

Olga was listening in. 'GCRs?' she asked innocently, winking slyly at Fanny. She saw what Fanny was up to. It wasn't the first time a client was crusty with them and the two had banded together to loosen the client up.

'Galactic cosmic rays composed mainly of high-energy protons and atomic nuclei, originating primarily from supernovae,' Rag Yang told her, 'called GCRs for short.'

'And your solution?' asked Olga, grinning widely.

'Deploying active radiation shields in GSO round Mars. They've protected our colonists from GCRs for four hundred years, although now we have a protective atmosphere, there's almost no need for artificial shielding. Still, there's sixty satellites round the planet with twenty acting as reserves. Before the satellites, when we began, we built our habitats in lava tubes, but otherwise we used inflatable igloo structures covered with sintered regolith bricks. Initially, that was our protection from solar and GCR radiation. Nowadays, you can still see some of the abandoned igloo structures.'

*Well done Olga. Between the two of us, we've got him talking.* And then Fanny took over, 'What's it like at the top?'

'You mean Olympus Mons? Well, if you were actually standing on the top of Olympus, you'd be able to see the other side of the caldera which stretches 80 klicks across, and drops 3 klicks onto the crater floor. Now there's drama for you.'

'I wouldn't mind going up there if there's time.' Ingratiating herself was hard work. She turned to Claymore. 'You ready to go to work?' Fanny asked Claymore, trying to get him to behave seriously.

'Always,' muttered Claymore drolly. Their quantum-computer expert was worth his own weight in platinum, but needed supervising in polite company.

The shuttle swung back around Olympus Mons and came to a rest on the roof of a building jutting out of a six kilometre high cliff.

# 2
# GRABWORMS

The Praut Agency occupied the whole of the 999th floor of the 3.8 kilometres high Europa Trade Centre. All of the Agency's space was controlled by the buildings q-machine; three tenth was the holo-deck reception area, one half the holo-deck offices, two tenth was Praut's private holo-deck living quarters-come-recreation area where he swam and loafed about.

After sending his team off with his new client, Praut needed to find a little thinking time. Time to mull over all the implications of the new contract he'd taken on. Time to make discreet enquiries about this wormhole technology, and especially time to finish his midday meal, even though it was well past midday.

Praut returned to his private quarters and reloaded his loafer-airship holo, and lay in the sun, scratching his head, *strange business, this. There's been so many accidents with this wormhole stuff, why would anybody want to steal it? We're making lots of headway with Warp, why waste time with this wormhole guff? Must be a reason!*

Finally, the auto-chef on the holo-airship proclaimed his meal was ready. His loafer floated over and settled in the stern of the airship gondola. The table was laid, and the sea bass with fennel melted in the mouth. He tasted lemon, basil, and olives…until a ping announced a com's arrival. The holo-message hung in the air above his eyes. Fanny's party had arrived safe and sound on Mars. The atmosphere in the Darhlburg lab was *pregnant with expectation*, she said.

*Fanny and her phantom pregnancies*, scoffed Praut. He knew Fanny wanted to get pregnant, but in an age of population control and strict lab births, it was unlikely. She kept using the word every chance she got.

These days people lived until two hundred, but it was at a price. All births were strictly controlled by licence. There hadn't been a natural pregnancy on earth for the last two hundred years. The population was stable and only increased according deaths. Off planet, it was different. There, the usual population chaos was the norm. On earth, everything was done in the lab. Inception, bringing to term, and finally birth. Infants were stimulated in lab conditions until the age of three and then handed to the nurseries. Man made nature and nurture combined to produce the best possible results via a lab.

Praut wanted to know, *why the hell any woman on this earth would want to get pregnant, old-style?* Contact sex was now merely recreational.

'Alert!' squalled his auto-sec. 'Com-line under attack.'

'Full firewall!' commanded Praut. 'Emergency lockdown and trace.' Praut gave the crisis password for the holo-deck to close. 'What is it?' he asked the auto-sec.

'A grabworm sir,' replied the automaton. 'It's trawling for coms. When the anti-viral trace locked on, it self destructed.'

'Any signatures?'

'All went down too fast sir.'

*Well, there's my answer.* Praut scratched his cropped hair. *Someone* is *trying to find out what went on with Rang Yang and me.* 'Get Edel in here,' he ordered the auto-sec. The holo-office reappeared, and so did Praut's clothing.

Gangly Edel Vartaplug, Praut's tech expert, rolled in a few minutes later. 'You wanted to see me Dil?'

'Yeah, listen Ed, we've just had a grabworm trying to trawl my com-messages. See if anything's left of it. Need to find out who's trying to bug me.'

'I'll do it from a dock outside. Let you know if I find anything.' Edel left with a wave of the hand and a toss of his dark hair.

'Bring the Agency to full alert,' Praut told the auto-sec. 'Send a warning to Fanny to be careful. Take the usual in-house countermeasures. Oh, and I'm calling an Agency conference for half an hour. Make sure everyone's notified.'

'Sir, Helmut and his team are still working on the Nafto Conspiracy, and Mykola and his team are busy chasing up the Dour-Chick Scam. Do you want them here?'

'No, let them finish. Anybody free—get them here.'

Ho Fu Liwei was the first to arrive. Harry to his friends, expert with a long range guided laser rifle, and nano-missile control. Dealt with all the Agency's nanomorphs. Harry was followed by Tilmore Krout. Close quarter combat and lock-picker extraordinaire. He had enhanced power implants in his muscles. A few minutes later, in came Meserine Monat—Praut's personal pilot and navigator. When needed, she ran the Agency's taxi service. Finally, Edel Vartaplug reappeared, shaking his dark head, looking perplexed. He was supposed to be a genius with any kind of machine, electronic or mechanical. Tech expert, and space mechanic fixer par excellence.

They draped themselves in the contour chairs, pouring and sipping drinks from the table.

'So Ed, what's the verdict?'

Still puzzled, Edel raised his dark eyebrows, 'Never seen anything like it. Completely new to me. Vanished without any debris. New tech, this thing. Nothing I've ever come across before. Even the logs are phased.'

'That right?' Praut didn't like the sound of that. 'So we've got zilch to go on?'

'Sorry guv. Did my best.'

'Don't let it worry you. I'm sure you did.' Praut heard the phrase, *new technology*. That meant there was a big player in the game. It could get nasty. Praut stood up. 'Right folks, why I called this meet.' Praut looked around at his people. They were a good bunch. 'We've just been handed a new job. Darhlburg of Mars. They've had an item stolen, and they want it back…real bad. Fanny, Olga and Claymore already gone there for a recky...do a prelim. I should hear from them tomorrow. You're all here because you're free. Nod if that's still the case.'

The four people round the table all nodded.

'Good. Now I'll let you in on my gut feeling about this one. I don't like it. Something tells me it's bigger than it seems. Ostensibly, it's a missing blueprint purloined from the Darhlburg system, but whoever did this, wiped the backup. Then there's the item. It's wormhole technology. I want all of you to have a think. Why would anybody steal wormhole technology? Seems nuts to me. Ed, you're the tech expert. Concentrate on finding out who would want to steal wormhole technology. Meserine, you're the pilot… have a dig around the warp scene. Find out where they're at…who's in front. Let me know how wormhole compares to warp. Tilmore, I want you to try to find out who's snooping us. Start with the grabworms. Liaise with Claymore; get him to write a grabworm grabber. See if you can chase the buggers back to their hole-in-the-ground. Have a word with Ed about our recent visitor. Harry, you check who's on the other side of the galaxy. I want a list of the big players out on the rim. Something tells me there's a connection. Right! Off you go. Report back as soon as you find anything. Keep me in the loop.'

To his auto-sec he said, 'I want you to take control of the other two jobs you mentioned. You have *my* authority. Only bother me in an emergency. Now, get me Lalepeth in Canberra. Use the secure comm.' After a few moments of nothing, a face came into focus half a meter in front of him. 'Hi Sam, how you doing?'

'Dil, what's up?'

'Can't a guy call his old buddy without something being up?'

'Don't give me that, mate. I know you. You only call when you want something.'

Praut smiled awkwardly. 'Give us a break. But since your going down that road…have you heard anything unusual from those techy labs in the outback?'

'Like what?'

'Warp drive, wormhole…anything like that?'

'There's a number of people testing new warp systems. Largest one is Boomer Industries. That what you mean?'

'What about wormhole stuff?'

'Very droll…you want to be squelched, be my guest. Wormhole? What's got into you? You know the stuff's no good. Warp is the future.'

'Yeah, so I'm told. Right, thanks. If you come over here, don't be a stranger.'

'You still in Frankfurt?'

'Sam you old rogue, I know you've got the address hanging in front of you. If you hear of anything funny going on with wormholes, let me know. Give my love to Lydia.'

The connection snapped shut.

*So the Aussies are playing dumb.*

'Get me Emanuel Alverado, in Estados Unidos,' he told the auto-sec.

'¡Hola Manny!' Praut said to the holo image of his American counterpart. '¿Cómo están las cosas?'

'Todo está bien, Dil. ¿Qué quieres?'

'Mind if we switch?'

'Be my guest.'

'I've got a job involving wormholes. Heard anything new on them?'

'Wormholes? That the garden variety?'

'Very goofy. You know the type I mean.'

'What you looking for?'

'Anything…'

'Bolguard, the people who invented the stuff, had a major fire in their facility on Pluto. That the type of stuff you mean?'

'That's *exactly* what I mean. Can you gemail me anything you've got on it. How are the kids? How's Washington?'

'Washington? Never heard of it.'

'Okay, I mean BolivarMet.'

'Now I recognise it. Run down as usual. Snowing hard. How's your pile in the sky? Still with the sauerkraut?'

'Yeah, same as usual. Look me up when you get over here. I'll force-feed you some.'

The connection snapped off.

'Put me through to Boris Nemtsov in Moscow,' Praut ordered his auto-sec.

A thick set face of Praut's counterpart in Moscow appeared in mid-air before him. Praut switched to Russian, «Pryvet Boris, kak dela? Kak Natasha? Dayte ey moyu lubov.»

«Nu ty znaesh, nekotorye dela horosh, nekotorye plokha. Natasha prykrasna. V chem delo?» Boris' face set into a query.

«Mozhem ly my menyt?» suggested Praut.

'Okay, same question...what's up?'

'I've got a job on wormholes. You heard anything unusual regarding them?'

'Like what?'

'Like anything.'

'There seems to be a lot of activity on the gq-net involving wormhole deletions. That what you mean?'

'Deletions, heh? Yeah that's what I mean. Anything else?'

'Not at the moment.'

'Thanks Boris. See you soon. Do svydanye.'

*So much for Moscow. Deletions...now what's going on?*

'Harry, where are you?' Praut snapped in his throat mike.

'Checking on who's who in the rim, like you asked me to, boss.'

'Drop that for a moment and get in touch with your pals in Peking. Find out if they've heard any talk about wormholes…anything at all.'

'Yes boss. Let you know soon.'

To his auto-sec, 'Do a gq-net search on wormholes. Put it in a meme-cap.'

'Yes sir.'

Bleep from his comm-sys. 'Yeah?'

'¡Hola Dil! Just thought I'd let you know,' it was Emmanuel Alverado in BolivarMet. 'An e-circular came round just now, not a moment after we talked. Someone's been deleting all info on wormholes on the galactic-quantum-net. There's a number of viruses trawling the gq-net and erasing anything they can find on the wormhole. We've been warned to keep our firewalls up…not to download anything until the techs get to the bottom of this.'

'Hey Manny, gracias. Told you something fishy's going on. Is this only earth-side, or space-side as well?'

'As far as I can tell, it's going through the whole Solar System...server to server.'

'In which case, it's doing the galaxy as well. This is definitely serious. Hear anymore, get back to me pronto? Hasta luego.'

'Yeah, sure. Hasta luego.'

*Now it's definitely getting creepy,* went Praut's mind. *Who's behind this? What the hell's going on? Why pick on a duff technology? All I've got is bloody questions and no answers.*

'Where's that meme-cap on the wormhole stuff I asked for?' demanded Praut of the auto-sec.

A meme-capsule materialised on his desk. Praut inserted it into the neuro-pad but didn't interface with it.

'How big is this?'

'Sixty terabytes sir.'

'Yeah, thought so.' He took it out of the neuro-pad. 'Put it in my e-pad but disconnect the pad from the gq-net. I want it standalone.'

'Yes sir.'

'Put an alarm tag on my e-pad. Anyone going near it without my explicit permission gets stunned. Is that clear?'

'Yes sir.'

*That's what I like with these machines, they never argue back no matter how hard you push them.*

'Dil, this is Harry. You there?'

'Yeah, go ahead.'

'My contacts in Peking report nothing unusual earth-side, apart from the wholesale erasure of wormhole info from the gq-net. However, a small outfit on Callisto was hit two days ago by a kind of self-seeking ultra-missile originating from outside our Solar System. Destroyed the lab. The outfit was doing work on the existing wormhole… trying to stabilise it. The weird missile was one smart cookie to navigate through the Oort Cloud and through Kuipers Belt intact. Must've travelled quite a distance.'

'How come no one's heard about it?'

'I asked the same question. They tell me it's all been hushed up. No idea why.'

'Any idea where the hushing came from?'

'Must be WorldGovSecurity on New Caledonia.'

'Thanks Harry. I'll look into it.'

*Two days ago, eh?* mused Praut. *I wonder if Sanjit would open up? He's got contacts in WGS. His brother works for them.*

‘Get me Sanjit Gupta in New Delhi,’ Praut ordered his auto-sec.

‘Yes sir.’

The image appeared half a meter in front of him. ‘Hi Sanj, how you doing?’

‘Namaste, Dil you old rascal, haven’t heard from you in a while. How’s Frankfurt treating you? Still got your head in the clouds?’

‘Still. Namaste. Been meaning to drop in when I’m in the neighbourhood. You know me, up to my eyes in sleuths. Your brother still with the WGS?’

‘You know, I was betting with myself that would come up. Yeah, he’s still there. What are you after?’

‘Ouch! Serves me right for neglecting you. Anyway, I’ve got a client who’s interested in wormholes. You know the stuff’s being deleted on the gq-net as we speak?’

‘Yeah, heard something like that. So?’

‘Well, I’ve just heard an outfit fiddling with wormholes on Callisto got hit. I’m reliably informed WGS is hushing it up. I’m interested as to why. Whatever happened to info freedom?’

‘Hmm! When was this?’

‘Two days ago.’

‘Let me have a snoop around. Get back to you ASAP.’

‘Thanks Sanj. I owe you one.’

‘I won’t forget.’

The connection closed.

*Why is it worth hushing up a missile strike? How come the media went along with this? More questions without answers.* Praut was getting annoyed. ‘Get a droid to do my neck, will you,’ he demanded of his auto-sec.

A droid in a white coat materialised. ‘Do your neck, sir?’

‘Go ahead. I need to relax and think straight.’

‘Yes sir.’

The droid's hands vibrated and massaged Praut's neck, starting gently on one side, rubbing the neck muscles down to the trapezium muscle, then switching to the other side. Going in deeply to work the muscles out from the centre of the neck and all along the shoulder and upper back.

'Ah! Yeah! That's it, keep going.'

Ping, and Sanjit's face appeared. 'Nama… What the Kali are you up to?' Sanjit inquired, seeing the contortions on Praut's face.

'That's enough!' he told the droid. 'No, Sanj, not you. I'm talking to the droid giving me a massage. Namaste Sanj. You got something for me?'

'Massage hey? Good idea, I'll have one myself when we've finished. Anyway, I had a chat with my brother and… this line secure?

'Yes, yes, it's secure.'

'He tells me they've got a problem with the peculiar missile. They've never seen the likes of it. Completely new tech. Full of exotic crystals no one's seen before. Until they sort it, they're keeping it under wraps.'

'That's the second time someone's thrown new tech at me,' Praut retorted. 'What are we talking of? What kind of new tech? What's with the crystals? What the hell's going on? Who's new tech?'

'Sure this line's good?' Sanjit repeated.

Praut's right eyebrow went up. 'Don't you believe me?'

Sanjit paused, then said, 'Alien…'

Praut sat back as if he'd been slapped. 'Are you… they…sure?'

'That's what my bro tells me. And for goodness sake don't spread this around. So far, we've not come across any aliens as we've spread through the galaxy…but now? Don't know what to think.'

'Well I'll be...' Praut sat shaking his head. 'Hang on...just had an idea. What if these aliens are using a wormhole...that might explain all this funny wormhole business?'

'Yeah, but why bother deleting it from the gq-net,' Sanjit asked. 'Another thing, why not just announce your own arrival. I mean, are they hostile?'

'If we *are* dealing with aliens, we don't have a paradigm to work from. Who knows what they want. So far they've not been too friendly.'

'You can say that again. Weird missiles and peculiar grabworms?'

'No Sanj, I'm not convinced. I'm going back to my original theory. I think an outfit on the rim has made a tech breakthrough and they're keeping quiet. I think all this stuff is human origin. But whatever it is, its something to do with wormholes.'

'You could be right. Anyhow, you owe me.'

'You're right, I do. Thanks, alavidha.'

'Alavidha.'

Connection closed.

# 3
# OFF PLANET

'*Dil, Dil, anybody home*?' Meserine's voice called out urgently from a holo-com. 'Time to get up and do some work,' her voice persisted.

'Will you quieten down,' Praut scolded her from across the room, cosseted in his silk bathrobe. 'Can't a man have a morning swim without you storming the Bastille all over again?'

'Sorry boss, I thought you were still asleep.'

'And if I was? Is that any reason to wake the dead?'

'I've got the report on the warp stuff you wanted. Do you want me to tell you, or leave it with the auto-sec?'

'As I'm standing here, you might as well tell me.'

'Here goes. I'll start with wormholes, since that's the shortest. Bolguard, the people who fabricated the wormhole in 2443, made a bit of a mess of it. Maybe cos it was last century's technology…they couldn't get the hole stabilised enough to be safe. Anyhow, they're okay as comm-gauge wormholes but anything solid going through the mouth tends to get squelched. The first-generation wormholes allowed transmission of information at faster-than-light speeds; they being the current comm-gauge wormholes. The second-generation enabled us to transmit and receive conventional data and create eavesdropping systems. The third-generations was the first to transmit tiny bits of matter, and the fourth-generations was to be the transporter. Only this fourth generation has turned into a disaster, known more affectionately as the squelcher. This is the one they're all trying to correct.

'Well, anyway, someone's set fire to Bolguard's Pluto lab a couple of weeks ago. The place is kaput. Then another lab on Callisto got hit two days ago. They were working on stabilising the existing wormhole...and they're also kaput. Nobody else knows anything about Darhlburg's efforts, but, as we both know, they've taken a hit. The wormhole has a great potential for travel to other galaxies, but unless it's stabilised, it's no good. If we could get wormholes working properly, together with warp, it would open up the whole of the universe for humanity to explore.'

'Great so far,' Praut encouraged her.

'Right. Well warp, that's another matter. It's development's in full flow. There's three main attacks on the problem. One, the drive we're using now, has always been especially promising. The current faster-than-light drive allows a spacecraft to travel at FTL by many orders of magnitude, circumventing the relativistic time dilation.' The pilot techy in Meserine was in full flow.

'Warp drive creates an artificial *bubble* of normal space-time which surrounds the spacecraft. Accordingly, spacecraft at warp can interact with objects in *normal space*. Warp 1 is equivalent to the speed of light, Warp 2 is 8 times, Warp 3 is 27 times, and so on. The propulsion method is the gravimetric field displacement manifold. It's a reactor which taps the energy released in a matter-antimatter annihilation. The reactor energy is then converted directly into huge quantities of electromagnetic radiation energy. Containing and *controlling* the annihilation reaction of matter and antimatter in a spaceship's warp core gives us our warp speeds. Humanity's been using this drive for the last two centuries. The developers, Boomer Industries, are based in the outback in Australia. They, and a number of others, are now tweaking the *controller* technology to increase the speed. Frankly, the driving force behind Boomer Industries is the Oort Mining Consortium, which is probably the largest conglomerate in the Solar System right now. They're the guys out mining the Oort Cloud asteroids, mixed in amongst the mass of comets, extending about 30 trillion kilometres out from the Sun. It's the Oort Mining Consortium that's demanding better warp drives so they can bring their minerals back to feed Earth's hungry foundries all the quicker from other systems.'

Praut asked, 'Aren't they the same people behind the Kuipers Belt Mining Consortium?'

'Yes, I think they are. What of it?'

'Nothing, its just that these outfits have far too much influence on Earth's economy for my liking. Too big for their own boots…and always trying to climb into other people's boots.'

'Dil, come now, humans need mineral resources now we're moving out into the galaxy. Someone's got to bring the stuff back here.'

'Okay, thanks. Is that it?' asked Praut.

'No. There's more on warp. Another type of warp drive's being worked on; the Krasnikov Tube, which is basically a modified Alcubierre drive.'

Praut interrupted again, 'Alcubierre drive? Never heard of it.'

'The Alcubierre drive is old twenty first century stuff, and it involves expanding the fabric of space *behind* a ship into a bubble and shrinking space-time in *front* of the ship. The ship would rest in between the expanding and shrinking space-time, essentially surfing down the other side of the bubble. When they came up with the theory, there wasn't the technology to put it into practice.'

'And have they made such a drive?'

'One lot claim they have…but haven't produced the evidence.'

'So let me see…the main contender is the gravimetric drive. Is that right?' Praut's eyes had narrowed.

‘Well, yes. Actually, it’s the only working drive. There’s a lot of hype going on about warp, but what they’re really doing is tweaking the existing drive, that’s all.’

Exasperated, Praut expelled, ‘So how does that effect the wormhole stuff?’

‘As far as I can see, it doesn’t.’

‘So then why are people stealing, destroying, and deleting wormhole stuff?’

‘You tell me.’

‘Great! We’re no further that we were yesterday.’ Praut was getting annoyed.

Meserine’s image shrugged her shoulders and lifted her eyebrows. As far as she was concerned, she’d done what she’d been asked to do; now it was Praut’s job to work it out.

‘Sorry Mes, you did good. I was simply hoping your info would throw a little light on our problem.’

‘While I was doing this report, I was thinking on why there’s this stuff going down on the wormhole,’ offered Meserine, ‘and what if it’s a Luddite thing. What if someone out there simply wants to destroy it because it’s a technology? What if they’ve got relatives who’ve been squelched and it’s a revenge thing?’

‘Revenge? Now I never even thought of that,’ Praut queried. ‘Revenge heh? Could be…but for one thing. Revenge doesn’t have advanced missile capability.’

‘It does if they’ve got the money,’ contradicted Meserine. ‘If whoever’s been squelched by a wormhole had rich relatives, or even better, were the big boss of a techy conglomerate, and their relatives were out to get the wormhole developers.’

‘Yeah, that might do it. Look Mes, you’ve finished with the warp report. How about chasing this up. We might as well grasp at straws, since we haven’t anything solid to go on. Find out who’s been squelched by the wormhole, and see if it includes anybody fitting your profile.’

'Sure thing Dil, get right on it.'

The com went dead; leaving Praut with the new angle Mes had come up with. Could it be that simple? He'd assumed there was a sinister reason for the wormhole carnage, like a rival company which felt threatened by a stabilised wormhole. Maybe people on the rim currently out of reach of central authority, threatened by its imminent arrival. But could it be as silly as a revenge motive? Someone with enough cash to cause this chaos? Wouldn't be the first time revenge caused such outrageous damage.

Ping. A com demanded his attention.

'Yeah, who's this?'

'Dil, its Fanny. Claymore's found how they broke into the computer.'

'Good old Clay. He's certainly good for one thing. So tell.'

'They used old DNA from the guy who's supposed to have done it, and was then ruled out. It's not difficult to get hold of someone's DNA if you're determined enough. Let me be clear; there's living DNA with negative superturns, and old DNA like a fossil. The quantum-computer access should have been set up to tell the difference. That was Darhlburg's mistake. So, a person in the lab has got hold of Wilgot's old DNA without his knowledge, and passed it on to whoever accessed the machine.'

'Wilgot, I'm guessing, is the guy originally accused?' Praut asked.

'That's right. On Clay's advice, they've now tightened security access to recognise only live DNA, but that leaves a *someone* who stole Wilgot's DNA. Olga's chasing this *someone*. She's got a sniffer on their tail. No matter how careful he or she's been, Olga's sniffer will ferret them out. They always leave a little behind...even if it's only a bad smell. Lucky for us, Darhlburg's security quarantined that access dock, so nobody's been near it since it happened.'

‘Great work,’ Praut congratulated her. ‘Tell Clay I said so. Best news I’ve had. Otherwise it’s a dead end. Now Fanny, make sure you catch this *someone*. I want a talk with whoever it is. Stuns and huggers only, no megajoules.’

‘Right Dil. I’ll call you again tomorrow with an update. Ciao!’

‘Ciao!’

The connection closed.

‘Hi Mes, where are you right now? Mes…if you can hear me please answer?’

‘Hi Dil! Sorry I was a little indisposed. What can I do for you?’

‘I need your taxi service.’

‘Where to?’

‘Callisto.’

‘When?’

‘Right now! I want to check out what’s going on up there. We’re going to do a little field work. I’ll meet you out in reception. Bring your zapper.’

‘Right.’

Praut made sure he had his own zapper with him. His jacket had everything else he would need. ‘Give me a meme-cap for Callisto,’ he told his auto-sec.

‘Yes sir.’ A meme-capsule popped into his outstretched hand. He loaded it into his neuro-pad and held it at the back of his left hemisphere.

Out in reception, Meserine waited to the far left, near the teleport interface. Praut waved at her and walked around the lake.

‘Hi Mes, you all ready?’ Praut asked as he joined her.

‘Yes Dil.’ She patted her belt to let him know she’d brought her zapper.

‘Right let’s do it.’

Praut gave their ships coordinates to the teleport operator and both stood inside the port-ring.

They rematerialised on board the *Faust* and Meserine walked calmly over to the captain's seat, while Praut sat in the co-pilot's seat to the right.

'How far is Callisto at the moment?' Praut asked.

Meserine checked the navcomp. 'Around eight hundred and fifty million klicks or five AU's. According to the navcomp, we should be there in three hours and twenty four minutes.'

'Good. Get this tub going and I'll fill you in on the mission.'

Meserine talked quietly into her throat mike, giving route instructions to the onboard computer. The ship gave a gentle shudder and the impulse engines kicked in. She sat back in her seat smiling with satisfaction.

'The outfit on Callisto which got hit was called Singularity Inc.,' Praut told her. 'They had a lab in a dome inside the Tornarsuk impact crater east of the huge Asgard multi-ring impact crater in the Northern Hemisphere. Tornarsuk is ninety-nine klicks across but the Singularity dome was only two klicks across. The strange missile hit the force-field protected dome, pierced it and depressurised it. Anybody not in a pressure suit was killed. I'm told only seven people survived. They were doing a bit of work outside the dome at the time of the missile strike.'

'How many dead?'

'They say around three and a half thousand.'

'Shit, that's rough. Who'd want to do such a thing?'

'That's what we're going to try to find out. I need to find at least one of those seven survivors. Find out what they know. And most of all…I want to see with my own eyes the damage done. You can tell a lot about a missile, even if it's weird, if you view the destruction.'

'That's true.'

'Mes, can you connect me with Fanny on Mars. She got in touch earlier but I forgot to ask her something.'

Meserine muttered sub-voce into her throat mike for a while, sounding as if she was getting exasperated. She put on an apologetic face and said, 'Sorry Dil, I'm being told there's congestion on the com-traffic transit beacons. There's at least a twenty minute delay to get through to Mars.'

'You can't be serious! This is getting ridiculous. It's occurring far too often. When are they going to upgrade those rotten relay nodes? I can get through to the Scutum-Centauri arm quicker than I can contact Mars.' Praut was venting his frustration with the lack of results on the case.

'Look Dil, you know as well as I do, there's so much e-traffic—it makes it difficult to route the bloody stuff effectively. Too many holes in the systems. Every facet of our lives is e-controlled now.' Meserine tried to calm her boss.

'Tell me about it. I can't go to the toilet without my auto-sec following me.'

'Humanity's spread throughout the galaxy. Some of our techy stuff isn't keeping up, that's all. Wormholes squelches people, but they allow us to communicate with your Scutum-Centauri arm almost instantly. That's gotta be a bloody miracle.'

'Yeah, I suppose.' Praut's anger was waning. 'While we continue to expand, we're adding more chaos to entropy. We don't seem to find time to consolidate our gains. Reminds me a bit of the Chinese Warring States period back in the dawn of civilisation. Little tin-pot empires appearing on various planets, jealously guarding their little plots of land.'

'Eh? Is that before warp?' Meserine smiled slyly.

'Yeah, before warp, and before your time. Should have known it's no use talking sensibly to a techy.'

'Well here's a thought from this tetchy techy. Half of our troubles you've been moaning about come from one lot of quantum-computers being put to work on wrecking other quantum-machines. That's why it's getting chaotic. One conglomerate trying to outdo their rivals, using q-machines as proxy bludgeons. Put some order into business practices and most of our troubles will sort themselves out.'

'Hmm! I can't argue against that; but isn't that what they've been trying to do for the last nine hundred years? We're the fathers of our inventions. I suppose you know we've got quantum-computers working on this problem, but our current struggling system is mostly down to our inbuilt survival of the fittest syndrome.'

'Mothers, not fathers,' Meserine said sternly. 'Mothers give birth, not fathers.' Meserine ignored his Darwinian tirade and picked up on her own agenda.

'Trust you to get sexist on me. But since you mentioned it—labs give birth, not mothers. As a modern day techy from earth, you must've been aware of that, surely?'

Meserine screwed up her face and stuck her tongue out at Praut.

'I should have known that would be your answer. Bach, Beethoven, Brahms, or Mendelssohn?'

'Oh, I think Tchaikovsky. I think staring out into space to the sound of Tchaikovsky Piano Trio in A minor, Op. 50 is somehow appropriate. All those stars twinkling to the sound of a hypnotic violin counterpointing with a cello…it seems just right.'

'Opus 50 coming up.' Praut spoke into his throat mike and the hypnotic opening bars came over the sound system.

Both he and Mes relaxed in their seats, settling down to listen for the forty-four minutes the Piano Trio played itself out.

At the end there was a moment of silence, followed by, 'Hang on Dil, I'm getting a *Mayday*,' she said urgently.

'Where's it coming from?'

'We've just swung round the curvature of the sun, and in half an hour we'll be coming up on Jupiter. It seems to be coming from the edge of the outer asteroid belt.'

'Have you got a visual?'

'Just coming up.'

The holo-image was trying to focus on a small craft drifting on the edge of the asteroid belt to their starboard.

'Slow to point one impulse,' Praut ordered her.

'I was just doing that,' grumbled Meserine. 'Dil, in space, let me play at captain.'

'Sorry Mes, force of habit.'

'Look, over there to our stern. It looks like a small cruiser.'

As Meserine manoeuvred the *Faust* closer, they could make out a large red S with a blue ellipse around it on the ship's hull.

'Hallo, can anybody hear me?' Meserine mouthed into her throat mike, while swinging the ship round to face the drifting vessel. 'I'll put this on the open mike for you,' she said to Praut.

'*Thank the space lanes*!' came the outburst from a gruff voice on the overhead mike. 'Hallo! This is the *Lilliput 2* out of Earth. We have a *Mayday*. Who's this?'

'This is the *Faust* from Earth. We picked up your *Mayday*. What seems to be the trouble?'

'Our engines have been disabled,' said the gruff voice.

'Disabled…nonsense, they've been sabotaged,' interrupted a woman's voice.

'Who's the captain of the vessel?' asked Meserine. She could see this getting out of hand.

The gruff voice said, 'Sorry for the outburst. This is Captain Lombardi of the Singularity Inc. vessel *Lilliput 2*. We've been hit by a meteor and it's knocked out the engines. If you'd be so kind as to port my passenger across to your vessel, I'd be much obliged.'

'This is Captain Monat on the *Faust*. Be happy to. I read two lifesigns on your ship. If your passenger could move to the stern so I can lock on, I'll initiate the port.'

'She's done that. Over to you captain,' said the gruff voice.

'Locked. Porting,' replied Meserine.

A middle-aged woman in an orange jumpsuit materialised in the stern of the *Faust*. She stood there, peering round the vessel.

'Thank you captain, for the rescue. But *I'm* right. It was sabotage. You'll see,' insisted the portly middle-aged woman.

Praut turned to face her, 'And you are?'

'Sorry, I should have introduced myself. I'm Randoline Walcott…CEO of Singularity.'

'Pleased to meet you Frau Walcott. I'm Dilmore Praut of the Praut Agency. We were just coming to see you on Callisto.'

Walcott's brow furrowed. 'Really? What a coincidence?'

'Well, not you personally, but Singularity Inc. in Tornarsuk crater. I've got a client who's worried by your lab's demise. I was coming to have a look at what caused it.'

A look of suspicion replaced her surprise. 'And what does the Praut Agency do?' asked the lady in the orange jumpsuit, coming over to sit on a seat behind Praut's cockpit seat.

'I run a discovery agency Frau Walcott. We find things out…things that people ask us to find out for them.'

Meserine was talking sub-voce into the throat mike all the while this was going on.

'Sorry to interrupt Dil. I'd like to go over to the *Lilliput* and run our antivirus stuff through their navcomp, if that's okay with you and the lady here.'

Randoline Walcott nodded her enthusiastic agreement. Praut said, 'If it's fine by Frau Walcott, its okay by me. Don't be long.'

Meserine adjusted some controls and went to the stern where her last passenger materialised. She snapped her fingers, and dematerialised.

'So now, while we're waiting, why not tell me why you think your ship's been sabotaged.' Praut rose from the cockpit and came to sit beside his new passenger.

'If you were coming to see the damage done to my lab, then you know what caused it. Am I right?' Walcott looked deep into Praut's eyes.

He flinched at the intrusive prying look and replied, 'May I offer you a herbal?'

'That's very kind. Make it a chamomile,' she responded, watching his every move.

'Chamomile, and a cappuccino,' Praut told the onboard computer.

The wall replicator unit produced, first the chamomile in a glass, followed by the coffee.

'Here we go,' said Praut as he handed her the drink. 'To answer your question, of course I was coming to see the damage. I was told it was a missile strike. You have my sympathies at loosing so many of your workers.'

The woman CEO shrugged. 'Thank you, but coming all this way; you're wasting your time.'

Now it was Praut's turn to be surprised. 'And why's that, may I ask?'

'There's nothing to see.'

'Nothing to see? What about the damage?'

'That's all been fixed,' replied the woman CEO. 'Nanobots. We have them spare just in case of meteor strikes. The nanobots repaired all the damage the following day. It merely punctured the dome, that's all. It was easy to repair. I was coming to see how our research stood. The depressurisation didn't damage any of the machines. We've hired more people and we'll continue. I'm not letting some bunch of hooligans wreck my life's work.'

'Which is?'

'To finish what Bolguard started. Bolguard was my grandfather. I'm determined to stabilise the wormhole. I consider it a matter of family honour.'

Praut was sipping his coffee and gently shaking his head at the same time. 'This current job is full of surprises. But if you're Bolguard's granddaughter, why aren't you with Bolguard on Pluto?'

'I disagreed with how they were approaching the work. I had a falling out with the Board. So I set up my own outfit here on Callisto. As it is, someone's out gunning for us both. You know Bolguard had a fire?'

'Yes, I'd heard. Anyway, maybe I could still come and have a look.'

'If you get me to Callisto, I'll personally give you the tour,' replied his uninvited guest.

'I'll take you up on that.'

Meserine rematerialised in the stern. 'We found it. I mean the antivirus found it. It's the same bizarre grabworm we got hit by. Left the same footprint…that is, nothing. I'm afraid our guest was right.'

'As I said,' confirmed Singularity's CEO.

'What about the meteor? Captain Lombardi said he'd been hit by a meteor.' Praut was puzzled.

'It was his assumption. The onboard computer was down so he guessed at the cause,' Meserine told him.

'So, is their ship back to normal?' asked Praut.

'Her captain thinks it is.' Meserine switched to the woman CEO. 'He's waiting for you. You should be able to continue your voyage now.'

'Thank you so much,' said the lady CEO, rising from her seat and going to the stern of the vessel.

'Ready to port?' queried Meserine.

'Ready!'

Singularity's CEO dematerialised leaving only the two original passengers of the *Faust*.

# 4
# CALLISTO

'So now what?' asked Meserine.

'We follow the *Lilliput* to Callisto,' smiled Praut. 'I have an invite to tour their facility.'

'Trust you,' Meserine smiled back. She watched the *Lilliput's* engines fire up and it pulled away towards Jupiter. Meserine ordered the *Faust* to follow, increasing speed to match the other vessel. 'Dil, I've been meaning to ask you. I've been with you only a year, so I don't know all the ins and outs of the Agency. For instance, this vessel. How come you named it *Faust*? And if this is the fifth, as the Log Book says, what happened to the other four?'

'As you're the captain, you might as well know. I've made a pact with the devil to fulfil my end of a client's contract come what may. So...*Faust* 1, 2, 3, and 4, went to the bone yard in the line of duty—but you should have seen the other guy.'

Meserine smiled at the clarification. 'That explains it. I knew you were a hell of a guy,' she told him.

'Hey, Mes, that's pure kitsch.'

'Sorry, but so was your gumpf.'

Praut admitted defeat and shrugged. 'You win. *Faust*, cos I like Goethe. As for the other previous four ships...I told you the truth.'

'That's better. Now I can like you again.'

'How's our arrival time?'

'We're coming up on Jupiter in ten minutes.'

'My, how time flies when you're having fun. By the way, don't be surprised when we arrive at the Tornarsuk crater. They've fixed all the damage. There's nothing to see.'

'That from their CEO?'

'Yep. Nano-bots. She's the granddaughter of Bolguard…the guy who invented the wormhole monster.'

'Well I never. So that's why she's so feisty. She's got something to prove.'

'I'll bet she's had some stick in her life.'

'Especially from relatives of those it's squelched. Hang on, we're coming into orbit round Callisto.'

'Look at the engines, they've gone into overdrive.'

'That's Jupiter. It's got a whopper of a pull. The magnetosphere is the most powerful in our Solar System. Don't worry, they'll hold.'

'They'd better, or I'm gonna demand my money back.'

'We're coming in on Tornarsuk,' she warned Praut. 'We'll land next to the *Lilliput* near that geodesic hangar.'

The *Faust* parked near the other ship inside the crater rim only a hundred meters from the massive geodesic dome. Roadrunners moved both ships into the airlock of the hangar. The doors closed and the hangar airlock was re-pressurised. The main hangar doors opened and the *Faust* was snagged by a robot tug and moved to the left, inside a massive oval dome hangar.

'Do we walk?' asked Meserine as she climbed out of her cockpit seat. 'This low gravity's gonna be difficult.'

'You'll get used to it. Put on the grip-shoes and it'll be okay. As for walking, there's a small maglev running down a connecting tube into the dome from here.' Praut was already waiting at the exit door in his grip-shoes, looking outside into the hangar. He discovered quite a number of large space cruisers parked on one side.

'Could have ported into the dome…been easier.'

'Waste of energy. This is just as good—get some exercise. The gravity here is great. The whole floor area is covered in grip tiles.'

'Since when have you been so keen on exercise?' countered Meserine.

'Since I hit a place that has thirteen per cent of earth's gravity, *and* it's got low GCRs so there's little background radiation to contend with.' Praut threw his head back and bounded over to the maglev in his grip shoes, where Randoline Walcott was waiting for them. She was accompanied by a solidly built man in a space captain's uniform. Mes arrived just behind Praut.

'Let me introduce you,' said Singularity's CEO to Praut. 'This is Captain Lombardi.'

Praut steadied himself, and nodded at the captain of the *Lilliput*, who nodded back, and the little party boarded the waiting maglev.

A *whoosh* later, they stepped out into the vast reception area of the geodesic dome—two kilometres across and half a kilometre high.

'Where did all that lovely muck come from?' Meserine asked the CEO, pointing at a few stunted trees growing within reception.

'We had it shipped from earth, where else? It's a purely psychological thing, but they're struggling in the low gravity. They're grown in containers but it gives our people a lot of comfort, I can assure you.'

'Yeah, a reminder of home. Why didn't you use a holo-image for the whole area. It's more realistic,' Meserine suggested.

'My problem. I'm allergic to holo-images,' the CEO retorted.

'Pardon the interruption, but where did the missile hit?' Praut asked, looking up at the dome.

'As I said, it's all repaired now, but if you look closely at the dome about a quarter of a klick up over there,' the CEO pointed to the left. 'There, it's just, just visible, that clean patch. Can you see it?'

Praut peered hard where she was pointing, 'No, can't see it.'

Meserine reached to the back of her belt and handed him a pair of holo-binocs.

'Thanks Mes.' He looked again and said, 'Ah, yes! The clean patch. Heh, its quite big, isn't it?'

'The dome was depressurised instantly.' Walcott told him.

A group of people appeared out of nowhere. A number of Singularity's Board had arrived and a lot of hand shaking and hugging got under way.

'This is my personal secretary, Ms Raffles.' Walcott told him. 'Please feel free to use her.'

Praut nodded at the little woman standing by her boss's side. 'A real live secretary? How quaint.'

'I prefer it that way. Sometimes I need a human touch,' replied the CEO.

'Back to the dome. What about the forcefield? Didn't it hold the pressure? I mean, isn't that what they're supposed to do?' Praut persisted.

'Now that's the strange part of the missile strike. It hit the forcefield and punctured a hole in the field…which remained open. When the dome was breeched, the hole in the field didn't close as it should have done. The atmosphere vented right through the forcefield. Something's wrong there. The WGS got real excited about that. We had to report the incident to WorldGov. They sent their agents up here and they took a lot of holo-vids. They took away any fragments of the missile they could find back to earth with them.'

'You don't have any fragments left at all?' Praut asked surprised.

'Nothing. They even confiscated all the CCHV footage from our security people. We've got no record of the attack at all.'

'Ehm, that's not strictly true, Miss Walcott,' interrupted her secretary. 'We kept a bit back for our insurance people. We needed proof of the attack, you see.'

'*Now* you tell me,' Walcott scolded her secretary. 'Where is it?'

'It's in the vault, ma'am. Do you want to see it?'

'Make a copy of it and give it to Mr Praut,' she ordered her assistant. To Praut she said, 'If you hadn't come along when you did, we might still be out there, falling into the meteor belt. This is the least I can do. I owe you my life. If there's anything else, don't hesitate.'

Praut gave her a grateful smile, 'If not us, then someone else would have come along.'

'You can't be certain of that. We were drifting into the meteor belt…and then we would *really* have been hit by a meteor. I'll go with my version if you don't mind.'

Praut shrugged. 'Thank you for the holo-vid. It should help in my investigation. Sorry I can't tell you why I need it, but be assured that I do.'

'You told me your client is worried about our demise. Since I'm working on wormholes…then I'm afraid, I can guess who your client is. There's not many of us working in this field. It can't be Bolguard. They're gone. The fire did a thorough job on them. The only people left doing wormholes are Darhlburg on Mars. They're doing the same as us. We're racing each other to get the job done…stabilise the torque fields doing the squelching.'

Praut looked innocently at her. 'I'm afraid I'm not at liberty to say anything.'

Walcott smiled, 'I didn't expect you to say anything. I'm simply letting you know…that I know who your client is. Why they've hired you, would be my only interest. They must've suffered some kind of calamity, not dissimilar to ours. Anyway, I won't press you on the subject.'

'What I can tell you is, I'm trying to find out who is behind these attacks on your wormhole technology. Which is why I'm here. And since you've managed to retain one item not confiscated by WGS,' Praut continued, 'maybe you could look for any bits of the missile that didn't get away?'

'I can try, but don't hold your breath.'

'Yes, I can see that would be a mistake up here. Thanks. By the way, I heard there were only seven survivors,' Praut said casually.

'That's right. Four were taken away by the WGS and three are still around here somewhere. Let me guess. You'd like to talk with them if possible.' She looked closely at Praut.

'You've read my mind. I just want to get a feel of what happened here.'

'I'll see if I can dig them up for you. You can have a chat to them later, if that suits?'

'That's absolutely fine. Anytime will do.' Praut smiled again.

'So, shall we?' Walcott asked.

Praut looked questioningly at the CEO.

'I promised you a tour. We might as well get started.' To her assistant she said, 'Hold everything until I finish with this gentleman. There's nothing urgent I suppose?'

'No ma'am.'

'Good, then Mr Praut, let me show you my brains.' She led Praut and Meserine to a massive building fifty meters away to their front. The single building occupied a lot of the dome's space.

'What astonishes me is how quickly you've normalised the disaster,' Praut mentioned as they walked. 'Apart from the obvious lack of people, there's no sign you've had any trouble at all.' Praut was genuinely amazed by the look of normality within the dome.

'And we're bringing in more people as we speak,' the CEO responded. She looked pleased at Praut's skewed compliment. 'You must've noticed the large number of space cruisers in the hangar...they're the replacements. I've tried to run this place as tightly as I know how. We've got budgetary constraints, so every credit counts. It's at times like this that my efficiency is paying dividends.'

Inside the building, in the middle, Praut found a large hall surrounded by quantum-computers. In the centre of the hall was a low round platform. Singularity's CEO headed straight for the podium, followed by Praut and Meserine.

'This is the only building that has pro-gravity underneath it. Gives the place Earth type gravity but it takes up too much energy. This is where the holo-images come up…it's where we tweak the wormhole. The computers have to be powerful enough to simulate and project a 10 meter holo-wormhole mouth onto this platform, and then allow us to adjust its configuration.'

'How many machines are there?' Praut asked.

'We've a bank of ten q-machines. They're the biggest cluster you'll find anywhere. Well almost anywhere. The warp boys probably have just as many. A wormhole simulation needs at least $1.5\times10^{77}$ q-bits, and these babies have enough spare capacity to run the rest of the dome. Anyhow, we have something in the $10^{128}$ quintillion region. I mean they're in their q-bit form of course, but that's the capacity.

'We eventually envisage creating a 100 km Schwarzschild traversable wormhole which allows travel in both directions and both ends are held open by a spherical shell of negative stress-energy tensor fields to circumvent the effects of the event horizon. We'll use exotic matter from scalar quantum field fluctuations to create the wormhole and the same exotic matter will be used to keep the wormhole mouth open. The remote mouth at the other end is coordinate dependent. The basic theory was expounded long ago in 1936 in the legendary Einstein-Rosen Bridge paper, but the technical feasibility only became available in the last century. I've memorised that paper backwards.'

'I have a q-computer expert who'd be very impressed by the explanation and the figures you've just quoted,' Praut excused himself. 'But I'm afraid most of this is well over my head. I'm a simple snoop, a good sleuth, so my clients tell me, but nevertheless, a sleuthhound. My captain here, is a far more able techy than I am. I expect you to remember all this,' Praut said to Meserine. 'There'll be a test when we get back.' He winked at her so the CEO didn't see.

'Anyway, the point being,' continued the CEO, 'we simulate the wormhole and try to stabilise it here on this platform. All the rest of the dome is merely support for this single enterprise.'

'Are you getting anywhere?' asked Praut.

There was a moment's silence while the CEO wondered how much she should reveal. Then she said, 'We're close. Another month should do it. The only problem that's cropped up, is that the people who *were* close, are all dead. A new bunch will have to start again. Not entirely from scratch, but it's going to take longer. All I can promise is, we will get there no matter how many hurdles are put in our way.' Walcott had set her face and features into a hard look. She was determined to finish this job. Then she softened and said, 'Now tell me, how long you would like to stay here?'

'As long as you will have us…eh, well not quite.' Praut smiled a weak smile. 'I have to be back on earth tomorrow.'

'Good! Then you'll dine with me tonight. Maybe you'd like to go and have a look at the rest of the place? I mean, there's not much to see after this main instillation here,' she swept her arm around the room, indicating the massed banks of q-computers. 'About teatime I'll send a comm to you when I've found those three people you want to talk to.'

'You must have a lot of work to do. I'm sorry I kept you from getting things back in order.' Praut meant it.

'As a matter of fact I have. The whole Board arrived a day ago to survey the damage. We need to meet and get things going again. However, *my* priority was to my saviour. Once again, I thank you for being out there when I needed you most.'

'Fraulein Walcott, it was my honour and pleasure.' Praut nodded to Meserine that they should leave the building and go outside.

'Till this evening,' said the CEO, still lingering near the simulation platform.

'Till this evening,' replied Praut, walking towards the exit, followed by Meserine.

In the cold recycled air of the dome, Praut stood on the steps of the building and looked around at the gigantic setup.

'Once upon a time, it would have been a tremendous effort to set something like this up. Now, with all the nanobot technology, I suppose it would only take a few months. What do you think?' he asked Meserine.

'Yeah, that's about right. Hey, I noticed you changed from Frau to Fraulein in there. What gives?'

Praut gave a small shrug. 'Her secretary called her Miss, so I adjusted.'

'You know…this mission's turned out okay. What'd you think? That *Mayday* rescue couldn't have turned out better even if you'd planned it that way.' Meserine chuckled under her breath.

'It must be the devil in me, but are you hinting at something?'

'Me? I'd never impugn my boss, boss.'

'Better not, you know I've got low connections.'

'Shall we take a stroll?'

'Lead on captain.'

They both went a little unsteadily down by the side of the building through alleys and blocks of housing, coming out into a small square. It took a little effort to adjust to the low gravity. To house all of Singularity's workers, a small village had been built at the back of the massive main building. The architects had put in a few old style shops and eateries to give the impression of earth like community—all for the sake of psychology. The small village square even had an artificial lawn with flowers, and trees surrounding the square. Praut spotted a small bistro nestling in amongst a low row of buildings.

'Fancy a drink?' Praut asked his pilot.

'Do I? I'm as dry as a dead dingo's donger,' Meserine spat out.

'A *what*?' asked a startled Praut.

'A dead dingo's donger,' she repeated.

'I send you out to check those outback warp merchants, and you drag this baggage back to me. I'd better be careful where I send you in future.' Praut smiled cheerfully at her.

She retorted back, 'Ace mate.'

Praut threw his hands up in mock horror. He walked quickly inside the Bistro followed by his new Aussie convert.

They sat at a table and Praut motioned at the few clientele, 'Must be the new workers they've brought in.'

'Fast of them, eh?'

Praut ordered into the table mike. 'I'll have a Blue Lagoon—and you?' He queried her.

'Make mine a Blue Island,' she said into the mike.

The drinks arrived and they sipped them leisurely.

From another table, two tables away, came, 'Psst! Psst!'

Praut wondered where the funny noise was coming from.

Again, 'Psst! Hey, you the guy looking for a piece of the missile junk that hit the dome?'

This time it was unmistakable. A small individual on a table with two others was doing the *pssts*.

Praut waved for the man to come over.

The short fellow left his table and arrived, looking around furtively. 'I heard you were looking for a piece of the missile junk that hit this place. Still interested?'

'We've only just got here. How could you have heard anything?' Praut was suspicious.

'I just overheard you talking to the boss. Well?'

'There was no one like you around when I was talking to her.' Praut didn't like the situation.

'Of course there was. You just didn't see them. We've got nanomorphs buzzing the Board. They've just arrived and we want to know what's happening. They've only just hired us…so are they gonna close the place down or not? They won't tell us, so we've bugged them. Well, do you want a piece of the junk?'

Praut was shaking his head at the idea of being bugged, while Meserine was grinning at the situation.

'What've you got?'

'It'll cost you.'

'If it's of any value, I might.'

'It's part of the missile, what more do you want? The WGS took the rest. They missed this piece.'

'Let me see it.'

'Not here. If you're interested, I'll meet you outside in five.'

Praut nodded. The little man walked back to his table.

'What'd you think?' he asked Meserine.

'Not sure. Depends on what he's got.'

'Yeah, suppose. You stay here. I'll deal with this.'

'Not on your life. You go out and I'll send this fellow to follow you.' She reached into her belt pouch and produced a nanomorph in its capsule. 'Two can play at this bugging game. I'll follow you after a small gap just in case this funny little man tries anything.' She patted her zapper, then spoke into her throat mike, programming the nanomorph.

Praut had a little laugh at his pilot's caution. But he knew she was right. You never knew what might happen in these shady deals. Wouldn't be the first time he'd ended up with a bump on his head, if he was lucky. He felt for his own zapper for comfort. He got up from the table and went outside. The little man was waiting for him.

'Well?' Praut demanded.

'I have it stashed at my place,' the little man started walking away. 'Are you coming or not?' he asked testily.

'I'm not as stupid as you think. I'll wait for you over there,' Praut pointed at the far end of the square, the direction the little man was heading.

The little fellow scowled but kept walking. Praut followed him to the edge of the square and then stopped, sitting down on a bench facing where they'd come from.

Fifteen minutes of waiting and the little man reappeared, walking back towards Praut as if he was carrying something...the low gravity disguised it, yet nothing was visible. He stopped by Praut's bench and put something down on the bench.

'What am I looking at?' asked Praut.

'A piece of the missile, as promised. Wait, it's cloaked. Let's get into an alley and I'll make it visible.' He lifted whatever it was and Praut followed him towards the nearest alley.

The little man put his load down, looked around, then uncloaked it. On the ground, there suddenly appeared a piece of mutilated dull composite. Varieties of strange coloured crystals were visible inside the damaged mechanism.

'What the hell?' Praut exclaimed in a hiss.

'What'll you give me for this?' the little man wanted to know.

'Name your price...and try to be sensible.'

'A million.' The fellow was holding his breath.

'Give you a hundred thou...and don't push your luck.'

The man's face dropped.

'Why not put it on the open market...you know...an auction. See what it brings,' Praut said dismissively.

A look of pain replaced the disappointment.

'Well? Do we have a deal?' Praut demanded.

Half-heartedly, the little man nodded.

Meserine appeared from round the corner, attempting to stride alertly into the alley. 'Everything okay?' she asked.

'Is it?' Praut asked the little man.

Again a half hearted nod.

'Good. Cloak it again, and I'll throw in a little extra for the cloaking device. How do you want paying?'

The little man opened his jacket and displayed a tiny screen with a number on it.

Praut looked at Meserine and nodded. She spoke into her throat mike.

'I've just transferred a hundred and ten thou to that number. It's in both our interests to keep this quiet.' Praut looked meaningfully at the little man.

The little fellow handed something to Meserine and sauntered off back to the Bistro. His step was visibly lighter and more contented. It seems he'd done better than expected on the deal, at least his pseudo dance step implied it.

'Let's hope we've not been seen. Now, how do we get this back to the ship?' Praut asked Meserine.

Meserine stared at Praut, 'Even if we've been seen, it's not in Singularity's interest to stop us, surely.'

'I'm not thinking of Singularity. If I were WGS, I'd leave a few snoops here just in case. Do a sweep right now for nanomorphs. See if we've been peeked.'

Meserine took out her terahertz scanner and swept the area. 'All I'm picking up is our nanomorph.' She retrieved the pesky thing and replaced it in its capsule. 'Got the whole transaction down on vid just in case.' She showed him the capsule.

'Good and bad. It incriminates us, but we may need to use it. Anyway of teleporting this out of here?' Praut indicated the cloaked piece of scrap missile.

'I'd have to activate the ship from here.'

'Try. It would solve our problems.'

Meserine spoke into her throat mike for a minute. Then she motioned for Praut to stand back, and she took a step backwards. The cloaked item decloaked while the teleport locked on and then it vanished.

'That's it,' Meserine pronounced with a look of satisfaction. 'It's on the ship.'

Ping, a com announced itself. A holo image of Walcott's secretary hung in the air. 'Your appointment with the three survivors is imminent. Please make your way to the second floor of the main building.'

'Copy that,' said Meserine into her throat mike. She put the cloaking control into her jumpsuit pocket.

'Got rid of that just in time, eh?' exclaimed Praut.

'Shall we?'

'After you captain.'

Both headed back to the main building. They found Walcott's secretary waiting in the second floor corridor.

'Before you go in, I have something for you.' She handed Praut a data cube. 'This is a copy of the promised CCHV missile footage.'

'Ah yes. Thank you,' said Praut, handing the cube to Meserine. 'And where are the witnesses?'

'Through here, in the next room. Would you like to see them individually or together?'

'Together I think; that way they can contradict each other and argue it out in front of me,' Praut told her.

'Yes sir.'

She led the way into the next room where three middle aged men sat on a contour couch.

Meserine stayed outside and after only ten minutes, Praut came out in a disgusted state.

'Nothing, absolutely nothing! They might as well not have been there. They saw nothing, heard nothing, and know nothing. The three monkeys know more than this lot. Simply idiotic,' he was fuming with the waste of time.

'They're probably ordinary workers and don't want to get themselves into trouble,' Meserine tried to placate him.

'Oh, no. They're all highly educated,' Praut said in disgust. 'These are scientist of the first order. Either they're taking the piss, or they're the most unobservant people in the galaxy. And frankly I'm not certain which.'

'So what now?'

'You know, I'm in the mood to get out of here. I know we've got a dinner date with the CEO, but if I can find a suitable excuse, I'll use it.'

'What about the emergency on Mars?' Meserine suggested.

Praut's eyebrows went up, 'What emer… oh, I see, yes, *the* Mars emergency. Those three in there have made me half-witted like them. Get in touch with Miss Walcott and tell her we've got the Mars emergency and we've got to leave immediately.'

'Yes boss.'

A short time later, they were leaving Callisto's orbit and heading back to Earth. Half way through the journey, Praut asked to be connected to Fanny on Mars. This time the connection came through instantly.

'Hi Fanny, how's tricks?'

'Hi Dil, I'm kinda busy. We're chasing this woman who stole Wilgot's DNA. Olga's got a sniffer hot on her tail. Look, sorry, I'll get back to you later.' The connection went dead.

‘Well I never. She cut me off,’ complained Praut.

‘Must’ve been something important for her to do that,’ Meserine tried to find an excuse for her friend.

‘Yeah, I suppose…oh what the hell.’ Praut settle down for the short journey back to Earth.

# 5
# MARS

The year was 2567. By the second half of the twenty-first century, quantum computers had made a qualitative difference to most people's lives. Financial Markets were put in order, the weather system fully addressed and the climate stabilised. The World Energy Grid came into effect, and goods were produced either by nano-manufacturing or by 3D-printing. Permanent colonies were established on Mars and the Moon.

By the twenty second century, Physics blossomed and the Field Theory had been successfully Unified. Global Air Control had to be brought in once flying cars became ubiquitous. All ground traffic was automated. Near and distant space lanes needed governing and ordering. Research made strides that had been held back by lack of computing power, especially in the medical and biological fields. A functional space elevator was built for earth. By the twenty third century, the terraforming of Mars had been well under way, although many people, known as *the complainers,* always looking backwards, objected to this gigantic violation of our pristine neighbouring planet. By the twenty fourth century, the warp drive was invented and anti-grav was commonplace. Replicators were replacing 3D printing as a source of manufacturing. Humans visited every planted of our Solar system…and then went beyond.

By the twenty fifth century, an artificial wormhole had been developed, albeit not perfected. With the help of interstellar warp ships, humanity spread to the farthest reaches of the galaxy. The Era of Expansion had begun. By the twenty sixth century, q-computers manipulated atoms via holo emitters, giving hard substance to any imagined hologram. Most people lived on q-machine controlled holo-decks, with their embedded omni-directional holo-diodes, enabling a change to their environments at a whim. At least that was the situation on Earth.

Out in the vastness of space, scientists predicted one in ten stars had a solar system like ours. Since our galaxy contained three hundred billion stars, it meant there were thirty billion solar systems out there similar to ours. Given such circumstances, humanity continued its self-imposed mission to spread itself throughout the Milky Way.

To date, no other sentient life forms had been encountered in the colonisation process. Already over four hundred planets around the galaxy had been terraformed and were accommodating migrants from earth. True, the immigrants roughed it in many ways, compared with Earth, but technology made an enormous difference. Warp ships, teleports, replicators, instant comm-gauge wormhole communication with earth, quantum-computers, holo-deck comforts, and a medical technology which allowed humans to live to two hundred, all made the move to the stars not only possible and inevitable, but necessary.

Humanity was spreading as it once did on Earth, into every niche that would sustain them. There were currently human colonists on the rim of the Milky Way looking longingly across the empty chasm of intergalactic space at our neighbouring galaxies, hoping a way would be found to bridge the chasm. That way was through a stabilised wormhole. Yet this last piece of the technological puzzle was evading them.

Now, out of nowhere, just as the scientists were on the verge of succeeding in stabilising the wormhole, someone or something, was sabotaging the one way of reaching the other galaxies. All the information on wormholes was under threat. Any enterprise trying to stabilise the wormhole was being attacked. The culprits had to be found. Humanities interstellar dream demanded it.

* * *

Fanny and Olga were following the sniffer, and it was hot on the trail of Wanda Hortynska, the Darhlburg employee who'd pinched Wilgot's DNA. They needed to know why she did it, and who induced her to risk such a stupid gambit. The why would probably turn out to be credits, but the who…well that was the more interesting question which needed an urgent answer.

After more grilling, Wilgot asked to take a memory scan. From the scan, after sifting through his memories, Olga discovered Wanda had playfully run her fingers through Wilgot's hair in the lab's diner four days before the theft of the blueprint. She'd been flirting with Wilgot off and on for days, setting him up.

The hair follicle contained live cells at it's root, and someone extracted DNA from those four day old cells, then reprogrammed the DNA to produce a skin sample large enough to submit to the q-computer's access scanner.

Once Olga had a name, she found Wanda's work station, and then set her sniffer to do its work with its q-circuit e-sensor. The sniffer, at its elementary stage, worked like the super nose of a Silvertip Grizzly bear, who's sense of smell is seven time more sensitive than that of a bloodhound. The sniffer chased the volatile organic compounds. They found a pair of sandals in Wanda's locker, and set the sniffer on to it. The sniffer followed Wanda's smell, discerning Wanda's molecular presence, to the lab's exit, where security's CCHV had her boarding the shuttle off the mountain.

Darhlburg's security was all set to send all their people out in pursuit of Wanda, when Fanny intervened and asked them to take it easy.

'By all means join in the search, but let us be the ones to apprehend her,' Fanny told Barnhart, head of Darhlburg's security.

The man looked puzzled at the request. 'Don't you want to catch her?'

'Of course,' replied Fanny, 'but I don't want to put her into a situation where she feels there's only one way out, that of doing away with herself.'

'So what about *you* taking the lead and my people taking orders from you?' Barnhart asked.

'Now that's what I was hoping you'd say. I want to make sure we take her alive. We badly need to question her.' The problem tossing around in Fanny's mind was, *who* had set this nominally loyal employee to do such a stupid thing?

Once off the mountain, Wanda switched to a hover, and trackers had her heading south-east past Peacock Mountain towards the Tharsis Bulge, then down into the Mariner Valley at the Night Labyrinth. She was hoping to throw her tracker off by disappearing off radar. The only problem was, her hover had an inbuilt tracker beaming her location up to the overhead traffic satellite, updating her location every few seconds. Wanda must've known this. There really was no place to run.

Wanda's holo-image coming from the pursuing sniffer, informed Olga the fugitive's hover was skimming effortlessly over the blue waters of the Mariner Valley, heading past Lus for the Melas Basin. This was a two hundred kilometre wide mid point in Mariner Valley. She was ineffectively attempting to disappear into the four thousand kilometre long canyon. She was like some animal looking for a hole to hide in. Had the valley been a lot narrower she might have succeeded, but with it being two hundred kilometre wide at the Melas Basin, she stood no chance of evading the satellites. The spy in the sky pinpointed her location to a meter as she sped her way over the waters.

The sniffer looked like a small thin oversized pencil floating in the air, trailing Wanda's every move. It was designed to make sure the pursuit was one-sided, stacked in favour of the chaser. It had her at a distance of a hundred meters out in front, her hover still skimming, occasionally changing direction as if undecided where to turn next.

*

A sniffer—through its atom sized e-circuits, and its frequency analyser, had the facility to analyse the whole of the electromagnetic spectrum from ELF to gamma rays. Via it's controller, it had high-speed network access to a quantum-computer.

All neurons emit weak radio signals across the ELF/SLF/ULF frequency bands, allowing the sniffer to use its remote neuro-signal acquisition algorithms, and its remote neural interface, with an onboard Electroencephalograph, to detect remotely, a person's thoughts at a distance of a two hundred kilometres.

*

'From her neuro-signal acquisition I'm reading she's extremely scared and panicky,' Olga informed Fanny.

'Is that the sniffer reading her brainwaves?' asked Fanny.

'Right! She doesn't seem to know what to do. The remote neural interface in the sniffer's brain wave analyser is showing her as volatile. We need to tread with care here or we'll push her over the edge,' Olga notified Fanny.

Olga maintained a tight control over her sniffer and kept her baby out of harms way. If Wanda was able to use a zapper, she could have destroyed the delicate sniffer, but as it was, she was too busy trying to control her hover and evade the mountain ridges sticking out of the water. Wanda had cut her com-links and shut down her camera feed at the outset, making it impossible to communicate with her.

Olga was in a hover, closing in on Wanda's location, while Fanny had taken her hover along the top right ridge of the Mariner Valley, waiting for an opportunity to cut Wanda off should she try to leave the canyon. Numerous of Darhlburg security's hovers were on either side of the Mariner Valley waiting for Fanny to give them the word and guide them in on the target.

'*Hey, where'd she go*?' burst out Olga on her com-line to Fanny.

'What's happening,' Fanny demanded in response.

'*She's vanished*,' cried Olga.

'What do you mean vanished?' Fanny was getting annoyed.

'Hey, I think she went in to the waters. It's the only thing I can think of. One moment I had her holo-image and the next, empty water.'

'Wait,' Fanny told her, 'I'm picking up her satellite trace. By josh, you're right. She's underwater and still moving down the canyon. What a sneaky thing to do.'

'You have an interstellar call from the *Faust.* Shall I put it through?' her comm informed Fanny.

'Yes, go ahead.'

'Hi Fanny, how's tricks?' came Praut's voice.

'Hi Dil, I'm kinda busy. We're chasing this woman who stole Wilgot's DNA. Olga's got a sniffer hot on her tail. Look, sorry, I'll get back to you later.' She disconnected. She'd explain her rudeness to her boss later.

'Yeah, I've got the same feed now, from the satellite. Look there…*she's stopped*,' Olga replied, getting excited.

'Right, just short of Coprates. Has anything gone wrong?' asked Fanny.

'What, you mean her hover?'

'Why's she stopped?' Fanny demanded. 'Wait, I'm coming down to join you. Something's not right here.' Fanny dove her hover down into the canyon and found Olga's hover in the Coprates Canyon stationary above the waters.

'Now what?' Olga asked. 'We can't just sit here doing nothing. I don't think there's any point sending the sniffer down under the water.' Fanny was her gaffer and it was up to her to decide what to do next.

'Wait,' Fanny replied. 'I'll get in touch with the lead Darhlburg security hover. They can get in touch with Darhlburg base and ask them to send a cruiser down here. The cruiser can use its tractor beam and pull her hover out from down there. There's no alternative.'

'Yeah, good idea. In the mean time I'll retrieve my sniffer.'

'Don't put it away just yet. Let's see what's happened. She might try to make a break for it.'

'Wilco.'

The two hovers waited twenty minutes until the heavy cruiser arrived. Then the cruiser latched onto Wanda's hover and grappled it with its tractor beam, pulling it up from below the deep waters.

'I don't read any life signs,' Olga warned Fanny.

'She must be in there somewhere,' Fanny retorted.

'Not according to my trace recorder.' Olga's sniffer atom configuration analyser had picked up a teleporter trace but she didn't say anything. She thought, *Let the captain tell her*.

'It must be on the blink. She couldn't have left the hover from down there.'

'Don't say I didn't warn you,' Olga told her.

'We have the hover on board,' said the captain of the heavy cruiser. 'We're just about to open her up. My people tell me there's no life signs on board.'

'This is ridiculous,' insisted Fanny. 'How could someone vanish from down there?'

'We're inside, and as I said, there's no one here. We've picked up traces of a teleport. There's your answer,' said the captain of the cruiser.

'*Oh fuck*,' exploded Fanny. 'They can't be serious? A teleport…but who…?' Fanny suddenly realised it was an open comm. 'My profound apologies captain, you weren't meant to hear that outburst.'

'Its okay, I've heard worse,' replied the captain.

'I'll bet it's the same bastard who got her involved in all this,' replied Olga.

'In which case, she's off planet by now.' Fanny felt immensely deflated at not having caught her quarry. She spoke quietly into her throat mike, 'To all hovers, this is Number One, the chase is over and everyone should return to base. Over.'

'Copy that, see you back in the lab.' Olga gave instructions to her hover to return to the Olympus lab.

Back in the diner of the Olympus lab, where Praut's trio had established themselves, they began to go over what had gone down with their fugitive.

'Hi Clay, you missed all the fun,' Olga teased Claymore, as they settled into chairs.

'No I didn't. I hacked into your holo-feed from your sniffer.'

'What? How?' Olga had been under the impression the feed went only to her.

'I used the q-computer here. It's only a frequency feed, isn't it? I know the frequency your sniffer uses for the feed, the rest is easy.'

Olga didn't like the sound of that. Her jealous instinct was to find a way to block anyone else's frequency analyser from probing her sniffers. She wanted to make sure the sniffer's feed stayed securely tied only to her.

Fanny said, 'So you know the guilty party teleported?'

'Yep.'

'I'm gonna have to change the frequency on my sniffers,' muttered Olga.

'Won't do you any good,' replied Clay. 'I can always hack those things.'

Olga decided, there and then, to stop him, but she ignored his remark for the moment and turned to Fanny, 'So now what? Where do we go from here?'

'Well, we know how the blueprint was stolen, and we partially know one of the perpetrators, but the main culprit's managed to elude us. Sadly to say, I'd say we're finished here.'

'What? Back to the office?' asked Olga.

'Looks like it…unless you have another suggestion.'

'Any way of finding out how and when this Wanda was contacted?' Olga suggested.

'You mean by her controller?'

'Yeah, the guy who's been pulling her strings.'

'I'd have to ask Barnhart if they've got CCHV footage of her over time.' Fanny wondered if they'd kept any footage of Wanda.

Claymore put in, 'What if she wasn't contacted here in the lab, but at home, or someplace outside?'

'Let's take it one at a time,' Fanny responded. 'I'll ask Barnhart what he's got on her…then we'll take it from there.'

Olga said, 'Listen Fan, I've got two ideas to put to you. Firstly, when a person teleports, it must mean a q-computer has disassembled the person atom by atom, and stored the original configuration, then reassembled that person in a different location…right? I want you to get Clay to check if any of Darhlburg's computers were used to port anyone at the very time that Wanda ported. We know the time, give or take a minute, when this happened. Secondly, I want to send a sniffer up above Mars to see if it can locate a trace of a ship in orbit in the area at the time in question.'

'Olga, you come up with some good ones.' Fanny turned to Claymore and told him to do what Olga suggested. 'As for the sniffer, you go ahead. It's a thin move but we have little choice. I'm gonna contact Dil and report in.'

Olga used her throat mike to reprogramme a sniffer to locate and follow the possible ship, if it managed to find this teleport ship. Then she sent it on its way.

Fanny muttered into her throat mike to make a connection to the *Faust*. 'Hi Dil, just thought I'd apologise for cutting you off the last time. We were kinda busy. Anyway, we're ready to go back to the office. I thought you might be able to come and pick us up.'

'Fanny, you're fired…I mean you were all fired up last time we talked.' Praut just managed to curtail his poor attempt at a joke. 'Apology accepted. Did you get who you were after?'

'No Dil, the party teleported off planet. Olga's just sending a sniffer up into orbit to see if we can pick up a trace. So, can you pick us up? I'll give you the full report on the way back to earth.'

'Lucky for all of you, we're just a short distance away. I'll be with you in an hour. Where do you want to be picked up from?'

'Simplest is the space elevator ASO. We'll be there soonest. Ciao.'

'Ciao,' Praut closed the come link.

Fanny looked relieved at leaving Mars. The trip was a failure and she didn't like failures. 'So has the sniffer gone?' Fanny asked.

'Yeah, just sent it off upstairs. See what happens, okay?' Olga looked pleased and disappointed at the same time.

Fanny stood up and faced her two companions. 'Dil is collecting us from the top of the space elevator in an hour.

Get your stuff together, we're going home.' Into her throat mike she asked Barnhart in security, 'Could you look for any CCHV footage of Wanda. Could you please send the stuff to the Praut Agency on Earth, and could you let us have a shuttle ride to the top of the space elevator. Thanks.'

# 6
# UNTIMELY DEATHS

Ping. 'Hi Dil, you there?'

'Yes Sanj, what can I do for you?'

'I've just had the big boys at WGS on to me.' Sanjit looked bemused. 'They want to know why you've been snooping around on Callisto. I told them to get in touch with you...but I thought I'd warn you. The WGS is after you.'

'Why ask you?'

'They must be bugging my coms. They know we've talked.'

'Thanks Sanj. Sorry for the trouble.' Praut smiled at this new hassle and disconnected.

They were all gathered in Praut's office for a review of their progress, or lack of it. Eight people spread round the room on contour chairs or contour couches.

'Olga, Fanny tells me you've got something to tell me.'

'When we got back, I had a report from my sniffer,' said Olga, relaxing in a contour seat. 'It sent an e-com through the Kuipers relay node while still chasing its quarry. It's found traces of a cloaked ship in orbit around Mars. The sniffer's positron-based q-sensor managed to detect the traces of a cloaking device. There's an ion trail leaving Mars orbit a few moments after Wanda ported up. My sniffer isolated the plasma decay rate, but can't tell what kind of ship it is. The ion trace from its engines is not in the database. So whatever was up there warped out through the Oort cloud and into open space soon after. I have my sniffer following their warp trail.'

‘Why can’t it identify the ship?’ Praut asked surprised.

‘As I said, it’s not in the database. It means there’s a ship’s ion signature out there that’s so new, it’s not been put into the database yet.’

‘Or…it’s never gonna be put into a database.’ Praut screwed up his brows. ‘Just when I’d began to opt for the revenge idea as a working hypothesis…I start getting this new techy stuff thrown at me again. Either someone on the rim has made one hell of a techy breakthrough or we are dealing with an alien technology…and I don’t like the implications of that. And to add to the shit, the WGS boys are getting involved.’ Praut wasn’t happy.

‘What’s this revenge thing?’ asked Fanny. First time she’d heard of the idea.

‘It’s something Mes came up with while we were en route to Callisto.’ Praut turned to Meserine, ‘You tell her.’

Meserine began, ‘I had this idea that someone out there might simply want to destroy the wormhole stuff because it’s a technology. What if this someone had rich relatives who’ve been squelched by a malfunctioning wormhole, and they’re out to get revenge. Maybe this someone’s had the big boss of a techy conglomerate squelched by a wormhole. Then their relatives went bananas and go after the wormhole developers?’

‘Yeah, could be,’ said Fanny thoughtfully. Then she asked Praut, ‘So are we going down that road, or are you changing direction?’

‘Keep an open mind for the moment. We don’t have enough info yet.’

Then Fanny asked, ‘Clay, what happened when you checked Darhlburg’s q-machines? Did you find one of them ported Wanda?’

‘Nah, nada. It wasn’t a Darhlburg computer.’

‘It was only an idea,’ Olga defended her suggestion.

‘So what now, Dil?’ Fanny asked.

'I've brought back something from Callisto I want Edel here to have a look at. I want his tech expertise to tell me if it's human technology.'

Gangly Edel Vartaplug raised his eyebrows in anticipation. 'Glad to, where is it?'

'It's in the next room. I can't make head or tail of it. It seems to be full of weird looking crystals.'

Edel pushed himself out of the couch and ambled next door.

'Tilmore, any progress on who's behind the grabworms? Did you ask Clay to write the worm grabber program?'

'Sorry boss, I forgot. I'll ask him in a minute. But the other thing; I did manage to trace the grabworm to a weird planet called Harmony in Sector O7 on the Outer Arm of the galaxy about ten kiloparsecs from here…at least that's what the circuitous route of the server logs show.'

Claymore hadn't been listening and now looked mystified at his name being thrown into the conversation. He looked questioningly at his friend and colleague, Tilmore.

'Good, well done Til. That's the first piece of positive news I've had,' said Praut. 'Well, apart from the piece of junk Edel is working on next door.'

Praut, as usual, was scrutinising their faces and noticed Fanny's reaction when Harmony was mentioned. She had a look of intense distaste.

'You know this planet Harmony?' he asked her.

Astonished at being noticed, Fanny responded, 'Me? No way. Just didn't like the name, that's all.'

Edel's head came round the door, 'Boss, can I borrow Til for a moment to give me a hand?'

Tilmore looked at Praut and the latter nodded his assent. Tilmore walked out to join Edel in analysing the strange missile fragment from Callisto.

'Fanny, find out how to get to this planet Harmony. If it's not too much of a hassle, I want you to go there and check out who's sending the grabworm. Take anyone you need.'

'You sure you want *me* to do this?'

'You got a problem with this planet?'

'No…not really. Just don't like the sound of it.'

'Fanny, you're my right hand. I need you on this. Take Clay and it'll all turn out okay.'

She sighed, 'Right Dil.'

Suddenly, from next door, there came a loud ***thwack*** followed by a ***whoosh***, which blew the door off its hinges right into Praut's office.

A momentary shock followed by, '*What the shit*?' from Praut.

The office holo-image shimmered for a split second and then stabilised. An e-alarm began to give off a high pitched racket.

Fanny and the others leapt from their seats. Fanny rushed next door, then stopped in the shattered doorway, standing looking into the room with a look of horror on her face. Praut joined her, and stared at the carnage. There were bits of mangled flesh everywhere, and blood splattered the whole scene; the walls, the floor, and even on the ceiling. Edel's and Til's flesh were spread in small pieces all over the bloodied room.

Nobody spoke.

'*What the hell's happened*?' Praut blurted out angrily.

Meserine joined Fanny and held her by the shoulders. Olga came over and joined them. Fanny and Olga were moved to tears. A stunned Claymore stood with Harry, looking at the bloodbath in the room.

Harry managed to say, 'It must've been booby-trapped.' He turned to look for the door, and found it up against the back wall, with a blackened scar across its middle.

'But....how? Why right now?' Praut wasn't able to sort out his anger from his devastation. He'd just lost two of his best people...and it was he who'd brought the bloody piece of junk back to the office, and paid a hundred thousand credits to do so.

Fanny, dabbing at her tears, spat out with venom, 'If I find whoever this rubbish belongs to, *I'll wipe them out.*'

The rest of her colleagues all agreed with her.

'From what I can see,' Praut motioned at the junk on the table, 'the damned thing is still as I found it. It's not exploded or anything...or been damaged. With the mess it's made, I expected it to be in small pieces.' He was throaty with emotion at the needless deaths.

'It's not a particle beam weapon, not with all this blood and flesh all over the place. Particle beams disintegrate. Must be some kind of weird scatter laser,' suggested Claymore.

Fanny said, 'Dil, we have to report this. Two people dead...the police need to be informed.'

'Yes, you're quite right.' Into his throat mike, he told his auto-sec, 'Get through to Polizeiobermeister Hanz Otto at Frankfurt Police Headquarters. Ask him to port up here. Give him my name and tell him there's been an accident and I need to see him urgently. Two people dead.'

'Yes sir.'

'In the mean time, Fanny, seal this room. It's off limits.' Praut ushered Clay and Harry off to another office.

Meserine, as a space pilot, was coping a little better. She'd seen worse in her time. She pulled herself together and led the other two women away from the dreadful scene, following Praut. 'I'll seal the room,' Mes told Fanny. She came back and put three chairs into the doorway of the disaster room, blocking the entrance.

A short while later Praut's auto-sec announced, 'Polizeiobermeister Otto here to see you.'

Before long, three men strode into Praut's office.

‘Hanz, Wie geht’s dir?’ effused Praut, as he went over to shake his friend’s hand. Glad to see you. I wish it were under different circumstances.’ Praut was staring at the two men accompanying the police

‘Dil my friend, I came as soon as I could.’ Lieutenant-Colonel Hanz Georg Otto returned Praut’s fulsome handshake. ‘Let me introduce Brigadier Shevchenko and Colonel Saunders from WGS. We were just talking about you when your call came through. They asked to accompany me. I hope you don’t mind?’

Praut nodded at the two WGS officers and said, ‘No, of course not. I half expected them.’

‘So what’s happened?’

Praut led them to the doorway of the devastated room. ‘We’ve sealed off the room. On the table, you’ll find the cause. I brought it back from Callisto with me.’

The two WGS officers looked meaningfully at each other.

Colonel Otto didn’t need to ask what happened. The carnage in the room told the story.

‘And that mechanism on the table did all this?’ Otto asked with surprise on his face.

‘We were all sitting in this room and I sent Edel Vartaplug next door to examine the mechanism and give me his expert opinion. He’s our tech expert. Next thing I know, there was a loud *whooshing* noise and this,’ Praut spread his hand at the scene in the room.

‘You say there were two people in there…?’

‘Yes, sorry, Edel came and asked Tilmore Krout to come and give him a hand…just before it destroyed them.’

‘I see. And what’s that thing on the table? I assume you think that’s what’s caused the damage.’

‘I’m certain that’s the cause. As to what it is…’ Praut stared at the two WGS officers. ‘I was told it was part of a missile that wrecked the Callisto dome. These gentlemen took away most of the missile, but they missed this piece.’

The brigadier was just about to say something, but Otto held his up hand to stop him and said, ‘First things first.’ He spoke into his throat mike, then turned to Praut and the WGS officers. ‘There’ll have to be an official inquest on this,’ the colonel said for the benefit of the WGS officers. ‘And the coroner will have to be informed. I’ll get my forensic people to go through this,’ he swept the room with his hand. ‘We’ll remove what we can salvage to the morgue. Forensics will reconstruct what happened here. Once we know the details, the coroner’s inquest can pronounce on it…and only then will we release everything to you gentlemen. This is Europol and German jurisdiction and German law *will* prevail. I’m its servant and intend to carry it out to the last letter of the law. We will do this by the book. And Herr Praut,’ Colonel Otto became formal, ‘I would like an affirmed recorded statement from all the people who were in this room prior to the accident.’

‘But of course.’

Both Praut and Otto could see the two WGS officers weren’t at all happy at this official turn of events. However, unless there was clear evidence of imminent world security issues involved, local law took precedent. Since the situation was static, then there were no evident urgent issues. WGS would have liked to hush this up, but a local senior police officer was preventing that, and there was little they could do about it.

The two WGS officers were staring longingly at the missile part lying on the table.

Praut spoke into his throat mike, ‘Clear glass, one and a half meters from floor.’

The office glass cleared and Praut looked out into reception. He watched as the forensics people materialised at the teleport and made their way round the lake to his office. Behind them came a group of policemen towing a hover box.

'I knew Edel, and you have my sympathies,' Colonel Otto said to Praut. 'He helped us out from time to time. Wizard with any machine. We'll miss him.'

'Thanks.'

'I'll try to make this as quick and as painless as I can. It'll be over in a week. I'll use my influence.'

Just then, four forensics came through the door towing a large hover bag. Otto pointed at the room but held his hand up to stop them.

Another of Praut's employees, a section chief called Helmut, popped in and asked Praut what had happened.

'It's alright, Helmut,' Praut soothed. 'Tell everyone it's all under control and they should continue with their work.'

The employee didn't look convinced, but shrugged in resignation and went to inform his other colleagues what their boss had said.

Then four heavily armed policemen towing a graded-Z shielded laminate hover box lined with lead, followed the forensics people into Praut's office from reception.

Otto ordered the P4 police sergeant in charge of the police squad, 'Go in there,' he pointed at the room, 'and you'll find a piece of junk lying on the table. Approach cautiously, and be careful how you handle it. It's very dangerous. Put it gently in the box and seal it…and don't open the box again until I say so. Take it down to lockup and put a sign on it that says, it's quarantined. Am I clear? No one is to go near it. Be warned, it's messy in there.'

'Yes sir,' replied the sergeant and got one of his men to move the blocking chairs out of the way.

When the police squad left, the forensics people donned protective suits and went inside.

'I'll wait till forensics have finished then leave you in peace to mourn your friends.' Otto was talking quietly as befitted the sad situation. To the WGS officers he said, 'Have you anything to say to Herr Praut here?'

The WGS brigadier shook his head. 'No, I think it can wait. What we really wanted was that missile part.' He turned to Praut, 'Pity you didn't hand it over to us as you should have done. It might have saved some lives.'

A flash of anger crossed Praut's face, 'If you hadn't hushed everything up, maybe I wouldn't have had to play cat and mouse with you. Did you think of that? What's so bloody important with this stuff that you can't tell the people? Why all this stupid cloak and dagger stuff?' He was just about to really let rip, when a look on Otto's face stopped him. 'I'll get started on the statements,' and he stormed out into another room where his people waited.

As Colonel Otto walked back through reception to the teleport station with the two WGS men, he said to the brigadier, 'I thought we agreed in my office, you would be discreet with Herr Praut. No heavy handedness.'

'I thought I was being discreet,' he responded innocently.

'That bit about handing over the missile piece to you…and saving lives? That's being discreet to the point of callousness,' Otto replied.

# 7
# HARMONY

The next day there was a solemn atmosphere that threw a dampener on everything in the Agency. Praut was sitting in the office with Fanny, Meserine, Olga, Claymore, and Harry.

'How's everybody else taking what happened,' he asked Fanny.

'With the rest of the office? What can I say? It's a bummer. Everybody thinks it's a bummer. Although, everybody is being very supportive.'

'In my judgement, the best memorial to Edel and Til, will be to catch whoever's responsible for that missile.' He looked around the table to see if they agreed.

'I second that,' Olga said almost inaudibly.

Meserine took up the cry, 'And me. I'm itching to get my hands on those responsible.'

'Yeah, count me in,' Claymore added.

'Don't forget me,' Harry chimed in.

'What about you,' Praut asked Fanny. 'You haven't' said anything.'

'I didn't think I needed to. Of course I'm in. Just say the word.'

'Well, the word is Harmony. Before Til went into that damned room, he said something about tracing the grabworm to a planet called Harmony in Sector O7 on the Outer Arm of the galaxy.' Praut addressed Fanny, 'Did you go through Til's stuff as I asked you to?'

'Yeah, Dil. His personal e-notes had lots of computer logs, but I didn't find much on Harmony. I had Clay look at the logs, and he confirms the grabworms seem to originate from Harmony. It's a way off planet. Very weird…it's gone back in time. It tries to live in a peculiar period of the mid twentieth century. Something called hippy time. That's five hundred years in the past. The people of that period took lots of drugs and tried to drop out of society. You sure you still want me to go there? Sounds like a nightmare.'

Praut screwed up his face, 'Sorry, but that's exactly what I'm proposing you do. We don't have many leads. Can you manage to overcome your reluctance? Remember, this grabworm is removing all wormhole stuff from the galactic internet. It's important to find out who's running it and why.'

Fanny shrugged in resignation. 'If I must, I must. Why don't you come with me?'

'I've got other stuff in the oven.'

'Dil, you don't know what it's costing me to go to this loony planet, but for the sake of yesterday, I'd refuse. I'm going for Edel and Til's sake.'

'As long as you go. Take anyone you want, but I'd still recommend Clay, since it's a computer thing you're chasing.' Then Praut changed his attentions, 'Olga, what about the sniffer. Where's the little perisher now.'

'Last time it reported in, the ship was leading it halfway across the galaxy. It's still locked onto that ship's trace. That's what you wanted, wasn't it?'

'Quite right. If it can follow the ship's trace, it must. No matter what the cost, we have to find the ship's hideout. Ride it to destruction if need be.'

Olga feigned shock at the idea of one of her sniffers being destroyed.

To Fanny, Praut said, 'I'm taking Olga and Harry, and we're chasing the sniffer. Mes is driving. As for *that* planet, I have a contact for you on Harmony. He's a friend of a friend…go see him. All the info is on this data cube.' Praut threw the cube gently so Fanny could catch it. 'Right folks, this meeting is over.'

* * *

Fanny and Clay were on their way to Harmony, a hippie planet ten kiloparsecs from the Solar system, in Sector O7 on the Outer Arm of the galaxy. Initially Harmony had been colonised by serious human migrants, but slowly over a short period, it had been turned into a sanctuary for the rabble of the galaxy, attracted by it's Outer Arm location. It became a haven for outrageous avant-garde artists, corrupt financiers, conmen, drug addicts, layabouts, thieves and other petty criminals kicked off of other planets. These odious immigrants had inserted themselves into the fabric of Harmony until the original settlers had had enough and left in disgust.

Ten kiloparsecs and two days later, as the starship *Calliope* dropped out of warp and approached the planet; the passengers were met by a kaleidoscope of dazzling colours, spread in space in an exuberant cosmic tableau. The tableau depicted a series of paintulptures, hanging in the largest gallery nature could provide.

The composers of these so-called works of art, dashed around in their garish spaceships, maniacally creating, distractedly reshaping their creations for the delectation of those on the planet's surface. During the hours of darkness, the paintulptures lit up the night sky with a psychedelic extravagance, proclaiming the artist's effusive rapture and the intense expression of their artistic ideals.

Fanny and Clay stood in the observation lounge on the *Calliope,* where in spite of Fanny's provocative distaste for all things artistic, she gaped in astonishment at the brilliant exhibition lighting up the blue darkness of space around the red-blue planet. Fanny had a sense of foreboding as she watched the outlandish dissonance of colours being traced by these Bohemian artist's on this haunt of good-for-nothing slubberdegullions.

‘Look at that one,’ enthused Claymore, pointing at a particularly garish paintulpture. ‘Isn’t it marvellous?’ He didn’t notice Fanny’s scowling face.

For Fanny, this trip was a total nightmare. This was the last place in the galaxy she wanted to visit. It had painful memories of a past she’d rather forget. Yet unbeknown to Praut, she’d arranged to visit this planet. Her reluctance was a carefully contrived sham.

As the ship touched down at Euterpe’s Spaceport, her mind went back to the day eleven years ago on Earth, when her father had run out on her mother and her. The callous act had broken her mother’s heart. He’d had this daydreaming quest for a fantasy Shangri-la and chose that day to pursue it. Five hundred years ago on old Earth, they’d have called him a dropout, a beatnik, or a hippie.

Yet six years ago, she had promised her dying mother she would make one last attempt to reconcile herself with her missing father. Some weeks before, prior to the current job, she’d hired a lawyer to trace that self indulgent seeker after sensualism, and two days ago the lawyer had named the planet Harmony. She was unbelievably shocked when Til, and later Praut, mentioned the place. Now she’d arranged to meet with her hired lawyer, and she was going to try to squeeze in some private business with her current assignment…without telling Claymore.

Fanny was a hard nosed individual, assertive and hard working, who’d spent most of her time pushing her way up within various Solar corporations until she’d come across Dilmore Praut. He’d just started the Agency, and in his first job, he’d been investigating the disappearance of a large sum from the corporation she was working for at the time. In short order, he’d uncovered a major fraud by the finance director. Praut and Fanny took to each other and with his usual directness; Praut offered her a job in his Agency.

To look at her, she could have fitted well into any fashion salon. She was tall, slim, had striking red hair, cold green eyes, and angular facial features. She was also calculatingly oblivious of the effect she had on the males, immersing herself in her work, gaining from her detractors the unmerited nickname of *the cold Aphrodite*.

The Id-checks at Euterpe were minimal, almost sloppy. With a swift retinal scan, she and Clay were out of the flower filled spaceport and into a waiting Hydro with what there was of their luggage. The Hydro lifted, and headed for Euterpe proper, the main commune on Harmony.

Enroute, there were more artworks, water sculptures, aerial sculptures, murals on billboards in the sky with actual old fashioned *paint* on them, visual dribbles, huge kinetic masterpieces forever performing some purposeless task. To add to the ocular cacophony; interspersed between the magna opera were the occasional anti-art toilet, turd, exhibited in a conventional holographic context. Yet again, they were attempting to make fun of all serious artistic declarations, the interminable challenge to the nature of art. In reality, the turds merely illustrated their creator's barrenness of any worthwhile talent. In endeavouring to provoke all art forms, the artist simply declared their inability to be original or say anything artistic.

At least this was her explanation of what she saw. The long-haired driver of the Hydro, himself a minor poet, with a red bandanna around his forehead, insisted on illustrating anti-art with some nonsense poetry.

*Help!* Thought Fanny, *everyone's thinks they're an artist, and I'm going to drown in all this crap.* She sat quietly beside Clay throughout the twenty-minute journey, trying not to encourage the talkative poet, come driver. Claymore on the other hand, listened attentively, and even put in his own two-bits worth.

Fanny butted in, 'How come you're driving this by yourself? Don't they have under-road guidance systems?'

The driver dismissed her interruption, 'Nah, this is Harmony not Urania. Don't need that crap here.'

An old style screen sprung to life in the roof of the cab, declaring *Gilgamesh Lives,* in bold cuneiform-like script. The hero of Sumerian legend, Lord of the city of Uruk, was performing live at the local Hippodrome, for the next two weeks. All twelve books of verse recounting the Epic of Gilgamesh would be performed by the *Ancient Epic Society*, including the devastating Flood. *Now that ought to be fun,* she thought, *maybe they could drown the audience and call it kinetic art.*

The Hydro stopped at the local Waldorf, and an android porter extracted their luggage. The architecture of the building was in the style of Gaudí, the gnarled imprint of nature festooning every cranny. She went to the desk to claim their reservation, while Clay settled with the hydro driver. To her disgust, walking through the foyer, she found herself included in a live action theatre performance group. They attempted to inveigle her to act as a suspect in a murder scene, and she threatened to carry out a real murder if they didn't leave her alone.

Above the reception desk, Théophile Gautier's ancient doctrine *l'art pour l'art*, was emblazoned in large neon-like lettering.

As Fanny led Clay to the elevator, she muttered to herself, *I've landed in a madhouse*. In the elevator, Hackmausen bleared at them from the sound system, producing the random dissonance that passed for highbrow music. They stepped off at the first floor and walked down the corridor to their adjoining rooms.

Fanny entered her room and found a large screen covering one whole wall. It was depicting a scene from the *Ramayana,* a Sanskrit epic of circa 300 BC, where Rama and his friend Hanuman, the monkey chieftain, strove to recover Rama's wife, Sita, abducted by the demon king Ravana. She noted a sign on the back of the door inviting her to an address to purchase any drug of her choice…even e-stimulants for neural implants.

She commanded, 'Next channel!' and the scene changed to the *Kalevala,* the Finnish national epic where the hero, Väinämöinen, had his horse shot from under him by the Pohjola Joukahainen. '*Next channel*!' she yelled, and *El Cid,* from the anonymous Spanish epic, had master Rodrigo Díaz de Vivar, fighting off the Moorish attempts to take the alcazar of Valencia; she quickly flicked through other channels and had, Homer's *The Iliad, The Odyssey,* Virgil's *Aeneid,* the *Nibelungenlied*, *Beowulf, The Chanson de Roland,* flash across the screen in quick succession; '*Off!*' she ordered in exasperation. *Isn't there any normal programming on this arts infested planet? Why do I have to be bombarded by these ancient culture vultures?*

A holo-com demanded her attention. There was a call from the lawyer she'd hired to locate her father.

'Miss Fanny Fester?' a dark face was asking.

'Yes.'

'I'm Mark Melpomene. You hired me to find your father.'

'And have you?'

'Yes. He's living in Euphrosyne, an obscure commune on the other side of the planet.'

'I'm staying at the Waldorf, can you come round.' *Best to meet him on my terms*, she thought.

'I'm calling from the lobby of the Waldorf,' he sounded full of himself.

'I'll be right down.'

On her way, she knocked on Clay's door and walked in. 'Listen Clay, I'm feeling whacked after that journey. Be a dear man and go see Praut's contact by yourself. Here's the address. Make sure you get a proper address on this planet where the grabworm came from.' She gave him the data cube. 'I'm going downstairs and have a small drink, then I want to lie down for a while. Will you do that for me?' She smiled sweetly at Clay.

'Sure Fan, no prob.' Then Claymore remembered to complain, 'They don't even have a clothes exchanger in my room. Would you believe it?'

'It's a primitive planet. I was surprised they had an android porter.' Fanny agreed.

'They had a clothes exchanger on the ship coming here.'

'Yes, but the ship had a q-machine. I doubt there a q-machine on this whole planet. Clay, you're gonna have to make do, that's all.' She left Claymore's room and went downstairs.

In the lobby, she met a tall dark haired man of what should have been around fifty. His features seemed nondescript, but the eyes were grey and hawk-like.

'Let's go have a schlapee,' she suggested.

As they sat down in the small hotel Café, to the pervasive sounds of chamber music hovering in the air; they eyed each other, both probing for a weakness.

Fanny said, 'The only reason I'm searching for my father is because of my mother's death bed wish. She wanted me to patch things up with him.'

Her dying mother's last action had been selfish. She wanted to make sure her daughter *met* her errant father at least once, face to face. She'd hoped to induce some remorse into her husband for his actions.

'The commune he's living in has a notorious reputation for tripping visitors,' he told her bluntly.

'Tripping?' she asked.

'In their drinks, or their food. Sending people unwittingly on psychedelic trips. They don't rob them or anything like that, but they believe *the trip* turns them into better people, changing them for the good. I'm telling you this, so you're aware of what you're letting yourself in for.' He looked at her for a reaction.

'And the authorities turn a blind eye to it?'

'What authority there is, warn people not to go there.'

'Fine state of affairs!' Fanny said in disgust. 'He won't leave the place, and now you're virtually warning me not to go there. So how do I get to meet him?' she looked at the lawyer.

'You may not like this; but my job's done. I've located him for you. The rest is up to you,' he sat back in his chair. 'You didn't pay for anything else.'

'Okay! So is there anything I can take to prevent the effects of their drugs?'

'Not I'm aware of.'

'You mean I've to take my chances? Is that what you're saying?' she looked at him with aversion.

He shrugged his shoulders, and said nothing. She sat sipping her schlapee for a moment, mulling over the disturbing change of events; chewing her lip, thinking.

'How does anything manage to function with all these Bohemians running amuck?' she finally said, changing the subject.

'The Government was franchised out some years back. At the beginning, the early colonists suffered years of mayhem, chaos, and anarchy, whilst the artistic factions fought each other to a standstill, and the criminals robbed everyone. Then, when the initial settlers left, the remnants held a fragile peace conference and decided to franchise the running of the Government out to Urania, the neighbouring system, who now provides the entire infrastructure on a contractual basis, strictly business. They put a stop to the more outlandish criminal enterprises…threw them out. Bad for tourism. Tourism and art sales fill this planet's coffers. Now the artists get on with art, and the franchise brings in the tourists,' he leaned forward to admire his client.

'But that's shameful. It's tantamount to admitting incompetence,' the control freak in Fanny was outraged.

'Not at all. It takes courage to admit you need help. They know they can't run the infrastructure, and so they've brought in professionals. I'm from Urania myself.'

'No offence meant, but I find it repugnant to have to hand over control to someone else.'

'Maybe you'll change your mind after you've seen more of the planet.'

'Now your being patronising,' she said.

'I can't win, can I?' he smiled.

'How do I get to Euphrosyne?' she ignored his remark.

'Take a shuttle. It's the easiest way. If you allow me; my office will arrange passage.'

'For tomorrow?'

'Certainly! I'll have the ticket waiting at the shuttle port.'

They parted in an atmosphere of polite mutual suspicion. He was wondering how to squeeze her credits; she was wondering how to keep him at arm's length, having a healthy distrust of all lawyers.

Back in her room, Fanny lay down and waited for Clay to return.

Some time later, there was a knock on the door. Fanny woke with a start. 'Wait a minute!' she shouted, climbing quickly to her feet. 'Yes, come in.'

'Were you asleep?' asked Claymore as he walked in.

'Just a short nap. So what did you find out?'

'Short nap? Its evening now. Anyhow, the fellow turned out to be a lawyer.' Claymore noticed Fanny screwing up her face at the mention of *lawyer*. 'Anyway, Dil knows some strange people. This lawyer told me there's a new outfit that's set up on Harmony called Zimmer Inc. It's very secretive and the company imported all its personnel here off planet. People are assuming it's one of those criminal enterprises that thrives in this sloppy environment. They're based about twenty klicks west of Euterpe. It seems the grabworm came from them. Thought we might go have a look. What'd think?'

‘We do need to have a look, but I’ve got something on for tomorrow. Dil asked me to do something for him,’ Fanny lied. ‘So I want you to do a recky on Zimmer’s location and we’ll meet tomorrow night and see where we go from there. Okay?’

‘Sure, whatever you say.’

‘Now we’ll go and have some food in the restaurant, and as it late, we’ll turn in.’

# 8
# VIRTUAL ZIMMER

The following morning, having sent Clay off to reconnoitre Zimmer Inc., Fanny boarded the shuttle for Euphrosyne, stopping at Polyhymnia, Kale, Erato, Aglaia, and Mnemosyne. The Musician's Union grabbed the opportunity of a captive shuttle passenger audience, to present them with the latest developments in musical compu-simulations. Piece after piece, written and composed through ancient computers, was delivered through proximity speakers. Fanny angrily hushed hers, but could still hear the overtones from her neighbour's racket. To her, the so-called music was utterly atrocious and she fumed at the stupid antics being forced on her.

The journey took her through some of the wildest countryside she'd ever seen. But then she was comparing everything with the neatness of Earth, and it was really unfair to this countryside. After putting the climate in order, Earth was lush and green again, a planet where one could dance in the green meadows. This planet was in decay with a lot of red soil, a dry land with lots of dust and dirt and a sore lack of moisture. The shuttle even travelled over a shallow sea that gave the impression it was struggling to survive. The planet badly needed terraforming but the people lacked the will and the credits.

At the first stop, Polyhymnia, they were met by a number of choirs which rushed to surround their shuttle, seemingly competing with each other in ancient sacred choral song. Other various communes they went through specialised in the art the commune was named after. Kale made itself as beautiful and enticing as possible, almost siren like. A number of passengers disembarked, caught up by its evocative appeal. The largest group got off at Erato, which specialised in love poetry. Bold banners could be seen through the shuttle windows advertising the Indian love Sutras, including the Kamasutra. For Fanny it might as well have been the infamous Porn City on Astarte—a hedonists paradise without meaning.

She nodded off through Aglaia, and awoke on the way to Mnemosyne. They circumvented the highest mountains on Harmony, the twin peaks of Helicon and Parnassus, covered in snow, rising majestically into the blue-red sky. The meagre waterfalls and rivers of these mountains fed the far off Sea of Nereid, filled with a vibrant local fauna.

The next stop was her destination, Euphrosyne. Again she reminded herself not to eat or drink anything during her visit; *get in there do what I came to do, and get out.* As the shuttle touched down at the shuttleport, the view from the window was of a somewhat dilapidated commune; colourful but run-down. When she'd disembarked and went into the commune centre, Fanny became aware of the total neglect inflicted on their residency by the inhabitants. The place was filthy, refuse in the streets, peeling paint, and the utter shabbiness of the surroundings made her shudder.

She approached one of the inhabitants lolling in the street near the shuttleport, asking him where she might find Gandalf Thalia. The fellow looked at her with vacant eyes, staring right through her. *This is Shangri-la?* She thought with contempt. *More like dystopia, or kakotopia.* She went over to a kiosk, where the dark-haired owner was busy reading a VidMag on his screen. He had shaggy long black hair and a portly indisposition.

'Excuse me, can you give me some information?' She hoped she put the right tone of deference into her voice.

'Huh?' the owner didn't bother looking up.

'Can you tell me where I can find Gandalf Thalia,' she was still being courteous.

'He's just bought that organic store over yonder,' he pointed at a two level building on the right, further down the filthy main street.

She headed towards the store, then through the large shop front window she glimpsed the outline of an image. Stepping closer, she stared through the glass and saw a tall thin old man standing at the top of a step ladder, his long light hair tied in a pony tail. Gandalf was stacking some shelves with some kind of containers. In the display window of the store, there were crystals proclaiming magical properties, and notices extolling exotic healing remedies, all backed by Earth's ancient *new age* wisdom. It was like going back thousands of years, to a time of ignorance and superstition.

Fanny was disgusted in having to be there at all. In a time of food replicators, warp drives, and nanobots, these people had reverted to irrational beliefs and sheer feeble-mindedness. *Well, here goes nothing.* She went into the store. Gandalf, oblivious, continued stacking his shelves.

'Hallo Gandalf!' she tried to put a pleasant tone into her voice.

Gandalf froze. Slowly he turned towards her. Then his eyes widened, 'Is that you Fanny?' His eyes narrowed, and she noticed a pronounced tic in the left one, as he recognised her.

'I thought you might be expecting me,' she responded nonchalantly.

'The thought had crossed my mind. I end up inheriting your mother's money, and you turn up begging,' his voice was full of sarcasm. 'You alone?' he looked passed her.

'Is that what I'm doing here?' she joined in the sarcasm, 'Begging? I see you've already started spending *my* money!' She swept her hand around the store.

'I was her *husband* and next of kin. The law says *I* inherit her estate,' he looked defensive in a maniacal way.

'*Husband*? You don't know the meaning of the word. So why did you run off, leaving her in the lurch? *Was that your idea of being a husband*?' Fanny found herself shouting at him.

He stood looking at her with some vehemence, yet alert. The way he kept looking around gave him a semblance of paranoia…even of guilt.

'You're a self obsessed hedonist, always on the lookout for what you can rip off. Look me in the face and deny it.' He seemed almost psychotic to her.

'And you're a cold emotionless anal-retentive brat!' He was trying to reassert himself.

They stood five meters apart, glaring daggers at each other. Then a look of animal cunning fleeted across his face.

'Look Fanny, I'm sorry we got off on the wrong foot. You're welcome to stay for a while. Why don't I make you a cup of coffee? Would you like that?'

'Oh yeah! Send me on a trip, and hope I don't come back from it. You must take me for the simpleton you thought my mother was.'

'Suite yourself! You're still welcome to stay. I live above the store. Why not go up and freshen up?'

'*That* at least I could do with,' and she headed for the stairs.

Upstairs she got out the bottled water she had bought with her, and reconstituted some dehydrated food, which she consumed straight away, not daring to leave it unattended. She cleaned herself up a bit, and after composing herself, went back downstairs.

'You got any transport?' she asked Gandalf.

'Round the back. It's a ground flitter. If you're going for a trip, be careful with it.'

She went out back, without answering him, found the flitter and climbed in. The flitter was old, and made a strange noise when it took off. She headed out into the surrounding desert, just going nowhere. She could think better whilst driving alone. About ten kilometres out, she halted amongst some scrub brush in a shallow ravine, and for the next two hours just sat there, on a boulder, trying to work up the courage to carry out her plan.

Finally, she came to a decision. Climbing resolutely back into the flitter, she lifted off and headed back to the commune. Back in the store, she confronted Gandalf again. He was still fiddling with the shelves in his obsessive over attention to detail.

'Morally, you've no right to my mother's legacy, and you know it.'

'Look Fanny, *you* may have a point; but *I've* got the money. Better get used to it!' He said with a tinge of hysteria and grim satisfaction. 'Why don't you try cultivating some charity? You've got a well paid job.'

'I intend to relieve you of *my* money, even if I have to kill you. I'll be damned if *my* mother's memory and hard work is going to subsidise your rotten life-style. Think that over!'

'You vicious bitch! I'm sure *glad* you're *no* daughter from my loins,' he spat out with venom.

'Now you mention it; so am I. I've known for some time you weren't my real father, but I went along with the charade for mother's sake. I know my father was a Space Captain, a *one night stand*...and I'm proud of it.' She looked insolently at Gandalf.

'Wait a mo. Did you just threaten me back then?' he looked around furtively.

'What do you think? You're the big wit. Work it out yourself! Why not look into your crystals? Maybe they can tell you?'

'We may be a small commune, but we still have *law*,' his voice was rising.

'You're hallucinating, Gandalf. The law has abandoned this place.' She could see beads of sweat appearing on his forehead.

She moved closer to the doorway; looked outside, saw the street was empty. She reversed the open sign and pulled down the roller blinds. Gandalf climbed down off the stepladder a little shakily. He picked up a pair of scissors off the counter and ambled towards her menacingly. From her pocket, she quickly removed a tranquillising zapper and as he approached, she fired a flash into Gandalf's groin. He collapsed and buckled to the floor.

She went over to the unconscious figure, knelt and prised open his mouth none too gently, then removed a plastic bottle from her pouch and placed a drop from a stopper on his tongue. The drop contained a powerful synthetic hallucinogenic, laced with alcuronium, a synthetic curare-like muscle relaxant, which would block the acetylcholine channels, paralysing Gandalf's muscles. The small dose of the muscle relaxant combined with the large dose of hallucinogen from the zapper, would point the autopsy, if there was one, in the direction of a long-standing well known self abuse.

She dragged the dying body of Gandalf into the back room of the shop, out of any peepers' sight, intending to sit tight for a couple of hours before reporting finding him like this. She'd come face to face with her *so called* father, as her dying mother had wished, but she had her own agenda for the meeting. She *had* been charitable; she'd put him out of his pathetic misery. She'd be damned if she let him enjoy her mother's inheritance.

As per plan, she staggered out of the store two hours later, claiming a headache and feigning confusion. The first person she came across was the kiosk owner, still reading his VidMag. He snickered as he saw her, assuming the commune had struck again, and *tripped* another visitor. He pointed her in the direction of the lone law enforcer in the commune, a Space Corps Ranger from Urania.

She reported to the sympathetic Ranger, of going into the store, then waking up just now to find the body of the old man, and of not really remembering what had happened to her. She said she'd accepted a coffee from Gandalf, her father, and that's the last thing she remembered. She'd come back to her senses, lying in the back room on the couch just a little while back and found Gandalf's body nearby. She was *almost* sure he was alive when she'd last seen him, before becoming unconscious.

She'd relied on a sloppy instant autopsy carried out on this backward planet; she wasn't disappointed. His death was immediately recorded as a misadventure, resulting from drug misuse. After another couple of hours, she took the evening shuttle back to Euterpe. She got through to Mark Melpomene on the shuttle comm and re-hired him to dispose of her late father's assets at the best price possible, and forward the sum it fetched back to her on Earth. The lawyer looked at her screen face in a wary curious manner, almost as if he suspected something. If he did, he kept it to himself.

As Fanny made her way back to Euterpe and the Waldorf, her conscience was at ease, and her mother's memory within her, at peace. Although it was late, Claymore sat waiting for her in the foyer of the hotel.

'You silly man, why did you wait up for me?' she reprimanded him as she neared him.

'I didn't have anything better to do,' he replied with a puzzled look. He was wondering where Fanny had been all day.

'You're looking a bit scruffy, Clay. So, what've you been up to? What did you find? Tell me all while we have a schlapee in the hotel Café.'

As they both sat down at an empty table, Claymore took a deep breath, 'Zimmer Inc. is a state of the art e-company; high tech brimming with defences and no way to access it from outside. It's real secretive...more suited to Urania than Harmony, but then on Urania, they would scrutinise this company closely, whilst here, it's as sloppy as could be, despite the Urania franchise.'

'So it follows the profile of what we're looking for. Any local whispers concerning the setup? Did you try pumping the locals?'

'I would if there were any computer geeks here. Locals are stum on what's happening out there.'

'So you went out there and sat and watched…is that it?'

'There's a strange looking hangar not far from the main office building. I tried peeking through the walls with the probe but the walls are fully deflected. I think the programming is done in the main building and the q-computer is in the hangar.'

'We're going to have to have another look at this hangar in the morning. Dig up anything else on the company?'

'From where? This dump hasn't go the tech to do a proper search. We'd have to go to Urania to do that. Anything else is useless. As for the hangar, I figured you'd want to have a look at it.' Claymore was getting upset at the frustration and lack of results.

'Okay,' Fanny put her hand up to stop him. 'It's getting late. I suggest we turn in and get an early start.'

As Fanny walked by the main desk, the desk clerk said, 'Miss Fester, a message just came in for you.' He handed her a piece of paper. Fanny looked at the paper with amazement. 'Hey Clay, look at this. They're still using real paper. Talk about backwards.'

'You sure it isn't plasto-paper?'

'No, it feels like real paper. How weird is that?'

'Told you they were a strange lot! What's it say?'

'It's cryptic; from Dil. He says he's heading our way. That's all. Signed DP.'

'So when's he due?'

'He don't say.'

'I'll bet its something to do with this company we're chasing.'

'Can't think of any other reason. Maybe he's found something?'

'Could be.'

'We'll find out soon enough,' was her last parting phrase as they parted, each entering their separate hotel rooms.

Early next morning, Fanny and Claymore hired an ancient Hydro from the hotel and sped twenty klicks westward out of Euterpe towards Zimmer's location.

'The entrance is just round the next bend in the hills, but there's a forcefield fence round the whole property. No way in,' Claymore informed Fanny.

'Where were you yesterday? You said you were looking at the hangar.'

'Stay this side of the hills and go to the top. Park just below the rise. If this was a government thing, they'd have satellite cameras probing the perimeter and we'd be spotted for sure, but with this company, using an orbital camera would attract too much attention from Urania. Remember they're trying to keep a low profile.'

Fanny parked the hydro below the knoll and both climbed out.

'Over here,' Claymore whispered.

'Why you're whispering?'

'Proximity acoustics. They'll have state of the art listening bots patrolling their perimeter.' Claymore reached into his pocket and pulled out a small box. 'I'm gonna deploy a few counter nanobots to hunt them down and shush them.' He let the nanobots out of the box.

'Won't that alert Zimmer security?'

'Specially made by me. Stealth mode.'

'I'm talking about they're security *not* getting a response from their listening bots.'

'My killer bots replace theirs. They won't know the difference. My lot mimic theirs, only they don't report the noise their supposed to.'

'Devious old dog,' Fanny complimented Clay.

'Play with the devil, act like the devil.'

'Where do you get these silly aphorisms,' Fanny smiled, while using her penet-scope to inspect the hangar. 'This is no good…can't see a thing. Their deflector shield throws the frequencies right back at me.'

'Yep, told you. Did the same thing to me yesterday.'

Fanny turned her attention on the main building which seemed to be made of compo-glass. 'Seems to be some kind of flap on. People are leaving the main building and heading for the hangar.'

'Yeah look, the hangar doors are opening.' Clay was keeping a sharp eye out on the hangar.

'Wait a mo, they've folded the deflector on the main building. What are they up to? I can see people lining up to teleport out. They're stepping on the port and disappearing. Where the hell are they going?' Fanny was getting annoyed at not knowing what was happening.

Claymore had his own penet-scope trained on the hangar. 'Now they've lowered the hangar deflector shield. *Shit, look at this*!' He was nudging Fanny's elbow to get her attention. 'It's a starship.'

'By cripes, you're right.' Fanny moved her penet-scope onto the hangar. 'They've got a starship in that building.'

'Holy mackerel, Fanny, look!' Claymore pointed at the main building.

'It's gone!' Fanny shot back. 'Must have been a holo-deck projection. That means they've got a big q-computer somewhere nearby.'

'It's on the ship. Has got to be. And its fairly powerful to reach out to fence the grounds.'

'Now the hangar's disappeared. Can't see any people anywhere.'

'They're all onboard the ship. They're leaving.'

Where there had been a large multi-floor building; now there was nothing, even the hangar had gone. All signs of occupation was disappearing before their very eyes. Then the starship shuddered and also vanished from sight.

'It's just cloaked,' cried Claymore, as he watched the rush of air and heard the *whoosh* of cloaked engines lift the ship up into the atmosphere, heading out to space. 'Now you see it, now you don't,' he added for emphasis.

'Look at that…nothing left,' Fanny sneered at the empty space left by what had been a fully functioning Zimmer Inc. a few minutes earlier. 'That is the most bizarre thing I've seen in a long time. Where's Olga when you need her? I could do with one of her sniffers right now.'

'What? To send after that ship?'

'Well of course. We need to know where that starship is heading. It'll set up somewhere else and be up to its old tricks in no time.'

'And set up as another high tech outfit on another planet,' Clay concluded for her.

'Right, let's get back to the hotel,' said Fanny, getting to her feet.

Claymore joined her in the hydro and they headed back to the Waldorf.

'Should we report what we've seen?' Claymore asked her.

'No point. The authorities either know already, or won't much care,' Fanny told him. 'Pity we didn't record this.'

'Who said we didn't?'

'Clay, tell me you did?'

'Yep! Got it all on the vidcube. Got a holo-camera on my hat. Thought it might come in handy when we reported to Dil.'

'I take my proverbial hat off to you. You are a genius.'

'So they tell me.' Claymore was used to being well regarded by his colleagues.

As Fanny and Claymore re-entered their hotel, Fanny spotted Praut sitting in the middle of the lobby, waiting for them. She waved, and he waved for them to join him.

'Dil, what are you doing here?' Fanny burst out eagerly as she reached her boss. She was pleased to see him.

'Well nice to see you too,' he joked. 'So where've you been?'

'Doing our jobs. Where's Olga? Is she with you?'

'Why? What's up? She's in the Café with Mes and Harry.'

'I need to get one of her sniffers to track a starship right away.'

Praut got to his feet and led the way to where Olga was chatting away to her colleagues.

'Hi Fanny,' Olga called out as the group neared. She nodded at Claymore.

'Listen Olga,' Fanny began, 'I need you to send one of your sniffers after a starship that's just left this planet's atmosphere.'

'What?' cried Olga. 'And have another one of my dears destroyed?'

Fanny stood aback at the outburst, puzzled as to what Olga was on about.

Praut explained, 'That sniffer we were following from Mars…it led us to this planet. That's why we're here. Only the ship it was following destroyed the sniffer somewhere between Harmony and Urania. Anyway, we lost contact with the sniffer. It's upset Olga.'

'Oh!' Fanny said not in the least surprised. 'I'm sorry for your loss, Olga…but that's the business we're in. Only we do need to move fast or we'll loose the trace of the ship that's just left this place.'

'Oh well, if we must. Have you got the coordinates of the ship?'

'I've got the *exact* coordinates for the sniffer.' She looked at Praut, 'And Clay's got some footage to show you that'll blow your mind.'

'We've left our ship at the spaceport,' Olga informed Fanny. 'I'll programme the sniffer from here, then launch it through the probe exit chute. There's one sitting in there already to go. Fanny, give me those coordinates.'

Fanny nodded to Claymore, who gave Olga the Zimmer Inc. galactic coordinates.

'The sniffer needs to pick up the starship's trace from that spot.'

Olga was talking quietly into her throat mike, giving the sniffer its instructions. Then she turned her attention to Praut, 'Dil, I'll take Mes and Harry with me, if you can spare them. I'm assuming you're not coming with me.'

Praut shook his head, 'No, I'm heading back to the office. We'll take the regular passenger warpship back to Earth. You go off…and keep in touch. I want a report twice a day. Morning and evening. And no heroics. I've lost two people already on this job, and I don't want to loose any more.'

# 9
# ASSASSINS

On the way back to earth, the small group had retired to a quite corner in the warpship's observation lounge. Occupying a cluster of contour seats, Praut viewed Claymore's vidcube footage of the dismantling of Zimmer Inc.

Praut commented, 'I knew this type of stuff was possible, theoretically, but I've never seen it in practice. Buildings, people, and *phut*, it all vanished in a shake of a lamb's tail.'

'They even had their getaway ship handy next door,' added Claymore. 'How many other outfits like that are there out there?'

Fanny tried to inject a modicum of sense, 'Let's face it Clay, our Agency office isn't much different. Most of it is holo-deck. We're parked 999 stories up, but after that, it's all q-machine controlled.'

'Yeah, but we got a proper address,' Clay told her, still feeling the Zimmer outfit had taken far too many liberties.

'No, Fanny's right. We've got to be on the lookout for this kind of thing. It's only possible on sloppily controlled planets…somewhere where there's little authority or central government. The revenue people make sure of that.'

'All only possible because of those damned computers,' Fanny mouthed just audibly in frustration.

'Fanny, I thought better of you,' Praut berated her. 'A computer is only doing what *someone's* told it to do. It doesn't do anything by itself. We all enjoy a beautiful laser display, but put to another use, a laser zapper can drill holes in you. Don't blame the laser for that.'

Claymore looked with dotting admiration at his boss for jumping in to defend his beloved computers.

'Sorry Dil,' Fanny said contritely, 'Having just seen Harmony and its backwardness, I shouldn't have said that. It's just that I get the feeling we're being given the run-around by some sharp conmen…and I don't like it. You're right; I shouldn't blame computers for Zimmer vanishing like that. I should blame whoever gave the orders.'

* * *

Two days later, back in their skyscraper office, Praut smiled at his audience of two and pronounced, 'For sure there's a guiding hand in all this mess…and all I know for certain is that they're out to destroy wormhole technology because it's some kind of threat to them. I wish I could work out what the threat was. We've been at this for almost two weeks and I'm still no wiser.'

In light of Praut's previous defence of computers on the warpship, Claymore decided to put in his suggestion, 'Has someone invented long distance teleportation? And is stabilising the wormhole interfering with their plans?'

Praut looked at his computer expert, surprised at the sensible question he'd just posed. 'Don't think its teleportation. A teleport needs a q-computer, and how are you going to stream the disassembled atoms over the millions of light years and then reassemble them at the other end? No, either someone's come up with a wormhole beater, or they don't want wormholes at all. It's the only thing that makes sense.'

'If you say so,' muttered Claymore.

'Fanny, its time we did our weekly report to Darhlburg Inc.,' Praut advised her. 'Re our progress on their behalf, can you put something together and send it off. Fill it with hopeful phrases. That'll be the second report saying no progress, but it can't be helped. We need to keep them informed even if we're not getting anywhere.'

'Will do,' Fanny replied. Fanny looked into the distance, slowly shaking her head at the lack of progress. As she finished her head movements, a bright flash exploded in the sky a good distance upward from them, but bright enough to attract their attention.

'What the hell was that?' asked Praut looking out through the window at the afterglow in the sky.

'I'd say it was one whopping explosion…somewhere high up above us. Probably about a hundred klicks away,' proposed Claymore.

'Yeah, that's what it looked like to me,' agreed Praut.

'Could it be a ship's exploding on entry?' asked Fanny.

'Yeah it could be…but I hope it wasn't. Nobody could survive that.'

Out in the reception area, people were running towards the western side of the building. Then out of nowhere, a large black shuttle bearing WGS insignia loomed closer, suddenly hovering next to the western wall of their skyscraper building.

'*Oh for fudge cake, what's going on out there*?' shouted Praut as he saw the WGS shuttle. He strode quickly out of the office and stopped in the doorway staring into reception.

The enormous black WGS shuttle now blocked out any view to the outside world. In the teleport bay, three figures materialised, all wearing black WGS uniforms.

Praut stood waiting. Clearly, the WGS uniforms were heading his way. Praut recognised two of the WGS men as Brigadier Shevchenko and Colonel Sanders from their earlier visit with Colonel Hans Otto on the deaths of Tilmore and Edel. They were being led by a tall hulk of a man marching out in front.

Fanny joined Praut at the office entrance, staring at the commotion in the reception area. 'We've got visitors,' she pointed out unnecessarily. Claymore was looking over Praut's shoulders into reception.

'I can see that,' mouthed Praut. 'They've brought in the big guns. That's a full general leading them.'

The three WGS men reached Praut. Brigadier Shevchenko said, 'Here we are again. Be assured, we mean you no harm. Mr Praut, may I introduce General Botha. He'd like a few words with you.'

'You'd better step into my office, gentlemen.' Praut led the way into his office. 'Fanny, I'll see you and Clay later.'

Inside Praut's office, he swept his arm at the chairs and said, 'Make yourselves comfortable. Can I get you some refreshments?'

'Thank you, no,' said the deep husky voice of the general as he parked his large frame in one of the contour seats. 'I'll get to the point. I assume you just saw the explosion above your building to the west?'

The other two WGS men sat on the contour couch, staring at Praut.

'Could hardly miss it. Was that your pyrotechnics?' asked Praut.

'Yes and no. We just intercepted a missile heading for your building…and dealt with it.'

Praut looked surprised, 'A missile…heading here?'

'Yes Mr Praut. It had your name on it.'

'Is this some kind of joke?'

'Do you see me laughing, Mr Praut.'

Praut sat there looking at the general, as if he'd just been slapped in the face.

'So now, Mr Praut, maybe you'd be so kind as to treat this job you've taken on…with a lot more caution than you have done to date.' The general was staring keenly at Praut's face, assessing the impact he'd made.

After a while, Praut looked the general squarely in the eyes. 'And maybe *you* would be so kind as to fill me in on what's just happened.'

'But of course. Brigadier…all yours.' Said the general to Shevchenko.

'We've been monitoring your airspace ever since that unfortunate mishap in your office,' the Brigadier began, 'We've assumed that someone would try to have a go at you sooner or later. Earlier today, our long-range radar near Pluto, picked up an incoming missile heading for Callisto. They, whoever *they* are, were going to have another go at the Singularity dome, but this time it was intended to destroy the whole complex. We intercepted it and neutralised it. We couldn't do that with the first one because we weren't expecting it.'

'So what happened to the long-range radar with the first missile? How come it got through? Why didn't your Pluto Station pick it up?' Praut gazed at the brigadier trying to see how he'd wriggle his way out of that one.

'Mr Praut, you're right, we did fail on that. We've become complacent as a result of not finding any alien threats in our galaxy. We're not as sharp as we should have been. That missile came up on the radar as a comet coming in from the Oort Cloud…it disguised itself as a comet. Our radar didn't pick it up as a threat. Now we know that whoever controls those missiles can do such a thing, we've adjusted our radar profile to accommodate such an eventuality. We've reprogrammed our q-computers.'

'You should thank the blaggards who sent the missile for sharpening your Solar defence systems.'

'That as may be. But an hour later, we had another missile on our holo-screens coming in through the Kuiper Belt, this time heading for Earth. We could have taken it out near Jupiter, but then you wouldn't have seen it.'

'You mean you let this one through on purpose…so I could see the explosion?'

'We've got to make you see how serious this thing is. This was our way of getting your attention.'

Praut was shaking his head at the idiocy of it all. 'What if it had got past your anti-missile security?'

The general shrugged his shoulders, and took over the conversation again, 'Now Mr Praut, my question to you is, what do you know about these missiles and their origins?'

'Come now general, I suspect you know far more about these missiles than I do. I don't have the equipment to track the missiles down. You must have extrapolated the missile's point of origin on your equipment. So you tell me where they come from.'

'Damn, you're one stubborn man to deal with,' exploded the general.

'You're confusing ignorance for stubbornness, general. Here you are, the premier World Security Agency, asking a simple *private* Agency for information. Doesn't this strike you as the wrong way round? You should be telling me what's what, not me telling you.'

'I should've let that missile do its job,' the general spat out angrily. 'Next time you might not be so lucky.'

Praut smiled at this tantrum. 'Yes, that would certainly add to my *security* from a World Security Agency. My tax credits well spent, eh? Now if you don't mind, I've an Agency to run.'

All three WGS men rose and walked hurriedly out of the office.

'You might want to look into wormholes for some answers,' Praut called after the general as the door was closing.

Fanny popped her head into the office, 'Have they gone?'

'You wouldn't believe what they've done.' The note of exasperation was clear in Praut's voice.

Fanny's set her face into query mode, eyebrows lifted.

'They only let one of those missiles through so they could explode it for my benefit. That's what we just witnessed.'

'Sorry, I missed that. Are you saying WGS let a missile through, and then exploded it so you could see the explosion?'

'That's what this general just told me.'

Fanny exploded, 'They've gone bananas. Totally and utterly bananas.'

'There, I can't disagree with you at all.'

'So, what's our next move. I assume you sent the WGS off with a flea in their ears.'

'I tried to. They must know more about these missiles than they're letting on. Would you believe, they're asking me to give them info about where the missiles were coming from? How am I supposed to know where they're coming from? They've got the whole resources of the government at their disposal…and they're asking me?'

Fanny didn't often see Praut worked up like this and she studied him, in a friendly manner, while he let off steam.

'As for where we go from here…have you heard anything from Olga? She's supposed to report in twice a day. That's what I told her to do.'

'Have you checked you gemail. I've got stuff from her. Nothing dramatic.'

'My auto-sec is supposed to alert me. Hey, how come I've not heard from the auto-sec?'

'Try it now,' Fanny suggested.

'Auto-sec…you there?'

He got no response.

'What the hell? Where's Clay? Get him to do a system check.'

'Aye aye boss,' quipped Fanny. She was about to call for Claymore, but Clay walked in to the room on hearing his name being used.

‘Good man Clay,’ Praut beamed at him. ‘My auto-sec isn’t responding. Can you do a system check and find out why…and check my galactic-emails while you’re at it. There should be a lot of stuff from Olga there.’

‘Right-o Dil,’ and Claymore disappeared again.

‘Fanny, I want you to put together a holovid news statement for the Frankfurter Holovid Studio. Get in touch with Friedrich Schiller at the studio, and tell him it’s from me. He’s an old friend of mine. This is to go out on the gq-net today at the latest. Something to the effect that, *the Praut Agency was informed by WGS General Botha that the WGS allowed a missile through their defences and then exploded it to attempt to intimidate the Praut Agency CEO. Is this really how we taxpayers expect our tax credits to be spent?* You know the sort of thing. Make sure it goes viral. I won’t put up with such behaviour from the WGS.’

‘Dil, they’ll go after you with a vengeance…you know that?’

‘As if they haven’t already. I want it to come out into the open. I don’t want to be chased down the alley ways. If they’re going after me, I want them chasing me down the boulevards, out in the open so all can see…and let the people judge them.’

‘I’ll get this out right away.’ Fanny left the office.

Unexpectedly Praut’s auto-sec announced in his ear, ‘You have seventeen gemails needing your attention.’

Shortly after, Claymore came back. ‘It’s another grabworm…and this one’s smarter. I’ve got rid of it, but it was blocking your auto-sec and all contacts with you. I’m in the process of chasing down its origins.’

‘Well done Clay! I’ve just had my auto-sec contact me. I thought it might be your handiwork.’

‘I’ve written a new routine that will stop this happening again…and I’ve increased our Firewall to Level Red protection. It shouldn’t happen again.’

‘Do me a favour Clay…sift Olga’s gemails for me. Leave the routine ones and tell me what the urgent ones say.’

‘Right Dil,’ and Claymore vanished again.

Fanny walked back into the office.

‘Fanny, I need another shuttle. Olga’s using our only shuttle chasing her sniffer. As I see it, we have three options. We can have one made using programmable atoms, or we can get nanobots to put one together, or finally we can put it out to one of the Additive Manufacturing corporations and they can Layer Fabricate the shuttle. I want your input as to which way to go. What do you think?’

‘Layered Fabrication is going to take the longest, simply because we’re tendering it out. Why not get Clay to talk to his buddies in our building’s computer department. Use programmable atoms *and* nanobots; it’s quicker. The building’s computer bods could probably put something together in a couple of days, depending on their workload.’

‘Can I leave it with you? Have a word with Clay and see if you can get me a shuttle ready in a couple of days. Use your best judgement as to which way to go.’

‘Right Dil.’ Fanny made to go.

Claymore came into the office in a rush, ‘Dil, Olga’s crashed.’

‘*What’s this*?’ shouted Praut.

Fanny halted and stayed to listen.

‘She’s come down on some planet called Barnaby in Sector N1 on the Norma Arm,’ Claymore told him. ‘Meserine’s last gemail was a *Mayday* to us. It said *we’ve been hit, going down…need help*.’

‘Fanny, we can’t wait for a shuttle to be built; I need that shuttle now. See if anyone can lend us theirs. Get on the comm and find out who’s got a spare shuttle.’

Fanny sprang into motion and began an urgent quest on her throat mike, making calls to various contacts.

‘That’s not all Dil,’ Claymore continued, ‘I’ve tracked down that grabworm. I chased the log down through a number of servers on various planetary systems; it seems its origin is a planet called…Barnaby.’

‘What, Barnaby *again*? That’s bloody it! We’ve got to get to this Barnaby…and I mean fast.’

Fanny shouted, ‘*Dil*,’ loudly interrupting his tirade. ‘Friedrich Schiller at Frankfurter Holovid Studios says he can let us have the studio warpshuttle. It’s a little bigger than we need but it’s available as of right now.’

‘Grab it…and tell Friedrich I’ll thank him properly when we get back. Tell him I owe him one.’ Praut spun on Claymore, ‘Pack your bags, we’re going to Barnaby…and that means you too, Fanny. Clay, make sure we well supplied with weaponry.’

‘Aye aye boss,’ both of them said in unison, then laughed.

Claymore suddenly asked, ‘Who’s going to pilot the shuttle?’

‘I suppose I’ll have to,’ Praut informed him. ‘I’m not as good as Mes but I have a space pilot’s licence.’

‘You won’t need to,’ Fanny informed him. ‘Friedrich says he’s loaning us their usual pilot for old time’s sake.’

‘Good old Friedrich! I owe him double. Fanny, did you send out the Press Release?’

‘Yes. Friedrich was happy to oblige. It’s out right now going viral as we speak.’

‘When’s the shuttle coming?’

‘Should be here anytime soon. Friedrich said he was sending it right over. We ought to head for the departure gate and get ready to board.’

‘Wait a mo.’ Praut spoke into his throat mike, ‘Helmut…Helmut, you there?’

‘Yes Dil, what’s up?’

‘You still busy with the Nafto Conspiracy affair?’

'Yes, but it's coming to a close. We've got a good result. I'm tying things up right now.'

'Good. Me, Fanny and Clay will be away for I don't know how long. I'm leaving you in charge. How's Mykola getting on with the Dour-Chick Scam, do you know?'

'I think he's almost done as well.'

'I'll keep in contact with you from a planet called Barnaby. Get both teams up to speed on this planet when you've finished with your current jobs. I may need your help. When you're done, make plans to join me…as a standby. That's your backup plan. Make sure you come armed. Am I clear?'

'Yes Dil, Barnaby. Wilco.'

'Right Fanny, now we can go to the departure gate.'

# 10
# BARNABY

Praut's critical rescue mission was under way on the *FrankfurterPresse* warpshuttle. For a little over three days, the borrowed *FrankfurterPresse* had been speeding urgently across the galaxy towards Barnaby's planet. The engines were pushed beyond their limits to squeeze every bit of warp power in a race against time. On an inwards spiralling course along the Sagittarius Arm, the distance from Sol was roughly twenty-five kiloparsecs as plotted by the navcomp.

Karl, their adopted space pilot was more than competent and knew his stuff inside out. Thus far, everything had gone as smoothly as an atom-clock mechanism.

Praut spent the onboard time pouring over all of Olga's gemails trying to extract the last gluon of information he could from them. Then he held a meeting to discuss their implications.

Apparently, Olga's sniffer had followed their quarry towards Barnaby, where she then wrote, *it had stopped sending back reports.* She'd closed in on its last known location and had been ambushed with a *whammy* hit to the *Faust's* engines. Major systems malfunctioned. Meserine had been forced to make a dash for Barnaby on the last vestiges of power left to the Agency's crippled *Faust* shuttle.

'Any observations?' Praut asked as he looked around his little group after reading out the last message.

Unexpectedly, Karl asked the unvoiced question, 'I know I'm new, but one of those people missing is a close friend of mine. Do you think they're still alive?'

'They'd better be, or we're going to a funeral…and if that's the case…*I will have vengeance.*' Praut looked like he was about to blow an air seal. Then he did a double take on Karl, 'Hey, what did you say about one of them being a close friend of yours?'

'I'm sorry I said that,' apologised Karl sheepishly. 'Mes asked me to be discreet about our friendship. But you're her boss, and I think you have a right to know. Me and Mes were both in the same space combat squadron. I've known her for years. Oh, and just in case you think otherwise…we're just close friends, that's all.'

Fanny said, 'It's all right, Dil. He only said what we all thought….about them still being alive, that is.' She looked hard at Praut to see if he'd disagree. She was rushing to Karl's defence.

Praut looked at Karl as if he was seeing him for the first time. 'Hmm, combat squadron, you say, eh? Well okay, then you know what she's capable of. Do you think she survived?'

'From what I know of Mes, she definitely must have survived…she's a survivor.' Karl shrugged as if it were self evident, and then turned his attention to the instruments, although they didn't need his attention. He was sorry he'd spoke.

'Karl Wolfe, welcome aboard the Praut Agency.' Praut patted the pilot in a friendly manner on his shoulder. 'Showing concern for one of my people, friend of Mes or no friend, makes you one of us. If you ever want to leave the Holovid Studios and join us, you'd be most welcome.'

Fanny raised her eyebrows. It wasn't everybody Praut invited on board. Then she remembered that they'd lost two of their own people recently and Dill might be on a recruiting drive.

'I'll keep that in mind, Herr Praut.'

‘All my friends call me Dil,’ Praut smiled effusively at Karl. ‘There, we have it; we’re *NOT* going to a funeral. Now, let’s have a food break.’

‘How far are we from Barnaby?’ Praut asked Karl, as they took their turns at the food replicator.

‘The navcomp makes it about three days,’ Karl told him. ‘We should be there two days after tomorrow. Then I’ll make a sweep of the planet…with your permission. Mes will have set off the *Mayday* rescue beacon. They’re designed to work no matter what. If they all stayed by the ship, we ought to be able to pick them up during the day.’

‘That’s assuming things are as we hope they are,’ Praut said quietly, tucking into his salmon salad.

‘Well yes, of course,’ replied Karl, biting into his Bratwurst.

‘Tell me Karl, does this ship have the standard modulated neutrino communication device installed?’

‘But of course. All the ships do, you must know that. Why do you ask?’

‘Interplanetary range?’

‘Naturally.’

‘Then even if the *Mayday* beacon isn’t working we should be able to pick up a message from Mes. I’ll explain when we’re ready to use it.’

Karl peered quizzically at Praut, trying to fathom his intention. Most communications was via entangle photons. Long distance was packaged through wormholes. Focused neutrinos was a backup system used only in emergencies.

Praut smiled sweetly and said, ‘Right, I propose we relax before turning in and listen to Mendelssohn’s Violin Concerto in E minor. Any objections?’

Everyone knew of the boss’s passion for classical music and all, except Clay, nodded in agreement.

‘Oh do I have to?’ Clay said quietly, almost to himself. ‘The bloody stuff’s seven and a half centuries old.’

Praut scowled but said, 'I'll never get through to you Clay. That q-machine's warped your brain. You can use your earphones and listen to whatever you want.'

That brought a smile to Clay's face.

Praut continued, 'If anybody else wants to join Clay, be my guest.' Nobody moved or said anything. 'Right then, first Opus 64, and then we get some sleep if we're to properly deal with what promises to be a heavy day tomorrow. I'll alternate with Karl at the controls. Fanny, you alternate with Clay at the comm. After the concert, Karl, you go get some sleep—you too,' he motioned at Fanny. Me and Clay will call you in six hours.'

* * *

Three days later, according to the galactic chronometer, dawn was creeping over the 3.8 kilometres high Europa Trade Centre back in Frankfurt. Karl noted the time on the console and yawned widely. He then deftly dropped his middle finger onto the control touch-panel bringing the ship out of hyperspace.

Praut stirred in his bunk, then abruptly threw his legs onto the floor and sat up. Yawning, he climbed onto his feet, left his cabin and went quickly onto the bridge. 'I felt the shudder. Have we come out into ISM?' He stretched his arms and stood looking at Karl, Fanny, and Clay.

'Yes, you're right. I just brought us back into the Interstellar Medium,' Karl told Praut. 'I'm taking a position between Barnaby's two moons.' Karl looked at Fanny at the comm. 'Please switch over to the *Mayday* beacon signal.'

'Will do,' Fanny prodded a panel in front of her.

Claymore sat by her side, looking at the comm panel with her.

'Well? Anything?' asked Praut.

Karl watched the control panel over Fanny's shoulder, and shook his head.

'That's odd,' said Fanny. 'Nothing's coming through.'

'Not a blip,' added Clay.

'Go to the other side of Barnaby,' Praut told Karl. 'Maybe something's interfering with the transmitter signal.'

A while later on the other side of Barnaby, there was still a deathly silence on the emergency frequency.

'Can you find the last position of the *Faust*?' Praut asked Karl.

'Didn't Olga include the coordinates in one of her gemails?' Claymore asked.

'Yes…yes…' Praut scrolled through his e-pad and found the relevant gemail. He showed the pad to Karl, 'Can you find that spot?'

'Let me enter the coordinated into the navcomp.'

Praut suddenly stopped himself, 'Wait. I've just had a bad thought. Look Karl, be careful. Whoever ambushed Mes and Olga might still have a sentinel waiting at the same spot. When we're approaching the area, make sure all the ships frequency sweeps are fully operational. Every detector the ship has, needs to be on the lookout for another ambush.'

'Dil, I'm an ex-combat pilot. It's the first thing I did…automatic reaction. I've already taken care of that. Don't worry.'

'Oh, right…' Praut knew when to back off. He watched as Karl manoeuvred the ship to match the given coordinates.

'I'm picking up a number of tracers bouncing off our detectors,' Karl told Praut. 'The closer we get to the last known position of the *Faust*, the stronger they become.'

'I knew it…the buggers are waiting for us. Karl, are the shields up?'

'Of course. The source of the tracers is coming from deep space. I can lock on them, but we're not a combat vessel. If they attack, I'll have to make a run for it.'

'Yes, I know…do your best.' Praut turned to Fanny. 'Anything from the *Mayday* beacon yet?'

'No Dil, I'm just switching to their wrist frequencies.'

Praut said to Karl, 'Now I can tell you how we're going to locate them. Every Praut Agent has a personal emergency beacon bracelet so that they can be located, no matter what.' Praut showed Karl the one on his own wrist. 'Good for a long distance. When activated, it sends out the *initial* of the person in trouble…to orbit level. Fanny's now looking for a combined beacon giving off OMH, or its combination, to our modulated neutrino collector channel.

'OMH?' queried Karl.

'Olga, Mes, Harry. OMH. If Mes is doing it right, she'll have connected the bracelets in series to boost the power. Before we land, I'll give you one. Fanny will show you how to programme the *K* into it. Look Karl, let's move from here…out of this ambush; head for Barnaby's exosphere. We'll circle the planet a couple of times. We should locate them from their bracelets by then.' As Praut finished talking, a shudder ran through the ship. '*What the hell?*' yelled Praut.

'It's alright, the shields are holding. We've just been fired on,' explained Karl to those listening. He looked at the control panel, 'It's a long range burst of red energy. Seems to be combined laser and microwave coming from deep space. Hang on! Get into your seats and strap in. I'm getting us out of here, hold tight.' Karl switched the ship to manual and gave it thrust. The *FrankfurterPresse* warpshuttle accelerated with such speed that it pushed its four occupants deep into their seats.

The ship shot round to the other side of Barnaby, using the planet as a shield, away from where the long range burst of energy was coming from. The ship parked amongst a cluster of comm satellites for added radar confusion.

Fanny was watching Karl manoeuvre the shuttle when Claymore suddenly shouted, 'Hey, the bracelet beacon's coming through…look at this.' He'd been sitting near Fanny, keeping an eye on the comm panel.

Praut shouted, 'Get a fix on their location.' Then added to Karl, 'Can you set the shuttle down where they are.'

'The beacon is coming in strong…somewhere in the northern continent,' Claymore told him.

'Be more precise.'

'I think this continent is called Serpedonia. The signal's coming from the north-central part of Serpedonia, about four hundred klicks inland from the northern coast.'

'Put a map of that place on the screen,' Praut told him.

A small light flashed on the map covering one of the screens, giving the precise location of the bracelet beacon. Karl input the galactic coordinates into the navcomp and flipped the controls back to automatic. The vessel skimmed the exosphere and began to hit the atmosphere into the three dimensional entry corridor, a flight path angle which caused the ship's shield to glow red in the process. A few minutes and they were gliding down to where the damaged *Faust* was supposed to be waiting.

'Look…there…I can see the *Faust*,' Karl pointed through the cockpit window, as the ship glided ever lower. 'There's a long dark streak in the snow where the shuttle crash-landed.'

The landscape was a frozen waste. The northern region's climate was a cold and harsh environment. Barnaby's axial tilt was similar to Earth's. Because of this, the northern polar region never received much sunlight, but instead obtained the sun's rays indirectly.

Karl settled the *FrankfurterPresse* warpshuttle on its landing legs beside the damaged *Faust* and switched off the engines.

Praut looked at his pilot, 'Karl, I don't want to be here any longer than necessary. Be ready to take her up if it gets messy down here. Oh, and here's the Agency bracelet I promised you.' Praut held a platinum bracelet out to Karl.

'Thanks boss.' Karl said with a warm smile.

'Right, let's get the weather proof suits on. Any life signs from the *Faust*?' Praut asked Fanny.

Claymore answered for her, 'Three. Looks like their all alive.'

'That's good news.' Praut led the way to the exit hatch. 'Karl, stay here and be ready to do a quick lift off.'

'Oh boss, let me go with you. I want to see if Mes is alright.'

'Oh, sure…I suppose you deserve that. Get your suit on then and follow us.'

Karl was the last one out of the exit hatch, following the three others as they all trooped over to where the wrecked *Faust* lay half covered in snow.

When the group neared, *Faust's* cockpit door shuddered once, shaking the snow off, and then slid open. Mes stood in the doorway, beaming at them. The party of four trudged past her and Karl brought up the rear. As the two friends saw each other, they spontaneously threw their arms around each other in a long hug. Mes pressed the door-close button over Karl's shoulder with her hand, sliding the door shut behind him.

'Thank god you're alive,' Karl exclaimed with a sense of relief. 'I knew you'd make it…I kept telling them, you're indestructible.'

'But what in the Sam Hill are you doing here?' replied Mes pulling herself out of the clinch.

'I'm the pilot.' Karl stated, as if it were self evident.

Mes followed Praut into the Faust cockpit. 'How come Karl's here,' she asked him.

'I was forced to borrow a shuttle from the Holovid Studios and Karl came with the ship.' Praut looked at Olga. 'Grab what you can and let's get out of here before the enemy comes a visiting.'

Harry butted in, ‘Dil, I need to use your ships computer urgently. OK if I go over there right now.’

‘Oh yeah, sure, go ahead.’

‘Dil, I want a little help to gather the rest of our sniffers,’ said Olga as Harry rushed out of the *Faust*. ‘There’s one stuck in the exit tube.’

‘What…do we really need them. I want us out of here quickly.’ Praut looked around at his people to see if they were complying with his order to leave.

Mes was climbing into her all weather suit, but Olga was standing visibly stubborn. She wasn’t about to abandon her sniffer if she could help it.

‘It’ll only take a few minutes Dil.’

‘Alright, but hurry. Clay, Karl, give Olga a hand.’

The trio proceeded off to the engine room, led by Olga. Suddenly there was an almighty ***wham*** from outside. It shook the *Faust*, throwing its occupants off their feet.

‘*What the shit?*’ yelled Praut, climbing back to his feet.

Mes was on her feet in a jiffy and rushed to the cockpit window. ‘Dil, come quick...look…over there.’ She pointed through the window to where the *FrankfurterPresse* had stood. In its place was a large hole in the ground as if a meteor had hit. Bits of the shuttle were flung all over the place.

‘Where’s Harry,’ was Praut’s next question. He’d said it quietly, as if he wasn’t expecting a reply.

‘Sorry Dil…,’ Mes said. ‘I think he’s gone.’

‘They’ll pay for that, damn them,’ Praut said angrily under his breath. ‘That’s three of my people they’ve wasted. I won’t stop until I get at those bastards responsible. Then I’m going to make them pay the ultimate penalty. Filthy lot, whoever they are.’

Olga, Karl and Clay rushed back into the cockpit as soon as they could. They caught the end of Praut’s last statement.

'*What's happened*,' asked Karl, alarm writ large on his face.

Praut told them.

'Oh no! I can't stand much more of this,' cried Olga. 'Not Harry. He was such a lovely man...such a good friend.' She stomped her feet in anger and frustration, then collapsed into one of the cockpit seats quietly sobbing. She even dropped the two sniffers she was carrying.

Karl said angrily, 'How am I going to explain to the studio about the *FrankfurterPresse?*'

Praut stood shaking his head. 'More to the point, how the hell are we going to get out of here?' he asked, not really expecting an answer.

He was met with sheepish silence, except for a couple of sniffles from Olga.

Mes was the first one to break the silence, 'Karl, come on now, let's put our survival training to good use. What's the first thing they taught us in this kind of situation?'

Karl bucked up, 'Well, stay calm and assess our resources.' He looked at Mes, 'Have we got comm with the outside world?'

'Afraid not,' she answered. 'Certain circuits are working, like the doors, and some power, but the antennae has gone and the ship's comm circuits are fried. Power's been draining for the last three days.'

'What about our private comms. Have we got gq-net access?' Karl persisted. 'Any comm of any kind…throat mike? Anything?'

'I've tried everything,' said Claymore. 'It seems something is jamming our outside frequencies. We're cut off.'

Mes continued, 'We don't have the food replicator but there's the dehydrated emergency rations. We've got emergency shelters.'

Praut added his voice, 'Mes, Karl, since you're the survival experts, I'm putting you in charge of organising our trek out of here. Is the baggage hover working? We'll need it if we're going to leave this ship…and I strongly urge we do, before the enemy decides to check on this wreck.'

'You're right,' Mes agreed. 'We need to get moving. Clay, check on the map exactly where we are and where we need to head for. Look, it would be best if I allocated specific jobs for everybody,' Mes looked at Praut to see if he agreed.

Praut nodded for her to go ahead.

'Right then. Dil, can you look out for any weaponry and transportation. We'll need them on our journey. Karl, I'm allocating shelter to you. Make sure we have the emergency shelter with us. Clay, stay with navigation. Make sure we're heading in the right direction. Fanny, please make sure we have adequate clothing and protective suits with us. Olga, I want you to look for any comm devices, mobiles…anything. Me, I'm going to make sure we have enough food with us to survive this journey.'

Praut raised his hand to get their attention. 'We'll need to build a sled of some kind. Karl, come and let's see what we can put together out of this wreck. And we'll see what material's left outside. We'll use the baggage hover to pull the sled.'

At the end of some furious activity, Praut had Clay inform them where they stood in terms of the map.

'The continent we're on is called Serpedonia. We're in the north of that,' Claymore indicated it on the map he'd drawn on the shuttle cockpit wall. 'We're roughly here, and we need to get to Ventura, Barnaby's capital, a thousand klicks to the south. There's a couple of mountain ranges we have to cross. It may seem a long way, but I'd guess we'll come across somebody on our route. They'll have a comm, and it should be just a matter of calling for a local taxi…' he stood smiling weakly at his attempt at a joke.

‘Fine,’ said Praut, ‘I can’t see a problem with that info. When we get to Ventura, if I have to, I’ll hire or buy another shuttle.’

‘What about my sniffers?’ Olga interrupted. ‘I can’t leave them here.’ She’d gathered up the two she dropped and hugged them close to her.

‘Now Olga,’ Praut tried to calm her. ‘We’ll come and collect your sniffers when we get another shuttle. Don’t worry, we won’t leave them behind. I promise you. By the way…how many have you got?’

‘Four.’

‘We’ll bury them in the snow before we leave, so no one else can get at them.’ Praut smiled reassuringly at Olga. ‘Now, me and Karl have put together a sort of sled. All we’re taking with us is now loaded on the sled, ready to go. The baggage hover is going to be working overtime, but I dare say it’ll cope.’

‘So, are we ready to leave?’ asked Mes.

‘I’d say so,’ replied Praut. ‘I’ve given a laser rifle to Karl, and kept one myself. You’ve each got a zapper and short range comms. Everyone is wearing all-weather suits and snow shoes. Once we leave, remember that the weather is our worst enemy…but keep a sharp lookout…and whatever you do, stay together.’

Olga kept looking back longingly at where they’d buried her four sniffers.

Praut looked at Olga in exasperation. ‘Come on Olga, they’ll be alright. Come along now. Karl, you bring up the rear…I’ll take point.’

# 11
# TUNDRA

One last lingering look at his beloved *Faust*, disfigured with battle charred black patches across the damaged engines, and Praut stomped off angrily into the wilderness, leading his group into the ice-covered tundra.

How in tarnation had it come to this? It all began innocently enough with a visit from Van Rag Yang, Darhlburg's CEO, only three weeks ago. Now they were marooned on a planet twenty-five kiloparsecs away from Earth, trudging through a frozen wilderness with no rescue in sight. Any other person might have felt despondent, but Praut merely felt angry and vengeful. He knew he'd survive *and* bring his people through this hardship. It wasn't the first time he'd been in such sticky situations, and reacted by poking his tongue out at what fate had in store for him.

The six resolute members of Praut's Agency left the damaged *Faust* and headed south, deep into the treeless tundra of Barnaby's northern continent, tramping over the permafrost at a steady two klicks per hour, heading for a capital a thousand klicks away.

The only plant life they encountered were various species of lichen and mosses, which had been laboriously transplanted from earth when they were terraforming the planet. Snow covered everything as far as the eye could see. The terrain was undulating and uneven, hampering their progress.

As the party slid through the snow, the wind suddenly picked up, causing problems to the improvised sled containing all their belongings being pulled by an overstrained baggage hover. In a short while, it turned into a sinister storm. The wind howled down from the north supported by stinging flecks of ice, wave following wave, hammering the landscape and its occupants. Raw shuddering gusts whipped up the snow and threw it about so their vision was cut to a meter before their eyes. Finally, Praut called a halt.

Into his throat mike, he told the others, 'Its no use. We'll have to wait this out. We'll only blunder about and get lost in this snowstorm. Is everyone comfy in their weather suits?' he observed all their nodding heads, then had them form a circle facing each other with the hover and sled in the middle, then got them to sit.

'We're not gonna get far today if this storm keeps up,' Claymore observed into his throat mike, voicing a mild complaint.

'Clay,' Fanny coaxed, 'we're in a wilderness…there's no way to control this situation. Relax and accept it.'

'Yes, and that goes for *all* of you,' added Praut. 'Be assured, we will get out of this mess…*and* hunt down the people who caused our misery.' It was only a short pep talk, but it put heart into his listeners.

The storm lasted for some two hours into the afternoon and then they set off again at a slow trudging pace. The snowstorm had blown drifts against the hillocks and otherwise flattened the landscape. It looked more desolate than ever.

By evening, the little group had accomplished twenty klick but were all utterly exhausted. Finally, Praut called a halt for the night. Karl hurried to unpack the single shelter from the sled and threw it into a shallow gully, which was to be their night camp. The intelligent circular domed shelter auto-erected and became rigid with weatherproof walls, and looked much like an ancient Mongol yurt. It was warm and utterly comfortable with eight inflatable camp beds round its walls. There was a double door entrance system with a short corridor in between.

‘Hey, we’ve even got room for a couple of guests,’ Karl informed them in bemusement, as he pegged the sides into the snow.

‘Maybe we should invite the locals to our party,’ Fanny joined the banter.

‘Karl, have we got any sort of light beacon?’ Praut asked. ‘I want to see if we can attract the locals Fanny just mentioned.’

‘Hey, Dil, I was only kidding,’ Fanny quickly put into her mike.

‘I’m not,’ Praut responded. ‘Don’t knock it, it was a good idea. I hope we’re far enough away from the *Faust* to be able to shout for help.’

‘You think there’s people out here?’ asked Olga in surprise. She’d been staring at the two moons of Barnaby; one larger than the other—both shining brightly in the night sky.

‘We won’t know unless we try to contact them,’ said Praut.

‘I don’t think we’ve got anything…’ then Karl stopped himself, ‘wait…what about a flare…an old fashioned flare. I think we’ve got a couple of those in the survival kit.’

‘Great, let’s get one out and send it up…see what happens.’

‘Yeah,’ exclaimed Claymore. ‘I could do with some rescuing. And yes, there *are* people out here.’

‘Don’t get your hopes up,’ Praut told him. ‘My guess is we’re too far north for anybody to be around.’

Olga screwed her face up, but inside her weather suit, no one noticed her disappointment. She continued gazing at Barnaby’s two moons.

Karl had parked the sled near the yurt’s outer doorway and was unpacking the sled’s contents into the yurt’s corridor. The others joined him lifting in the gear, and shortly trooped inside. Once the inner door was sealed, most began to remove their suits.

Karl kept his suit on and pulled out what seemed to be a small tube from the pile and went outside. There was a *whoosh*, and the flare rocket went up into the double moonlit sky. He returned, removed his suit, and said, 'Well, I've sent it up. Now we wait and see what happens.'

Praut nodded, 'Yeah, let's hope it gets a result. Mes, how about some food.'

'Olga, give us a hand,' Mes asked, as she began to sort out the stuff from the pile on the floor of the yurt near the doorway.

'Did you know where the origin of breakfast comes from,' Fanny asked Praut as he listened for any reaction that might come from the flare going up.

'You're kidding me, right? You can't be serious.' He looked at her as if she'd flipped.

'No, I'm serious. It came from breaking the nights fast,' she informed him. 'Come on Dil, lighten up. We'll go bonkers if we take this disaster too seriously.'

Praut stared at her fine features for a moment, then smiled, 'Okay, you win. You got any more gems like that before the rescue party arrives?'

'Not at the moment, but I'll work on it,' she returned his smile then went to help Mes and Olga with the food prep.

'Olga, get some snow from outside into this container,' asked Mes, handing her a popup bucket. 'We'll use it to rehydrate the food. Put it through the yurt's purifier-decontaminator first though.'

'Fanny,' Karl called, 'can you show me how to programme the *K* into my wrist bracelet.'

'Coming,' Fanny called back.

After the food, the group sat cross-legged in a circle in the middle of the yurt, as Praut asked Olga to explain exactly what happened to her in the *Faust*. Mes sat next to her, ready to corroborate her story.

'We arrived,' Olga began, 'at the point where my sniffer vanished, some way out from Barnaby, when we suddenly felt a mighty ***whack*** on the engines at the rear of the shuttle. Mes knew immediately what had happened and tried to take evasive action. The shields were down cos we didn't expect such an attack. She was wonderful. She managed to bypass the worst damaged systems and get some of the backup systems operational. The self-repair e-systems made an effort to patch up the damage, but the hit was too serious. A reroute to the backup got smashed up as well. We owe her our lives. Her quick thinking saved us. There was a lot of damage. She got the *Faust's* engines to tick over enough so we could limp onwards towards Barnaby. Life support was at minimal but held, thanks to the inbuilt self-repair circuits. The entry heat almost got us, but these shuttles are tough little birds. It held together enough until it crash landed in the northern continent where you found us.'

Praut put his arm round Meserine and hugged her gently, 'Now you know why I hired Mes. She's saved my skin a number of times. Mes was a combat pilot and her reactions are second to none. Oh, and Mes, *vis-a-vie* our talk on the way to Callisto; that's *Faust V* gone. *Faust VI* coming up. Now you know how that happens,' Praut informed Meserine.

'Well, anyway, the *Mayday* beacon was being jammed,' Olga went on, 'so Mes pooled our bracelets and sent out our distress call on the modulated neutrino comm channel. We waited in the shuttle for three days. I was certain you'd show up. Anyway, a little while later…you appeared. We thought that was it. We were saved….' her voice chocked away to nothing. She was thinking of their current circumstances.

'Olga, look at me,' Praut ordered. 'Are we snug and safe or not? You've just eaten well, and we'll sleep cosily tonight. What more do you want?' He was saying this for everyone's benefit.

Olga smiled, 'Sorry Dil, of course we're comfortable. I just weakened for a moment.'

'That's alright…it's understandable. But have faith and keep heart. Remember what I said earlier…we *will* come through this *and* get those we're after. Right?'

'Right!' the other five voices in the yurt shouted in unison.

'Now, I want us to understand where we are,' Praut told the little circle. 'Clay, you got the mapping job, didn't you. How much do you know of this planet? Tell us all you can.'

Claymore got his e-pad out and flipped through it for a short while, then put it back in his pocket. 'I've been putting this info together ever since we left earth, at Dil's request. I've even had a meme-capsule on Barnaby. What you all now know is that the *Faust* crash-landed on the north-central part of Serpedonia,' he began in a lecturing style, 'about four hundred klicks from the northern coast. Ventura, Barnaby's capital is a thousand klicks to the south-west. Barnaby has three continents. Serpedonia is the largest continent in the north with two major cities: Ventura with a population of 3 million, and Argos with 2 million. Both are on the southern coast, one in the west the other in the east.

'Celestica is a smaller continent nearer to Barnaby's South Pole; its capital city is New Kyiv with 1 million, and that's on its northern coast. There is also Asterica, an even smaller continent straddling the equator; the main city is New Knossos with a million people. The area is dotted with lots of small islands. The ocean between Serpedonia and Celestica is called the Krethys Sea.

'The *habitable zone* planet Barnaby was discovered 150 years ago in 2417, revolving around a G2 star with four other planets in this solar system. Barnaby already had three continents and a large ocean, so making it habitable for humans meant some minor adjustments to the atmosphere and flora. There were no large fauna. Ten years later after the terraforming, the first settlers arrived. The local fauna was carefully augmented with chosen terrafauna…the atmosphere had been stabilised to accommodate humans. Then ten years later, the first planetary based q-machine arrived. Now there are four large cities. Two on Serpedonia, and one each on the other two continents. The planetary population has reached a respectable 9½ million based on the 2567 stats.

'According to the info I've gathered from the gq-net, Barnaby is divided into two factions: the minority faction favours continued contacts with Earth, while the majority faction wants complete independence. This has been a recent phenomenon. This second faction is supported by Stimmer Corp., a large new off-planet outfit that suddenly arrived a year ago and swung the vote heavily in favour of the independence faction with a massive injection of credits and tech savvy.'

'Hang on, what did you call the outfit? Stimmer?'

'Yes Dil, why?'

'Anybody notice the similarity?' Praut looked at their blank faces. 'Stimmer…Zimmer?'

'Hell yes…I see what you're getting at,' burst out Fanny. 'I'll bet they're connected.'

Praut's people looked puzzled as to why they hadn't noticed this obvious similarity.

'Come on folks,' cajoled Praut. 'Wake up. Get your brains in gear. I don't want to have to do all your thinking for you.' Then he nodded for Clay to go on.

'The last bit of info concerns our immediate situation,' continued Clay. 'When they brought in the settlers, because of the harsh climate up here in Serpedonia, the local Governor imported a number of Sámi settlers… with their reindeer. The Sámi were willing and were needed. You remember reindeer; the large Arctic Earth deer with large antlers. Well they brought in a mass of frozen embryos and presto, there's whole herds supposed to be roaming up here now, tended by their Sámi herders.'

'So that flare Karl sent up might actually get a reaction?' Praut asked in surprise.

'I was trying to tell you earlier,' Claymore replied.

'Well I'll be!' Praut laughed aloud. 'See,' he added to everyone, 'Things are looking up already. There's people close by.' He was trying to boost moral, but not really expecting reindeer herders to come storming their yurt.

'If Stimmer is behind the independence drive,' Praut continued, 'then its clear we have to contact the other side…those against independence. They're the ones we ask for help. Make sure you're all clear on that; the pro-independence people are our enemy. Be sure whom you're talking to when we get to Ventura.'

Then Praut looked at Mes and said, 'Mes, as head of this agency, I'm officially thanking you for such a fine bit of survival. I'm glad to have you, Olga and…' then he stopped. He was just about to say Harry, but he pulled himself up, reminding himself that Harry was no more. 'As you might have guessed, I was just about to mention Harry, but with deep sadness I managed to stop myself; I'm aware that Harry was killed a short while ago. I'm thankful for those now present…and vow with all my being that I will hunt down the cowardly people who killed Harry…*and* Edel, *and* Tilmore. I was hoping to finish on a brighter note…I've not had such casualties since I set this agency up. Someone is going to pay for this, but now I suggest we all turn in. Good night.'

* * *

After breakfast, early next morning, the little group of six were back trudging through the snow until mid-morning, trying to keep the pace and their spirits up.

Praut had walked back and was talking with Fanny, when the sled gave a mighty *shlop* and came to a halt. The baggage hover strained its anti-grav engine to get it moving again, but it was no use. The sled had got itself lodged in a shallow gully and was wedged in at an angle, and the baggage hover didn't have enough power to pull it free.

'It's no good,' bemoaned Karl. 'We'll have to pull it out by hand. The little hover is simply underpowered for such work.'

'Sorry folks,' announced Praut. 'I should have seen that gully since I was out on point. My fault, *mia culpa*. Got distracted.'

Praut was the first into the gully, followed by Karl and Claymore. All three had jumped down into the small gully, got their shoulders below and behind, and pushed. Fanny, Mes, and Olga pulled on a graphene rope from the front; until bit-by-bit, the sled began to move and then nudged free.

'Trouble is, the bloomin runners get frozen into the snow,' grumbled Clay. 'All it needs is for them to be stationary for a mo, and they'll get stuck fast.'

'They're free now,' Praut admonished. 'So let's get moving. A little further on and we'll stop for some food and a short rest.' And to Claymore, more as an aside, he said almost tetchily, 'I'll try to keep my attention focused on what I'm supposed to be doing, okay.' He resumed his lead and was keenly watchful for more snow filled gullies, so as not to embarrass himself a second time.

Some time further on in the afternoon, after what seemed like many klicks of difficult travelling, and following the promised short rest and meal break, the group came across their next impediment to their journey south. This was in the form of an impassable crevasse, which presented them with a deep ravine of about ten meters wide and seemingly running many klicks in both directions, blocking their route to the south.

‘Now what?’ mouthed Praut angrily. ‘Bloody terrain seems determined to hamper our crossing. Right folks, I want a consensus on which way we go. East or west? We’ll follow a majority decision. Personally I can’t see any break or benefits in either direction.’

‘I vote we head west,’ voiced Karl.

Praut raised his eyebrows in his weather suit, although no one could see it. ‘Any particular reason,’ he asked.

‘Only that Ventura is to the west of the continent.’

‘Good point. Anybody else?’

‘I’ll go with Karl,’ Meserine muttered.

‘Sorry, couldn’t hear that,’ said Praut.

‘I’m voting with Karl to go west,’ Mes said louder.

‘I’ll call a halt to this democratic shindig,’ smiled Praut. ‘Karl mentioned Ventura was to the west, and I think that swings it for me. I’d forgotten that little point for a mo. West it is.’

They set off once again and after more trudging, being careful to stay back from the meandering ravine, they came to a gently sloping hill. It was early evening and the light was just beginning to dim. Because of the drift, it was a difficult climb, but once over the rise, they were brought up short—and they stood on the hill staring in disbelief.

Claymore was the first to shout, ‘Is that a bloody bridge or what?’ he said pointing at the structure across the ravine.

Everyone stared at it as if they’d never seen a bridge before.

‘I told you there were people here,’ Praut said loudly. ‘Or more to the point…Clay here, told you there were reindeer herders in this area.’

Suddenly people began to dance in the snow, shouting and whooping as if at a carnival….then they stopped and stared some more.

'How wide is it,' asked Olga, looking at an inordinately wide structure.

'Must be around twenty meters,' replied Meserine.

'Must be,' agreed Karl.

'Why so wide?' asked Fanny, head to the side in thought.

'What do you suppose this bridge is for?' asked Praut of Fanny.

'No idea!' she replied.

'Go on…have a guess,' Praut encouraged.

'Traffic…I don't know…' she shrugged her shoulders in the weather suit.

'Anybody else?' Praut asked them.

'My guess would be reindeer,' ventured Karl.

'Precisely,' said Praut loudly. 'Thank you Karl. The only thinking person here,' and Praut smiled at them, indicating he was having a bit of fun, and not to take him too seriously. 'Reindeer…the herd would need a wide crossing.'

'Pity the snow storm wiped out all traces of them,' said Olga wistfully. 'We could have used their tracks to follow them.'

'We'll find them, don't you worry,' Praut soothed her. 'We must be on a main highway if they've put up a bridge like this.'

'What's it made of,' asked Clay, ever nosy in a geeky way.

The group had slowly been walking towards the bridge as they were speaking. Now they stood at one end, looking across to the other side.

Karl peered closely at the material. 'Some kind of composite carbon. Probably graphene. Everything's made of graphene nowadays.'

Praut told his group, 'Now that gives me an idea… thanks to Clay and Karl. I want everyone to have a good look around the bridge…see if they can find any electronics…any kind of control box.' He added, 'Be extra careful in this dusky light.'

'It'll be solid state. You couldn't tamper with the circuits,' Mes advised.

'I don't want to tamper with the circuits…I want to wreck them. If my guess is right…they'll be to do with an alarm to warn whoever's keeping a distant eye on this, that the bridge has become unstable.' Of Karl and Mes, Praut asked, 'Would they build something like that into a bridge?'

'I've heard of that,' Karl replied. 'On Earth it's a standard part of construction. Damage alarm linked to traffic control.'

'I'm grasping at straws here,' Praut told them. 'But if such a box exists, and we disable it…someone must come to find out what's up. All we have to do is wait here for them to turn up…what'd think?'

'I'm for it,' Fanny said.

'Count me in,' came from Olga. 'Beats trudging in this snow.'

The rest of the group nodded their agreement, and then began to look carefully for any form of electronics attached to the bridge.

After a while, Clay shouted from the other side of the bridge, '*Found something.*' He was leaning over the side of the bridge floor looking underneath with a torch. Olga was holding down his legs by sitting on them.

'Good man,' Praut told him as he reached the spot. 'Where is it?'

'Under there, Dil,' Clay said, pointing underneath with his torch, at where the bridge met the ravine embankment.

'Can you get to it with a zapper and *whack* it? Be careful!'

'I think so.' Clay swung himself over the edge and disappeared onto a strut holding the bridge up, then popped up again and took the zapper Praut offered him. A short while later, a *zap* was heard from underneath, and then Clay's head reappeared some moments later.

'Well?' demanded Praut.

Clay's head was wearing a broad grin in his weather suit. 'It's well and truly wrecked Dil, I promise you. Now let's hope they come to investigate.'

'Cross you fingers everybody…we're camping here until further notice.'

# 12
# A SÁMI WELCOME

Since they were expecting the emergency inspection team to come from the southern side of the bridge, Praut instructed Karl to raise the self-erecting yurt on the southern side, in what was left of the fading daylight. The problem was, people felt far too excited to bed down, and sat round nervously in a circle talking energetically after their evening meal.

'What gets me…is this Zimmer, Stimmer, could be causing all sorts of chaos out there,' Mes threw her hand into the air, 'and we're stuck here helpless to do anything about it.'

'I'll repeat a phrase you're all familiar with by now,' said Praut. 'What you can't control, you need to get relaxed about. Getting all flustered about something that's happening in places you can't reach, will give you grey hair before your time. Be assured…we will get back into this game. It's just going to take a little time…that's all. Look at Karl…he's completely relaxed. Take a leaf out of his proverbial book.'

Karl smiled at Mes, and shrugged his shoulders.

'By the way, has anybody checked if we're still being jammed on our comm frequencies?' Praut asked, looking at Clay.

'I've been keeping an eye out and checking from time to time. We're still being jammed,' Clay reported.

'Oh well, it was just a thought.'

'I'm still struggling to understand,' Clay went on, 'if our comm frequencies are being jammed, then how come we think the bridge alarm transmitter is going to send its *malfunction* message through to its controller? Why wouldn't *it* be jammed? Edel would have understood it, he'd of explained it to me...' he let the sentence drift off. Clay had relied on his friend Edel to explain things like that to him, and only remembered too late that his friend was no more.

The reminder of Edel's death subdued the atmosphere and everyone sat silently for a while with sad thoughts.

Suddenly, Clay said quietly to Praut, 'Dil, can I ask you a question?'

'But of course,' Praut told him, wondering what Clay had come up with now.

Clay kept his voice low, 'Dil, why do you keep playing that old music...you know, the Beethoven and the like?'

Praut looked startled at such a silly question. '*That old music*, as you call it, is timeless. It's rightly called *classical*. Clay, it's like asking why they keep the Mona Lisa? Or why the Coliseum in Rome is still standing? Why the Rijksmuseum is still open to the public? You could equally ask why the pyramids are still standing? In human history, there are works of unique genius, like Beethoven's music, or Bach, or Mendelssohn. It's our combined human heritage.'

Clay looked puzzled, 'But Dil, a q-machine produces music just as good as the stuff you're listening to...and it's up to date.'

Praut shook his head, 'Do you know what derivative is? It means that your q-machine hasn't produced anything original in all the time it's been churning out the so called new music. A machine is *only* a machine. It can only produce what humans have programmed into it. All the worlds' music is now in storage but the machine can only extrapolate what it has in storage. A q-machine can produce a Rubens that is just as good as the original, but it's still not a Rubens. It's copying, mimicking, or extrapolating, but it's not *original*. Can a q-machine invent an artificial wormhole? It takes humans to think of the original…only then the q-machines are used to help develop the final item. Clay? Do you understand what I'm saying to you?'

'Yes Dil. I suppose I've never really given it much thought…until now. Thanks Dil.'

Praut smiled and said loudly, 'I think its time to turn in. We may have visitors tomorrow.' Praut rose and headed for his bunk. The rest followed his example.

*

Half an hour after the lights were dimmed in the yurt; the area outside the yurt was ablaze with a brilliant luminosity that lit up the night sky, vying with the light from Barnaby's two moons. A loudspeaker blared from outside, '*Those people in the shelter...could they please show themselves!*'

Praut was on his feet, 'I think we won't have to wait till tomorrow for our visitors.' He struggled into his all-weather suit.

Karl jumped into his all-weather suit and made for the inner door. In the excitement, he struggled with the inner door seal, then went through and unsealed the outer door. Cautiously Karl waved a white hanky out of the door, then went outside with both hands in the air, closely followed by Praut. The others were squeezing their bodies into their all-weather suits as fast as they could.

At the yurt entrance, Karl could see the blazing lights were coming from the underbelly of a medium sized hover that hung ten meters in front of the yurt. He was gently indicating for it to land with his hands, motioning to it in a downward movement. Praut joined him, then so did the others, all indicating for the hover to land.

It took another ten minutes or so before the hover decided it was going to land, and then it settled in the snow in front of the yurt directly opposite the bridge. The hover door opened and someone dressed in fur, pointing a laser rifle, came guardedly out. He moved a few steps in the direction of the yurt and stopped.

Praut came forward, arms raised as a sign of peace. The man in the furs motioned him forward, and Praut went to meet him. They talked for a long while until Praut's people noted that the man in the furs finally lowered his laser rifle. Praut turned and gestured for his people to come forward. They rushed forward and crowded round Praut and the man in furs.

'I've explained our situation to this Sámi herder and he seems surprisingly sanguine about getting us out of here,' Praut informed his group. 'I've offered to pay for the damage to the alarm box, but he tells me there's no need. The bridge build is modular and they'll replace the box in no time. Anyway, grab your gear and get aboard the hover. Oh, and let's clear everything carefully. I don't want to leave anything behind to indicate we've been here. We're going back to civilisation.'

An almighty cheer rose from the five stranded individuals. Karl turned and led them back to deconstruct the yurt, while Praut climbed into the hover and continued to talk with the Sámi herder.

The Sámi then excused himself, went to a container, pulled out a replacement alarm box, and went out to replace the damaged alarm box. Praut watched this activity with bemusement. He reminded himself to apologise yet again for the damage they'd caused to the old alarm box.

After a while, all the gear was stored aboard the hover and people sat in the hover's lounge-come-canteen, chatting and drinking various beverages as it whisked them to wherever they were going.

Praut told Clay, 'Apparently, there's a trapdoor above the alarm box you zapped. The herder has yanked out the old one and fitted in a replacement in no time.'

'Where are we headed,' Meserine asked as she sipped her drink.

'Back to the Sámi base camp. We'll be there shortly,' Praut told her.

Fanny joined in, 'Just out of curiosity, when would someone have come across the bridge, if we hadn't zapped their alarm?'

Praut grimaced and said, 'It seems we'd be still waiting till next year if we hadn't done that. Early next spring is when the herds come through here again, heading up north in their spring migration.'

'It's September back on Earth. Is that the same here on Barnaby?' Olga inquired.

Praut nodded, looking at Clay, who confirmed his assumption.

'Then it would have been one hell of a long wait,' Fanny muttered.

'So what's next?' asked Olga.

'The herder says he can get us to Ventura by tomorrow. Listen up—I've told him we crash-landed due to engine failure…everyone, make a note of that. Make sure you stick to that story until further notice. That reminds me, Karl, you'll have to prepare a report for Friedrich Schiller at Frankfurter Holovid Studios as to what happened to the *FrankfurterPresse.* I'll prepare a supporting report of my own for your studio…and then I'll have to prepare a report about the *Faust* for my insurance people.'

Karl nodded and sighed in resignation at the work involved. Reports were not his favourite pastimes.

'Fanny, I want you to get in touch with our office and let Helmut know we're okay. Use the gq-net. Leave a forwarding comm number. Tell Helmut to be ready to come to Barnaby at a moments notice. Get Helmut to buy another shuttle, a large one. Money no object. He's to come to Barnaby as soon as he's settled everything at the Agency. Tell him to bring all my people, armed to the teeth. He's to stand off a parsec from Barnaby in comm range. Stay there until called for. I'm going to leave that in your hands. Clay, how's the jamming?'

'Gone!' replied Clay. 'I'm through to the gq-net on my e-pad.'

Praut smiled, 'Good Clay, get through to WGS and tell them what's happened. Address it to Brigadier Shevchenko and mark it urgent. Ask for some assistance. You never know, we might need it.'

'That's a first,' interjected Fanny. 'You've never asked for help from the Government…not in all the time I've known you.'

Praut shrugged, trying to dismiss it as inconsequential. 'I'm beginning to smell a big corporate rat in all that's been happening to us, and I think we might need some big outside support. What with these Zimmer and Stimmer corporations. If they're mixing in planetary politics, then we'll need Earth's Government help. Clay, help Fanny to get through to our office. She'll tell you what she needs. By the way, be wary what you say with the Sámi herder around. We don't know which side he's on.'

Just then, the Sámi's blonde head came round the door, he shouted, 'Landing in ten minutes,' and disappeared.

Praut wondered if he'd heard his last comment.

A while later the hover touched down and the Sámi herder reappeared. 'Grab your stuff and I'll take you to our communal lodge hall. You can bed down there for what's left of the night.'

Praut's people re-donned their all-weather suits and gathered their gear. The Sámi herder led the way and the hover pilot brought up the rear. The little column trooped through the moonlit snow to a large oblong structure two stories high, set in a space in the middle of a group of buildings.

The herder opened the door and ushered his guests inside, leading them off to the left into a side corridor.

'You'll find guest rooms on either side of the corridor. Make yourselves at home. There's a kitchen at the far end where you'll find all sorts. Help yourselves. It's midnight, so I'll leave you, and see you tomorrow morning. Goodnight, and sleep well. By the way...here we start early.'

Praut thanked the herder on behalf of his group. 'We're grateful for your kindness in putting us up…but especially for your rescue. We're in your debt. We'll talk more tomorrow. Goodnight.' Praut made sure the herder had gone, then looked around to see they were alone. 'Clay, can you check for bugs.'

Claymore pulled out his terahertz scanner and scrutinized the area. 'Clean,' he pronounced.

'Right, listen up,' Praut began to his group. 'I can't emphasise this enough; watch yourselves. I don't want to loose any more people. This is a *deadly* game we're in. No loose talk. Make sure *who* you're talking to—are they friend or foe. Those people on this planet wanting to stay with Earth are our friends…those angling for independence and siding with Stimmer, are our enemies. It's as clear cut as that. Starting from now…we're on full alert. No letting your guard down and make sure you have your zapper with you at all times. Okay, now let's hit the sack. Sleep well.'

* * *

The next morning, Praut and his people woke to the sound of strange music coming from a sound system embedded in the walls of the building. The music floated on the air from a *fadno*, a Sámi reedpipe, a *lur*, a long horn trumpet; the two instruments were accompanied by a Sámi drum beating out a steady rhythm. The combination was uplifting, as it was hypnotic.

'*Breakfast is being served*,' came a loud shout from the corridor.

Praut stuck his head out of his door and found the same Sámi herder from the previous night, standing there, grinning at him.

'The canteen is on the other side of this building. You'd better get your people to hurry. I'm here to show you the way.'

Praut voiced into his throat mike, 'Rise and shine you lazy lot. Out in five or we go without you.' He called the Sámi over and asked, 'Do you have a first name?'

'Ailo,' replied the Sámi.

'I'm called Dil. May I ask you a personal question?'

The Sámi nodded, 'Why not.'

'I'm told Barnaby is impatient to gain its independence from Earth's control. What's your view of this aim?

Ailo looked quizzically at Praut, then made his mind up, 'No Sámi will vote in favour of such a proposition. We have too many close family connections with the Sámi community on Earth…and we intend to keep that close bond. What would independence give us, except rule by a bunch of local yokels? No Mr Praut…we're not in favour. And yes, I did hear what you said on the shuttle. My hearing is twice as keen as yours. And yes, this recent Stimmer lot are behind this new independence fad…and we Sámi don't like it.'

Praut stood there amazed at the long speech, and the venom in Ailo's last words. 'Now I know where you stand, and it seems you know our position only too well. Let me be candid with you. Our shuttle didn't just crash, it was shot down by people, I believe, associated with this Stimmer Inc. Frankly, I think our lives are in danger from anyone associated with the independence movement. When you give us a lift to Ventura…by the way, is that still on?'

Ailo nodded.

‘When we get to Ventura, could you be discreet about our arrival…and could you put us in touch with the anti-independence people?

‘I was going to do just that anyway,’ replied a smiling Ailo.

Praut’s people had joined them in the corridor and were listening in on the tail-end of the conversation.

‘Now shall we get some breakfast…I’m starving,’ said Ailo, leading the way out of the corridor and through the main hall to a flight of stairs.

‘Stairs?’ Olga motioned at the steps. ‘How quaint?’ she quipped.

Claymore just gaped at the idea of climbing stairs… speechless.

Ailo laughed aloud, ‘There’s a lot here that will startle you. We don’t rely on technology to the extent you do, not even on Earth. When you were stuck out there in the wilderness, all you really needed was a pair of reindeers pulling a sled and you could have got here under your own steam. People are far too pampered with all this techy stuff.’

Claymore’s brow furrowed in irritation, but he kept his tongue under control.

‘For instance,’ Ailo continued as he led them upstairs. ‘We were offered a teleport for this base camp and refused, then it took them all their efforts to sell us the shuttle…the one we used yesterday. We prefer to be cut off from their civilisation…prefer not to be too contaminated by it. The one concession we made to techy stuff was the bridge you saw. It simply made sense to go that route.’

‘I must admit, I couldn’t work like that,’ Praut responded, ‘but each to their own…right?’

Ailo looked at Praut, ‘Right! If we don’t get sucked in…we don’t get absorbed. That’s our guiding principle.’

‘I can see some sense to that,’ Praut shot back.

They’d reached the first floor and all trooped through a door into a large canteen.

'Well here we are, our canteen. You'll find hot food on hot-plates on the side tables against the wall. Get a tray and help yourselves.'

The canteen was empty, which surprised Praut. 'Where are all your people?' he asked Ailo.

Ailo smiled and said, 'They've all had their breakfast and are out busy with the reindeers. I told you last night we start early here.'

Praut led the way to the food. There were trays of hot reindeer sausage, blood sausage, hot blood pancakes, smoked reindeer, dried reindeer, and simple hot homemade flatbread. All to be washed down with fresh reindeer milk. Praut took a sample from each tray and took it to a table where Ailo waited with his food.

'This is a bit rich for me for breakfast,' Praut gently complained. He began to sample each of the foods in turn, as the rest of his group joined him.

'It wouldn't be if your next job was to round up reindeer, or prune reindeer antlers. Out in the cold, you'd appreciate the calories,' replied Ailo, digging into his own meal.

'Yes, I suppose I would…but then again…I'd be wearing an all-weather suit and wouldn't feel the cold.' Praut decided most of the food was indeed very tasty, if a touch strange.

His Agency people were fiddling with the food. Karl and Mes were clearly delighted by it and got stuck in. Clay dabbled at it. Fanny was making a good stab at enjoying it. Olga was tussling with it.

'If you were wearing one of those suits,' Ailo shot back, 'you wouldn't be bothering with reindeer. We lead different lives with different life philosophies. I'm a Sámi… you're a…?' He paused and concentrated on munching away with enthusiasm, leaving the question hanging in mid air.

The group's ears pricked up. Would Praut divulge his origins?

'Yes, you're right, my beginnings have been obscured somewhat by this headlong rush for progress. By the way, this sausage is delicious. Anyway, my people originated from eastern Germany, Brandenburg…then they emigrated to Canada. Now I've set up my agency back in Germany. What we have in common is, we're both standing on a strange planet 25 kiloparsecs from our origins. Also we're both vehemently opposed to the planned break with Earth, some people here, are being pushed into. Because I solemnly do believe this is not a homegrown movement. I think this Stimmer lot are pushing people into something against their own sensibilities. It's for reasons I'm not yet clear, but I intend to find out why.'

'I wish you luck,' replied Ailo.

'I'm afraid I'm going to need it. So far, I've lost three people and two space ships…and I've got little to show for it. I still have no idea why or who.'

Praut's people suddenly stopped at the reminder of their losses. They became quiet.

'I can tell you that whatever's happening,' said Ailo, 'it didn't originate on Barnaby. All our troubles began when Stimmer arrived a year ago...from Beaivi knows where. They stirred up the local malcontents into this full-blown independence movement.'

'Beaivi?' Praut interrupted, puzzled as to this reference.

'Oh sorry, yeah you wouldn't know, would you,' smiled Ailo. 'She's our great Goddess of the Sun, the mother of humankind.'

'Oh, I see.'

'Well, I'm finished,' Ailo said, looking at Praut. 'Ready when you are.'

'Ventura?'

'You've got it.'

'Where in Ventura?'

'I'm going to off-load you on Max Barkin. He's my contact with the anti-independence people.'

'What's he do?'

'He runs a hover repair place on the outskirts of Ventura.'

'We usually dump bust hovers back on Earth,' interjected Claymore. 'It's easier to print or replicate a new one.'

'We're short of q-machines here,' Ailo replied. 'We've got a couple on order, but with this independence business, I think Earth's dragging its feet over the supply.'

'So Earth's aware of what's happening here?' Fanny asked, cutting into the conversation for the first time.

'That's my supposition,' responded Ailo.

'So why aren't they doing something about it?' asked Meserine. She'd finished her food and was sitting back, listening to the talk.

'What can they do?' asked Ailo. 'Send the Space Fleet in…sanitise the planet? How would that look? I think they're waiting for this to play itself out before they interfere.'

'Makes sense I suppose,' said Praut, pushing his plate away and getting up.

Ailo was already on his feet and urging them back to the exit door and the stairwell. Back down in the hall he suggested they collect their belongings and meet him outside.

Back on the Sámi shuttle, everyone settled down for the ride to the capital. It took them thirty-five minutes to get to the outskirts of Ventura, flying as low as safety would allow, to avoid leaving a radar signature for whoever might be watching. On the eastern outskirts of the city, outside of the fourth ring road, the shuttle slowed and settled down in a huge circular frost encrusted field by a large dome hangar. The circular field overflowed with scrap hovers.

# 13
# VENTURA

'He knows we're coming,' Ailo responded to Praut's querying look.

As the little group approached the hangar door in the early morning light, Praut could see the tip of a laser rifle barrel protruding from the entrance.

'Max is cautious,' explained Ailo leading them to the entrance.

Just inside the doorway stood a heavyset individual, the owner of the laser rifle. He nodded to Ailo and jerked his barrel inwards to indicate they should go in. On entering the hangar, they came across another two tough looking thugs staring daggers at them on the other side of the door, both totting laser rifles.

'I must say,' Praut said quietly to Ailo, 'I'd rather have this bunch on my side than against us.'

Ailo chuckled at this, treating it as a huge joke.

On the far side of the huge hangar, Praut could see a number of cubicles and offices spaced around the walls. Ailo led the group towards a large office to the right. In the middle of the hangar, people were busily working on some kind of large contraption unfamiliar to Praut. A man with a backpack was climbing onto a platform in the middle of the apparatus. Ailo's group skirted the contraption and came to a door. Ailo knocked, heard a voice, and entered, followed by Praut. He told his group to wait outside.

In a chair behind a desk sat a big man with a pleasant grin on his face. 'Ailo, good morning, great to see you again. This the fellow you mentioned to me?' He nodded at Praut.

‘Morning Max. Yes, let me introduce you to Mr Praut of Earth. His group needs your help. It seems Stimmer shot them out of the sky and they crash-landed on our patch. I think he wants to get back to Earth.’

Praut leaned across the desk and shook a large fist. ‘Mr. Barkin, good to meet you. I hear we have a mutual enemy in common.’

‘You mean Stimmer? Those rascals are causing my friends and me a lot of trouble. I’d sorely like to know where they came from.’

Ailo turned to Praut and said, ‘I’m going now. I leave you in good hands. If ever you want to visit me, you’re always welcome. Goodbye for now.’

‘Goodbye Ailo, and thank you for all you’ve done for us.’ Praut shook the proffered hand and watched the Sámi herder leave.

‘Bye Max,’ Ailo shouted over his shoulder. ‘See you soon.’

‘Bye Ailo, see you soon.’ Barkin waved and returned his attention back to Praut. ‘Now Mr Praut, have a seat.’

Praut sat on the only free chair.

‘Tell me something about yourself,’ Barkin said amiably. ‘There’s green tea on the table; help yourself.’

Praut poured himself a glass and took a sip. ‘Nice, lemon green tea?’

‘Yes, I’m fond of it. Settles my stomach.’

‘I’ll start at the beginning,’ Praut smiled to reassure his host. ‘Some three weeks ago I had a visit from a new client who asked me to discover why his wormhole stuff had been deleted from his q-machine.’

‘Sorry to interrupt, but what’s your business?’

‘I run an Investigation Agency on Earth. People bring me their problems and I try to solve them. Anyway, as a result of chasing up this deletion, I’d discovered a fly by night corporation called Zimmer Inc. on a hippy planet called Harmony, seemingly involved in sabotaging wormhole technology, and we followed this Zimmer to Barnaby. This is where my shuttle was ambushed and shot down. Thanks to Ailo, he managed to rescue me and my people from the tundra…and here I am.'

Barkin sneered, 'Zimmer…huh? Sounds like Stimmer by another name…what do you think?'

'My very thought.'

'So you say this lot are trying to get rid of wormhole technology? Any idea why?'

'I've been puzzling over this very fact for the last three weeks. I'm still no nearer to an answer. Mind if my people come in here and listen in on our talk. I need to keep them abreast of what's happening.'

'No, go ahead. I'm afraid they'll have to stand, unless they want to sit on the floor.'

'Thanks.' Praut stood up and went to open the door, calling his people in to the office.

Barkin noted Fanny's tall, slim physique, her dazzling red hair, and looked away from her ice-cold green eyes.

'Listen and learn,' Praut told his group. Returning to his chair and Barkin, 'Why does Stimmer want independence for Barnaby?'

'We've been working on that for a while. The only thing we've come up with, is they want a power base not controlled by Earth. As to why…we haven't a clue. They've given nothing away so far. Mind you, your new input about this wormhole stuff could be a clue. How it fits in…we'll need to think about it. By the way, call me Max.'

'I'm Dil to my friends…of whom I hope you're going to be one.'

'Count on it.'

Karl and Mes slid to the floor, sitting with their backs to the office wall. All the others followed suit.

'So Dil,' continued Barkin, 'how can I be of assistance to you and your people? Since we're fighting the same war, I'll help in any way I can.'

‘My first thought when we crash-landed,’ said Praut, ‘was to get off this planet, but that was just a reaction to what happened. Since I’m now convinced this Stimmer entity is at the core of my inquiry, if I want to clear up my client’s problem, then I’m going to have to stay here till I get to the bottom of who and what Stimmer is. Can you put up with us for a while?’ Praut turned and looked at his group, sitting on the floor. He wanted their reaction to what he’d just said.

They all nodded almost in unison, agreeing to his course of action.

‘In that case Dil, welcome on board.’ Barkin smiled broadly. ‘Maybe you can do what we’ve failed to do for the past year. Get behind the Stimmer façade.’

Praut tried to look diffident but failed, ‘I’m told by my clients, I’m quite a good sleuth. Now’s my chance to prove it, eh? If me and my people can unmask Stimmer for the blackguards they are, I’ll have done you and Earth a service, and I believe, moved my client’s cause closer to a solution.’

Barkin asked, ‘Where do you want to start?’

‘What have you got on Stimmer so far?’ Praut replied. ‘Give me all you have on this corporation in the form of a meme-cap and let me absorb it, then we’ll have a conference to see where we go.’

Barkin looked apologetic, ‘Sorry, no can do. We’re right out of meme-caps. No access to q-machines.’

The shock on Praut’s face was easy to see. ‘What *NO* q-machines *at all*? How can that be? I was told you had at least one on the planet.’

‘You were told right. The only q-machine on this planet is in our hands,’ Barkin admitted, ‘but it’s disconnected and in storage so the other lot can’t get at it.’

‘But what good is that?’ exploded Praut.

‘Just as Stimmer came on the scene, we thought that if those independence loons led by Laudo, didn’t have access to a q-machine, their movement would fall to pieces.' Barkin's features weakened. 'Unfortunately, that didn't happen. They seem to have access to another q-machine from Stimmer. We didn't bargain for that. Now, we can't reconnect our q-machine without giving away where it is. Our opposition is now far weaker than the other lot. The tables have turned. If we reconnect our q-machine, they'd come and wreck it in no time and we couldn't stop them. We're not ready for an open battle. We need to find a way of crippling Stimmer before we take them on in a full frontal assault. Let's hope you can come up with something.'

'I'll try,' Praut said. 'So then let me have what you have on Stimmer in any way you can.'

'That I can do.'

'From what I could see when I was coming in here, you're prepared for a serious confrontation, am I right?'

'Oh, you mean my men?' Barkin smiled. 'That's nothing, you should see the other lot…armed to the teeth and eager to use them.'

'I can vouch for that…that's why I'm sitting here.' Praut spread his arms. 'Can you tell me, how's your lot structured…I mean have you got spies in the other camp?'

Barkin hesitated answering. He paused for a moment, then said, 'It's a delicate matter.' He looked over to where Praut's people were sitting. 'I assume you'll vouch for them,' he nodded in their direction.

'With my life. You can trust each one of my people as if they were me.'

'Then, yes we have some people inside the other camp.' Again Barkin hesitated. 'That's all I can say for the time being. You'll have to meet the leaders of our movement. I'll arrange that. They'll check you out with Earth, of course. That's just a sensible precaution. You don't have any problems with that, do you?'

'No, no problems.' Praut looked awkward. 'If your checking with WGS, be warned, I'm currently not their favourite guy, but I'm a hundred percent loyal to Earth.'

'That's good. Should be no problem then.'

Praut poured another tea, 'Any idea what Stimmer does, as a corporation, I mean?'

'New technology, so their e-brochures keep advertising. I've come across some of it….why are you looking at me like that?' Barkin stopped in mid-sentence.

'I'm sorry,' said Praut, 'but I've been hounded by this so-called new tech stuff ever since this thing began. It's getting on my nerves.'

'What new tech stuff are you referring to?'

'New type of Grabworms, disappearing corporations, missiles with strange crystals inside them. I've lost two good men to such a missile. Did you know that whoever is behind Stimmer has already fired three missiles inside the Solar System? Twice at a dome on Callisto and once at me personally?'

'What, Stimmer's lot have fired a missile at *you*?'

'WGS intercepted it and blew it up not far from my office building.'

'Sounds like you've been in the wars just as much as we have.'

'Tell me, have your two factions come to blows yet?' Praut took another sip of this palatable tea.

'We did at the beginning, but when we saw their firepower, we pulled back.' Barkin seemed to be remembering something painful. 'No point in sacrificing lives unnecessarily. We did a tactical withdrawal. It's been guerilla warfare ever since then. Hit and run…then hide. Out in the open, the two leaders, Catz and Laudo, talk and debate, making things look civilised, but behind the scenes, its daggers drawn. There's still quite a sizeable faction of undecided, just under a third of the population. Both sides are vying for their vote. Like it or not…there will have to be a referendum on this independence business. All activity is building up towards it. Earth will insist on it.'

'Let's hope we can swing it to our side. In the final analysis, Earth's Fleet will intervene, I'm fairly certain of that. I've sent a report back to WGS asking for help.'

Barkin's eyebrows lifted in surprise, 'You did that?'

'Yes, while we were on the way here.'

'Who did you contact at WGS?'

'Brigadier Shevchenko, why?'

'It adds standing and credibility to your position with our leaders. We have a couple of the brigadier's people here with us…monitoring the situation.'

Praut's brow furrowed in return at the information. 'Really? That's a bit of good news. I wasn't expecting that.'

'Now, let me take you into the next room.' Barkin rose and led the way to another door.

Praut took a last sip of his tea and followed, leading his own people after Barkin.

The next room was a war room with maps on the walls, models on tables. List after list on a white board.

Clay was disgusted at the primitive state of affairs. He would have preferred a series of screens and a mass of holo-models with tactical simulations, with q-machines feeding them idea after idea. The other members of Praut's group felt almost as disgusted as Clay. They felt the primitive nature of Barkin's approach boded no good.

Barkin was a sharp observer and noted the aversion on his audience's features. He laughed out loud, 'Look at their faces,' he said to Praut. 'What modern technology has done to people.'

Praut also chuckled at the scene. 'We've been spoilt, no question. I'm used to my meme-caps, my holo-decks, my teleports and the like. I'll be glad to get back to them but… if this is what we have at our disposal, then I'll use anything I can get my hands on to accomplish my aim.'

'Bravo, well said Dil. I can see we're going to get on just fine. Over there is a small model of Ventura. Come and get acquainted.' Barkin encouraged them to gather round it.

Praut was drawn to the model; it was the first overview he had of Barnaby's capital. The first thing that struck him; every building was round. There wasn't a straight line anywhere in the city. All the tall buildings were capped by domes. Parks were circular. The access roads were in the form of ever-increasing rings outwards from a huge spherical plaza in the centre of the city. Four ring roads in total around the central plaza.

'In the middle of the plaza,' Barkin pointed at the model, 'is the central dome, or theme centre, which housed the quantum-computer, the core of what was then the cybernated system of Serpedonia. All computerised communications, networking systems, admin, health and educational facilities, stemmed from there.'

'And the other buildings?' asked Fanny.

'The buildings surrounding the central dome provide the community with centres for cultural activities such as the arts, theatre, exhibitions, concerts, and various forms of entertainment.'

'Where do the people live?' asked Karl.

'There's eight residential districts surrounding the core. In those districts there's a variety of spherical buildings for the various occupants needs. Each home is embedded in what passes for a garden here on this planet. The outermost city perimeter is used for outdoor recreational activities such as hover biking, sky surfing, athletics and the like. Some of the tall buildings you see round the plaza are indoor hydroponic facilities. Others are vertical farms and agricultural buildings. Before this crisis began, we had high hopes of getting more q-machines so we could turn to replication instead of having to grow our food all the time. That would have released all the hydroponic buildings. Now I don't know where this will end.'

'Max, you're beginning to sound like a tour guide,' Praut joked. 'What about the maps on the walls?'

'One is of the inside of the dome.' Barkin pointed at one of the maps. 'Stimmer has taken that over and set up house in it. We don't know how many changes they've made inside, but we're trying to keep an eye on it…hence the map. That other map next to it, is the tall building where Laudo's lot have set up their command centre. Note, it's almost next door to Stimmer in the central dome.'

'Just a mo, Max.' Praut held up his hand. 'Has anybody had a look inside the dome since Stimmer moved in?'

'We've sent four lots of people to try to get inside… nobody came out. They vanished. The last lot was a month ago. I've got no more plans to waste more people.'

'Sorry, but I had to ask,' Praut apologised for digging into a mental wound. Praut nodded to Clay to stay and study this map.

'Not your fault Dil. Recently we had one bit of luck…' Barkin broke off, wondering if he should continue to tell Praut. 'Oh what the hell, you're either in or you're not. One of our spies inside the opposition told us Laudo's lot were testing a new camouflage outfit. We sent in a large group and hijacked it. We're testing it right now. Now my experts tell me it's not a camouflage outfit at all, but a new piece of technology; a contour force-field suit that shields its wearer. You know, like a force field round a space ship. You probably saw it as you came in. It's in the centre of this dome.'

Karl bucked up at hearing this. 'A personal force field suit? Our military's been trying to perfect one of those for years…and you've got a working model?'

'Looks like it.' Barkin looked smug for the first time. 'The opposition's been hunting for it ever since we took it. They've turned most of Ventura upside down looking for it.'

‘How did they get the force-field output module down to a size where a person could wear it?’ Karl asked.

‘That module is now a backpack. We’re still trying to understand it,’ Barkin replied.

Praut put his head to one side, ‘I’ve a vague feeling you’d get the WGS to take you really seriously if they knew you had that,’ he smiled. ‘You could name your own price.’

‘We were going to use it a few times and then pass it on to them. My people are trying to ascertain if they can replicate it.’

‘If you could do that…now that would be a game changer,’ interposed Mes, just as interested as Karl in the new equipment.

‘I must agree with my pilot there,’ Praut added.

‘We’re not a backward planet,’ Barkin explained. ‘We’ve got people here well able to deal with this sort of thing. The one problem that’s giving us a headache is the lack of our q-machine.’

Again Clay frowned at the hole in his life—no q-machine to play with.

‘Are we staying here with you?’ asked Praut, wondering where all this talk was going.

Barkin shook his big head. ‘This place isn’t safe. The room you’re in, is booby trapped. There’s explosives in every part of this dome. All I need to do is press a button. We’ve been expecting a raid for the last week…which is why my people all carry rifles. No, I’ll move you to a safe house nearer the centre. I want you to meet our former Governor. He’s been ousted from his post by Laudo’s rigged election, but amongst us, he still performs that function. He’ll want to talk to you.’

Praut wondered aloud, ‘Is it safe for us to go out there?’

Barkin grinned, ‘I’m in the hover repair business so I have a legit reason for moving around Ventura. If I’m stopped, I’m test-driving a repaired hover. I don’t have to be coming from anywhere or going anywhere. It's been safe so far. I'm afraid there's no other choice.'

'Max, we're in your capable hands. Frankly, I've only just met you, but I would trust you with my life.'

'Which is what you're just about to do,' replied Barkin, his grin getting wider. 'Now, let's have a quick peek at what my people are up to out in the dome, then I'll hover you out of here to your safe-house.'

Barkin led the group out into the dome centre to observe his scientists grappling with the personal force-field suit.

'I'd love to have a go at wearing that,' Karl said without caution, pointing at the man on the platform.

Suddenly a burst of laser fire came from one of the machines, aimed at the man with the backpack on the platform. He stood with his hands on his hips, safe from harm. The laser beam hit the force field at his midriff and stopped, unable to penetrate it.

'Damn that's impressive,' Karl said exuberantly. 'What'd you think,' he asked Mes, who was standing by his side.

'Yep, seems to work nicely,' she responded. 'Like to get my hands on it.'

'So would a lot of people,' Barkin told her.

'Max,' Praut said as they were standing a little way off watching Barkin's people at work. 'I've got a couple of ex-military combat pilots here in my group. If you ever need such people, well I'm sure they'd be only too happy to help you out.'

'Now that's good to know. Yes, I'm sure we'll need them when the time comes.' Pointing at the bustle in the centre of the dome, Barkin asked, 'Make any sense to any of you?'

Praut gave a sigh. 'The person who could have made sense of this…was killed recently. He was my technical wizard. He was one of the people killed by a missile fragment I was careless enough to bring back from Callisto.'

'Oh come on Dil, don't reproach yourself. It wasn't your fault,' Fanny leapt in, placing her hand gently on Praut's shoulder.

'You mustn't keep blaming yourself,' Olga added.

'Any one of us would have made the same choice,' put in Meserine. 'You didn't know it was going to happen.'

Barkin watched this performance and his eyes twinkled with pleasure. 'You've got a right loyal crew here. I like that. Makes you out to be a real leader.'

Praut winced with embarrassment at such a compliment. He always thought of himself as diffident.

Barkin raised his hand, 'Now, if we're ready, we'll find a working hover and make a move.'

# 14
# SAFE HOUSE

Outside in the frosty field with the derelict hovers, Barkin motioned Praut's group to the open side door of a cargo-hover standing amongst a number of other seemingly derelict hovers. 'I use this hover to move our people around. Get in. You'll find laser rifles on the floor in case we're stopped. I assume you have people who can use them?'

'They're all trained to use them. Some are better than others,' Praut replied, leading the way into the back of the hover.

The hover lifted from the field bearing outwards from Ventura into the midmorning winter sunlight, heading towards the eastern highway. On the Great Eastern Road, it swung right and travelled back down towards the centre until it came to the fourth ring road, and then went along it towards the Great North Road, following what there was of ground traffic.

'I do this to try and confuse air traffic control,' Barkin told Praut over his shoulder. 'My experts tell me it leaves a question mark on monitors radar screen. Are we ground traffic or hover traffic? We'll head in a circle to the northern side of Ventura and come in from that direction into the city centre.'

Praut puzzled over how it was possible to confuse ground traffic with air traffic. Surely, both had distinct and differing spatial coordinates on a screen? What were Barkin's so-called experts thinking?

There were four major highways leading out of Ventura emanating from the central plaza heading west, east, north and the short road south to the sea. These were the only straight roads anywhere in the entire city.

Barkin reached the northern highway after some twenty five minutes of high-speed travel and then swung left heading inwards towards the central plaza. After a while, the hover turned right again along the second ring road for two hundred meters and landed under the overhang of a tall round building. Barkin did something to the controls and a large pair of doors slid apart in front of them, opening a cavern in the building. The hover manoeuvred forward until it was inside and the doors slid closed behind it.

'For you information, this is Hydroponics Building 23A and you'll be housed on the $2^{nd}$ Floor. It's a floor devoted to growing oranges. Make a note of the address,' Barkin told Praut. 'Now let me introduce you to your new host.' Barkin climbed out.

The rear hover side door slid open and Praut and his crew disembarked, following Barkin in between lanes of massive vats containing various liquids.

'These tanks are filled with nutrients for the plants,' Barkin explained to Praut, waving his hand at the huge containers, as he led the way through them ever deeper into the interior of the building. Finally, they came to a round pillar with a door. Barkin pressed a button and the doors slid open revealing a lift.

'Weird place this,' commented Clay to no one in particular. 'Primitive lifts, no q-machines or teleports, and architects that find it difficult to think in a straight line.'

'Stop complaining. You're alive and being taken care of,' admonished Fanny. 'Say thank you instead of moaning.'

Praut lifted his finger to his lips, indicating they should both be quiet.

The group crowded into the lift. The doors closed and the lift vacuum *whooshed* upwards two floors. The doors opened onto a lush green forest filled with hydroponic orange trees that stretched as far as the eye could penetrate.

The air had a tinge of citrus wafting at them as they came out of the lift.

‘Down this way,’ Barkin led Praut, while the rest followed.

‘Looks like everything is automated,’ Praut observed, taking in the lack of people.

‘The building is huge,’ replied Barkin, ‘but only around ten people are needed to actually monitor production in the whole building. I’m just taking you to the Director of the place. He’s one of ours and lets us use a couple of rooms as a safe house.’

In the far corner of the eastern side, Barkin led them to a door. Barkin didn’t bother knocking, just slid the door aside and walked in, followed by Praut and his people.

The room was sparse with a long table in the middle, and what looked like food preparation area along the left wall. More laser rifles stood by the doorway to the left in a rack. Tinted windows covered the outer wall, while bunk beds were stacked against the right and back walls. Below the tinted windows stood a bank of screens; clearly gq-net access.

Clay tried to look nonchalant as he rushed over to a terminal and tapped the screen. His face brightened as the screen came alive.

‘I think you’ve made one of my people happy,’ Praut informed Barkin, nodding in Clay’s direction.

Barkin smiled at this, while watching Clay’s performance. ‘I’m informed the Director of this building is on the top floor at the moment, but he’s coming down as we speak.’

‘Thanks,’ Praut responded. ‘We need to get a plan of action going otherwise my people will stagnate. I’m sure what’s happening here on Barnaby is moving fast and is urgent.’

‘Yes, that’s an accurate observation.’ Barkin’s attention focused back on Praut. ‘This evening I’ve been told, one of our leaders will come here and have an in depth chat with you. I think you can expect things to start moving after that.'

'I'm glad to hear that. It's midday now…' Praut broke off as the door opened.

A large elderly man with a bald head strode confidently inside. He smiled broadly at Barkin, and made a note of the females in the room.

'May I introduce you to Director Hamrod, the chief of this enterprise,' Barkin said to Praut.

'Dilmore Praut of the Praut Agency,' Praut held out his hand. 'And these are my people.' He waved his other hand round the room.

'Michael Hamrod at your service; my friends call me Mike. I gather you need to stay here for a few days?'

'If that's okay with you? Call me Dil.'

'I'm at Max's disposal. You're most welcome, of course. You'll find all you need in this room. If your people fancy an orange or so, please feel free.' He gestured to the orchard outside the room. 'I'm afraid you'll have to share this room,' and he nodded at the women.

'We're not planning to undress, and as for the oranges…we'll try not to take them all,' Praut smiled.

'Over here,' Hamrod continued amiably, pointing at the ceiling over the door, 'you'll note the green light, which is on at the moment. Next to it is a red light. If that should light up, you'll have two or three minutes at the most, to grab a rifle and make a run for it. The red light means a raid. They won't ask questions—they'll shoot to kill. One of your people must monitor these lights at all times. It's a life or death thing. As soon as the red comes on, head down in between the tanks into the orange grove, away from here. Do not, repeat, do not go the way you came in. The enemy will have that covered. Keep going into the orange grove until you find a wide path running through the middle, down the length of the building. Then keep going until you come across the third stairway and wait at the top. Barkin's people will have sent a rescue team to help you. There's a team stationed nearby. You should be able to escape with their help. They're recognition signal will be *Barkin-Praut*.'

That created unease in Praut…his name in a signal?

'Barkin is updating that as we speak. Don't worry, our comms are well encrypted. You and your people may have to fight your way out. Any questions?'

'What's the likelihood of that happening…I mean having to fight our way out?' Praut asked, thinking of how he should prepare in that eventuality.

'Fifty fifty. We're due for a raid. Things have been getting rougher recently and you should prepare for what I said.'

'I'm taking note of that,' Praut told Hamrod.

Barkin held out his hand, 'I've got to go back to my place. See how my people are getting on with that thing we have.' He winked at Praut. 'Good to have met you Dil. Good fortune. I'm sure we'll meet again.'

'Count on it Max.' Praut shook Barkin's hand.

'I have to go as well, back to the top floor again,' Hamrod told Praut. 'I'm likely to be up there all afternoon. Make yourselves comfortable, and this evening, someone from the defence council will come and interview you. If you need me, use your throat mike. To make sure we're on the same frequency, I'll test it when I'm outside. I'll use that comm to let you know when to expect your distinguished visitor this evening. Any questions?'

Praut said, 'Thanks, and no questions.'

With that, Hamrod left with Barkin.

Praut invited his group to park themselves around the table. 'Listen up. I want your impression of what's just happened. What you think of Barkin and his setup? What you think of where we've ended up? *Clay!* Stop playing with that terminal and join us. *Now…!* This is a brain storming session. The rest, take your time. Sort your thoughts out.'

Clay reluctantly joined them and took a seat. 'What's the point Dil?'

'The point is to get on top of our situation. Karl and Mes are combat people and always on top of their surroundings. Here we are in the middle of a serious conflict. I want to know if anyone has noticed a flaw, a danger to us that I might have missed.'

'Before we begin, Clay, can you make a sweep of this room…make sure it's clean.'

Clay pulled out his terahertz scanner and went around the room with it. After he'd finished he told Praut, 'No sign of bugs Dil.'

Through Praut's earpiece came, 'Testing, testing, one two three. Can you hear me?' It was the voice of Hamrod checking the comm equipment.

'Receiving loud and clear. Over and out,' replied Praut. Then turning back to Clay he said, 'Right, thanks Clay. Please sit down.' Praut then addressed Mes, 'I'll ask Mes to begin.'

'I think this place is a death trap,' Mes began. 'Barkin is okay, if a bit rough. I still like that tech suit he's pinched. Hamrod seems alright. But the main thing is to explore this place and find our own exit. Is there an underground escape route?'

Praut looked at Karl for his input.

'I'm with Mes,' Karl replied. 'This place needs exploring. I don't like being cooped up here like this. Gives me a bad feeling.'

'Fanny?' Praut picked her out next.

'Apart from what Mes and Karl have said, with which I agree, I'm not sure what we can do. This planetary situation is so big…it's beyond our group's capabilities. I feel like we're being swamped by it. I'd like to focus on Stimmer. I want to know how they fit in to all this?' Fanny sat back and looked grim. 'Other than that, I didn't notice any other problems.'

'Olga?'

'You said we'd go back and pick up my sniffers Dil.' Olga looked annoyed.

'Olga, can't you think of anything but your damned sniffers?'

'You hired me to deal with the sniffers...I'm dealing. As for the rest, I'll leave you to pull us through.'

'Olga, you're impossible. You must know that without a q-machine, your sniffers value has been reduced by fifty percent.'

'That still leaves fifty percent,' Olga retorted.

'Clay, how about you?'

'I'm with Karl and Mes. I'm a bit lost without my q-machines. Still, going after Stimmer seems like a good idea. Let these people bloody each other's noses; we should concentrate on getting to the bottom of this Stimmer mob. That's what we've been hired to do.'

Praut looked at Clay, and not for the first time said, 'I often think you act the clown, but now, you've said what sounds like common sense. Well done Clay.'

Clay just shrugged and looked over to the terminal screen he'd been playing with.

'I've been informed this place could be raided by our enemy. Those laser rifles near the door. I want each one of you to grab one from the rack and familiarise yourselves with it. Make sure it works. Your life may depend on it. After we've had a bite to eat, I want two of you, preferably Karl and Mes, if they'd be so kind, to go out and do a recky of this place…then report back.'

Karl said, 'Will do.'

Mes just nodded her agreement.

'Now let's find what food there is.'

There were freezer cupboards above the food prep area stocked with a good variety of ready self-heat meals. Each picked out what they wanted and readied their food.

After they ate, Praut said, 'It's mid afternoon now, which leaves us a couple of hours before I have to meet with one of their leaders, whoever he may be. But remember this, we haven't any access to nanobots or nanomorphs, or any of the other trappings of a q-machine, whilst the enemy has. I want you to be especially aware of that so you don't get taken unawares. That also means teleports. If you have to fight, fight back to back. Keep your wits about you at all times.'

'Hey,' cried Karl, standing by the rifle rack. 'Two of these are maser rifles.' He picked one up and handed it to Mes, then took the second for himself. 'The microwave beam will penetrate walls.'

Mes was scrutinising the bulky rifle, hefting it against her shoulder, trying it out for size.

'Back soon,' Karl called out, as he and Mes left on their reconnaissance mission, both hefting their newly discovered maser rifles.

'The rest of you are free. Go get some oranges, use the gq-net, or just relax.' Praut went and sat at one of the terminals next to Clay.

Olga and Fanny sat at the table and chatted away with serious looks on their faces. A couple of hours passed by like this until Praut's earpiece informed him to expect a visitor. Karl and Mes still hadn't returned and Praut was beginning to get worried about them.

There was a quiet tap on the door, followed by *Barkin-Praut* in his earpiece.

Praut went to the door and gently opened it. In front of him stood Karl and Mes, hands on their shoulders.

Praut smiled, 'Where have you two been? I was getting worried.' Then Praut remembered the code word in his earpiece.

Karl and Mes walked through the doorway, followed by two tough looking individuals, laser rifles aimed at their backs. Behind them walked a tall thin looking individual with an aquiline nose. 'Mr Praut?' asked the sharp featured gent.

'Yes. What's happening here? Why are your men pointing rifles at mine?'

'Let me introduce myself. I'm Aldo Catz.' Catz motioned for his people to lower their rifles. 'Just a small misunderstanding. We found these two wondering about in the tunnel...and since we didn't know who they were, we took them into custody, just in case. I'm glad we've cleared this up.' He nodded at Karl and Mes, who now sat next to Fanny and Olga at the table looking nonplussed.

'Catz? Ah yes, now I recognise your name. It was me who sent these two off to reconnoitre an escape route just in case this place is raided, as I've been told it might be. I see they didn't come out on top in the encounter. Ah well, thanks be that no shots were fired.

Catz frowned, 'I thought Hamrod gave you instructions as to what to do if this place was raided.'

'I've survived this long in a dangerous business by double checking everything, including escape routes,' replied Praut severely. 'Now, shall we talk in here or have you another place in mind?'

'No, this place will do just fine.' Catz had his two men rack the maser rifles taken from Karl and Mes and then they went outside. He sat at the table at the other end from Karl, Mes, Fanny and Olga.

Praut joined him. 'I gather you have some questions for me.'

Catz composed his thin face, 'I've had a chat with Barkin and he's filled me in on what you've told him. Shevchenko's men say they're aware of you and what you're trying to do. They've okayed you. What can we do for you...and more importantly, what can you do for us?'

Praut sat back and thought for a moment, then smiled. 'What you can do for us is to help us get to the bottom of who this Stimmer lot are. And at the same time, that's what we can do for you. I gather you're stumped as far as this conglomerate goes…and they are at the root of your problem as well. Have I summed the situation up?'

Catz looked thoughtful and then the beak relaxed and he smiled back at Praut. 'Well, yes, I can see that we might be able to do business.' He looked deep into Praut's eyes. 'As for summing up the situation…I think that's fairly accurate. Our problems began with Stimmer, and if we can take them apart, we might be able to end this nonsense once and for all. Laudo and his mob are only a front for them.'

'So, any idea how we can get inside Stimmer?' Praut returned the penetrating stare.

Catz lowered his voice, 'We have someone inside Stimmer, but keeping in contact with her is proving nigh impossible. All their people are chipped and monitored. She can't make a move without them knowing. All we know for certain is, Stimmer is from off planet, and at the moment we don't know where its home planet is…but it's somewhere in this region.'

'She must have given you more than that?' Praut didn't look convinced.

'We've got three suspect planets we're looking at.' Catz shifted his position to a less confrontational one. He sat back and looked more casual. 'All three might be already overtaken by this Stimmer plague. We're certainly next on their menu. I'm loathed to mention this, but a number of my people seem convinced there's an alien influence here.'

Praut sat up. 'This isn't the first time this idea has surfaced. The strange crystals in the missiles I saw had me thinking the same. Eventually I put it down to someone coming up with entirely new technology out here on the rim. I was trying to follow this up when they shot me out of the sky.'

Catz paused a moment, 'I don't know what to think. The suggestion that there may be aliens involved seems such a far-fetched idea. We've no paradigm for such a notion. Barkin mentioned something about wormholes. Care to elaborate.'

'I started this investigation chasing people who were deleting wormhole technology from q-machines and the gq-net,' replied Praut. 'They were sabotaging wormhole work at various enterprises in the Solar System. So whatever Stimmer is up to, involves wormholes…you can be certain of that.'

'Is this where the aliens fit in? Did they arrive via a wormhole? If so, which galaxy? Damn, questions on questions. We need facts not more questions.' Catz slapped the table.

Now Praut was chuckling quietly to himself. This was exactly the point he'd got to a couple of weeks ago. 'I'm sorry, I should explain my mirth. You're at the position I was a week ago.' Praut shrugged, 'I can't see any other way except getting inside Stimmer…one way or another. That's where we'll find the facts.' Then an idea hit Praut, 'Have you tried abducting Stimmer personnel and forcefully questioning them.'

Catz frowned, 'No good. The bastards croak as soon as they're taken. Self-destruct. I told you, they're closely monitored.'

'Anyway of disabling the self-destruct?'

'Our people are working on it,' Catz informed him.

By now, all of Praut's people were pretending to do other things, but in fact were listening intently on the progress of the conversation with their boss.

Praut shook his head slowly, 'In that case we'll have to get inside Stimmer. No other alternative. I'll work on this with my people…and maybe you could help by seeing if there's anything you can do from your side to help me gain access to the Stimmer dome. Is there an offshoot of Stimmer anywhere which is less well guarded?'

'This is Barkin's province,' offered Catz. 'Let me put it to him. He'll get back to you tomorrow at the latest. He's made off with something that might help.'

'You mean the personal force field suit?' suggested Praut.

'Is that what it is?' exclaimed Catz. 'I'm supposed to be briefed on it later on. You must've seen it when you were with Barkin. Sloppy security!'

'Either you trust me and my people…or you don't,' challenged Praut, eyeing Catz closely.

'I trust you. Trust you enough to let you call me by my first name, Aldo. Now, I must get back to my place… more meetings.' Catz stood and held out his hand. 'Having had this chat with you, I'm trusting you to get to the bottom of this Stimmer outfit…and that means solving my whole problem. That's more trust than I have in my own people.' Catz smile was sincere.

'Good to have met you Aldo. My name is Dil.' Praut shook Catz's firm hand and the leader of the opposition made for the door.

'Good luck Dil, and good hunting. I'm relying on you.' Catz called back as he disappeared through the door, closely followed by his entourage.

# 15
# ESCAPE AND SUB

Praut watched the door close and then turned his attention to Karl and Mes. 'What happened?' he asked softly as he sat back down near them. He could see Karl was somewhat dejected, as was Mes.

Karl looked at Mes, and she nodded. 'We'd gone through this floor to the end,' Karl began, 'and found little to help us escape. Then I suggested taking the lift down as far as it would go. We came out three floors below ground level. It opened up into two tunnels heading in opposite directions. One north, the other south. Both of us assumed they led to the adjoining buildings on either side. We rock-paper-scissored it and that chose the southern tunnel. Half way down the tunnel, the two gents you saw behind us when we came in, appeared out of nowhere. I'm guessing that there's alcoves we didn't know about all along the tunnels. The rest you know. They led us back here non too gently. I just feel like someone's shot me in the back due to carelessness.'

'*Not* carelessness!' Praut said loudly. 'I repeat; *not carelessness*. We're in unfamiliar territory. It could have happened to any of us. Let me ask you now; what would you have done differently with hindsight?'

'I don't really know,' Karl replied. 'Crept along the tunnel wall? Maybe we should have been back to back going down that tunnel?'

'Should have been back to back,' added Mes. 'Silly to get caught like that.'

'And what did I tell you just before you left? If you have to fight, fight back to back. Keep your wits about you at all times. With an enemy like this, you'll only get one chance. Karl and Mes are lucky; they get a second chance.'

Karl hung his head even lower in embarrassment at allowing himself to be taken so easily. Barely in a whisper he said, 'Sorry Dil. Back to back, right. Try to do better next time.'

Mes put her arm gently round his shoulder, trying to buck him up. 'Don't take it so hard. We survived. It'll be okay you'll see.'

That brightened Karl up somewhat. He smiled at her reassuringly.

Another couple of hours at the gq-net screens and more chit-chat before Praut announced, 'Now, I propose we bed down. It's been a long day and we don't know what tomorrow will bring.'

*

A repeating piercing e-note shrieked into the room, waking Praut's group from their deep sleep. The light went on in the middle of the room and Praut jumped out of his bunk onto the floor. He looked at the light above the door and the green had been replaced by bright red.

'*You've got two minutes to grab your gear, grab a rifle and head for the door*,' shouted Praut at the top of his voice.

Mes was already dressed and at the rifle rack, closely followed by Karl. Fanny was close behind Praut grabbing a rifle. Praut stood by the door holding it open for his people. He'd gone to bed fully dressed, as had most of them. Clay was the last, closely behind Olga. Praut pushed Clay through the door and followed his people down in between the hydroponic tanks containing the orange trees.

Karl was running out in front leading them down through the middle path he'd reconnoitred earlier. They all rushed headlong towards the appointed third stairwell where they were to be met by Barkin's rescue team, assuming all went as planned.

After a hundred meters, at the first stairwell, they came across an anxious Hamrod who was shouting and gesturing at them, '*Hurry, keep going, they're almost with us.*'

Praut was bringing up the rear urging Clay along. As his people hurried past Hamrod, a laser shot fired from below the stairwell caught Hamrod in the back. Praut returned the shot and felt certain he'd hit the shooter, since the firing stopped. Hamrod, however, had fallen, and died with a plaintive look on his face.

Praut threw one last look back at the bald-headed elderly man who'd given his life for their safety, and winced at the barbarity of another needless death. In casting that last look, he noticed a head appearing, coming up the stairs, and he blasted it with his laser rifle in anger and reprisal for Hamrod.

Running through more of the orange orchard, after another hundred meters, they came to the second stairwell, where all seemed quiet as they rushed past it. However, Praut heard shouting coming from somewhere behind them and from down the second stairwell. The enemy was close behind. Olga tripped and stumbled while Clay jumped over her and kept going. Praut grabbed her by the scruff of the neck and lifted her back to her feet, shoving her forward.

'*Keep going*,' he shouted. Throughout their flight, all the time in his heightened state of awareness, Praut was aware of the tangy scent of citrus wafting up his nose, contradicting their life and death struggle.

Another hundred meters and the third stairwell came in sight. Praut caught up with Mes and swapped his laser rifle with her maser rifle. He wanted to see if he could slow the progress of those coming up behind them. Fanny was panting heavily. Olga was rubbing her knees where she'd stumbled. Clay was wildly looking all around him. Karl was looking down the stairwell.

It seemed folly to wait at the top of the stairs where they'd been told to wait, what with Laudo's people almost on top of them.

'Quick, down the stairs,' Praut told Karl and Mes who were leading his group. 'I'll try to stall them up here. When you're down safe, holler up and I'll join you.'

Praut watched his group descend the stairs, then he turned and swept the orchard with his maser rifle, driving a microwave beam through everything. Then he concentrated his fire down the route they'd come from. It seemed to prove effective if the shouting and noise was anything to go by. He heard yelling and shouts of pain coming from that direction. He wore a grim satisfied smile as he gave them one last burst.

Praut heard Karl's voice from below shouting for him to join them. One last glance into the orchard, and then he hurried down the stairwell to the bottom, where he found a group of dark clad men waiting by a dark hover, side door open. Scattered around the base of the stairwell lay a large number of dead bodies, implying a fierce firefight had taken place.

'Hurry, get inside, we can't hang around,' urged one of the dark clad men in a hoarse gruff whisper, motioning Praut with his laser rifle. They shoved him inside to join the rest of his group and the door slammed shut. A split second later the hover lifted, hugging the ground as it sped off into the darkness.

'Shit that was close!' Claymore burst out, looking at his trembling hands in the red darkness. The hover had a dim red light in the middle of the roof.

'Mind your manners, people present,' admonished Praut.

'Sorry Dil. Just the adrenaline talking,' defended Clay.

Suddenly laser cannon fire lit up the sky as a burst missed their hover, but only just. The hover made a sharp swing to their left, followed by a sharp swerve to the right. Their human cargo in the back tumbled about, trying not to break any bones.

'*Hang on to something*,' shouted Praut needlessly, managing to get onto his knees from the floor of the hover.

People were feeling bruised, having been thrown about like rag dolls. The hover was now running steady and everyone quickly took the opportunity to sit firmly on the floor, their backs to the wall and hands holding on to tie straps attached to the floor. If there were more turbulence, at least they wouldn't be thrown about.

The firing ceased and the hover ran steady for what seemed an eternity before coming to a gentle landing. Those in the back had no idea what was happening outside, as they had no access to an exterior view.

They heard what seemed a huge door *swish* open and the hover move forward, then a *swish* closed behind them. Finally, the hover side door opened and a dark clad individual's head appeared and motioned them out with his gloved hand.

Praut stepped out into what looked like a long low hangar; a strip of bright light ran down the centre. He noted people were busily scurrying around their hover trying to lock the four hover legs to the floor. That seemed strange. Two other black hovers stood nearby in the hangar, dark clad people toting laser rifles were climbing out of them. Others were locking those hover legs to the floor. Further away, at the far end, stood a weird low flat dark craft that looked distinctly sinister. Suddenly the floor tilted forward and remained like that leaving Praut with a puzzled expression on his face.

A huge dark clad figure approached. 'We're submerging. That's why the floor's tilted,' he explained. 'Sorry, let me introduce myself. My name is Tim Rogers.

I'm in charge of your rescue squad. Leave your laser rifles on the floor of the hover please.'

Eyebrows lifted, all Praut could say was, 'Submerging?' Karl and the rest of Praut's group crowded round him, minus their rifles, listening in.

'Yes, we had to bring you aboard our sub.' Rogers was smiling at Praut, trying to reassure him. 'We had intended simply to stash you in another safe house, but for some reason, they used a larger assault force than usual. We were cut off from where we wanted to go…so we brought you out here. It's safer here, but more difficult to operate from.'

Praut relaxed and smiled back, 'I was told you had moles inside the opposition…looks like they've got moles inside your organisation as well.'

Rogers shrugged his shoulders in resignation. 'We assume they must have. It's the nature of this conflict.'

'By the way, you need to tell whoever needs informing, that the director of the hydroponics building was killed as we left.'

'Mike Hamrod?'

'Yes. He was waiting for us at the first stairwell and some tyke coming up the stairs shot him in the back. My commiserations.'

'That's a great pity…he was a good man. Big hearted. Generous to the core. We'll have to inform his missus.'

'Damn! He was married?'

'Afraid so. Not your worry. Now, Mr Catz is waiting in the forward lounge. He asked me to take you to him. Please follow me.'

Praut followed the burly Tim Rogers. 'I haven't thanked you for rescuing us. Thanks. You seem to have had some trouble at the third stairwell?'

'The enemy blocked all the stairwells into the building. Normally we have to deal with four or five of them per stairwell. This time there were fifteen of them waiting there. No problem, we dealt with them.'

'So I noticed.'

'There were only two choices really; leave you there or deal with the hindrance. Which would you have preferred?' There was a twinkle in Roger's eyes as he looked at Praut while they were walking.

'From my point of view, you made the right choice. I don't know what your bosses would have thought had you chosen the other option.' Now Praut returned the mischievous smile that Rogers had worn.

'They would have lived with the misfortune as they've been forced to live with other tragedies that have befallen us recently.'

'What's the size of this sub?' Praut changed the subject. 'Must be enormous by my simple estimation.' Rogers and Praut were leading the group through wide corridors and through spaces filled with people perched over instruments. It was a hive of activity in spaces that would have seemed normal on land, but not on a sub.

'Length is 250 meters; beam is 75 meters, that's width to you landlubbers. It's the size of a large space cruiser, probably even larger. Built on Asterica, just outside New Knossos where they've got a good shipyard. It was intended as a research vessel to map Barnaby's oceans, but we commandeered it as the situation deteriorated. Now we use it as our main HQ.' Rogers led them through a huge communal space with a restaurant and café bar. People were relaxing in their break moments. 'It has a q-machine which enables us…' Praut pulled up sharply in the corridor, forcing Rogers to stop as well. 'What's the matter?' asked Rogers.

'I was told you had only one q-machine and it was disconnected,' Praut eyed Rogers with suspicion. 'Stored away somewhere and unused.'

'Disinformation I'm afraid. We tell everybody that. No, the machine is here on this sub, where it's harder to locate.' Rogers resumed walking, followed by Praut and his people.

Clay's hazel eyes narrowed. Having just heard there was a q-machine on board, he was fuming at being lied to. On the brighter side, he was close to a quantum computer once again, and he soon relaxed his mind in anticipation. Olga had picked up the info and added it to her sniffer info. Karl and Mes made a note of the tactics these people used with strangers. Fanny was staring all around her trying to grasp the enormous size of this submarine they were being led through.

'I'll let Mr Catz fill in the rest, if you don't mind,' Rogers concluded.

Finally, the group came to a large double sliding door. It opened automatically and Rogers led them through into the forward lounge. Ahead, Catz was seated in a comfortable contour seat, and he motioned for them to join him on the two wide contour settees near him.

Beyond Catz, were two large curved windows with a panoramic view of the ocean beneath the waves. Strange long red slender creatures with small gleaming yellow eyes, almost like swimming ropes, were whirling around just five meters off ahead of the sub. The ocean colour was bluish green, reflecting the mineral composition of the sea.

Catz told Rogers, 'Thank you Tim. You're free; resume your duties.'

Rogers nodded and walked out the way he'd come.

Then Catz turned to Praut, 'Good to see you again. Make yourselves comfortable. Well Dil, what do you think of my little sub?' asked Catz as Praut and his people seated themselves.

'Stunning. Very impressive Mr Catz. I've just been informed you have a q-machine on board. Is that true?' asked Praut brusquely.

Catz gave a small shrug, ‘Call me Aldo. Yes, we have a q-machine on the sub. Why do you ask?’

‘Barkin told me your only q-machine was in storage, disconnected. Now I’m told by Rogers that this was disinformation. I’m supposed to try to organise an attack on Stimmer, and it makes one hell of a difference if we have a working q-machine, or not. Surely you must know that.’

‘Sorry. I can see you’re irritated by our diversions. Barkin had only just met you and he gave you our standard line. Now we know more about you, you’ve been told the truth. We’re at war against an unknown enemy, make no mistake. I make no apologies for any disinformation. It’s part and parcel of such a conflict. You’re a practical man; surely you can appreciate our tactics?’

Praut relaxed his anger and sat back. ‘Yes, I suppose you’re right. It’s just that I need my allies to be straight with me if I’m going to help solve their problem.’

‘As I understand it, you’re primarily solving your own problem. We’re just an offshoot of your client’s predicament. Solve our problem and you solve your own. Am I right?’

‘Yes, you’ve hit the nail on the head.’ Praut had to admit Catz was correct. ‘So Aldo, let’s now get to the nub. How am I to get inside Stimmer from this sub?’

‘Right Dil, you didn’t happen to notice another craft in the hangar?’

‘Now you mention it…I did. A weird dark looking craft...that the one you mean?’

‘That’s the one. It’s our stealth flying sub. Usually we stay submerged. Coming up to the surface was an exception this time to retrieve our hovers. The stealth craft has no radar profile. We’ve removed the satellite GPS so it doesn’t report its position. It’s virtually invisible to radar. It has a coating of nanobots that absorb all radar frequencies aimed at it. We go in low and fast. That’s our usual mode of getting in and out of Ventura. That's how you'll get to Stimmer.'

'Any further info on Stimmer?' Praut inquired.

'We've been monitoring comm traffic off planet for a while, trying to determine the direction it's going from Barnaby. We've narrowed down the origin to two planets in our sector. We may have got Stimmer's home world. It's either Lowry or Fourex.'

'What are the comms saying?'

'We haven't broken the comms. They're using a code we've never encountered. My experts tell me they're dealing with a language they've never come across. They've got no references or paradigms for this code. The q-machine can't break it. We need more computing power.'

'Another *new* piece of nonsense. This is really getting too frustrating.' Praut seemed to be getting annoyed. 'This *new* business is getting on my wick. I'm determined to break down this *new* thing of theirs.'

Catz was looking at Praut, with a gentle smile. 'Yes, I can almost see an aura of frustrated determination. Well, I'll help in any way I can. Tell me what you need.'

'You wouldn't happen to have a cloaking device I can borrow? Might be useful to get past the guards.'

'You must know cloaking isn't effective.' Catz was surprised at the request. 'Any thermal imager can see through it. Put on a *cold* suite to block the thermal, and a maser sweep will fry you. There's detectors for the cloaking light deflectors. Cloaking is for party gimmicks not for serious work.'

Praut smiled weakly, 'Yes I know…just thinking aloud. I really need to take my people into another room and do a brain storm.'

Catz rose to his feet, 'I've got to do my rounds now Dil. Why not use this space. Your throat mikes will auto-tune to our q-machine. If you need anything, you can get in touch with me anytime. I'll leave you for an hour, if that's okay by you? Is that time enough?'

'I'll call you if we need more Aldo,' Praut rose and shook Catz's hand.

Catz left, leaving Praut staring after him. 'Right folks, lets begin.' Praut resumed his seat. 'I want ideas on how we're going to get inside Stimmer. We'll start with what we might expect to encounter from the enemy. What kind of defences do we imagine they have? Fanny, why don't you start the ball rolling?'

Fanny turned serious, 'Okay, so we're trying to get inside the Stimmer dome. Has it got a force field protecting it? Now we have access to a q-machine; can we teleport inside?' Fanny nodded at Mes to take over.

Mes frowned and said, 'I remember someone saying all their people are chipped. That means their personnel are monitored 24/7 and the whole place will be e-probed for non chipped individuals. I assume all their access points are closely scrutinised.' She looked at Karl to take over.

'I'd be looking for intelligent laser and maser turrets blasting anything it doesn't recognise. I'd assume there's thermal imaging on the access points.' Karl looked at Olga to take up the story.

'I'd assume the area is swept for teleports and they'd use disrupters to prevent it happening.' Olga pointed at Clay.

Clay coughed to clear his throat, 'I'd assume nanomorphs patrolled the area using visual recognition, and they'd have pressure sensors on areas not used by humans, include acoustic analysers in every area. They'll have their q-machine looking out for anomalies.'

Praut looked pleased with the brain storm, 'So, to sum up: all people with access are chipped and monitored 24/7. Special access corridors are screened for cloaking with thermal imaging. Intelligent laser and maser turrets blasting anything it doesn't recognise. No teleport allowed.

Nanomorphs patrolling the area using visual recognition. Pressure sensors on areas not used by humans. Acoustic analysers. We'll have to check with Barkin if he's aware of a force-field round the dome. Did his people try teleporting inside? How did they try and fail? Is he aware of other protective measures? Yeah, we definitely need to have a word with Barkin before we decide how to do this. Did I miss anything?'

People smiled at him and shook their heads.

'Just in case, I want you all to keep nibbling away at this problem. Then let me add; is there anyway of conning Stimmer to suspending one of the protection points? Can we sabotage any of their protections? We can't fiddle with their chips because their q-machine would know, unless Clay can come up with a way of fooling their q-machine.' That last idea had Praut looking questioningly at Claymore.

Clay nodded; he would give this some thought.

When Catz returned, Praut asked if he could get Barkin to come and talk to him.

'It'll have to be tomorrow. Is that okay?'

'Sure. Now can we get some food? I'd like my people to get some rest and take the day off, if you have no objections?'

Catz shook his head, implying he had no objections. 'Get something to eat and then feel free to have a roam around the sub, get acquainted with it. If you need anything, holler; my aide Johnsy will help you. I'll be busy in meetings all day.'

Praut thanked his host and took his people away to relax for the rest of the day, just prowling around the huge sub, eating and drinking, familiarising themselves with their new environment.

# 16
# PRAUT'S IDEA

The second day on the sub was a sheer delight for Praut and his people. The atmosphere was relaxed; all the tension had gone. Their sleeping quarters were sumptuous—each person had their own large bedroom with all mod cons. Breakfast had been excellent with the replicator delivering their favourite food. Most of them felt as if they were back home on Earth leading a normal life.

Catz had Johnsy, his aide, allocate them a large permanent office space near the forward lounge. This was to be their operational headquarters. The flying sub was placed at their disposal. All they needed now was a viable plan of action. This they didn't have yet. Following breakfast, they retired to their new office to discuss this.

As they were settling down for the analysis, the door slid open and Barkin popped his head inside. 'May I?' he inquired with a broad grin.

'Max, please. Just the man we've been wanting to see,' enthused Praut. 'Come in and join us. Sit here by me. We've got a barrage of questions for you.'

'You know about Mike Hamrod?' Barkin asked as he walked over to the seat, his face becoming grim, replacing the grin.

'We were there when he got it in the back. Nothing we could do. I know he'd still be alive if not for us…' Praut shrugged helplessly.

'It's this dammed conflict,' Barkin said sitting down. 'Not your fault. He was a good man. If not you…then someone else. It's the nature of the struggle. No one's blaming you.'

'Still….' Praut looked down hiding his emotions.

'Yeah, I know. Anyway, what's all these questions?'

'Right.' Praut bucked up. 'We need to know as much detail of your peoples failures to get inside the dome. Sorry if it brings up painful memories. What do you know of its security regime. If you think there are any weak points. We're assuming we can't just teleport in.'

'There's an anti-teleport disrupter sweep over Ventura preventing all teleports from functioning. I mean you can teleport, but what you'll look like when the q-machine reassembles you, I'd hate to see. What have you come up with so far?'

Praut showed Barkin the previous day's e-list brain storm on the e-pad he'd been given.

'I can confirm all of these,' Barkin responded, looking down the list. 'I can add a satellite sweep of Ventura checking for any anomalies. I've just come aboard using the flying sub and I'm worried this will get picked up one day. Then we're in trouble.'

'So, Max, how did you try to get inside?'

'First go was via the sewers. They let us get past their camouflaged laser turrets before they opened up.' Barkin was grim as he spoke, the memory still painful to him. 'The next time was as part of a special delivery team. They'd ordered a number of plants to replenish those in the massive auditorium, and we muscled in on the operation. The plants came from one of the hydroponic buildings. The delivery people weren't chipped so we took advantage of this. As soon as we deviated from the delivery schedule, they picked us up. Each one of my guys disappeared.'

'I can see this is going to be difficult,' Praut thought aloud. 'Bye and bye Max, I've just remembered a question. Have you tested that suit you've got against masers?'

'Yep, all okay,' Barkin replied, smiling. 'There's a counter to the microwaves. A special composite material in the suit that shields and blocks them.'

'Good, that's what I'd hope to hear. What about the third attempt. I remember you telling me you had three goes at the dome.'

'The third attempt was through the sewers again. This time we went in with force. We knew now where the turrets were and we blasted them to pieces. Then we forced our way upwards to the lift shafts and tried getting higher using the lifts. The lifts wouldn't work…they'd disabled them. My people got stuck above the sewer lever on the third basement floor. There's three basement floors and then the sewer level below that. The enemy brought up reinforcements through the sewer, cutting off our retreat. After that, it was a mopping up operation for them. That was my last attempt.'

'You must have known you wouldn't get anywhere using force, surely?' said Praut.

'I suppose,' returned Barkin. 'Anger got in the way of sense…and my people paid for it. I regret doing it now, but I was furious then. Should have been sacked by Catz for doing it…but he was lenient.'

'Any other ideas on how to get inside now?'

'I'm in favour of using a neutron bomb to clear the place. It'll leave the place standing and get rid of those chipped morons inside.'

Praut looked hard at Barkin to see if he was really serious. He noted the mischievous tic on his face, barely repressing a chuckle.

'For a moment I thought you were serious,' Praut told him.

'If it were only *my* decision…' he left it hanging and sat back laughing quietly to himself.

'Right! So now we've identified how we can't, the next step is to identify how we can…and…I've just had a whopper of an idea.'

Barkin sat up eyes wide. 'You've got a way in?' he asked surprised.

'Maybe, but I need to talk to those WGS men you mentioned.'

'Dil, you devious bastard,' Barkin said amiably. 'Trust you to come up with something.'

All the people round the table sat up and looked with interest at their boss. Would his legendary deviousness get on top of this seemingly hopeless situation as it had done many times in the past? They were eager to find out how he would do it.

Praut sat for a moment in thought, then said, 'Max, arrange for me to meet the WGS guys. You decide where. I've got a proposal for them which might be mutually beneficial.'

'No prob. How soon?'

'As soon as poss.'

'Right. Tonight suit you?'

'Suit me fine.'

'Want to give me a hint what you have in mind?'

'I want to run it past WGS first. It's too radical. I'll look a prat if they turn me down. Did you know, that's what my enemies call me; Mr Prat. Anyway, you'll know soon enough.'

'Fine, be secretive.' Barkin didn't take offence and just chuckled. 'I'll confirm where and when over your comm system later on, okay Dil?'

'Thanks Max. You're a good friend.'

Barkin rose from his seat, waved to Praut, and left.

'Listen carefully,' Praut addressed his group. 'Keep this strictly under your hat, but my idea is to ask WGS to get WorldGov to send in an Inspection Commission to Barnaby. We're going to be part of it. Fanny, me, Clay and Mes. I can't see Stimmer's lot refusing WorldGov. If they did, and WorldGov insisted, it would force their hand. They would either have to offer armed resistance or be forced to leave Barnaby. Either way, we get inside Stimmer.' Praut sat back and waited for the clamour to begin. He knew his idea was audacious. It would push things here on Barnaby, to a conclusion.

Fanny was first, and burst out, 'Dil, you're a rogue. You never cease to amaze me.'

Meserine rose from her chair and came over to clap Praut on the back.

Olga was clapping her hands and chuckling aloud, 'He's done it again.'

Clay was gently gyrating around the room saying *bravo* over and over, until he got near the computer terminal.

Karl was the last to join in. He waited for the commotion to die down, then said, 'Dil, I've made up my mind. If the offer is still open, I'd like to come and join your firm. I've not had this much excitement since my combat days. Life with the Holovid Studio is mundane compared. Will you still have me?'

Mes was looking pleased at this proposal, and hopeful that Praut would agree with Karl's request.

Praut beamed with pleasure, 'Welcome on board Karl.' To the rest he said, 'Say *hi* to your new work colleague.'

Fanny said, 'Dil, what with your Stimmer breakthrough and the new addition to the Agency, can we go and have a small celebration?'

'You bet we can. Let's head for that food place we were at yesterday.' Praut rose from his seat and made his way to the slide door, followed by his people, who were pushing Karl ahead of them in jest, patting him on the back for making a good choice.

*

Later, after all their celebrations, when Praut eventually returned to his quarters to freshen up, he heard from Barkin.

'Dil, hi, can you hear me?' Barkin's voice came through in his tiny earphone.

'Yeah Max, loud and clear. What have you got for me?' he said into his throat mike.

'I've set up the meet with the two WGS operatives. It's for eight this evening in a little dive just off the main plaza in Ventura. The senior guy is called Major Fernandez. The other one is Captain Pham Van Dung. The meeting is in a nightclub called *Havana*. It's used mostly by our activists, and ought to be safe. I ought to warn you, it's mostly ancient Latino music they play down there. In any case, don't be late. Bye.'

'Thanks Max, and see you.' Praut then spoke into his throat mike, 'Karl, can you hear me?'

'Yes Dil, what is it?'

'Tell Mes that the meet with the WGS people is for eight this evening. You and Mes are coming with me, so be ready. Make sure you bring your zapper with you; same goes for Mes. I'm taking you two because you're both familiar with hand-to-hand and I'm not sure what to expect from another visit to Ventura. Bear that in mind.'

Karl's voice lowered, 'I'll warn Mes. We'll look after you Dil, don't worry.'

Praut could hear Karl chuckling. 'If you don't,' he told Karl, 'you'll loose your boss and your job, remember that.'

Praut went to see Catz's aide, Johnsy, and asked for the use of the flying sub for the evening. Praut explained the schedule, who he was taking and for what purpose…just in case.

'No problems,' replied Johnsy. 'Always let us know where you're going. That way, if you don't return, we'll know where to look. Good luck and good hunting,' he said smiling widely.

Later that day in their special room, when they were getting ready to go to Ventura, Praut noticed Fanny looking glum. Taking Karl and Mes with him seemed to have upset Fanny, and Praut noted this.

He called her over to the other side of the room out of earshot of the others and said, 'Fanny, I see you're not too happy I've left you out of this trip.'

'Oh no, Dil, it's quite alright. I don't mind, really.'

'Fanny, I know you better than that. I can see you're upset. I've only done this for your own good. Karl and Mes are combat ready, and I'm not sure what to expect in Ventura. I need people who can kick arse with me. I don't want you to get hurt. You can stick your neck out some other time, okay?'

Fanny bucked up when she heard this, 'Okay Dil. I'm alright.'

'Good, now go and encourage Olga, and keep an eye on Clay. See he stays out of mischief.' Praut led her back to the others. When he and Fanny sat back in their seats, Praut said to Olga, 'When we return, I'll see if I can get Catz to send the flying sub off to retrieve your sniffers. You'll have to go with them to show them where you've buried them. Is that okay with you?'

Olga beamed, 'Oh Dil, thanks. I was wondering when you'd get round to remembering my sniffers.'

Praut looked at his watch. 'It's 18:30 now. We should go. Are you two ready,' he looked at Karl and Mes, both on their feet and eager to go.

'Ready,' both replied at the same time.

'Then let's get to it.'

The flying sub was prepped and ready to go. Tim Rogers and a couple of his men went with them as escort.

The pilot hovered the flying sub into an open nearby doorway that slid open and closed behind it. The sea-exit compartment was flooded and an outer door slid open in the side of the huge submarine revealing the green blue vastness of the open sea. The pilot launched the flying sub into the sea and headed north underwater at forty knots, then around half a klick from the mother sub it climbed steeply and burst out into the night sky, flying north on a course for Ventura.

Praut looked at his watch and it said, 19:05. 'Am I going to make the eight o'clock appointment?' he asked Rogers, who was sitting beside him.

'Stop worrying. It'll take us half an hour to get there, and you'll make it in plenty of time,' Rogers informed him.

The trip went smoothly and at 19:40 the flying sub slowed, hovered, and set down.

'We've made good time,' Rogers told Praut. 'We're down behind the ring of buildings circling the central plaza. Behind Building 9; it's a nanobot lab. It has Building 9B in large lettering on the front; try to remember that. We'll wait here for you till you return. Go down the alleyway to your left and you'll come out into the plaza. Turn right and the *Havana* is just a short distance along. You can't miss it. There's a laser display out front. Good luck. See you soon.'

The slide door opened and Praut led Karl and Mes outside. Praut stopped and checked his zapper, then hurried down the designated alleyway. As he came out of the alley, he noted the huge composite dome in the centre of the plaza. It was the first glimpse of his enemy's hideout; Stimmer Inc. He stared at it for a tic and then led the way in a casual stroll towards the *Havana*.

'Is that our target,' asked Karl in a low voice, tilting his head at the dome.

Praut nodded, 'That's it. Doesn't look sinister does it?'

'Amazing what camouflage can do,' intervened Meserine.

'It's winter out in the wilderness, but there's no sign of snow in the city. Feels weird,' observed Karl.

During the short distance to the nightclub, the three peered sideways at the dome, trying somehow to get under the mask of this unknown entity. Stare as hard as they may, it remained the same innocuous dome by the time they reached the nightclub.

The laser display outside announced…*Havana*, in big lettering, the only amazing *Latino* nightclub on Barnaby. It invited customers to listen to the ancient rhythmic sounds of a bygone era.

The bouncer out front nodded to them and indicated they should go down the stairwell.

Praut shrugged and led the way down the stairs. Karl had his right hand in his pocket, fondling his zapper, ready to use it at a moments notice. Music met them bouncing up from down below; a tango was cascading off the walls, gyrating its way out to the plaza above.

Praut relaxed when he heard the tango. It wasn't to be a trap, at least not by the sound of the music. Mes had been tense until she heard the music.

They arrived down at the foyer with a brunette desk clerk behind a counter. She seemed disappointed they didn't have coats she could take.

A swarthy dark haired individual dressed all in white came towards them. 'Mr Praut?' asked this fellow.

'And who might you be,' asked Praut, being ultra vigilant.

'I'm Salvo Hernandez. I own this club. Max told me to expect you, and to give you my full cooperation.'

'Then I'm certainly Praut. I'm sorry but I've not found Ventura to be that friendly. I was just being cautious. These are two of my people,' Praut indicated at Mes and Karl.

Hernandez nodded at Mes and Karl, 'Very wise. It used to be the nicest of places until recently. Until you know who settled round our necks, making neighbour suspicious of neighbour. Can't get rid of them soon enough.'

'We're supposed to meet two gents down here. Know anything about it?'

'I have a side room reserved for you. They're waiting for you in there. They've just arrived. Please follow me.'

Hernandez led them around the club floor, past some tables and through a dazzling laser display. The tango had finished and a spicy salsa rhythm had taken over. They came to a door guarded by a heavyset waiter. He opened the door for them and ushered them inside.

At a round table sat two large individuals dressed in black.

The nightclub owner introduced them, 'This is Major Fernandez,' one of the men stood, extending his hand.

Praut shook a firm hand.

'I'll leave you to get acquainted,' Hernandez left and closed the door behind him.

'And my colleague is Captain Pham Van Dung,' said the major.

Praut shook the other proffered hand.

'Pleased to meet you both,' said Praut. 'These are two of my people,' he indicated Karl and Mes. All took chairs and sat round the table.

'Now what can we do for you,' asked the major.

'I have something to propose to you…or rather, I should say to WGS. I'd like you to pass this on to General Botha or Brigadier Shevchenko, whichever you see fit.'

A query rose on to the major's face. It asked for an explanation that needed no words.

'I assume you're aware of the Stimmer entity?'

'Well of course,' replied the major. 'They're our prime interest. It's why we're here.'

'Exactly. And I want access to the dome in the plaza.'

‘So do we. Believe me, we’ve asked to see inside. They keep on stalling.’

‘Right. And they’ll keep on stalling until it’s too late. So, I’d like the WGS to ask WorldGov to send an Inspection Commission to Barnaby...and I want to be part of that commission; me and three of my people. I think both WGS and I are interested in the same thing. Finding out who these people are? Where they come from…and whose behind them? I’ve had words with General Botha, when he asked for my assistance; now I’m asking for his.’

Suddenly the music stopped and shouting could be heard from beyond the door.

Hernandez came rushing in, slamming the door behind him and locking it. ‘*It won’t hold them for long*,’ he shouted. ‘Laudo’s men are smashing the place up again. There’s panic outside. I’ve come to help you to get away.’ He hurried over to the far wall and kicked at something below their sight. A panel in the wall slid aside showing a dark passageway. ‘Quick, in there. It leads out to the back door. Hurry, they’ll be here any minute...and be careful, they may be waiting for you out there as well.’

The major was through into the passageway, followed closely by Karl, Mes, and Praut. The captain brought up the rear, and the panel door slid closed behind them. As the panel door closed, lights came on in the tunnel.

‘*I’ll try my damnedest to make your commission happen*,’ cried the major over his shoulder, as he ran down the passageway. He added, ‘This is the last straw. These bloody thugs will pay for this.’

The tunnel ended at the bottom of a steep flight of stairs going up. The quintet climbed the stairs as silently as they could, straining their ears, listening for tell-tale sounds of people waiting in ambush at the top.

The major reached the top and waited until the others had joined him. He held a zapper in his hand.

‘I’m going out first,’ whispered the major. ‘Wait until you hear me call. Don’t show yourselves till then.’

Ever so cautiously, he pushed at the door. Nothing…it wouldn’t budge. He stood there for a second, then cursed under his breath. He pushed sideways and the door slid open. He peeked out into the darkness…no sign of an ambush. He walked out and had a look around, then called for the others to come out.

‘I think we’re in the clear. How are you getting out of here?’ asked the major of Praut.

‘There’s a vehicle waiting for us over there,’ Praut pointed to the right.

‘Fine, we’ll chaperone you to it,’ whispered the major.

Keeping to the shadows, all five people walked the short distance to where the flying sub was supposed to be waiting, but there was no sign of it.

The major stated the obvious, ‘Seems they’ve gone.’

‘Seems so,’ replied Praut, wondering what to do now.

The major looked at Praut, ‘Well you can’t hang around here. You’ll all have to come back to our hotel. You’ll be safer with us.’

# 17
# SECOND ESCAPE

'Quick, this way.' The major hurried his three charges past darkened buildings heading for the northern end of the plaza. 'We'll stay on the 1st Ring Road all the way. It'll be safer at the back of the buildings. We'll soon be at our hotel. It's not far.'

'I'm sorry to put you to all this trouble, Major. That wasn't my intention when I came.' Praut was trying to think what he was going to do next while excusing himself with the WGS officers.

'You didn't put me to this trouble, as you put it. *They* did that,' and the major threw his hand backwards, meaning Laudo's thugs.

'I'm just wondering how we're going to get back to the sub.' Praut wore a worried expression.

'Oh, don't fret about that,' scoffed the major. 'I'll simply get in touch with Max and he'll come and pick you up. Then it's just a matter of connecting with transport.'

'You think its going to be that simple?'

'Sure, no prob. As for the Commission, I'll get to work on that right away. Should have thought of it myself.' The major seemed confident things would work out.

After some walking, they came to a long road leading out west.

'This is where the 1st Ring Road crosses the Great Western Road,' the captain informed Karl.

They took the moving pathway under the road; that rode them down and under, coming up and out on the other side of the road.

‘Another distance similar to the one we’ve come, and we’re home,’ the major reassured Praut.

‘What the hell possessed them to invade the nightclub?’ Praut asked the major.

‘I’m guessing, but I think they’re getting worried things are getting out of hand,’ the major offered. ‘To date they’ve done a solid job of controlling everything. Now, a leak in Catz’s organisation must’ve put you in the frame. They’re worried you might upset their cosy applecart.’ The major was walking with a frown, which was visible to Praut despite the darkness.

‘They’ve left you alone so far, haven’t they?’ Praut asked.

‘Yes, so far. Tonight is the first time they’ve dared to threaten us. That’s why I say they’re getting worried.’

Karl suggested from behind, ‘You’ll have to put in a complaint to the Governor, or there’ll be more threats. You can’t let them get away with this type of thuggery.’

‘I’d already intended to do that,’ said the major. ‘First thing on my agenda when we get back to the hotel. Captain, make a note—official complaint to their so-called Governor regarding tonight.’

‘Yes sir.’

‘We’re nearly there. Just down that next alley and we come out into the north end of the plaza—then left and voilà, *The Caledonian Hotel*.’ The major slowed and looked around.

‘When you get in touch with Salvo Hernandez again, offer him my apologies for tonight’s fiasco,’ Praut said earnestly. ‘By the way, will they be waiting for us? What’d think?’

‘Bound to be. We’ve had a tail ever since we arrived. Two of them permanently stationed outside the hotel, keeping an eye on our comings and goings. As for Salvo, I’ll do that for you, but he’s used to it by now. It’s not the first time they’ve wrecked his place.’

'The two goons outside your hotel, controlled by chips?' Praut asked.

'Must be. We've been told that if they don't do as they're told, the chip can be made to give them a jolt.'

'I think they call that classical conditioning,' said Praut.

'No, you must mean operant conditioning. What's that gringo's name who invented it. The Americano....just slipped my tongue.' Major Fernandez's Latino background was coming to the fore.

They reached the alleyway and the major took them down it, still in the lead just ahead of Praut.

'You mean Skinner,' interposed Karl from behind. 'He used to experiment in shaped conditioning; mostly with pigeons.'

'That's him, sometime in the twentieth century, wasn't it? They called the Estados Unidos the United States then.'

'Shit, that's almost six hundred years ago,' scoffed Mes. 'Altmayer mapped the whole brain in 2167. Surely he deserves more credit than Skinner?'

'What's time got to do with it? We're still quoting Plato, Kongzi, and Aristotle, and that's more than three millennia in the past,' interjected the captain.

'Yeah, your right. Anyway, those chipped morons are still there, look.' The major pointed at two men sitting in the distance.

They'd come out into the plaza and were coming to the hotel front entrance, emblazoned with a large lit sign proclaiming, *The Caledonian Hotel*. On the other side of the road, in the plaza gardens, facing the hotel, sat two burly men in grey jumpsuits. As they spotted the group coming to the hotel, they began an animated report into their throat mikes, telling whoever was listening that the two WGS men had returned and had three others with them.

The major hurried through the entrance into the hotel lobby, followed by his entourage.

'This place is run by a friend of Catz's, so you'll be quite safe,' the major informed Praut. 'He'll find a room for you three on our floor. Might even find rooms next to ours. It's only for a short time until Barkin picks you up.'

'Thank you Major Fernandez, I'm glad we met you,' replied Praut. 'Coming to Ventura, I've found to be a dangerous business.'

'It shouldn't be. Hopefully when we're through, all this can be put behind us. This Stimmer nonsense has turned a nice peaceful planet into a conflict zone. It's got to be stopped.' The major was looking serious and getting heated.

'Let's get them registered,' said the captain, trying to defuse the left-over anger from the nightclub raid.

'Oh, right,' the major said, calming down. 'Why don't you go find Gordon,' he told the captain. To Praut he said, 'He's the owner. I'll have a quiet word with him and he'll settle you in.'

Gordon McTavish, the mild mannered owner of the hotel, had them registered and settled them into a room adjoining the WGS officers in no time. 'Any problems,' McTavish winked at Praut, 'let me know,' he said, closing their sliding door behind him.

'The wink, I presume refers to Laudo's louts,' said Mes, going to the window to see what the outside looked like.

'Who else could it be,' answered Karl on Praut's behalf.

'Where am I sleeping?' asked Mes, turning and glancing around the room.

'Mes, sorry, but I've got us into one room for safety reasons,' Praut told her. 'If we have to move fast, then at least we won't have to go around looking for each other. You use the bedroom; Karl and I will stay out here. Don't get undressed. It's only for one night, until Barkin picks us up…and keep your zappers at the ready.'

'Tonight was a complete shambles,' said Karl, as he made himself comfortable on one of the two sofas.

'Just hold on there,' responded Praut. 'Remember what we came for. We've achieved that without any hassle thanks to the shambles…and without any protracted arguments. I thought I would have to spend time and energy trying to convince our WGS officers to relay our request to WorldGov back home. Laudo's thugs managed to convince them far quicker than I ever could.' Praut smiled at the memory of escaping through the tunnel.

'Heh, didn't think of it from that point,' Karl replied.

'Not only that,' continued Praut, 'but Major Fernandez is keen on pushing it forward because of the shambles. Laudo's thugs are doing our job for us. That's a good Judo principle…employ your opponent to do your work for you.'

'Don't tell me you're a martial arts expert as well?' asked Mes in surprise.

'I have a few tricks up my sleeve that I don't advertise. I save them for when they're needed.' Praut stopped pacing the floor and sat on the other settee. 'Now I suggest Mes, you retire to your room, and we'll all turn in. We don't know what tomorrow will bring.'

A short while later the lights were dimmed.

*

The commotion in the corridor sometime during the night was loud enough to wake them. Praut woke to shouting beyond their door. Karl sprang to his feet, zapper in hand. Mes opened the door of the bedroom, zapper peering out first. The noise continued until the WGS officers were heard demanding to know what the hell was going on. The major's voice was heard shouting at the intruders, insisting they leave or he would use his weapons. The noise stopped.

Praut heard more talking, but with lowered voices. He didn't catch what was said. Praut cautioned Karl and Mes, 'Have your zappers ready in case they come through the door.'

Instead, a gentle tap came on their door from the corridor.

'Who is it?' asked Praut, ear to the door.

'Major Fernandez,' came the reply.

Praut pressed the door lock open and the sliding door became transparent one way. He noted the figure of the major on the other side, and stood back from the door. 'Come in,' he said lowering the zapper in his hand.

As the door slid open, the major's erect figure stepped over the threshold. 'Thought you might be cautious,' he said, looking at Praut's zapper.

'You live longer that way,' replied Praut. 'What's just happened?'

The major came in, followed by the captain. Both looked angry.

'More of Laudo's thugs,' spat out the major. 'The desk clerk wouldn't tell them where we were, so they went floor by floor, breaking down doors and intimidating the guests.'

'That much we guessed. How did you get rid of them…I assume you did?'

'Yes, they're gone. By the time they reached this floor, we'd been warned by Gordon and I came out and confronted them. I gave them the option of leaving or having Earth's Space Fleet make them a visit.'

'Yep, that would do it,' smiled Praut. 'But the audacity of invading the hotel…it's positively outrageous. From what's just occurred, my guess is whatever they had planned, has been moved forward. We urgently need to get back to the sub to warn Catz. How soon can you get Barkin here?'

'Within the hour,' said the major. 'Gordon is just contacting him now. It's still dark outside. I'll go and hurry him up.' The major left.

'It's five in the morning. Don't Laudo's thugs sleep?' Mes asked drolly.

'Must be those zombie chip implants,' Karl added with a sneer.

'Gordon has the hotel's run-around standing by out back of the next building,' the captain informed Praut. 'I'll take you down to the cellar and through the tunnel, out to the next building…then into the hotel's hover. You'll meet up with Barkin's hover on the Great Northern intersection of the 3rd Ring Road. Grab your things and let's go.'

'You heard the man,' Praut told Karl and Mes.

The captain led them to the lift. Down in the second basement, they came out into a cavernous area lit by a red light.

Gordon McTavish was waiting for them as they came out of the lift. 'Sorry for all this mess,' he apologised, as if it were his own fault. 'We're really not such a bad hotel. Don't let tonight put you off.'

'Look Gordon, I'm grateful for all you've done. No one is blaming you for Laudo's thugs,' Praut consoled the hotel owner. 'As for your hospitality; I consider it excellent. Can't wait to come again and stay for longer at *The Caledonian.*'

It put a shine on Gordon McTavish's face. 'Thank you. Now let's hurry, come this way and we'll get you into the tunnel.'

McTavish led them to a wall, then did something to a small contraption on his wrist, and part of the wall facing them morphed into a doorway. 'Through there,' he said leading the way.

'Say goodbye to the major for us,' Praut told the captain as it was obvious he wasn't coming with them. 'Tell him thanks and he knows where he can get in touch with us regarding the outcome of the other matter. The sooner the better.'

McTavish led them down the underground passage to basement of the next building, then up a set of stairs and out the back to a waiting hover, *The Caledonian* in elegant calligraphy on its back panel.

Under McTavish's control, the back door of the hover lifted and Praut, Karl, and Mes climbed in.

'It's only a short ride. We'll soon be there,' McTavish soothed over his shoulder.

'Can't get used to everything being manual,' Praut confided to Karl and Mes.

'You mean the controls?'

'Well yeah. Look at Gordon over there; he's actually driving the damned thing himself. How primitive can you get?'

Gordon flew the hover up the Great North Road and swung left on the 2nd Ring Road to Building 28, where he stopped at the front entrance. Over his shoulder, he informed them, 'This stop is part of my ruse to confuse any of Laudo's agents who might be trailing us. It's just in case.'

McTavish got out and went through the front entrance. A short while later he emerged with a uniformed guard who walked him back to the hover.

'Sorry again,' Gordon was telling the guard. 'Must be a wrong address…or a hoax. You sure nobody ordered caviare and champagne?'

'Positive. Too rich for our workers here. Be off with you.'

'Right-o. Well toodle-oo. I'll be off then.' Gordon got back into the drivers seat and lifted off, making a U-turn, then veering left into the right lane of the Great North Road again. At the 3rd Ring Road junction he swung right and stopped outside Building 1, Leisure and Relaxation, next to another hover with its side flap open. Inside the cargo hover sat one of Barkin's men.

Gordon said over his shoulder, 'I'm going to open up my back door. I've parked so that my flap joins the lifted side flap of the cargo hover. All you have to do is move from my hover to the other hover under cover of the two open flaps. That'll reduce overhead surveillance…and remember your promise to visit again. Bye bye, now.'

'Thanks Gordon,' Praut said to the back of Gordon's head.

Praut climbed from Gordon's hover into Barkin's cargo hover as fast as he could, quickly followed by Mes and Karl.

Barkin's hover door closed and the hover lifted off, heading down the Third Ring Road to the Great Eastern Road and out east to Barkin's field. After a while, the hover touched down and the side door lifted open. It revealed a cheerful Max Barkin standing in the dark frosty field, hands on hips, grinning with delight. Four of his henchmen totting laser rifles stood behind him.

'Welcome back Dil. I knew you couldn't stay away.'

'Hi Max, nice to see you too. We've been driven into your arms this early by some friends of yours.'

'With friends like that, who needs enemies?'

'Yeah, I guess you're right.'

Barking nodded a hallo to Karl and Mes. 'Let's get under cover. Who knows what's lurking in the skies.'

Barkin led them into the dome, followed by Praut, Karl, and Mes, with Barkin's henchmen bringing up the rear.

In the middle of the dome, under the bright lights, the experts were still fiddling with the personal force field suit.

'How's that coming along?' Praut asked Barkin, pointing in its direction.

'The analysis is being finalised as we speak,' Barkin told him. 'They think they can replicate it and the blueprints are being put into the computer right now. Then we'll do a simulation on the sub's q-machine and see how that goes. My people tell me they're fairly sure they've got it licked.'

'That's great. Have you been keeping abreast with our little saga. The Hotel and Nightclub raids?' Praut asked.

The group stood a little distance off from the middle of the dome, watching the scientists on the platform working on the suit.

'The major filled me in when he called for help to get you out. I gather you urgently need to get back to the sub.'

'All these raids suggest to me that Laudo and Stimmer have upped the anti and are getting ready to make a take over bid,' Praut told him. 'We've got to pre-empt it. We have to announce the imminent visit of the Inspection Commission from Earth. I need to apprise Catz of this and get him to contact the major and get him to inform Laudo this is going to happen.'

'I thought you only just put in a request to WorldGov for the Commission.'

'Yeah, but things are moving a bit too fast. These raids imply they're almost ready to strike and don't seem to care for the consequences. We've got to disabuse them of that. The only way I know is to announce the imminent arrival of a WorldGov Inspection Commission to determine Barnaby's reasons for their insistence on independence from Earth.'

'It'll take at least a week for any commission to arrive, even if they left now.'

'It took us six days to get here. It'll take them longer, but coms from Earth are almost instantaneous thanks to the wormholes. If Earth tells Laudo they're coming, it might hold them off for a week until they actually arrive.'

Barkin called one of his men over and told him, 'Get in touch with Catz's sub to send their flying sub over here to pick up Dil and his people. Tell them it's urgent.'

# 18
# LAUDO ACTS

Johnsy, Catz' aide, stuck his head round the opening slide door and said, 'Mr Catz will see you now.'

They'd been back on the sub for over two hours and Praut was getting impatient, sitting in the special room allocated to his group, waiting while Catz was in a meeting.

Over his shoulder as he left, Praut told his group, 'Try to find ways of exposing Stimmer when we're going through the dome.' Then he followed Johnsy down the corridor to Catz's lounge.

'Sorry I took so long,' Catz apologised. 'There's a bit of a flap on. We think there's something brewing in Laudo's camp.'

'That's what I've been waiting to tell you,' responded Praut. 'I think they're about ready to strike.'

Catz looked alarmed, 'Good grief, why didn't you tell me earlier?' cried Catz.

'I tried to, but your aide insisted you couldn't be disturbed...top level meeting and all that.'

'That Johnsy is too damned protective. Anyway, so tell me what you've found out.'

'We had a meet with the WGS officers last night, and that was raided by Laudo's thugs. The flying sub left without us, I gather now because of an imminent threat to it. Major Fernandez took us to his hotel…and Laudo's thugs raided that. By all that's happened, I've concluded that Laudo's boldness means he's just about ready to move against you…come what may. Maybe even today. You've got to warn all of your people. Stay armed and be vigilant.'

'Damn them. It sounds like your right. I'm not sure what we can do to stop them.' Catz talked rapidly into his throat mike, giving instructions to be sent out to all his personnel, warning them to be on their guard.

'Well, that's why I wanted to see you so urgently. I have a plan. It involves the WGS and WorldGov. I saw the WGS officers last night to ask them to organise an Inspection Commission from WorldGov to visit Barnaby. Remember, I told you about that idea before I left. Well if we can tell Laudo that the Commission is on its way…I think he might hold off from whatever he's about to do.'

'The Commission in itself is useless,' grumbled Catz.

'True…but it's what's behind the Commission that'll worry Laudo and his backers…Earth's Space Fleet.'

'I see what you mean. Of course…in both cases it's the ultimate threat of force that decides the issue. Laudo has superior firepower here on Barnaby…but the Space Fleet cancels it outright. They've got enough firepower to blast Barnaby back to nowhere. If Laudo bucks WorldGov, then he faces Earth's Space Fleet. It's an argument clincher.' Catz looked more relieved now he'd reminded himself of that scenario.

'That's what I'm saying to you,' insisted Praut.

'Right, so how do we proceed then?'

'We have to get the Major to inform Laudo that the Commission is on its way…that'll give him and the WGS time to convince WorldGov to send the Commission. We can only hope they move quickly.'

'Cart before the horse, surely?' voiced Catz.

'No choice…we're being pushed into this. It'll take any Commission at least six days to get here. The major will have to stall Laudo as best he can…no other choice.'

'I'm with you…all the way,' Catz looked encouraged. Then he sagged into the couch as it all sunk in. 'You're right…can't see any other way. Hope this bloody thing works.'

'At least we'll get to see what's inside the dome...see if there's any bug eyed monsters running the place. It may stall Laudo for the moment, from doing anything. I know it's a stopgap, until I or you come up with a better plan.' Praut wasn't exactly pleased, but he thought this little trick might buy some time. 'Can you get the major to come here to the sub?'

'No prob.' Catz talked into his throat mike. 'Right, I've sent the flying sub to pick up the major.'

'Can you contact WorldGov from your sub?'

'Thanks to the q-machine, we've got a channel to the local relay node. Then it's just a matter of the local comm-gauge-wormhole. What had you in mind?'

'To back up Major Fernandez' request, I'd like you, as leader of the opposition, to send a personal request to WorldGov to send an urgent Inspection Commission to Barnaby. You have reason to believe another planet is interfering in your internal affairs and this is the first step on a slippery road to a local empire building process, which inevitably will end up threatening Earth.' Praut paused, rubbing his chin. 'What do you think? Will it work?'

'The bit about *empire building* is a little devious to say the least,' chuckled Catz. 'But I'll do it. I'll send it.'

'Good. When the major gets here, he can use your comms to contact WGS and WorldGov. The combined pressure of you and the major might get the ball rolling a lot quicker. Now I think I ought to tell you something. This must stay between us two only, no other soul. It's my backup.'

Catz looked intrigued, but nodded his agreement.

'I assume the room is clean?'

Again Catz nodded, 'Swept just before our big meet earlier on.'

'Good. Well, I have a spaceship parked a parsec from Barnaby in comm range. The rest of my Agency people are on it armed to the teeth. When we crashed, I couldn't get in touch with them because our coms were being jammed. Now I think its time to bring them in. Can you see any reason not to?'

'I'd counsel waiting until it can join the WorldGov Inspection Commission shuttle,' Catz suggested.

'What, you think Stimmer might have a go at it?'

'With the heightened state of aggression, I think it a distinct possibility. After all, they blew you out of the sky, didn't they? No harm in waiting a few days, eh?'

'Put like that, I have to agree. I've had enough of my people killed.' Every time Praut had a reminder of those unwarranted deaths, a resurgence of anger tinged with sadness seared through his mind. 'On another note, do you think it might be possible to send your flying sub over to where my crashed shuttle is, to retrieve a piece of vital equipment?'

'Is it important?'

'It might be. They're called sniffers, and Olga, one of my people operates them. If Stimmer is forced off this planet, then it will head for home and what it considers to be safety. Olga can send a sniffer after Stimmer and determine the precise location of Stimmer's home planet. That way we can finish with them once and for all. Olga will have to go with your people to show them where she's hidden the sniffers.'

'In that case by all means, I'll give orders to the flying sub when it gets back.' Catz talked into his throat mike to one of his operatives for a short while, giving the appropriate orders.

Johnsy came hurrying in, '*Sir*, bad news. We've just received a message that Barkin's field has just been raided and the whole place is a wreck.'

Catz's face became livid, 'Is Max alright?'

'Yes sir, but he's injured.'

'Badly?'

'I don't think so sir. I'm told it's a minor shoulder wound,' Johnsy looked just as annoyed as his boss.

'Is the suit safe? Did they get it away in time?'

'That's what I'm told. They've taken the suit and the people working on it to the Sámi outpost. It ought to be safe out there.'

'What about the other thing his boffins were working on?' Catz looked anxious.

'That's safe as well,' replied his aide.

'Any progress with it? Did Barkin manage to tell you?'

'He told the major on the way here. He asked him to convey the info to you.'

'Anything else?'

'All our safe houses have been raided…and the hotel as well.'

'You mean *The Caledonian*?'

'Yes sir, it's been taken over by Laudo's men. We've managed to rescue McTavish and he's on his way to the sub with the major and Barkin.'

'So Barkin's on his way here to the sub as well?'

'Yes sir, him, the major and McTavish.'

'Good. We've got better care facilities here.' Catz then turned to Praut, 'Well, you were right. They have begun to move against us. Thank goodness, they've managed to salvage Barkin's two major projects. We'll definitely need both…soon.'

Praut peered quizzically at Catz, 'Can I inquire what the other project is? The suit I know about…but the other one?'

'Right, I suppose you should know that as well. You've been told how Stimmer controls their people?'

'Yes, I've been told it's by putting a chip in all their personnel.'

'Not just any chip…this is a biochip. Something we've never come across.'

'A biochip? What kind of biochip?' Praut was intrigued.

'This is going to take a little bit of explaining, so relax and let me finish,' Catz told Praut. 'Damn thing had us stumped for a long while. We catch their people…but the next thing…they fall down in a seizure and die. When our medics open them up…there's no sign of any chip. Just a blockage of the aorta…heart attack so it seems. That's what Barkin's boffins were trying to get to the bottom of. The missing chip. Finally they came up with a cryogenic stasis cubicle. As soon as they caught one of Laudo's people, they dumped them in the stasis cubicle…freezing them instantly. Then scans revealed the biochip at the base of the cerebellum. It seems that it's programmed to produce nanobots when the person is captured…nanobots that feed through the blood vessels to the heart and block the aorta… making it look like a heart attack. The damned things are smart and elusive…until now. Hopefully, what the major is going to tell me is that we've found a way to neutralise the nanobots and remove the biochip. If we can't, then all of Laudo's people are as good as dead, even if we win. That's a lot of innocent people…and so this is more important than that suit you know about. If we can't sort this out…then even if we win…we loose.'

'Any idea of whose biochip it is…I mean who made it?'

'Absolutely no idea. Our scientists say at the present it's beyond our capability…so your guess is as good as mine. They've never seen anything like it. Not only is the biochip a killer, but it manufactures nanobots, *and* controls the person via its neural connections in the person's brain. The chip feeds info back and forth to a central control… triple frequencies and encrypted, and all of Laudo's people have one in them, as far as we can determine.'

Praut was flabbergasted. He finally spat out, 'This is about as sinister as it gets. They've turned ordinary people into zombies. This has got to be stopped.'

'I'm glad you feel that way. Now you see what we're up against. We must find a way to rescue those people.' Catz was incensed as he spoke.

'Well first things first,' said Praut. 'You immediately need to make a strong protest to their so-called Governor regarding all the takeovers. It might just slow the attack down.'

'What's the point? Governor Pergman is Laudo's puppet,' grumbled Catz. 'He's probably chipped as well.'

'That as may be, but you have to follow the game. Remind the Governor that the Inspection Commission will not turn a blind eye on what's happening. He won't stay Governor for very long if he doesn't do something to stop this. Tell him what's happening is illegal and someone will be brought to account when the Commission arrives. While you're saying all this to the Governor—you know who will be listening. Laudo may hold off if he thinks the Commission is a done deal…and is due.'

Johnsy was also listening to Praut's advice. 'Shall I put a protest note together based on Mr Praut's suggestion?' he asked Catz.

'Yes, do that. Don't know what good it'll do, but who knows, it *might* just slow them down.'

Johnsy left to send the protest note to the so-called Governor.

Praut and Catz discussed the deteriorating situation for a while, tossing ideas around, until Johnsy interrupted them again, arriving with the major and McTavish in tow.

'Major Fernandez, glad you could come,' Catz welcomed. 'And Gordon, I'm so sorry about your hotel. When this is all over we'll fix it up like new; that's a promise.'

Gordon McTavish beamed at this but remained quietly standing behind the major.

'Mr Catz, Dil,' the major acknowledged them. 'I've been asked to tell you Mr Catz, that Barkin is in the subs medical facility as we speak. We brought him in with us. He's alright.'

'Thank goodness he's safe. Thank you for that info, but I'm told you might have more to tell me…from Barkin.'

'Ah yes, Barkin asked me to tell you they've found a solution to the chip problem…at least his boffins have.' The major came and sat on the settee near Praut, facing Catz. 'It seems that removing the chip isn't necessary. They were attacking the problem from the wrong end. The nanobot specialists came up with this. They've found a way of programming their own nanobots to attack the chip's nanobots *before* they get to the heart to block it. Destroy the chip's nanobots, and the chip self-destructs anyway. The latest information was, they're perfecting the nanobot programming so they get to the chip's nanobots as quickly as poss. That's the message Barkin asked me to convey to you.'

Catz sighed, 'That's the best news I've had recently. It's been worrying the hell out of me. Thank you major, I needed to hear that. It gives me hope.'

'I've also been hearing some of what's going on,' continued the major. 'It's getting more serious as we speak. Have you got a comm to Earth? I need to get through immediately and report. Maybe they can put a halt to this.'

'I've just given orders for my own protest to be sent to WorldGov demanding they do something. If you would like to put something together and let Johnsy have it when he gets back, he'll get it transmitted to Earth via the local relay node. Hopefully both reports will get them off their backsides and announce a Commission.'

Just then Johnsy returned and told Catz the protest note had gone off.

The major pulled his e-pad from his pocket and handed it to Johnsy, who stood nearby, 'I was putting this together while we were on our way here. It's addressed to General Botha at WGS and marked Imperative Action Needed. It asks that an Inspection Commission be sent with all speed by WorldGov to determine Barnaby's rationale for their insistence on independence from Earth. It demands that Governor Pergman be replaced and Monitors be appointed to oversee fair elections here on Barnaby. That of course requires the presence of the independent Galactic Electoral Commission. The GEC oversees all planetary elections—and that it didn't oversee the last election here might be solid grounds to declare those elections null and void. Mr Catz, that would put you back in the Governor's chair.'

'Yes it would,' replied Catz with a smile. 'But they'd never go for it, not Laudo, not Stimmer. They're too deep in the plot. For them it's all or nothing, especially now, surely?'

Praut intervened, 'You're probably right, but all we're trying to do is buy time. If we can stop them for a couple of days…a week…then the whole picture changes. They can't refuse the Commission,' insisted Praut. 'All we're after is for them to hesitate. If they go ahead, there'll be a bloodbath. Will you give in and allow them to take over?' Praut looked into Catz eyes.

*'NO!* Never…and most of my people feel the same. We'll go down fighting if need be.' Catz's eyes blazed with fury.

'So there's the rub. We've got to find any way we can to delay Stimmer's plans until help arrives, otherwise there *will* be a bloodbath,' Praut said passionately. 'And Major, could you mention to Earth, I and three of my people want to be included in the Inspection Commission. I'm sure four more won't overstaff such a Commission. Best way to do that is if my people and I are part of the welcoming group at the spaceport when the Commission lands.'

The major retrieved his e-pad from Johnsy and began to amend his report, while Catz and Praut looked on.

After a short while, Praut added, 'It might also be an idea if you could include, that we have a new kind of personal force field suit for Earth's defence forces. It might make them more forthcoming.'

The major smiled at Praut but looked at Catz. 'I've taken the liberty of doing that already in my report…I hope you don't mind? I thought it would wet their appetite.' The major handed the e-pad back to Johnsy.

'No I don't mind. I hope it helps.' Catz then turned to his aide, 'Johnsy, go quickly and send the two comms to Earth...mine and the Major's. Ask them to send an acknowledgement. And take Gordon here,' Catz motioned at the patiently waiting McTavish, 'and put him in one of our best rooms.' To McTavish he said, 'I'll have a chat with you later.'

'Yes sir, right away.' Johnsy left with McTavish to carry out his given tasks.

'Let's settle ourselves on the settee and I'll send for some refreshment,' invited Catz.

As the three settled down, Praut said to Catz, 'Next, I'd like you to get in touch with Laudo and tell him you'd like to have a talk with him, P2P. I want you to tell him of the imminent arrival of the Commission and warn him not to do anything silly before they arrive. Instead of the major telling Laudo about the Commission, inform Laudo you have a WGS Major with you. Remind him there's an Earth's Space Fleet behind the Commission. Also, remind him that the Galactic Electoral Commission didn't oversee the last elections here, and that they're likely to be invalid. Demand he remove his thugs from *The Caledonian*, and all the other places they've taken over…and also remind him that someone will have to answer for all the needless deaths that have taken place recently.'

'Yes, now that sounds like a good idea,' agreed the major. 'Even if he's not responsible for Stimmer, he's probably answerable *to* Stimmer. Let's see if Stimmer can be forced to back off.'

Praut nodded, 'All we need is a few days leeway and a bit of inaction from Laudo and his thugs.'

Catz frowned, 'As soon as Johnsy comes back I'll get him to contact Laudo. I'm not looking forward to this…but it's got to be done I suppose.'

'Look Aldo, you'll have to sound convincing,' Praut urged. 'You'll need to put some anger into this, some outraged indignity for Laudo's outrageous behaviour.'

'Don't worry Dil, I know how to be indignant.'

The major watched with amusement at Praut and Catz's performance. His military mind was busy on outmanoeuvring Stimmer's attempted takeover of this planet, yet here were these two working out how to behave in front of a thug. It tickled his funny bone.

Praut got to his feet, 'I think I'll leave you to do this in private. I'll take the major and introduce him to the rest of my people. If there's a message from Earth, please let me know,' and with that Praut left, taking the major with him to meet his group.

# 19
# UNDER ATTACK

Praut, standing side by side with the major, gazed at his group sitting round the long table. 'Mes and Karl you know already,' he said to the major. 'Fanny, our red haired beauty over there is my personal assistant. Olga, the dark haired lady is our sniffer specialist, and Claymore over there, sitting next to her, is our computer wizard. Say *Hi* to Major Fernandez of WGS.'

Almost in unison a weak, 'Hi,' came from the group.

'Oh *come-on*, you can do better than that. He's saved my neck and deserves a better thanks than that. Try to forget he's WGS.'

This time there was a loud, '*Hi*,' from them all.

'That's better,' Praut looked pleased.

The major began, 'Pleased to.....' which was interrupted by a strong shudder through the floor of the sub. '*What the hell?*' cried both the major and Praut.

A loud electronic alarm began beeping intermittently, followed by a disconnected voice, '*Action stations, action stations*, we're under attack. This is the Captain speaking. Repeat, we're under attack. All sub's personnel to their battle stations. Prepare for deep water. All civilian personnel—stay calm. The situation is under control.'

Karl and Mes were on their feet. Praut and the major were heading for the slide door, followed by Karl and Mes.

'Stay put and stay calm. I'll be back in a mo,' Praut shouted over his shoulder.

All four headed towards Catz's lounge. They encountered various people running down the corridors, until they came to Catz's door. It slid open and the four worried people rushed inside.

They found Catz talking furiously into his throat mike, while nearby, Johnsy fretted over him. 'Yes, yes, I understand Captain, of course, do as you see fit. I have full confidence in your abilities.' To the newly arrived, Catz said, 'It seems there's a large shuttle above us, firing missiles at our position.'

'But how did they find us?' asked Praut.

'Our comms to Earth,' replied Catz, casting a glance at his aide, as if it were his fault. 'They located us via our comms. We've got a solid anti-missile missile component on board. The shudder you felt through the floor is our missiles taking off to knock out their missiles. We even have a forcefield round the sub, but air and water are different mediums. Our forcefield is against other subs, not air born attacks. The Captain's heading out into deeper waters…but if they use a sonic beam weapon up there, it might penetrate our forcefield. The deeper we go, the less they can penetrate through the water.

Another shudder went through the floor of the sub.

'That's another missile on its way,' said Catz cautiously. 'By the way Johnsy, did we receive acknowledgement of our comms to Earth?'

'Yes sir, we got it just before I came to you. They confirm they've already sent a Commission two days ago. It's on its way…should be here in four days.'

'What? They've already *sent* a Commission? But, but….' Catz looked flabbergasted.

Praut looked dismayed at having his supposedly brilliant idea entirely pre-empted.

The major pricked his ears up at this news. 'Must be my earlier reports,' he suggested to Catz.

Catz turned to his aide, recovering his composure, 'Did we send the major's earlier reports?'

'Yes sir,' Johnsy replied. 'The major gave them to Barkin, and he passed them on to me.'

'So anyway, the Commission is on its way…that's the good news.' Catz enthused. 'All we have to do is survive this current onslaught for the next four days.'

'So all my hard thinking on the Commission was for nothing?' bemoaned Praut.

Suddenly Catz became distracted, listening to info coming in on his earphones. Then he said, 'Yes, yes, do what needs to be done. I said I'd leave all that up to you.' He was almost shouting into his throat mike.

'May I speak,' it was Karl.

Surprised, Praut said, 'But of course.'

'The flying sub, is it armed?'

Catz turned his attention keenly on Karl, 'Not as well as it could be, but it has a few weapons systems. Why?'

Mes intervened, 'It would be silly if we didn't take it out and had a go at the shuttle.'

Catz and the major looked amazed. Praut on the other hand understood their rational. They were combat pilots, and here was a combat situation. They were reacting to their training.

'I have to explain,' offered Praut. 'Mes and Karl are highly trained combat pilots, and they're looking to use their skills. You'd be well advised to listen to them.'

'Well bless my soul. Are you sure you want to go out and have a go?' Catz was being careful. He didn't want their deaths on his conscience.

'Very sure,' Mes and Karl both declared.

Mes continued, 'We need the practice…and they need to be taught a lesson. So with your permission we'll go out and start teaching.'

'Right, well be careful.' Catz talked into his throat mike, giving instructions to the flying sub people to allow these two combat pilots to take out the flying sub.

* * *

'What do you think, an *eagle* or the *crow*?' asked Mes, now happily ensconced in the captain's seat of the flying sub. Karl sat in the co-pilot's seat to the right.

'Let's go up and then we'll decide,' answered Karl.

The external doors of the flooded sub compartment slid open, giving access to the dark forbidding sea. The main sub was now around two hundred meters deep under the Krethys Sea and still diving. Mes took the flying sub out and headed eastwards for a klick before coming up into the air. The flying sub broke surface and climbed further east, then swung back on itself, climbing higher.

'Take her about a klick above the shuttle,' advised Karl.

'Understood,' Mes replied. 'I favour the *crow*, if it's all the same to you.'

'Fine. You're the captain,' responded Karl.

The Earth crow was renown for bombarding its targets with stones from above and the Space Combat Manual had used this behaviour to produce a terse one-word adjective to describe smart directed bombing from above. The eagle on the other hand dived on its prey and that was another cryptic term used to describe a combat manoeuvre.

'Let's see if they're expecting us?' Karl said, arming a missile and targeting the enemy shuttle's engines. 'Pity this ship hasn't got a good solid laser canon. Missile's armed. Right Mes, ready to fire.'

'Okay, let them go.'

Smart stealth missiles left the flying sub, following a tortuous path, first up, then zigzagging northwards, finally going up high before heading downwards towards the shuttle. The shuttles defences managed to neutralise the missile with a thunderous explosion. What the shuttle's defences failed to notice was the second missile that had tailed the first half a second behind, deceiving the defences, hiding behind the explosion, and getting through to hit the shuttle's engines. Mes and Karl watched on their view screen as the shuttle's engine caught fire.

'Hey, what's going on?' called Mes. 'That should have blown them out of the sky.'

'It should have done...but it didn't,' confirmed Karl. 'Look its breaking off the attack and heading inland.'

'Well, we've managed one thing at least. That lesson you mentioned...seems they're learning,' smiled Karl.

'Any comeback?' asked Mes.

'No, no one is targeting us. They weren't expecting that. Might not be so easy the next time.'

'Nothing's ever easy...law of life,' reminded Mes.

'Yeah, but this one was too easy. I'm not comfortable with them giving up like this...without a fight.'

'Stop moaning. Let's get back to the sub. I'll head south a good distance before going under. Might throw them off.'

* * *

Back on the main sub, the captain's voice came over the tannoy, 'Now hear this, this is the captain speaking. The emergency is over for the moment. The shuttle has been driven off. Stand down but stay vigilant. That's all.'

Fanny was shouting, 'Good old Mes. One in the eye from us all.'

'And Karl, don't forget Karl,' demanded Olga.

'Yeah, and good old Karl,' added Fanny.

Clay was drumming a victory roll on the tabletop, and stamping his feet.

Praut looked amused, gently clapping his hands. Praut had left the major with Catz; they'd begun to discuss something. He'd returned to his own people.

'Olga,' Praut focused on her, 'I've asked that the flying sub be used to retrieve your sniffers. You'll need to go with them and show them where you've hidden them. When Mes and Karl come back, you might ask them if they'll fly you there themselves, next time they take the flying sub out.'

When Mes and Karl returned, they were forced to walk through corridors filled with clapping people, congratulating them on their triumph. They were slightly embarrassed by the accolade, but not unduly. They simply shrugged it off as part of the job.

They reported back to Praut's room, where Praut shook them by the hand and said, 'Well done. Very impressive work. Glad you're with us.'

Karl stopped him, 'They left too quickly. I'm afraid they're up to something. That shuttle should have gone down…instead it shuddered as if it was throwing off something nasty, and then fled inland.'

Mes took over, 'Dil, I'm afraid Karl's right. We hit the engines smack-on. No way it could have stayed in the air. Something's wrong there.'

'If they come back, you can go out again and finish the job. Don't worry about it,' advised Praut.

'It's not that,' replied Mes. 'What we're doing is post-op analysis. We need to know why the shuttle didn't go down…or at least speculate on the reasons. Then we can modify our approach for next time and knock it out of the air.'

'Oh, right, I see. Post-op analysis,' mused Praut. 'Well you go ahead and analyse, but let's go and see Catz. He'll have a few things to say to you. I should think he'll want to thank you.'

In Catz's lounge they found the Captain of the sub, some of his senior officers, and the major, all were smiling and grinning with pleasure. As Mes and Karl entered, they began clapping and saying, 'Well done,' over and over.

Catz raised his hands and said, ‘On behalf of us all, a big hearty thank you for your performance. It’s an honour to have you with us.’

‘The congratulation might be premature,’ Praut told them. ‘These pilots tell me it went too easily. The shuttle should have gone down, but it didn’t…and that’s odd. They think we’re likely to see some more of them…so be prepared.’

That dampened down the celebratory enthusiasm.

‘Never mind, chalk one up for our side,’ insisted the Captain.

‘Quite right,’ added Catz. ‘We don’t have many to chalk up at the moment.’

# 20
# ACTION STATIONS

The next day just as they were having breakfast, the electronic alarm sounded again. Over the tannoy the Captain's voice was heard again, '*Action stations, action stations.* This is not a drill. This is the Captain speaking. We have hostiles above us. All sub's personnel to their battle stations. All civilian personnel—stay calm. The situation is under control.'

Mes and Karl jumped from the table, waved a cursory goodbye to Praut and the group, and rushed off to the flying sub. It was simply an ingrained instinctive reaction on their part. Once a combat pilot, there could be only one reaction.

'Damn, I'm getting worried on their behalf,' Praut confided to Fanny after they'd gone. 'I don't like them putting themselves in the firing line like that.'

'You'd be just as concerned if they didn't go, wondering if they could have made a difference,' Fanny replied. 'Let's face it Dil, you're just a worrier.'

'Don't rub it in.'

'It's why we like you so much Dil,' added Olga. 'You look after us and worry over us like a real boss should. Not like some of those insincere pally jokers; one moment you're a pal, the next moment they fire you.'

'Now steady on. I've already been accused of having an inflated ego…you're just adding to the rumours.'

'Shall we go back to our room?' Fanny asked, smiling innocently.

'Might as well.'

Praut stood and led the way out of the large dining room. On the way, the ship's floor shuddered again.

‘I suppose that’s another missile heading out,’ Fanny asked Praut.

‘Let’s hope it is. Anything else isn’t good.’

The floor of the sub began to tilt downwards.

‘The Captain must be taking us even deeper,’ Praut told Fanny and Olga as he noticed frowns on their faces. ‘Don’t worry, these tubs are well designed.’

Both gave a weak smile. Clay, on the other hand, was treating it as hilarious fun. He hadn’t had so much excitement in ages.

* * *

Up above the sub, Mes was keenly looking at her battle screen. ‘They know we’re here…I can feel it.’

‘Even through our stealth config?’ asked Karl.

‘I feel it in my bones. They may not have a visual, but the enemy knows we’re out here.’

‘Right, so let’s get to the *elbow*, we’re too far from the *control zone*.’

‘I’m being cautious,’ replied Mes. ‘We’re four klicks out and stable. Turning now…two targets on the screen. Now let’s see if that added maser canon works.’

‘Targets locked. I’m launching the smart distracter missiles, now,’ Karl informed her.

Two missiles shot out of the flying subs tubes and headed high upwards into near space, from where they would track a *pure pursuit course* down onto their two targets—the two enemy shuttles. They would likely be intercepted…but the enemy’s attention would be divided.

‘We’re coming up to the *control zone*,’ Mes informed Karl.

‘Priming maser canon,’ Karl called back. ‘Over to you.’

‘I don’t think they’re prepared for the maser, at least I hope not. Targets locked.’ Karl pressed the lever and an amplified coherent electromagnetic beam surged out of the maser canon, the shaft of energy shooting downwards to hit the first shuttle. Then Karl switched to the secondary target, the other shuttle.

'Direct hits on both targets,' Mes called out.

'One's going down, the other is wobbling… stabilising. Shit, what's going on? Why isn't the second one going down?' Karl sounded exasperated.

'It's in trouble alright, but it's somehow managed to stabilise and is heading back inland. Those two hits should have mashed the pilot's deck of both shuttles.'

'What if there's no pilots?' suggested Karl.

'Could be…shielded and pilotless eh?'

'That might explain it. Controlled from the dome?'

'Yeah, could be? I'm returning us to the sub right now. We'll give it some thought in our post-op analysis. Okay?'

'Fine by me, Captain.' Karl smiled in satisfaction at their performance.

* * *

Back on the main sub, as Karl opened the flying sub's cabin door, both pilots heard a huge cheer come from the hangar deck. Shouts of, '*Hooray*!' echoed round the cavernous interior. Karl peered out and saw a sea of noisy faces cheering them. On the hangar floor, people wanting to wish them well, surrounded them, looking to pat them on their backs.

Once again, the corridors were filled with a throng of fans, cheering them on, thanking them for *whacking* the enemy on their behalf. It was difficult for Mes and Karl to get through the clapping crowd, all insisting on congratulating them on their triumph.

As the door slid open to the group's temporary office, the lights dimmed, highlighting an oversized *tart myrtilles* topped with extra fruit, placed in the middle of the table. Praut, Fanny, Olga and Clay stood by it grinning like kids.

'*My favourite*,' cried Mes, looking adoringly at the large tart. 'You'll love this,' she said beaming at Karl.

'Fanny's idea,' said Praut, as if trying to distance himself from all the sentimental mush.

Catz, the Captain of the sub, and then the major, arrived to join in the congratulations.

'I've been meaning to ask you,' Praut said to the major, 'How is Captain Pham Van Dung managing? Is he safe? Why didn't you bring him with you?'

The major smiled conspiratorially, 'Oh he's safe. He's doing another job for me. Believe me; he can take care of himself. His martial arts skills are second to none.' The major winked at Praut and lowered his voice, 'He's keeping an eye on Laudo's HQ. It's a building close to the dome on the eastern side of the plaza. I'm confident he'll be okay.'

Mes had a slice of the *tart myrtilles* perched in her hand and was admiring it before taking a bite out of it.

The day remained fairly quiet after the enemy shuttles were dispatched, and the group settled down to relaxation and planning, following all the congratulations and celebrations.

Mes and Karl were locked in their analysis of their two combat operations.

'As I understand it,' Karl said, 'the Captain has now dived the sub down to a thousand meters. We're sitting in some kind of trench near the bottom. How's that going to effect our comings and goings?'

'Should be okay, I've had a word with the second in command, and he assures me the flying sub can take the pressures. It's built for space as well as water and the materials are all composites used in standard spaceship builds. They're also trying to add more firepower for when we take her out again. It'll be okay.'

Later in the afternoon, Mes and Karl took Olga out in the flying sub to retrieve her longed for sniffers. On the way back they checked on Barkin's boffins at Ailo's Sámi settlement, and brought back news that the nanobot programming had been completed and tested.

Karl was telling Praut what he'd been told. 'It seems Barkin's second in command set up a rendezvous with Catz's spy in the Stimmer dome. When she arrived at the meeting point, Barkin's people snatched her and rushed her to the nearby cargo hover. Inside the hover, they'd installed a cryogenic stasis cubicle. They flew her to the Sámi settlement and there, they inserted the specially programmed nanobots into her veins. She was the first test subject for clearing her of the biochip.'

Olga had laid a largish pack on the table and removed four long objects from the pack. She was admiring them.

Praut couldn't contain himself, 'Well? Did the nanobot thing work?'

'Let me finish Dil,' continued Karl. 'Yes it did work…and to their horror, when they'd cleared her of the alien nanobots, they discovered that she was in fact a double agent. Catz and Barkin thought she worked for them, but she was feeding them false info and spying on them for Stimmer. Anyway, it seems they've found a way of clearing people of the nasty biochip while still keeping them alive.'

'Have you informed Catz of this?'

'Yes, while we were walking here through the corridors via the throat mike. He's pleased the cleansing worked, but less pleased by the info she was a double agent.'

'Is the woman alright now?' asked a concerned Praut.

'Confused and a bit muddled but recovering,' Karl replied.

'What about the reason you went out?'

‘As you can see,’ Karl nodded at Olga, who was gently rubbing down four long objects, ‘we’ve retrieved her four sniffers.’

‘No problems in doing so?’

‘Nah, it all went smoothly.’

* * *

The next day remained relatively quiet, but around midday, the Captain informed Catz and Mes by throat mike, that a large spaceship had taken station above them and was probing the deep waters, looking for them.

Catz came over to Praut’s room with the major, and no sooner was he inside, he began telling Praut, ‘We’ve been monitoring the waters above us, courtesy of a hack by your computer wiz-kid, Clay over there, who’s hacked into the satellite feed above us. We cut that contact as soon as the spaceship arrived, but here’s a snapshot of the ship.’ Catz handed Praut a plastic sheet with a holo image of a spaceship on it.

‘What do you make of it?’ asked Praut.

‘Clay told me he recognised the ship straight away. He tells me it’s the Zimmer ship from Harmony. I’m here to ask you what that means?’

‘Clay could have told you himself. We were chasing a lead on our Agency’s wormhole problem, and it led us to the planet Harmony in Sector O7 on the Outer Arm fifteen kiloparsecs from here. I was told that Fanny and Clay were observing an outfit called Zimmer that was operating on that planet, when this outfit suddenly upped stakes and left on *that* spaceship. Olga sent a sniffer after it, and it led us here to Barnaby.’

‘I sort of see…or I don’t…I don’t think I understand,’ Catz complained.

Fanny intervened, ‘Proof of theory; I said that Zimmer and Stimmer are one and the same.’

‘Oh, now I see what you’re getting at,’ Catz said catching onto what Fanny had just said.

‘You and I are chasing the same people…that’s the crux of the matter,’ Praut told him. ‘Might have different names, but they’re up to the same no good.’

‘Right! And if that’s the case, then there’s at least one more planet they’ve infected. Stimmer’s home planet.’ Catz now had it clear in his mind.

‘And although we may, or may not stop them here on Barnaby, *I* will have to pursue them all the way back to their nest. I can’t have them killing my people and getting away with it.’ Praut was getting heated.

‘If we can rid Barnaby of this infestation, I promise you Dil, I will give you my full support in chasing them down, wherever they are. I swear that on the sacred bodies of all my dead people.’ Catz became solemn as he spoke.

‘I think I will probably be forced to hold you to that,’ answered Praut seriously. ‘I’m getting the impression this thing is far bigger than I initially thought. Me and my people could use some friendly help.’

That evening the Captain of the sub seemed worried as they all sat round the dining table in Catz’s lounge.

‘What’s on your mind?’ Catz asked gently, trying to prise the troubles out of him.

‘I’ve managed to evade the spaceships attentions so far, but just before I came here, my technical officer told me he thought the vessel above us had us located.’

‘What made him think so?’

‘He’s picked up faint fluctuating frequencies probing our position. They’re not on to us yet, but it’s simply a matter of time.’

‘I wish that Commission ship would hurry and arrive,’ voiced Praut. ‘It’d take the focus away from us.’

‘How many days to go?’ Karl asked distractedly.

‘This is the fifth day of their trip,’ replied the major. ‘All we need is to hold on one more day.’

That suddenly got everybody's attention. They were so preoccupied with the daily battles that they'd lost track of the Commission's imminent arrival.

'Really? The fifth day, eh?' Catz had the beginnings of a smile playing on his face as he mulled over the thought.

'So the Commission should be here tomorrow, all being well?' Praut looked at the major to confirm this.

'That's my calculation.'

The atmosphere round the table changed to one of bonhomie as the possibility of a looming *Gunship Rescue moment* sunk in. At the outset of the dinner, pessimism had reigned supreme around the table, but now, that had been replaced with an abundance of optimism and hope. After dinner and the usual chitchat, people retired to their own rooms for the night on a high note, full of plans for the morning.

During the middle of the night, the sub suddenly gave an all mighty lurch, followed by a strong shudder, which brought people rushing out of their rooms into the corridors. The piercing e-alarm sounded loudly throughout the sub.

Karl spotted Praut peering out of his room, 'We've been hit,' he shouted to Praut.

'Yes, that's my conclusion as well. Karl, gather our people and head for our meeting room. We'll try and sort things out there. At least we'll all be together.'

'Yes Dil.' Karl fetched Mes, and the others from nearby and followed Praut to their temporary office room.

Before Praut could speak, the tannoy announced, 'This is the Captain speaking. Please stay calm. Everything is under control. We've suffered some minor damage and the repair crews are fixing this as I speak. I repeat, please stay calm. All crew members to report to their stations at the double.'

'Yep, we've definitely been hit,' said Praut. 'That announcement confirms it. Wait, I'll try to contact Aldo, see if he's got any more info.' Praut talked into his throat mike for a minute, then turned to his people. 'It seems the spaceship above us managed to locate us and sent down some smart torpedoes. Catz tells me he's been informed by the Captain that a torpedo has breeched our forcefield and disabled two of our four water turbo jet engines. The engine room is flooding and there's been a number of casualties. We're limping in towards land, heading for a port.'

'How did they locate us?' Olga wanted to know.

'Are we sinking?' asked a worried Claymore.

'How did the torpedo get past our forcefield?' Karl asked.

'Hang on, there's more info coming in,' Praut held his hand up. Praut listened for a while then told them, 'Catz tells me the sub was attacked by three smart torpedoes. One analysed our forcefield frequency and inserted an opposing frequency, that made a small breech in the forcefield, so the Captain tells him. The second torpedo exploded inside that small breech and opened the forcefield some more, and the third torpedo passed through the breech and hit the engines. The damage is greater than the tannoy suggested. Fourteen people have lost their lives so far, according to the Captain. He's heading for the nearest port as fast as we can on the remaining two engines.'

'How the hell did they get us so far down?' Karl demanded. 'Those are some smart torpedoes…'

'Should we take the flying sub out and try to drive the spaceship off,' asked Mes.

'No point. It would be suicidal. I don't give much for your chances against a big well armed spaceship, especially if it's who I think it is. No, they've succeeded in driving us to a port, which is presumably their aim. I'm assuming Laudo's louts will be waiting for us. Best thing we can do is arm ourselves to the teeth. I'm not going quietly.'

'I'm with you Dil,' Karl said grimly.

'Me too,' joined in Mes.

'Don't forget me,' added Fanny.

'If you're all so eager, I'm going with you,' Olga informed them.

'Oh good, another chance to get killed,' said Clay. 'Count me in.'

As the night turned into morning, no further attacks were reported and an abject complacency took hold of Praut's people.

'This is intolerable,' muttered Karl. 'At least let me take the flying sub out.'

'Dil, please get in touch with the Captain and ask if we can go out for a recky,' pleaded Mes. 'This sitting around and doing nothing is too depressing.'

'Only if you promise to stay out of harms way.'

'We promise,' both said in unison, with fingers crossed behind their backs.

After a short chat into his throat mike, Praut told them the Captain had reluctantly agreed.

The two combat pilots understood that to mean the Captain had approved but Praut was reluctant to let them go.

'Be careful out there,' Praut insisted before they left.

* * *

A short while into their recky mission, Mes radioed back, 'Please inform the Captain that the spaceship has vanished. There's no further sign of it, and the threat seems to have vanished with it.'

'Wilco, can you take a look at the port area we're heading for. Do we have a reception committee waiting for us? Are we to expect hostilities?' asked the sub's comm.

'Roger, will do. Let you know in a while. Over and out.'

'Weird eh? The bugger's buzzed off and didn't even say goodbye,' Karl smiled at Mes as she piloted the flying sub towards land.

'Good riddance to bad rubbish I say,' retorted Mes.

'I'd like to see one of our Cruisers take it to pieces,' said Karl vindictively. 'That would teach them to fire on the sub.'

'Look down there!' exclaimed Mes.

'Yeah, what am I looking for?'

'The *absence* of activity,' she replied.

'Oh yeah, I see what you mean. Too quiet for my liking. Seems completely normal activity in the port area. What do you make of it?'

'What can you make of normality? I'll report back that all's quiet…but they should be on their guard.'

'Well, let's head back. Nothing else to see out here.'

'Wouldn't mind having a peek at the spaceport,' Mes suggested.

'Why the spaceport?' Karl asked.

'I'll bet the Commission spaceship's there. It's the only thing that makes any sense.'

'Hey, I'll bet you're right. That's why they've all gone quiet,' Karl agreed. 'Leave the spaceport for the moment. We'll get there soon enough if you're right. Let's head back.'

Mes swung the flying sub back towards the main sub. They spotted the big sub on the surface roughly where they expected to see it.

'The Captain must be worried about the damage the sub's sustained if he's broke cover like that,' commented Karl.

Mes didn't respond but put the flying sub down into a dive and landed on the main subs flight deck and came to a halt near an open hangar.

# 21
# THE COMMISSION

'You've probably hit the nail on the head,' Praut was telling Mes and Karl. 'If the Commission spaceship's landed, then that would explain why Laudo's thugs have all gone quiet.'

'Only one way to find out. Get in touch with the spaceport,' suggested Mes. 'See what they say.'

'No, I've no standing in this. I'll let Aldo Catz do that. It's his show after all. He's the real Governor of Barnaby.' Praut talked into his throat mike for a few minutes. Then he turned and explained to his people, 'It seems things are moving fast,' he told his group gathered round the table. 'The spaceport has been in touch with Catz. Apparently the Commission was met by that so-called Governor Pergman, but the head of the Commission refused to recognise him as the Governor. Something about the elections not being legal. They want to talk to the legally elected Governor.'

'That means Aldo Catz, surely,' put in Fanny.

'Right,' Praut agreed. 'So now Commissioner Souza won't leave the spaceport until they produce the duly elected Governor. It's turned into a bit of a farce. That's one of the reason's the sub's surfaced. Catz is getting ready to use the hovers to fly to the spaceport.'

'You going with him?' asked Fanny.

'Yes, and so are you. Mes, Clay, spruce yourselves up, you're coming too. We're now part of the Commission.'

'Has Helmut's shuttle landed with them?' asked Karl.

Praut shrugged, 'No news of our people yet. I hope he's at the spaceport but I've not heard. We could use some reinforcements.'

'Have you tried the comm?' Olga asked.

'Damn, didn't even think of that. Hold on a mo, let's see if I can get through to him.' Praut talked into his throat mike, giving connection protocols…and then a huge grin broke onto his face. 'Helmut, good to hear from you. Everything okay?' Praut listened for a while, then said, 'Right, see you soon,' and broke the connection.

'Helmut's fine, so are the rest of our people. They came in with the Commission as advised,' Praut informed them. 'Helmut says there's a heavy Earth Battle Cruiser in orbit around Barnaby…just in case. It seems Major Fernandez's reports have caused quite a stir back in WorldGov and created a lot of concern as to what was happening here on Barnaby. Helmut's been having a chat with one of the senior officer on the Commission ship, and he's been told in confidence that Admiral Zheng Zhen is standing by with Earth's Second Battle Group, should they be summoned.'

'Hold on, Catz is on the comm. Yes, Aldo, we're ready. Okay! See you on the flight deck.' Praut told his group to pack everything up, clear their rooms and to meet him on the flight deck up above. 'We've got an appointment with Commissioner Souza at the spaceport. We won't be coming back here.'

Once on the sub's flight deck, Praut announced, 'Fanny, Olga, and Clay, you're with me. Mes, Karl…Catz wants you to take the flying sub up one last time and fly gunshot over the two hovers carrying this delegation to the spaceport…just in case. Stay well above us and keep a sharp eye out for hostiles. They may try for one last desperate go at us. You'll be taking two pilots with you; they'll bring the flying sub back here.'

Two hovers stood ready for lift off. They were newly painted, sides and top, with the WorldGov logo. The first hover would carry Catz and his people, Praut, the Major, Fanny, Olga and Clay. The second hover was an armed escort of Catz's elite force from the sub, in fresh new light blue uniforms.

Praut led Fanny, Olga and Clay into the hover after Catz and his people, settling themselves down for the journey to the spaceport.

'It seems Laudo's thugs have left all the places they occupied recently,' Catz explained to Praut, as they sat next to each other in the hover. 'McTavish can go back to his hotel. Pity though about Barkin's dome.'

'Did he set off all those explosive charges?' Praut asked.

'I'm afraid so. How did you know about the explosives?'

'Max told me about them. By the way, how is Max? I haven't seen him recently. He still in the sick bay?'

'Afraid so. Septicaemia—blood poisoning. He's been fighting for his life since he arrived. I didn't know this until recently, but Max was hit with a guided poisoned nanodrone. It's a dirty trick.'

'I've been meaning to drop in on him, but didn't get round to it,' Praut apologised. 'Give him my regards if you see him, and tell him to pull his socks up.'

'I will. Do you know Commissioner Souza?' Catz asked both Praut and the major.

'Not personally,' replied Praut. 'He's the Foreign Affairs Commissioner for WorldGov; deals with all the scattered planets in the Galaxy. Supposed to be quite sharp.'

The major declared, 'I've never met him.'

'You know my biggest problem,' admitted Catz. 'I don't really know who's behind Laudo. I mean we have the name Stimmer floating around…but who runs Stimmer? Who's behind all this? I'd like a name and a face, something I can punch.'

'That's something I can't help you with at the moment. I'm as much in the dark as you.'

Catz continued, 'I mean Stimmer appeared out of nowhere one and a half years ago, and a couple of months later Laudo began to agitate for an election. Kept on at me until I caved in; me thinking I'd be certain to get re-elected. I got the shock of my life when Pergman got elected instead. Now I know those elections were rigged. Soon after, Stimmer took over the central dome. That was nine months ago. Since then both Laudo and Pergman have been going on and on about independence from Earth. Of having planet wide elections to secede from Earth's domination. How did he think he'd get away with it? I mean Laudo.'

'I think Commissioner Souza will want to know the same thing, and I'll be keenly interested to see what Laudo has to say for himself...and Stimmer.'

Catz smiled at the thought. Laudo finally on the back-foot, having to defend himself and his behaviour. 'What do you think; will we flush the people behind this out into the open?'

Praut frowned, 'I've been mulling this over ever since yesterday's dinner. I've a feeling we won't…my gut tells me they'll conceal to the last, until they're forced out, until the knife is tickling their throat. Then they'll make a run for it.'

Catz sighed in resignation. 'I was afraid you'd say that.'

'I'm sorry, but I'll have to agree with Mr Praut here,' added the major. 'Only the threat of heavy force will bring this to a conclusion.'

The hovers flew over the southern half of Ventura on the way to the spaceport. When they arrived and landed near the Commission's space shuttle, Laudo's people guarding the perimeter of the WorldGov Commission spaceship were respectful, until they saw who it was in the newly arrived hovers; then they turned hostile, refusing to allow them through the perimeter, even with the major in his WGS uniform. Catz's guards faced off with Laudo's thugs and things were looking ugly.

Commissioner Souza came out of his spaceship, followed by a platoon of marines, and approached Aldo Catz, demanding that Catz be allowed through the perimeter, or Souza would call in the rest of the marines on the Battle Cruiser stationed in orbit above Barnaby. It made the difference. Laudo's thugs stood down, but ever so reluctantly.

'Governor Catz, please come this way,' Souza said loudly, nodding at the major, 'and bring your people with you.' Souza lifted his chin up and led the way to his spaceship, giving those watching a clear message as to who was in charge here. Commissioner Souza had the backing of massive firepower orbiting above him should anyone question his authority.

Praut connected with Helmut and told him to keep everyone in their shuttle until he contacted him again.

Ensconced in the WorldGov spaceship's lounge with the formalities and introductions out of the way, Souza got to the point and asked Catz, 'Now what the hell is going on here. Are you the Governor or aren't you? I got the impression someone called Pergman was passing himself off as the Governor when I arrived.'

Praut was on the far settee with Fanny, Olga, Mes, and Clay, listening but keeping quiet. The major sat with Catz facing the Commissioner. Karl stood uncomfortably by the door.

'I'm afraid the opposition here have been playing at thuggery for the last year or so. You must have read the Major's reports,' answered Catz firmly. 'He lays it out fairly clearly. Here he is, ask him yourself. He'll confirm those reports.'

'It's because of those reports that I'm here,' Souza reaffirmed. 'Which brings me to the question as to why I was sent here. Do you, or do you not, need my help to sort things out on Barnaby?'

'We most certainly *do* and would be most grateful for any help you can give us. Things have really got out of hand.'

'Right, then I'm authorised to bring in Admiral Zheng…and I propose to do that right now. Have you any objections?'

'Certainly not. I'm as eager as you to put things back in order. Please send for the Admiral.'

'Excuse me.' Souza talked into his throat mike for a few moments and then said, 'Right that's done. He'll be here in two days time. He was en route as a precautionary measure. Now would you kindly fill me in on what's been going on?'

The major began, but Souza interrupted, 'No offence Major, but I'd like to hear it from the Governor here.'

Catz seemed pleased at having his title restored and repeated the story he'd told Praut about Stimmer and the fraudulent elections. About the biochip and the people entrapped by it. How he had no idea who this Stimmer entity was, but that he regarded it as the culprit behind Laudo and Pergman. Catz concluded with, 'Stimmer and Laudo need sorting out and removing from this planet.'

Souza sat there and thought for a moment. 'I'm a great believer in the doctrine of *rapid dominance…* otherwise known as overwhelming force. It saves on messy fighting and ends the argument quickly. I therefore propose when Admiral Zheng arrives with his Second Battle Group in two days time, we use his marines to round up all of Laudo's people and have them de-chipped. That gives you two days to prepare the equipment to carry out this operation. Do you think you can do that in the time given?'

Catz looked startled. 'I'll have to get my people to replicate at least a thousand cryogenic stasis cubicles. I'll have to give the order right now.' Catz talked into his throat mike for a time. 'I've got my people sub contacting all our manufacturing facilities. We'll be ready…I hope. How are we going to grab Laudo's people?'

Souza's features became determined, 'We'll teleport them straight into those cubicles. Admiral Zheng has the computing power on his ships. With the Earth's Second Battle Group above us and the marines on the ground, I don't think Laudo and this Stimmer will give us any trouble. What do you say to that?'

Catz chuckled and said, 'I've taken to you Commissioner. You're a man after my own heart.'

'Now Mr Praut,' Souza turned to Praut with a quizzical gaze, 'How do *you* fit into all this? I'm told you want to join our Inspection team. I've had your Agency shuttle join my entourage coming into Barnaby. I'm puzzled as to what you're doing here?'

'Commissioner,' Praut said innocently, 'I'm just a humble Earthling trying to make a living in this hostile galaxy.'

'Yes, yes, I've heard General Botha telling me all about your humbleness,' Souza said with a smile. 'Now can we stop the play acting and get to the point of what you're really doing on this planet?'

Praut shrugged, 'Pardon me Commissioner, that was me simply trying to protect my people with a little theatre. As to what I'm doing here; didn't General Botha give you any theories?'

'He did. Something about wormholes. Could you kindly elaborate?'

'My pleasure Commissioner. I have a client who's hired me to find his stolen wormhole blueprints, lifted from his q-machine. I've chased, who I believe is the culprit, firstly to a planet called Harmony, and that has led me here. It seems Mr Catz and I are entangled with the same people. What the connection is, I'm not certain. But this Stimmer lot are behind his troubles…and behind the deaths of three of my people. I want to know who this lot are, and what they're doing. And of course I want to retrieve the blueprints. Hence my shuttle and me.'

'Yes, that mostly tallies with what I've got from WGS,' Souza responded. 'They also added you might be seeking revenge…but we'll let that go. Right now, I'm minded to acquiesce to your request to join the Inspection team…but on two conditions. That you don't cause my people or me any problems. And, if I ask you to do something, you're to do it without giving me a big argument. Subject to those two conditions, you can join the team. Agreed?'

'Agreed!'

'Now I'd like a word with this Laudo character.' Souza sat for a moment and composed himself, then talked into his throat mike, 'Put me through to Bartholomew Laudo.' A little wait ensued, then, 'Mr Laudo…no, *you* listen…if your thugs aren't out of this spaceport and off the streets of Ventura within the next hour…I'm calling down the Battle Cruiser I've got stationed up above. The marines will then place you under arrest and deal with your thugs… do I make myself clear. One more thing…I want you, and this Stimmer Corporation I've been hearing about, out of Ventura's central dome and all of your people disarmed and the rifles back in the dome's arms repository. The dome is the Governor's domain and I want it handed back to Governor Catz at once. I'll be inspecting it in my tour. You've got one hour to comply. Out.'

'Damn, I wish I could have done that nine months ago. It would have saved a lot of lives and we wouldn't be in this mess right now,' Catz exclaimed.

'Better late than never,' Souza told him.

Quietly Catz said, 'Commissioner, thank you for what you've just done.' His voice broke on the last part of the sentence and he turned his head away.

Praut stood up, 'Aldo, let me get you a green tea. Max told me you like that.'

'Thanks,' Catz said recovering his composure. 'I could do with one.'

Praut looked round for the replicator and located it in the wall behind Souza. He enunciated his request clearly into the grille, waited, and then lifted the flap. He picked up the glass of green tea and took it to Catz. 'Careful, it's hot.'

'I'm just hearing from our Captain,' announced Souza. 'The armed guards are being withdrawn from the spaceport as we speak. Seems Laudo does understand the language of *rapid dominance.*'

'Commissioner, my compliments. I don't see how anyone could fail to understand a fist under their nose,' chuckled Praut. Then he contacted Helmut and told him to smarten his people up and bring them all to the spaceport lounge...zappers only, and to be discreet.

'So shall we go and have a look?' Souza asked Catz.

'Maybe this time we can do the greetings to your arrival properly as protocol intended,' Catz told Souza. Then Catz talked into his throat mike and arranged things with his uniformed escort. Catz left, with Praut and the major in tow, to see to the arrangements.

This time, when Commissioner Souza ventured out of his space shuttle, a Barnaby guard of honour in their crisp light blue uniforms greeted him, and there was a red carpet from the shuttle steps to the spaceport entrance.

Governor Catz stood there with his entourage, waiting to officially welcome WorldGov's Commissioner to Barnaby. Praut was trying to be unobtrusive, so he stood behind Catz, and the major stood on his other side.

Once the greetings were over, Souza said, 'Now let's have a look at this dome of yours.'

Catz seemed uncomfortable and informed Souza, 'We're having a problem getting into the dome. The major tells me he has a colleague keeping an eye on Laudo's HQ.

This Captain Dung is watching the plaza as we speak and says that a crowd dressed in some kind of brown clothing are pouring into the plaza. A lot of them are entering the dome...and it would seem that Laudo's thugs are refusing to vacate it. I'm going to have to take you to a comfortable hotel opposite the dome until this is resolved. The hotel is owned by a good friend of mine.'

'As soon as we get there, I'll want to have a word with this Laudo,' Souza replied. He didn't look too happy. He spoke into his throat mike and then turned to Catz, 'I've asked that the rest of the marines in orbit be sent down to secure the spaceport. It'll give us backup if we need it until Zheng arrives.'

Six hovers lifted from the spaceport and headed into Ventura along the Great West Road. On coming into the main plaza, it was obvious that something was going on. A lot of people dressed in brown clothing mingled in front of the dome's entrance. Others had brown armbands indicating they were part of the same crowd.

The six incoming hovers parked brazenly in front of *The Caledonian Hotel* and disembarked its occupants. Souza and his aides, Catz's people with the major, Praut and his full agency compliment, now some twenty-one people, all hurried up the steps into the hotel, lugging a lot of luggage with them. WorldGov marines, led by their colonel, together with Catz's guards, took up positions outside the hotel entrance. The colonel sent others to secure the hotel perimeter and park the six hovers round the back.

McTavish met them in the lobby. 'Aldo, welcome,' blurted out McTavish looking quizzically at the rest.

'Look Gordon, let me introduce Commissioner Souza from Earth's Government. We're going to use your hotel as a temporary HQ, with your permission, until we can recapture the dome. I hope you don't mind?'

McTavish bowed slightly to Souza, then said to Catz, ‘Of course, you’re welcome. Anything you want, let me know. I’m at your disposal.’

‘I’m sure the Commissioner could do with some food and refreshment…I know I could.’ Catz looked questioningly at the rest of his company. They all nodded politely.

‘I’ll go and organise a small banquet. Give me about half an hour.’ McTavish went to consult his chef.

‘Now, let’s get ourselves comfortable in the lounge,’ suggested Catz.

‘First things first, let me get through to this Laudo fellow,’ Souza said firmly. ‘I want him here in front of me. I’ve a few things to say to him.’ He spoke into his throat mike, then heaved a sigh, as if preparing himself for the encounter. Finally he relaxed back into the deep armchair.

Praut, Fanny, Helmut and the major were looking out into the plaza from the wide front window.

‘What do you make of it?’ asked the major.

‘I think it’s a final gambit,’ Praut smiled. ‘I’m looking at a demo organised by Laudo…or Stimmer. Note… nobody’s armed yet they’re milling around the dome entrance as if daring anyone to push through them. Do they think by putting a lot of people into the plaza, they’ll use people power to intimidate…or somehow tip the balance in their favour. I think we’re winning…that’s what it looks like to me. I think it’s a clear mark of desperation, them doing this. Does Laudo really think that Souza’s going to rush back to the spaceport and flee back to Earth after seeing this pathetic demo?’

‘Bloody day’s disappeared. It’s almost evening. I don’t like it,’ sneered the major. ‘You’re right, they don’t seem to be armed, but I’ll bet the arms are close by. I can’t really see them giving up without a fight.’ The major looked round to see Souza calling him. ‘Excuse me, I’m wanted. I think Captain Pham Van Dung has finally arrived.’

Praut nodded and turned to Helmut, 'Now then Helmut, make your report,' Praut smiled encouragingly at his newly arrived agency member.

'All went fairly smoothly, Dil. I've brought fourteen people with me armed to the teeth, as you ordered. Mykola is minding the shuttle as we speak. Fanny's been filling me in with what's been happening here, while we were in the hover coming to the hotel. Sorry about Harry. My condolences; he was a good guy.'

'Yeah, well someone's going to pay for that. Listen up Helmut; tell the people with you what's happening, and stay close to me. I've a feeling things are about to get hotter. Are the laser rifles still in the hover?'

'No, we've brought them in with our luggage.' Helmut pointed at the stack of luggage waiting by the entrance.

'Keep them handy. Zheng arrives in two days and that should tip the balance our way…but till then, stay alert. Now let's go and see if the food's ready.'

# 22
# STIMMER INC.

The next morning McTavish hurried into the breakfast room wearing worry all over his face. 'Laudo's here,' he told Catz. 'He's waiting in the foyer. He insists, we're expecting him.'

Catz looked meaningfully at Souza. 'Your show I believe.' Of McTavish he asked, 'Is he alone?'

'No, he's got Pergman with him. They're still strutting around as if they own the place,' McTavish said with disgust.

'Your right, it is my show. It's time to take them down a peg or two,' vowed Souza. He threw his napkin on his plate and rose from the table with purpose. 'Colonel Moran, you're with me,' Souza ordered his marine commander.

'Yes sir.' The colonel rose from the table and followed Souza.

The people around the breakfast room looked meaningfully at each other. Catz had been having breakfast with Souza, as befits their ranks. The major had the newly arrived Captain Dung with him, and on the next table, Praut sat with Fanny and Helmut, deep in conversation, trying to devise a plan to deal with Stimmer.

'We'll use your office, if we may,' Souza said to McTavish. To the colonel he said, 'I want four burly marines at the office door and four inside the room. See to it. Oh, and put Pergman under arrest for impersonating a Governor.'

'Yes sir. Be my pleasure.'

Laudo was ushered into the office by a strident marine staff sergeant, who virtually drove him inside before him. The four burly marines stood at attention on either side of the door…the staff sergeant joined them. They tried to meld in with the furniture but their presence was loud and ominous.

'Thank you for coming Mr Laudo. Please sit.' Souza was writing something and didn't look up at Laudo.

'What's all this about?' Laudo asked irritably. 'Why have you arrested Governor Pergman?'

'Just a moment and I'll be with you. I have to deal with this communiqué from Admiral Zheng,' snapped Souza.

A few moments of silence passed as Laudo took in the implications of Souza's words. He looked at the intimidating marines, then back at Souza.

'Right,' said Souza, finally looking up at Laudo. 'The Admiral is arriving tomorrow with his Battle Group. I want to make sure everything's ready for him. Now what can *I* do for *you*?' Souza asked innocently.

'Commissioner…you called *me* in, remember. You tell *me* why.' Laudo was loosing some of his assurance.

'Ah yes. Well, when I arrived at the spaceport, I was presented with someone called Pergman who was passing himself off as the Governor. I'd like an explanation, since you seem to be behind this. Impersonating a Governor is an offence, hence Pergman's arrest.'

'We had an election a while ago and Pergman was elected as the new Governor…yet you seem to have completely ignored our people's election.' Laudo thought he'd scored a point.

'Yes I've ignored those fraudulent elections.' Laudo's face clouded over at being told this, but Souza continued, 'Were they overseen by the Galactic Electoral Commission as they were supposed to have been?'

'I don't see why we have to have those busybodies interfering in our lives all the time. The people decided who they wanted for Governor—and he was installed.' The last part was almost a sneer.

'As I understand it, a minority here elected this puppet of yours, which is why you're having all this trouble. You're trying to impose a regime change here and the majority of the people here don't want it,' Souza raised his voice '…and WorldGov won't stand for it.'

'It's got nothing to do with WorldGov what we do on this planet. We can't have some planet twenty five kiloparsecs away on the other side of the galaxy dictating what and what we can't do in our own home.'

'*Some planet? Some planet?*' Souza shouted at Laudo. 'Have you completely lost your sanity? This is humanities *home*, not *some planet* we're talking of. We've carefully ventured into the galaxy from this home planet of ours, using it as our base. Barnaby could not have come into existence without *this planet* you so easily dismiss. Most people here understand this, yet somehow you've managed to conveniently ignore this fact.

'WorldGov is not interested in *ruling* over each new planet it colonises, or being a busybody in its affairs. We ensure that a Governor is elected by the colonists to look after the interests of the planet's inhabitants, but we insist that the GEC oversees each election. It's to prevent fraud and ensure democracy. It's to prevent a minority from grabbing power…as they've done here.' Souza watched as Laudo began to fidget. 'Mr Laudo, until a GEC election is held on Barnaby, Mr Catz remains the legally elected Governor. Mr Pergman is simply an ordinary citizen, as are you. Now Mr Laudo, please explain to me who put you in charge of organising this coup?'

Laudo seemed to begin to bluster, and then went red in the face. 'Coup? You call an election a coup? What contempt for people power is this? People put me in charge…they chose me to lead them. How dare you suggest otherwise?'

'Is this the same people power who are now milling around in the plaza outside?' asked Souza sneeringly.

'What if they are? People have a right to demonstrate against invaders. They want the Governor *they* elected, not the old one that lost the election.' Laudo was bridling at his treatment, and seemed to regain some of his normal oppressive self. He rose to his feet as if to tower over Souza until a pair of firm hands clamped on his shoulders and forced him back in his seat. The staff sergeant had intervened.

'Mr Laudo, there's over three million peaceful people in Ventura, yet you have a few thousand thugs creating an uprising and trying to take over the planet. I asked you to vacate the dome, yet you've ignored my request. Since you have all the intention of causing Governor Catz further trouble by continuing this rebellion to civilised order, I have no alternative but to place you under arrest as well. Sergeant, take him below into the cellars…lock him up…let him join his friend Pergman. Let's see if this Stimmer lot can get you out of this?'

'Be my pleasure Commissioner,' answered the staff sergeant. Two burly marines hoisted a shocked Laudo to his feet and frogmarched him down the corridors into the hotel cellars, throwing him into a dark storeroom and e-locking the door.

Laudo's last words came from a distance as he was being marched away, 'But…but…you can't do this to me…' and then his voice petered out.

Souza re-emerged from McTavish's office with a wide grin on his face. He collected the colonel, who'd waited outside. 'Colonel, reinforce the front entrance guard…I'm expecting unfriendly visitors.'

'Very good sir.' Colonel Moran marched off to carry out the order.

‘What’s going on?’ asked Catz as Souza rejoined him in the lounge. ‘Did I just see the marines march Laudo off towards the cellars?’

‘You did.’ Souza put his hand up to ward off any more questions. He spoke into his throat mike for a while then turned to Catz, ‘I’ve just been told that the rest of the marines have come down and the general is bringing them here from the spaceport. Now we’ll see if we can flush this Stimmer lot out of their hideout.’

Understanding began to dawn both on Catz, the major, and on Praut; and on all the others who’d been listening in.

‘So that’s it,’ smiled Catz. ‘You’ve deliberately imprisoned Laudo and Pergman to see if Stimmer can be forced to surface.

Souza nodded. ‘If Laudo and Pergman are mere pawns in this; then I want to know who I’m dealing with. Also, I’ve been told there’s a lot of activity in the building next door…to our right.’ Souza looked at McTavish. ‘Do you know anything about this?’

Praut sauntered off across the foyer to some rendezvous.

‘Sorry Commissioner, they’re my people,’ Catz intervened. ‘They’re installing cryogenic stasis cubicles on all the floors next door. Sly old McTavish seems to own it, as well as this hotel. We’re trying to be as quiet and discreet as possible. It’s to de-chip all those people. We’re going to need somewhere close at hand. I thought the building next door would be ideal. McTavish suggested it.’

‘Splendid, yes,’ said Souza enthusiastically. ‘When Zheng brings in the computing power tomorrow, we’ll teleport all those in the plaza into the those cubicles. Will you be ready in time?’

‘I think so,’ said Catz. ‘I’ll be able to tell you more tonight. That’s when they’ll do a dry run. They’ll nab a couple from the plaza and try to de-chip them. If all goes well, I'll let you know just before we turn in.'

'I have to warn you that there's an anti-teleport sweep running over the dome,' the major told Souza. 'That will have to be disabled before we can teleport anybody anywhere. At least Max Barkin says there is.'

'Don't worry about that,' Souza reassured the major. 'Zheng has people who will deal with such technical problems.'

'I just thought I'd let you know,' shrugged the major.

Souza turned back to Catz, 'A wicked idea has just surfaced in my head,' Souza told Catz with a wry grin. 'If the dry run is successful…why not do Laudo and Pergman as well? I assume they're both chipped?'

Catz joined in the sardonic smile and said, 'Why not indeed? I mean if they're not chipped…no harm's been done. We'll know when we get them inside the cubicle. There's a low profile scanner in there to observe the biochip.'

'Now, where's that fellow Praut got to?' asked Souza, looking around and then at the major. 'I always want to keep an eye on that chap. Don't know what kind of mischief he's likely to get us into. Loose cannon you know.'

'It's alright Commissioner, he's having a talk with his people in the bar on the other side of the foyer,' the major told him. 'He's got over twenty people with him now…a new lot just arrived yesterday…with you.'

'Yes, I know. Any more news of the demo outside?'

'More people have arrived. The plaza is getting packed. What do they think they can achieve?' the major wandered over to the window with Souza and both looked out onto the early morning plaza. Catz remained seated on the settee.

'Whatever it is, they've only got today to do it in. The Admiral arrives tomorrow…then their little game ends,' declared Souza. 'How many are out there, in your estimation?'

'About ten thousand, by my assessment. I don't like the look of it,' insisted the major. His eyes narrowed at what was happening to the crowd near the hotel. 'Now what?' he said in mock alarm.

As both men peered out at the demo, some of the people began sauntering towards the hotel, ever so slowly, but with determination, as if someone, or something, had focussed them in that direction.

'If we had Zheng's computing power here, we could've thrown a forcefield round the crowd, put in a little snooze gas and then teleported them off into a compound somewhere,' the major suggested.

Souza ignored the wishful thinking and said, 'Where are those marine reinforcements?' He looked down into the plaza and added, 'I wish the general would hurry.'

The mob had now reached the twenty or so marines defending the hotel entrance and began pushing and pointing at them. The marine colonel stood behind his men, directing their actions. Suddenly some object was lobbed at the marines—it produced a purple smoke and the marines began to fidget. All had biohazard suits on yet somehow the gas penetrated through their protective barrier. First one keeled over, then another. More of these smoke bombs were hurled and the colonel gave the order to fire into the crowd. The laser rifles were set on *stun* and initially some of the mob out in front went down, then the *stun* setting seemed to loose its effect. The colonel ordered the laser setting changed to *kill* and the crowd began to fall in large numbers.

Souza watched from the window, horrified. '*Colonel Moran!*' Souza shouted into his throat mike. '*Cease fire immediately.*'

The shooting stopped and well over a hundred people lay in front of the steps in the immediate vicinity of the hotel. The rest of the mob had stopped in their tracks as if waiting for orders. The plaza went deathly quiet.

Catz's curiosity got the better of him and he joined the others at the window. He opened his mouth in shock. Praut had heard some of the commotion and hurried in, followed by Helmut, Fanny, Mes and Karl.

'Son of a bitch!' cried the major, sounding angry. 'What rotten bastard told them to try to breech the hotel entrance? They must've known this would happen.'

Just then a large flotilla of some forty hover shuttles swept into the plaza fanning out from the direction of the Great West Road.

'Ah! The cavalry's arrived. General Kapoor with the rest of the marines. Just when we needed them the most,' exclaimed a delighted Souza. Into his throat mike Souza said, 'Yes general, we see you. Yes, that's a good idea. Hem them in and clear the plaza. Yes thank you, we're quite safe…yes, yes, see you soon.'

The forty hovers descended in an arc sweeping south and north until they formed a circle round the outside rim of the plaza, then the hovers landed. The hatches were thrown open and twenty-five marines hurried from each hover, fanning out until the dome was surrounded by a perimeter of a thousand marines walking slowly in a decreasing ring towards the dome, laser rifles thrust before them. General Kapoor's lead hover landed near the hotel with the slide door open. The general climbed out and came to take up position on the steps of *The Caledonian Hotel*, just in front of Souza, directing operations.

Souza was still unable to keep his eyes from all the bodies littering the front of the hotel. Colonel Moran saluted the general.

The mob with their pseudo brown dress began retreating towards the dome's gaping entrance as the marines closed in. The entrance had been flung wide open and the people now filed inside in a very orderly fashion.

The way the people filed into the dome raised eyebrows in the hotel, on the hotel steps, and amongst the enclosing marines. They behaved more like a bunch of robots rather than humans under pressure. It was the lack of panic that was so shocking.

In a short time, most of the plaza had been cleared of the crowd, all having crammed into the dome. As the encircling marines shrank their perimeter and closed in on the dome, laser firing abruptly erupted from the dome roof, somewhere high up near the zenith of the building. A number of marines fell, despite their protective suits, while others returned fire. Marines rushed to take cover and any further progress came to an abrupt halt.

General Kapoor gave the order to pull back to the tall buildings surrounding the plaza. They had the advantage of giving the marines some height to get level with the dome where the firing was coming from. The time was around noon, and all throughout the rest of the afternoon, this stand-off persisted. There was intermittent firing from both sides but no further attempt was made to take the dome. Souza insisted the general wait until Zheng arrived.

'I see no need for more senseless deaths if they can be avoided. All for the sake of a day or so,' Souza explained to General Kapoor. 'They're not going anywhere.'

'I could easily demolish this dome,' insisted the general.

'That's precisely what I mean. There's at least ten thousand people crammed in there at the moment. Why would you want to kill them all?'

'Sir, this is war.'

'No general, this is a small police action on people who are under some kind of alien control.'

'Aliens?'

'I don't mean *alien* alien, I mean foreign. These people don't know what they're doing. When the admiral arrives, we'll clear the biochip out of them and they'll wake up. At least that's what I'm told is going to happen. I'm prepared to listen to them. I'm ordering you not to make any more moves without my say so, is that clear?'

Kapoor wasn't too happy, 'I'm under your command, Commissioner. Reluctantly I obey.'

'Good!' returned Souza. 'Now please secure the perimeter round the dome in such a way that no one can sneak out. Rotate your men; let some of them have a rest.'

'But Commissioner, they've been resting all the way here. It's time for them to stop resting. Mind you, I myself could use a little refreshment.' The general smiled mischievously.

'The bar is over there,' Souza pointed towards it. 'Come, let me buy you whatever takes your fancy.' Souza led the way to the bar.

Throughout that evening, and into the night, a deadly hush descended over the plaza. The firing had entirely ceased and all signs of life disappeared from view, hiding in various nooks and crannies. A pre-battle silence hung loud in the wintry night air.

Inside the hotel, a small banquet was in progress with all the recent arrivals digging into the sumptuous fair provided by Gordon McTavish. He was keen to show his gratitude for being able to reoccupy his hotel. The atmosphere was permeated with the expectation of Admiral Zheng's imminent arrival. Whatever was happening in the dome was deemed to be of no consequence. Stimmer was down, but not yet out. With the Admiral's arrival in the morning, that would change.

* * *

The following morning as people gathered for breakfast, they found Praut already up and gazing out of the window of the breakfast room. Fanny was fidgeting nervously by his side.

'Praut, what are you up to,' Commissioner Souza demanded of Praut's back. 'Loose cannon,' he muttered to himself under his breath.

Souza joined Praut and stared at the scene unfolding in the plaza.

'What the devil's going on?' Souza queried yet again.

Out in the plaza a small group of five people looked to be inching their way forward towards the dome. They were overdressed with strange backpacks, rifles, and moving forward cautiously, clearly aiming for the dome's entrance.

'*Who are those people*?' Souza was now shouting in Praut's ear. 'I gave strict orders that no assault was to be made on the dome until Zheng arrives.'

'I think Max Barkin's trying something out,' Praut replied, straight faced.

'Barkin, Barkin…who the hell's Barkin?' Souza demanded.

'He's the Security Chief on Barnaby,' said Praut. 'He arrived late in the night.' Praut had been woken in the middle of the night as a result. Praut was so glad to see him recovered that they sat talking into the early morning.

The ruckus near the window was drawing a crowd round Praut and Souza, although their attention was soon diverted to the peculiar developments outside.

'*They'll get fried*,' shouted General Kapoor, having just arrived. He stood watching the group of five continue to inch forward towards the dome's entrance.

'Barkin doesn't think so, general,' Praut responded to the outcry.

'I'll bet you've got something to do with this,' Souza muttered at Praut.

From high up in the dome, there came laser fire at the group in the plaza. To the amazement of the onlookers, it had no effect. A shimmering field of energy seemed to be cloaking the little cluster, still intent on continuing to inch forward.

'What *is* going on?' shouted Souza again at Praut. 'Speak or I'll have Colonel Moran here, take you down into the cellars, under arrest.'

'Now Commissioner, there's no need for that,' Praut tried to placate him. 'All we're doing is testing out the personal force-field suits.'

'What suits? What are you talking about? Explain yourself.' Souza was loosing his cool.

'Max Barkin has replicated a few personal force-field suits and is in the process of testing their effectiveness. The suits protect the wearer from laser and maser fire. That comes from the backpack their wearing.'

General Kapoor's ears pricked up as he heard the explanation, and he came closer to Praut to listen in on the conversation.

More firing came from the dome, again without any effect on the target. The group of five were now near the entrance—then one of them threw something at the entrance.

There was a loud ***wham*** and the entrance doors to the dome were shattered, leaving a gaping hole. The little group of five gingerly shuffled inside.

In the hotel, Souza jerked his head, then held his hand up. 'People, I've just been informed that Admiral Zheng's Second Battle Group is in position around Barnaby.'

A cheer went up from everybody.

'One moment….and I'm just hearing that the anti-teleport sweep running over the dome has been neutralised.' Souza turned to Catz, who'd just joined him. 'Are your people ready with those cryogenic stasis cubicles?'

Catz excused himself and spoke into his throat mike. Turning back he informed Souza, 'My people tell me they're ready to go. It's almost as if Barkin's group going in, and Zheng's arrival was coordinated, certainly serendipitous.'

Souza grimaced at the suggestion, 'Right then, I'll order Admiral Zheng to start teleporting those inside the dome into the cubicles,' said Souza.

'Commissioner, if we connected the teleport operator on the admiral's ship with the cryogenic operators in the building next door, it would go more smoothly. What do you think?' Catz looked at Souza.

'Good thinking. Get your people to uplink with the teleport.' Souza seemed to relax and was looking over at the table. 'What about some breakfast, eh?' he turned to go but Catz stopped him by holding his arm.

'Look,' Catz said, pointing to the top of the dome.

'*Now what*?' exploded Praut. 'What *are* they up to?'

# 23
# CHASE RENEWED

A huge summit section of the dome vanished. One moment there was a complete dome, then no crown, as if someone had sliced off the top. Out of the gaping hole rose a ship—it hung in the sky for a fleeting moment, then *it* vanished.

From the back of the crowd of avid watchers came the clear cry of Claymore's voice, '*It's that bloody ship again!*'

Souza said to Catz, 'I'm hearing from the admiral. They've latched onto the ship…and lost it. Huh?' Souza began shouting into his throat mike. Souza wandered off still shouting into his throat mike.

'It's cloaked hasn't it?' Catz asked Praut, throwing his arm at the vanished spaceship.

'Yes…looks like it. But the Battle Group should be able to pierce the cloaking device,' Praut told him. 'But if what I heard from Souza's shouting just now, it seems the fleets sensors have lost the bugger.'

'But the cloaking stuff is not supposed to be effective. At least that's what they've been telling me,' complained Catz.

'*Olga…Olga,*' shouted Praut. 'Where is that woman?'

'Yeah Dil,' Olga was pushing her way through the crowd towards Praut.

'Olga, get a sniffer up there,' Praut pointed towards the dome's summit. 'Get one of your sniffers to follow that cloaked ship…hurry.

'Right Dil, I'm on it.' Olga turned and rushed off to locate one of her sniffers.

Praut was staring up at the hole in the dome. 'That Stimmer lot must've put a holographic top to the dome. It's the only explanation that makes any sense.'

'By Jove your right,' Catz agreed. 'So the firing was coming from the ship, not the dome? A holographic top, eh? Crafty sods.'

'How's your lot doing next door?' Praut asked.

'Hang on, I'll get an update.' Catz talked into his throat mike, then said, 'Seems to be going okay. They're getting overloaded with de-chipped confused people. They've processed around five thousand people, so they tell me. There's about forty five thousand in Ventura to do yet. We're taking possession of the nearby buildings to make more space for them, so they have temporary resting places.'

'Good, good, I'm glad it's going smoothly.' Praut was preoccupied in thought.

'Dil, you don't look too happy,' inquired Catz.

'I'm trying to work out my next move. It looks like Barnaby's fixed. All this chaos is gonna take some time to put right, but I'm still no closer to finding out who this Stimmer lot are.'

'My offer still stands,' Catz reminded him. 'Any help you need from me and mine…consider it yours. All you need to do is ask. Now I'm officially Governor again, the resources of this planet are at your disposal…and just for starters, I'm going to supply you with a replacement shuttle…you know, to replace the one you lost when you came here. Then I'm going to supply you with those five personal-force field suits that slipped into the dome before the Stimmer ship appeared. I'm glad you didn't tell Souza I approved of that stunt. By the way, have you heard from your people?'

'Yes, just now. Mes called in. She and Karl are both okay. So's the rest of the group. Oh, and I like Max…he thinks like me.'

‘Yeah, Max told me he’s taken to you as well. Look, if you go off chasing that spaceship, I’m going to send some of my people with you. I’ve not finished with this Stimmer lot until I know the end of the story. When they’re ground into dust, then I’ll consider Barnaby safe. I think Max and some of his men might want to join your expedition.’ Catz stood waiting for an answer.

‘Thanks Aldo. Yeah, that suits me fine.’ Praut smiled at Catz. ‘Look, if you’re going to supply me with another shuttle…could I ask you to put some weapons on it...arm it to the teeth. I get the feeling we’re going to need them where we’re going…and that goes for Max’s ship as well. If we don’t chase this Stimmer thing to its nest and wipe it out, they’ll try to infect some other planet…and we’ll have to start all over again.’

‘That’s my thinking as well…and that’s why I’m going to support you all the way.’ Catz’s face turned ultra serious. ‘Look, we’ve had a taste here on Barnaby what this infection is, and it’s got to be eradicated. I can justify any amount of expense on this. You can’t allow this Stimmer lot to go around chipping people and turning them into robots. If WorldGov had any sense, they’d support you all the way. I’m going to make it one of my tasks to get WorldGov behind you…count on it Dil.’

‘Thanks Aldo, you’re a good friend…and I’m going to accept any help you can give me. I owe that to my Agency people. By the way, can you put some weaponry on another of my shuttles that’s at the spaceport?’

‘No prob.’

Olga appeared, easing her way through the crowd of people waiting for news of any progress. ‘Dil, I’ve just sent one of my sniffers after that ship. It’s picked up the ion trail and is following. Are we going after it?’

‘Certainly we are. Go give our people the news. They should get ready to leave Barnaby. Tell Helmut to get the people he brought, back onto his shuttle and wait for me.’

'Wait a mo!' Catz intervened. 'Why don't I try to appropriate one of Zheng's battle cruisers to take you and Max, and all your people, to wherever you need to go? All on one ship, heh?'

Praut raised his hands in surprise, 'They'd never go for that, surely?'

'You won't know until I try. Let me go and speak to Souza, see what he says.'

'I'll come with you, give you support.'

They found a stern looking Souza at the bar, drinking and conversing with General Kapoor.

As Catz and Praut arrived, Souza said to Praut, 'Just the man I wanted a word with.'

'I'm at your disposal Commissioner.'

'I suppose you're going to go after that ship?'

'You suppose right, sir.'

'And how do you propose to follow it?'

'With my nose, sir.'

Souza scowled at Praut's facetious response.

'I assure you I'm not joking sir. I have at my disposal sniffers, and as I speak, one is currently hot on the trail of that spaceship that managed to evade your fleet's sensors. It's following the ion trail. All I need now is to board another ship and go after it, which is why we're here.' Praut stopped and looked at Catz to take up the story.

Souza's scowl had transformed into a quizzical stare. He had no idea what this loose cannon was talking about.

'Mr Souza,' Catz began, 'I would like to ask a favour of you and WorldGov.'

Souza smiled at Catz, 'If it's in my power...I'm disposed to grant it, seeing that it's the legitimate Governor of Barnaby asking. We should have come to your aid sooner.'

'Well sir, I was wondering if you could possibly put a battle cruiser at my disposal. I assure you it is for the safety of Barnaby that I ask.'

Souza thought for a moment then said, 'If you think you need one, then I will order the Admiral to do so. What is your purpose…I assume you have one.'

'My security chief, and Mr Praut here, want to put an end to this Stimmer business once and for all. They're going after that spaceship.'

Souza glanced at Praut as if to say, *there he goes again*. 'Do you intend the cruiser to go with them?'

'Yes Commissioner. If we're to finish with Stimmer, they must be followed and dealt with. It's in both our interests, WorldGov and Barnaby.'

'Yes, I think you may be right. I put one condition on this loan; that your security chief is in charge.'

Catz looked at Praut, who nodded his head. 'Agreed.'

Praut then asked Souza, 'Now sir, what do you know of Lowry, I mean the planet of course?'

'Lowry, eh?' Souza was thoughtful, 'Well, it's a planet we have on our *watch* list. We've had peculiar reports from people who've visited it. Nothing specific, but people say there's a strange atmosphere on the planet…a subdued mood of acceptance…almost too nice to be true.'

Catz and Praut looked meaningfully at each other.

Souza continued, 'There's no crime on the planet, everything is orderly, and we've had no complaints from anybody…and that's what's sticks out. Our q-machine algorithms throw this out as being out of the ordinary.'

Catz intervened, 'Might I suggest that Barnaby would have become like that if Stimmer had won.'

'Ah! I see what you're getting at,' Souza exclaimed. 'Those dammed biochips again.' He nodded at the general, who was quietly sitting on a stool, listening.

'Precisely!' said Catz.

'You sure your next target is Lowry?' Souza asked Praut, but looking at the general.

'Fairly sure, but I'll let the sniffer make the choice. Wherever it goes, we follow,' Praut told him.

'Fine, but if what you suspect is true…it becomes more serious. Let me in turn make a better offer to the Governor. I'm going to put Zheng's Second Battle Group at your disposal. Leave them parked here in orbit round Barnaby; your security chief takes the battle cruiser with him, and you can call for assistance from the fleet if and when you need it. What do you say to that?'

'I'm overwhelmed by your generosity, Commissioner,' Catz enthused.

'Generosity my eye,' replied Souza. 'Wasn't it you who pointed out that it was in both our interests to deal with this scourge. We don't want this spreading throughout the galaxy, do we? So who's your security chief?'

'Max Barkin, Commissioner,' Catz told him. 'General Max Barkin,' Catz added.

Praut did a double take at hearing Barkin's new title.

'Barkin…Barkin…I've heard that name just recently,' said Souza.

'He's the chap who ordered those five into the dome this morning,' Kapoor reminded him. 'The plaza group? Those with the personal force-field suits on?'

'Ah yes, I remember,' Souza affirmed. 'General, I believe you had a question for the Governor on that theme.'

'Mr Catz, any chance of my people having a look at your special suits?' asked the general.

'General,' replied Catz, 'we have a couple of suits ready for you…to keep. It was always our intention to share them with Earth's military. It's our way of saying thank you for your timely appearance and rescue.'

'That's most kind of you,' replied the general. 'By the way, where did the suits come from?'

Catz looked embarrassed. 'I'm afraid we pinched one of them from the Stimmer people and then had our experts analyse it and test it…then we replicated it. Part of further testing was this morning's display.'

Kapoor grimaced, 'I'm thinking that this isn't good news for your expedition to Lowry. I read a WGS report whilst I was coming here…about you Mr Praut.' Kapoor turned to Praut. 'You seem to think someone on the rim out here has made a tech breakthrough…is that right?'

'A WGS report about me? Hasn't WGS got any thing better to do?' Praut said irritated by the news.

'Now don't get huffed up, Mr Praut,' Kapoor said trying to sooth Praut's ruffled feathers. 'Half our Intel on this situation comes from keeping an eye out on you and your wormhole business. It's been very useful. And if your theory's right…what else have they got up their sleeve that's like it? Be careful…very careful.'

Praut answered, 'Oh we intend to be. Barnaby's been a good wakeup call. I never thought something like this could happen…biochipped people turned into robots.'

The general turned to Souza, 'Why don't we send in the fleet to Lowry? We could deal with them in one swift move and save Mr Praut the trouble of going there.'

'There you go again general,' Souza said through clenched teeth. 'Don't you know what would happen?'

General Kapoor looked at Souza in a puzzled way.

'Haven't you been listening? Our Battle Group appearing around Lowry would cause a planet wide catastrophe. The whole population would end up dead…the biochips would see to that. I'm sorry general, but you are being a bit dull in this. Force is not *always* the answer. Praut's idea is the right one. Go in carefully and de-chip people when you can…the way they've done here on this planet.'

'What we still haven't found out is how it happens… how they insert the biochip,' Catz said, interrupting Souza's flow. 'Clearly people don't simply roll over and let them do it…they must sneak it in somehow without the person being aware of it happening. We'll have to question our people here to see if they can remember anything.'

‘What a horrid thought,’ Souza spat out. ‘That ends any dithering. I’m ordering Admiral Zheng to give you full support. Can’t have this nonsense going any further.’

Later that day, Praut met his people in a room in the hotel and was telling them what their next move was. ‘Make no mistake, this is going to be dangerous. Anybody not up to it, say so now and I won’t think any the worse of you.’ He stared around the room.

Barkin was sitting in on the discussion, looking at Karl and Mes with friendly admiration. It was they who’d come up with the idea of trying out the personal force-field suits and getting into the dome using them.

Turning to Barkin, Praut said, ‘Congratulations Max on your promotion. You deserve it and earned it.’ Then he quickly continued to his people, ‘Right, that means we’re all committed to going to Lowry. Governor Catz has given us his personal war cruiser and upgraded Helmut’s shuttle with weapons. We’ll have a battle cruiser for escort. Max over there is nominally in charge of this expedition, but he’s kindly allowed me to take the lead. Max will be in his large ship with his people armed to the teeth. When we get to Lowry, we have to assume every person we meet is biochipped. It would be dangerous to do otherwise. A whole bay of the accompanying battle cruiser will be devoted to cryogenic stasis cubicles. The captain thinks he can manage six hundred cubicles. That should allow us to de-chip quite a few…but I’d guess they’ve got the same anti-teleport sweep running, but this time I suspect it’ll be planet wide. We’ll have to give that some thought. The people that came here with me originally, will go in the new cruiser. Helmut’s people will go with him in their shuttle. At the moment, I’m treating them as backup. My team and I go in first. I’ll shout if I need help. Any questions?’

No one said a word.

‘Right, we’re following Olga’s sniffer no matter where it leads. I’m still assuming it’s towards Lowry…but we'll see. We have our two shuttles; Max with his large shuttle, and all his people. Then there's the Admiral's battle cruiser. Should be enough, eh? We leave for the spaceport in an hour.'

Fanny motioned to Praut she has something to say.

'Well, what's up?'

'I'm putting together our report to Darhlburg Inc. re our progress to date. You have anything to add?'

'No Fanny, you know what needs doing and what needs saying. Tell them its slow but we're moving forward on their behalf. Oh, and tell them I have the end in sight.'

Fanny looked at Praut quizzically, 'Right, I'll send it off when we get under way.' *The end in sight*, she thought. *What's he got up his sleeve?*

* * *

The *Faust VI* was an elegant cruiser. It had belonged to Barnaby's Governor before being reassigned to Praut. It now brimmed with upgraded weaponry and it needed both Mes and Karl as pilots. Helmut and his people were in their ship, the *Humboldt*, which stayed close to the *Faust*. Max and his people were in a large cruiser called the *BS Catz* in honour of the Governor. Out in front of the expedition was the WorldGov battle cruiser, the *SSS Lazarev,* under command of Captain Sinclair, leading in the chase following Olga's sniffer.

'The sniffer is still on course to Lowry,' Olga reported to Praut.

'Mes! Are we still on three quarter speed?' asked Praut.

'Yes Dil. Six kiloparsecs to Lowry. Two days to get there at this speed.'

'Don't forget, you're to stand off a kiloparsec from Lowry…no closer. I don't want to warn them we're coming.'

‘Dil,’ called Karl, ‘I’ve just had a message from the *Solar System Ship Lazarev*. Captain Sinclair’s compliments and would you care to join him for dinner this evening?’

‘Hallo, Sinclair’s getting impatient. He’s after info. Probably wants to know what my plans are.’

‘He’s asked Barkin and Helmut to join the dinner party,’ added Mes.

‘Then it’s time we had a confab,’ Praut announced. ‘Link Helmut and Barkin with me.’

‘Right Dil,’ said Karl.

A holo image of Helmut appeared near the control panel, followed by Barkin’s image.

‘I thought it time we had a chat about what I’m proposing for us when we reach Lowry. Olga tells me her sniffer is still on track to Lowry, so I’m going to assume that’s where we’re going. I want us to be on the same page when we meet Captain Sinclair tonight. Any news before I begin?’

The two images shook their heads.

‘So what I’m proposing is a sly but gentle approach on Lowry. I want to find a small settlement; something isolated like a homestead, then nab them and quickly de-chip the people. I’m going to take the *Faust* in alone, but I’ll want at least four cryogenic stasis cubicles on board. It’ll be a night landing, probably sometime tomorrow night. Then I aim to bring our de-chipped people out here where you’re waiting, well away from Lowry. The people will be confused, but we can get Sinclair’s psyche people to talk to them and see if we can find out what’s been happening on Lowry.’

‘Sounds like a plan to me,’ Barkin’s image agreed.

Helmut’s image said, ‘I’m with you all the way Dil, you know that. Whatever you decide has been good enough for me so far.’

'Okay then, that's what I'm going to tell Sinclair. Thanks guys. See you both later. Out!' The images disappeared.

* * *

'Welcome aboard, Captain Praut,' Captain Sinclair said, standing there smiling, as Praut rematerialised.

'Steady on Captain Sinclair. I'm only wearing this uniform in deference to you and tonight's dinner. I found it hanging in the captain's cupboard aboard my ship.'

'Thoughtful of Governor Catz to fully stock your ship then. Anyway, it suits you. Captain Schulz and Captain Barkin are already waiting in the wardroom. This way,' Sinclair led the way along the corridor to the wardroom, one floor down from the ship's bridge. 'By the way, is it Captain Barkin or General Barkin?'

'He's the captain of his ship; you pick.'

They found the wardroom almost empty except for Barkin, standing uncomfortably in a crisp new sky-blue uniform, nursing a glass of some blue liquid, and Helmut reclining in a chair, in a spotless white uniform, similar to Praut's and Sinclair's, it being the normal dress uniform of Earth's Space Fleet. Only the insignia were different.

'Dil,' Helmut said, climbing to his feet to greet his boss.

Praut smiled at Helmut and said to Barkin, 'Max, how are you?'

Barkin shuffled his shoulders in the new uniform. 'Not used to this type of dress. Too crisp for my liking.'

'Captain Sinclair, any news before we settle down to your meal?' Praut asked.

'Not good news I'm afraid. My nav-people report we've been probed at least twice today. I'm assuming its Stimmer's lot. They know we're chasing them,' replied

Sinclair. 'On that basis gentlemen, I've brought the ship to battle stations. I've recommend your ships do the same.'

'They know I've been chasing them for the last two weeks…ever since Harmony. So it's nothing new then,' scoffed Praut. Then he stopped and asked, 'How come you can detect the probing? I was under the impression that Zheng lost the Stimmer ship when it left the dome…all down to *not* being able to detect it with his sensors.'

Sinclair smiled knowingly, 'When that happened, the admiral got his tech boys to find out why. Apart from getting round the jamming, they came up with fine-tuning our sensors way beyond what we thought necessary. I have the results built into my sensors. So far it's worked. The Stimmer probes are ultra low frequency so that we wouldn't normally pick them up, but with the fine-tuning; we just manage to detect them.'

'Good work…now can you get your people to serve some food; I'm starving,' Praut suggested.

To Praut, Sinclair said, 'I had a word with Ms Fester, and she said you liked sea bass with fennel, lemon, basil, and olives. That right?'

'She's a tell-tale…but yes, that's right.'

'Captain Schulz? We have Sauerbraten made with venison for you…and Captain Barkin; there's succulent reindeer steaks for you. I hope that's satisfactory?'

At the table, Praut outlined the agreed plan to Sinclair.

'So you'd like to have four cryogenic stasis cubicles installed on the *Faust VI*, if I understand you right?' Sinclair said between mouthfuls as he was tucking into his Chicken Cacciatore.

'If you can spare ten…that would be better, just in case,' Praut told him.

'No problem. I'll get my people to liaise with yours and we'll have them installed in no time. My tech people will upgrade your sensor systems at the same time and do the same fine-tuning that was carried out to our sensors on Barnaby. We'll do it for all three of your ships. As for the plan…I've no criticism of it.' Sinclair sat back and looked closely at Praut. 'Sounds like a good cautious enterprise. My only word of advice is…trust nobody. If in doubt…cut and run. I'll be waiting within comm distance if you need me.'

'Thanks…I'm hoping I won't need you. When I get back, I hope we'll have a better lead on what's happening on Lowry.'

# 24
# NIGHT RAID

The morning began quietly following the Captain's dinner party. All four spaceships were in a four-finger formation moving through space at three quarters speed, when without warning, the alarm klaxon broke the breakfast silence on the *Faust*.

'*What's happening*?' shouted Praut at Mes and Karl from where he was sitting, munching on some vanilla *brioche*.

'That's been kicked off by the *Lazarev*,' Karl called back. 'They must've got wind of something. Hang on, I'll check with them.'

Before Karl could make a connection, Sinclair's voice was heard over the *Faust's* tannoy system, 'Echelon formation on me, starboard to port. Incoming missiles. Stand by battle stations.'

The spaceships changed into the echelon formation with the battle cruiser *Lazarev* taking the lead and the brunt of any possible attack, seemingly from up ahead to starboard.

'Damned, but I was half expecting that,' oathed Praut. 'I knew my breakfast was too quiet.'

A brief flash glared on Karl's external viewscreen. 'I think Sinclair's ship just intercepted one of the missiles,' Mes called out to Praut.

The first flash was repeated, but closer in, and a slight shudder ran through the hull of the *Faust*.

Sinclair's voice came over the *Faust's* tannoy, 'Stay tight in formation. I'm dealing with their attack. Two down, six to go. For Captain's info only; the attack is coming from somewhere round one o'clock to starboard.'

'I think my upgraded sensors have them,' Karl announced. 'Permission to engage?' Karl's request was aimed at Praut *and* Sinclair.

'Is that the *Faust*? What do you have in mind?' Sinclair's voice asked over the speaker.

'My combat pilots have the enemy on their sensors,' Praut announced via his throat mike. 'They want to respond to the incoming salvoes. If all four ships send our response, we might drive Stimmer off, and maybe scare it off from trying any further attacks. What do you think Captain Sinclair?'

Just then, another six flashes lit up near space in quick succession, indicating that the other six missiles had been intercepted and dealt with.

'Have all the three ships got sensor contact?' Sinclair asked.

Barkin, Helmut, and Praut all replied '*Yes!*'

Praut spoke into his throat mike, 'Olga, have you got the whereabouts of your sniffer right now…the one following Stimmer?'

Olga's voice replied, 'Dil, the sniffer shows to be about a thousand klicks up ahead to starboard. Why?'

'You sure?' Praut had to be certain.

An indignant Olga responded, 'Of course I'm sure. I know where my sniffer is.'

Praut passed on the info to Sinclair to add to his calculations of the enemy's whereabouts.

After a second of silence, Sinclair announced, 'Right, Captain Praut and Captain Barkin, maser cannon. Captain Schulz, laser canon. I'll send a salvo of warp threshold missiles. See if that deters their lunacy. On my mark……*fire*!'

Pulses of D-band amplified microwave radiation hurtled out of Praut's and Barkin's maser canons, then bursts of exited gigajoules of photons were pumped out of Helmut's laser canon. Sinclair's warp missile salvo joined the outburst, all speeding in the direction of Stimmer's hypothetical position.

'I've lost contact,' Karl reported to Praut.

'You mean with the enemy?'

'That's right. Must have moved out of range.'

'It means they've fled. We've achieved what we wanted.'

'Bloodied their nose,' added Mes.

'Right!' said Praut. 'We've sent a message. We're on to them…and we're after them. They can't attack us with impunity.'

Fanny suddenly appeared with Clay in tow. 'We been in a battle?' she inquired.

'Cease fire,' Sinclair's voice came over the tannoy. 'I think the enemy has fled. Thank you Captains.'

Fanny was startled by the tannoy. 'Was that *Admiral* Sinclair?' Fanny asked sarcastically. She had little to do and felt restless.

'What was that remark in aid of?' inquired Praut angrily. As far as he was concerned, they'd just had a successful engagement.

'I thought you were in charge of this expedition?' retorted Fanny.

'When it comes to space battles, Sinclair is the expert, and *he's* in charge…is that clear?

Fanny looked upset at being put down, and quietly left the ship's bridge. Clay went over to have a look at what Karl was doing. Clay was looking for someone to replace Edel as his pseudo-guru and seemed to have latched onto Karl for the job.

'Right, stand down,' Sinclair's voice announced on the ship's speaker, 'but keep your sensors sharp and alert.'

Karl smiled triumphantly at Mes. 'I did enjoy that. Fed up with that Stimmer getting away with things. Now the table's are turning…and I'm looking forward to punching their light's out.'

'What gets me,' voiced Mes, 'is we still don't know who this Stimmer is…I mean what's their aim? What are they trying to achieve?'

'Oh come on? It's obvious…they want to take over the galaxy. Can't you see it?' Clay's eyes were wide as if he couldn't believe they didn't see this.

Praut stopped to look at Clay; as did Mes and Karl. They seemed surprised at Clay's outburst—and by what he said.

Olga had been listening at the doorway, and now joined in, 'Okay Clay, say you're right…it still doesn't answer who they are?'

'I don't know who they are,' Clay defended himself, 'but they're no good. We need to bloody their nose.'

'Now *there,* we're all agreed on that,' declared Praut. 'We need to squash them for Edel, Tilmore, and Harry. Is that right?'

'*Yeah!*' they all shouted in unison.

The unified *yell* of solidarity, lifted the tension of the recent engagement.

'How far are we from Lowry now?' Praut asked Mes.

'We reach the one kiloparsec boundary in a couple of hours,' she replied.

'Olga, where's your sniffer now?' Praut asked.

'It's off after the Stimmer ship, and it is heading directly for Lowry,' Olga reported.

'Do we have Lowry's planetary info in the system?' Praut demanded of Mes.

'Must have. Karl's just putting it on the screen.'

'So when is night on Lowry?'

'From the screen info, in about four hours,' said Karl.

'So we have four hours to organise ourselves into two snatch squads. Karl, from the maps, find me a solitary outpost somewhere on Lowry. You know what we want. An isolated farmstead or a weather station with four or five people in it. We'll have to disable the satellite that's covering that area—make it look like a meteor hit it. We go in as quietly as we can. Karl, you lead one squad. Mes, you lead another. Eight people per squad. I'll bring up a backup squad in case either of you get into trouble. Get in touch with Max, tell him we need eight of his armed bruisers to join us in two hours.' Praut looked animated when organising an action outing.

'Dil, I'm coming with you aren't I?' Clay asked, not wanting to be left out.

'Unless you want to join Helmut on his ship? But Clay, I've got an important job for you before we go. I want you to get in touch with the *Lazarev* and ask their tech people to supply us with sensor absorbing nanobots. I want to cover the *Faust* with them. Will you do that for me? Make sure the little buggers are programmed correctly. You've got two hours.'

'Right Dil. I'm on it.'

'Mes, warn me when we get to the one kiloparsec range.'

'Will do.'

An hour later, Barkin materialised with seven of his most ferocious goons.

'Max,' Praut acknowledged him. 'By the looks of it, you're intending to join our little expedition.'

'Be fair Dil, I can't let my people have all the fun while I sit around twiddling my thumbs. It would drive me potty. How do you want my people distributed?'

'I want two to go with Karl's squad, two with Mes, and four with me.'

'In that case I'll go with you and these three.' Barkin pointed at three of his people. 'You two, and you two,' Barking was pointing, 'go with him and her. If anything goes wrong, don't come back,' Max growled at his chosen men.

‘Steady on there,’ objected Praut. ‘This is only a snatch mission. I want everyone back, and that includes the captives, alive and in good health. Avoid trouble at all cost—unless it’s really unavoidable.’

‘It’ll go okay,’ soothed Barkin. ‘I’ll be holding your hand,’ he chuckled and patted Praut on his back. ‘It’ll go smoothly.’

‘It had better. Our purpose this time is simply to gather info on what’s happening on Lowry…that’s all.’

Barkin eyed Praut, ‘Why not send in one of your famous sniffers? Surely it would get the info just as well as this snatch mission.’ He’d seen Olga standing near Clay.

Olga jumped in to defend her robotic pets, ‘The sniffers are for *following*, not for gathering in depth info. For that, we need real people…like the ones Dil’s gonna snatch. We need to question the people, *and* receive plausible answers.’

‘So much for the sniffers,’ Barkin scoffed, all the time a wily smile playing on his face. He was having a bit of fun at Olga’s expense.

Praut intervened, ‘Now Max, behave yourself, you know how sensitive Olga is about her sniffers.’

At that point, Olga understood Barkin was pulling her leg and she smiled at the floor in embarrassment, and began to shuffle to the corridor to escape.

A couple of hours later, Mes announced, ‘Dil, we’ve reached the kiloparsec boundary. All ships have come to a halt.’

‘What the hell,’ came from Karl. ‘Look at this!’ He was staring at his external screen, watching a faint stream of particles crossing the space vacuum, coming from the *Lazarev* towards the *Faust*.

‘Oh goody,’ cried Clay, ‘right on time.’

‘What are they?’ demanded Karl.

‘Dil ordered them,’ said Clay, as if that was enough.

‘Ordered what?’ growled Karl. ‘Can’t you be more specific?’

‘Oh, they’re nanobots,’ smiled Clay. ‘They’re sending them over for the *Faust*. They’ll absorb any sensor thrown at us…with no feedback.’

Karl sat for a moment, looking at his frustrating colleague. Clay was far more childlike than he’d suspected. He maybe a genius with a q-machine, but he behaved as if he was hardly out of his nappies. He decided he was going to have to treat him with kid gloves.

‘Are they going to embed by themselves? Do we have to do anything?’ Praut asked Claymore.

‘No Dil, it’s all automatic. Every nanobot has its position on the ship allocated for it in its programming.’ Clay looked pleased at the space ballet being performed round the *Faust* by the nanobots.

‘Good job Clay. Right people, listen up.’ Praut rose to his feet. ‘We leave here in two hours. It’ll take us around four hours to reach Lowry. That should put us on Lowry bang in the middle of the night. Karl, have you chosen a spot for our first snatch mission?’

‘Yes Dil. It’s on the southern continent…in an arid part of the planet. Single household, probably a single-family residence. We hit the spy satellite covering the area as we go in, then land in a small dune below the horizon. I’ll take my squad and snatch the people; bring them on board and you’ll have to de-chip them as quickly as you can. I don’t think we’ll need more than one squad to do the job. What do you think?’

‘No, that’s fine. I think you have it just right. Eight of us rounding up one family group.’ Praut was thoughtful for a second. ‘We’ll have about three hours to complete our task, then we’ll have to be off the planet before we’re discovered.’

‘And as I understand it,’ Mes added, ‘Sinclair’s going to be two parsecs away covering our getaway.’

Praut nodded, ‘That’s it. Now get some food and rest before we set off. Max, make sure my people are properly armed.’

‘Yes boss,’ smiled Barkin. He was just about to give a mock salute, but changed his mind.

* * *

The *Faust* left the *Lazarev* parked a parsec behind them and headed off towards Lowry. Praut relied on the nanobots to mask his arrival and proceeded directly for the satellite that needed demolishing.

‘We can’t use energy weapons on this thing. That’ll get noticed.’

The *Faust* had stopped and was stationary about five hundred meters from the spy satellite.

‘I’ve got an ancient Glock 17 pistol,’ Karl offered. ‘If we get up close, the 9x19mm cartridge can cause quite a lot of damage.’

Praut’s eye brows were raised, ‘What? In a space vacuum? And why the deuce have you been carting that museum piece around?’

Barkin intervened, ‘If you think that’s a museum piece, wait till you here this one. One of my crew’s got an RPG-7 launcher in his bag. He restores them.’

‘RPG-7? What the hell is that when it’s at home?’ Praut asked in surprise.

‘It’s a five hundred year old rocket-propelled grenade launcher. That antique will put that satellite out of action in no time. No energy trace on that,’ Barkin assured him.

‘Whoa there. What’s going on here? How come we’ve got all these ancient weapons on board?’

‘Sorry Dil,’ Karl was the first to answer. ‘The Glock’s been in the family for a long time. I just cart it around for good luck.’

Praut looked at Barkin.

Barkin shrugged his shoulders, 'Don't look a gift horse in the mouth. Do you want to use the RPG or not?'

'Is it safe? Will it work in this vacuum? I mean its not going to blow up the ship or anything like that?' Praut was serious. He had no idea of what these old weapons were capable of.

'It's safe…it'll whack that satellite in no time. It's rocket propelled.'

'Okay, let's give it a go. We're loosing time.' Praut had made a decision. 'Suite your man up and I'll open the external hatch. He can give that spy a pop shot from there.'

A short while later, a rocket-propelled grenade was on its way, and caused a decent explosion as it hit its target.

'Now Mes, get us down to that southern continent,' ordered Praut. 'Enough playing with antiques.'

The *Faust* hit Lowry's atmosphere at the precise angle to gain access to the re-entry corridor and began to plane down towards the planet.

Praut shouted to Clay over the engine noise, '*How's the heat going to effect the nanobots*?'

Clay shouted back, '*Oh, they're okay, they're fry proof.*'

A little time later Mes aimed the *Faust* at a spot marked on her screen map...a gully in the landscape, and brought the ship to rest in a small dune below the horizon.

As the engines closed down, an eerie quiet settled within the ship.

'I picked up only one lifesign in the house,' Karl informed Praut.

'Just one?'

'That's it.'

'Well, what are you waiting for…an invitation? Go get your quarry.'

Karl jumped to it. He went towards the ship's hatch, where his squad was waiting and led them out into the arid land surrounding the parked ship.

Praut whispered in the hushed atmosphere, 'Mes, keep the external screen on Karl's squad. I want to know what's happening all the time.'

'Yes Dil.'

'I'm just leaving the gully,' Karl's voice whispered over Praut's earphone. After a few minutes silence, there came an outburst, '*What the shit*? Hey Dil, there's some guy coming towards us in the dark…and he's carrying a large sign….with a lit-up notice…it says…"Welcome, please don't shoot. I come to you as a friend."

'Are you sober?' Praut asked Karl over his throat mike.

'I'm not kidding. There's a guy out here coming towards our group…with a yellow fluorescent sign. Hang on…he's just stopped about ten meters away from us. Now I've got him on my ear mike. He's just repeating what's on the sign…not to shoot and he's a friend. Oh, and he says he's not chipped.'

'Well don't just stand there, bring him in,' instructed Praut. 'But be careful.'

Some time later, in the canteen-come-lounge of the *Faust*, sitting opposite a light brown skinned individual, Praut smiled and said, 'Now tell me, what's all this about? How did you know we were coming?'

'Let me introduce myself. My name is Adam Rubin. Dr Adam Rubin. I was watching from my veranda, what I thought was a shooting star coming down, when I realised it had to be a spaceship landing. I immediately knew it wasn't that lot from Stretford, otherwise they'd have landed in my front yard, so I quickly knocked up a sign and came to meet you. I assume you're from off world.'

Praut was weighing up his visitor. 'Well Dr Rubin, I need you to let me do something to you. It's a precautionary measure to check your health. There's a cubicle next door I'd like you to climb into of your own free will. Will you do that for me?'

Rubin smiled at Praut, 'If you want to check if I'm chipped, I can save you the trouble…I'm not. Not that they haven't tried…but I've managed to squirm out of it each time.'

Praut's ears pricked up at the information. 'I'm sorry doctor, but I simply can't take your word for it. Please, it won't take a minute…and then I can be sure. Then we'll talk. Okay?'

'If you must, you must, but you won't find anything. I'm clean.' Rubin shrugged, got up and followed Barkin down the corridor to the room with the ten cryogenic stasis cubicles.

When Rubin came back, Praut saw Barkin shaking his head, indicating that no chip was present.

'Well now Dr Rubin, you are one impressive individual. How is it you're *not* chipped?' Praut curiosity was roused.

Rubin was nursing a hot drink and cleared his throat, 'Oh they've tried, I can assure you of that. But not since I moved out here. Let me start from the beginning.'

Praut held his hand up, 'Just a second, I need to give some orders to my pilot. He spoke into his throat mike, 'Mes, can you get us out of here, back to where Sinclair's waiting. I'll explain later.' Praut returned his attention to Rubin. 'Now sir, please continue.'

'Please call me Adam. Let me see, it all began about one and a half years ago when Rimmer Inc. arrived on Lowry.'

Praut's eyes shot a question at Rubin, 'Rimmer Inc.? Would that be the same Stimmer Inc. I've been chasing, also known as Zimmer Inc. on Harmony?'

'Probably. Sounds about right,' continued Rubin, 'Anyway, this Rimmer lot landed in the Middle continent and set up an advanced electronic works just outside Lowry's capital, Stretford. Rumours started circulating about the people that worked there. How they seemed like zombies. Next thing we know, the Governor began to be all pally with Rimmer Inc. Then it crept through our society like a raging wildfire.'

'What did?' Praut interrupted.

'Why the zombie look on the people's faces. I worked in Stretford as a researcher in xenobotany, the branch of biology dealing with alien genetics, but as a sideline, I toyed with some private work on chip implants controlling humans. That's before Rimmer arrived. I postulated that people could be controlled by having neural chip implants to alleviate minor behavioural disorders, and I ran numerous simulations to back up my theories, but ethical considerations would hamper any such implants being installed. I mean we've all had chip implants for statistical purposes to identify us for hundreds of years, but using them as a neural controller has always been taboo...until now.'

'Well that explains a lot,' Praut interrupted again. 'I mean how you guessed about the chip implants. Sorry, go on with your story.'

'When friends I'd known of old, turned up with vacant expressions on their faces, I began to suspect Rimmer of being responsible. It was the only arbitrary factor to have entered our lives. I then spent most of my time with my back against a wall, literally. People kept trying to pat me on the back, and I became suspicious it was the way the chip was introduced. Finally, I abandoned my research post and fled to where you found me, on the Southern continent. I've lived here for the last year, and surprisingly, the people in Stretford have left me alone. I've assumed it was because I was no threat to them.'

Praut then spent some time explaining to their guest what it was they were doing and why they'd sneaked onto Lowry.

‘I’ve been wondering when WorldGov would finally catch up with Rimmer,’ Rubin said. ‘It had to happen sooner or later. I did hope it wasn’t going to be too late.’

‘Now Dr Rubin, this is important; can you estimate how many people are chipped on the planet?’ Praut waited for the answer, knowing he probably wouldn’t like it.

‘I’d make a guess that you wouldn’t find many like me on Lowry.’

‘I was afraid you were going to say that. This mess is going to take some thinking and some planning. Mes, tell Captain Sinclair we’re heading back to the boundary.’

# 25
# CALL IN THE FLEET

'I've asked you to meet me here to get some advice on to how to proceed with this Lowry mess.' Praut was speaking to Sinclair, Barkin, and Helmut, but the rest of the Praut's Agency people were also present in Captain Sinclair's Ready Room on board the *Lazarev*. The place was crowded. 'This thing is beyond my competence,' continued Praut. 'I'm simply running an inquiry agency, yet here I am for the second time, trying to resolve the problems of a planetary nature. On Barnaby they gave me no choice by knocking me out of the sky. Luckily there were a lot of people I could turn to for help.' Praut looked at Barkin and smiled encouragingly. 'On Lowry, if what Dr Rubin is saying is true, then the whole planet is chipped, with very few exceptions. I simply can't think of anything I can do on that scale. I open the floor to suggestions.'

'This ship has six hundred cubicles to de-chip people. Why can't we just collect six hundred at a time and go through the planet that way?' This suggestion came from Mykola, who'd been listening.

'And how do you propose to get them into the cubicles?' asked Helmut.

'The same way we did on Barnaby,' came the reply.

'On Barnaby we had a functional teleport; here there's an anti-teleport sweep planet-wide,' Karl informed Mykola.

'Can't we snatch people the way we did with this Rubin fellow?' Clay asked.

'No Clay, sorry,' Praut told him. 'We'd possibly manage a couple of hundred people before this Rimmer-

Stimmer lot got wise to our game. Then they'd put a spanner in our works. We're talking of a planet with millions of people on it.'

Sinclair cleared his throat to call for attention. 'If I might suggest…I think we need to call in the big guns on this. Captain Praut is right…this is big, and on a planetary scale. May I suggest getting in touch with Admiral Zheng on the flagship and asking for his assistance. His tech people can neutralise the anti-teleport sweep, and the *SSS Baochuan* has enough room to accommodate all the cryogenic stasis cubicles we left on Barnaby. I'm suggesting calling in the whole Battle Group to Lowry.'

The scale of Sinclair's suggestion brought a hush to the room and stopped any further discussion. Everyone was looking at Praut to take the lead.

'I can't think of another move that might avoid calling in Earth's Second Battle Group.' Praut was resigned to the inevitable. 'Thank you Captain Sinclair, I think we should proceed with your suggestion. My compliments to the Admiral, and please get in touch with him. Tell him we need all of the cryogenic stasis cubicles left on Barnaby. He should install them on his ship. We have a planet to de-chip.'

Sinclair nodded and replied, 'I'll do that right now.'

*

Back on the *Faust* Praut said to Mes, 'We'll have to sit here a couple of days while the fleet arrives. Keep the sensors scanning for our enemy.' He switched to Fanny, 'How's our guest doing?' he asked her. She was looking after Rubin.

'He's putting together a full report for WorldGov on what's been happening on Lowry. Its going to be an eye opener. He's articulate and seems to know what's going on.'

'Does he know who Stimmer is, or is it Rimmer now?' Praut was itching to know the answer to that damnable question.

'He thinks they're from the local planetary group. I've told him it can't be Barnaby, so that leaves a planet called Fourex. But as to who they are, he's just as in the dark as us. Nobody seems to be able to get inside Lowry's Rimmer, and come out again. They're all absorbed.' Fanny felt like a mother hen looking after Rubin. She'd taken a fancy to him.

'Where is he right now?'

'He's in the cabin you gave him torturing his e-pad. He's producing page after page of this report.'

'You have the bridge, Mes,' Praut said as he left to find Rubin.

'Ah Dr Rubin,' Praut said upon entering the xenobotanis't cabin. 'Do you mind? I have a few more questions for you.'

'No, not at all, do come in. I'm just tidying up that little piece you asked me to produce.'

'What I want is for you to clue me in on Lowry. The planet, the population and its industry. I could probably get it from our database, but you're much more up to date.'

'As you probably know; there's two major continents; Middle and Southern. The north is one vast ocean. Middle is the major continent, with two million inhabitants, and Stretford, with a million inhabitants, is the capital. Stretford's on the southern coast, and Pendlebury with another million, is the other major city on the western coast. Salford is the major city on the southern continent, about a million inhabitants. The southern continent is somewhat arid and still being terraformed. Total population of Lowry about four million, mostly all living in cities. Industry is mainly solid state electronics. There's four quantum computers on the planet, all now under Rimmer's control.'

'Sounds like its locked down tight.'

‘If you’re thinking of taking down Rimmer, I would recommend the direct approach. Take out Stretford and the battle’s won. Don’t play with them…don’t go for any fancy tactics. Hit them fast and hit them hard.’

‘You may not be aware, but we’re waiting for Admiral Zheng and Earth’s Second Battle Group to arrive. When I talk to the Admiral, I’d like you to be there with me. Can you manage that?’

‘When’s the fleet coming?’

‘Should be here tomorrow. Tell me, Stretford’s admin centre, is that where Rimmer’s made its home?’

‘It’s a tall square building in the middle of the city… can’t miss it…and yes, Rimmer has settled in there. It runs everything from there. Used to be the Governor’s residence…officially it still is, but I know who’s in charge, and its not the Governor. Some malign influence has gripped our planet and its spreading like a plague.’

‘Well, we’re here to disinfect that plague. Its them or us. Can’t have some rogue entity chipping humanity, turning us into zombies, now can we? I’ll leave you to finish your report. Thanks for the info.’ Praut left Rubin and went back to the bridge. He walked in on a discussion between Clay and Karl.

Clay was saying to Karl, ‘Strange how every planet seems to look like earth. Almost creepy. Mars, Harmony, Barnaby, and now Lowry. Is that what we’re doing throughout the galaxy? Creating Earth-look-alikes?’

‘What would you have them do? Let me ask you Clay, what kind of home do you want to live in?’

‘Well, yeah, a comfortable one, sure. But that’s a home, not a planet.’

‘A planet is a home. Throughout history we’ve cleared land and built homes to suit ourselves. Sometimes we’ve caused chaos in the process, but we’ve always put it right…eventually. Now we’ve spread out into the galaxy, we’re doing what we’ve always done, cleared land and built ourselves a home. Only now we terraform instead of clearing land, and we make ourselves as comfortable as we can…as earth-like as we can…so we feel at home...and it's not as if we're displacing another planet's indigenous population. This is a big venture for us all; its our future… going out into the galaxy. It's our children's future, humanity's future. You'll understand this more when you find yourself a soul-mate and start having kids.'

Clay looked down, his face tinged red, embarrassedly. 'Awe, Karl, you make it sound like its inevitable. I'm too young for that kind of thing. Anyway, who'd look after the q-machines if I did that?'

Mes put in, 'Karl, don't push the kid. Clay's going to get hitched to a q-machine and have lots of little q-machines, isn't that right Clay?'

The whole room erupted in laughter at Clay's expense.

'If you haven't anything better to do, I can soon find something for you,' snapped Praut, trying to ease Clay's predicament. 'Karl, can you make a thorough check of all our armaments, rifles, cannons, and the like. Make sure they're in tip-top condition and in easy reach. Clay, I want our computer systems linked with the *Lazarev's* q-machine, ready for when we go in on Lowry. Olga, call in your sniffer and drain it of all the info its been gathering. Fanny, see that Rubin's report is ready for the Admiral tomorrow when he arrives, then take a rest. And Mes, as First Officer on this ship, I want you to make sure we're battle ready, then rotate with Karl and get some rest. Look lively, let's get back into our normal routine. Now I'm going to lie down until this evening when I take over the watch. Call me if its urgent… but not otherwise.' Praut hadn't slept for over twenty four hours, nor had most of the crew.

* * *

The abrupt cacophony of the klaxon sounding, woke everybody up.

'This is Captain Sinclair, we have multiple teleports in progress. Everyone to battle stations. Prepare to repel boarders.'

Praut jumped out of his bunk and grabbed his zapper. The door slid open and he rushed onto the bridge. '*What's happening*?' he shouted at Mes.

'Grab a laser rifle Dil. Enemy trying to teleport in,' she shouted back at him. 'Karl and some others are already searching the ship. Sensors indicate we're clean but we're making sure. The enemy shouldn't have been able to do this. It'll teach us not to lower our shields.'

'How's Helmut's ship?'

'A couple of fire fights but clear otherwise. Looks like the *Lazarev* and the *Catz* took the brunt.'

'The enemy made a big mistake there. Those guys can look after themselves.'

Barkin's voice came over the tannoy, 'The ship's littered with their corpses, but we've finally cleared them out. No losses on our side.'

'The situation is pretty similar over here,' Sinclair's voice announced. As the enemy materialised, we teleported half of them back into outer space. What we've got left is a few dead zombies.'

'Dammed waste of lives,' Praut spat out, to no one in particular.

'They're obviously desperate,' Mes called out, trying to put sense into what just happened.

'Not desperate enough to throw their own lives away,' retorted Praut. 'Whoever's guiding this mess…where's their corpses?' Praut wanted to know.

'We'll get them,' Mes assured him.

'You got a bead on their ship?' Praut demanded irritably of his first officer.

‘Nothing! We’ve tweaked our sensors, and they’ve tweaked their signatures in response.’ Mes seemed apologetic. ‘It’s a cat and mouse game. We’re going to have to get the Admiral’s techs on to this, or we won’t be able to locate this Rimmer-Stimmer lot at all.’

‘It gets on my wick that this Stimmer keeps trying to attack us. They’re so incompetent at it. That stupid missile attack, and now this teleport thing. All a waste of time. It’s not going to stop us, they must know that. It’s not even going to slow us down, just irritate the hell out of us.’

Karl returned and caught the last of Praut’s tirade. ‘Dil, your just cantankerous you can’t get your hands round their throats, admit it?’

‘You’re bloody right I’ll admit it. But when I do get my hands round their throats, I’ll have no mercy…count on it.’

‘Well Captain, I’m reporting back that we’ve no boarders to repel…nobody you can throttle,’ Karl reported.

‘So it’s Captain now is it?’ Praut smiled at Karl, then turned his smile at all those on the bridge, showing he’d calmed down.

Over the tannoy, ‘Hear this, this is Captain Sinclair. I’m letting all the ship’s Captains know that Admiral Zheng’s flagship is within hailing range and the Second Battle Group should be with us in two hours at the most. Sinclair out.’

‘That’ll put a stop to this Rimmer nonsense. Now its our turn to kick butt,’ Mes told Karl with some unexpected venom, as he joined her at the pilots console. She’d caught some of Praut’s earlier irritation and was letting it out of her system.

‘Right folks, let’s bed down for what’s left of the night. We’ve got a busy day scheduled for tomorrow. We’re going to retake Lowry from the zombie makers,’ Praut said the last part with grim satisfaction.

* * *

When Praut came back onto the bridge the following morning, the empty vacuum of space, occupied by the four ships of the previous evening had gone, and this local vicinity was now crowded with over sixty newly arrived spaceships. Earth's Second Battle Group had filled the void.

'It's breathtaking, don't you think?' gushed Praut as he looked at the external view screen over Karl's shoulder.

'Yep, anybody at the wrong end of this lot is in for serious trouble,' Karl agreed.

'And we both know who we hope that is, don't we?'

'What's all this?' Mes asked as she came onto the bridge. 'Who's in for serious trouble?'

'Dil was just looking at the Battle Group and hoping Stimmer would attack again,' Karl informed her.

'Oh, that's nice.'

'Nice? Nice? What kind of fighting talk is that?' Praut asked her, trying to suppress a chuckle. 'Nice is for flower arrangements and cocktail parties…not butt kicking.'

'Oh come on Dil, I've only just woken up. Give us poor working pilots a break.'

'You've got half an hour for breakfast, then its back to the grind stone. You want a longer break, then go back to the Space Corps.' Praut stood there looking smug but benign.

'Slave driver!' Mes turned and stomped out in mock disgust, but only into the nearby lounge-come-canteen.

'Has Sinclair been in touch?' Praut asked Karl.

'I had a message ten minutes ago suggesting we meet with Zheng and Souza on the flagship *SSS Baochuan* sharp 09:00,' Karl informed Praut. 'Battle Group Staff meeting.'

'Souza? What's he doing here?'

'Probably here to keep an eye on his loose cannon,' Karl grinned at his own wit.

Praut was surprised. 'What? Has *that* story gone the rounds then?'

'Everyone in the agency is now aware that Souza thinks our boss is a loose cannon…with the cannon ball aimed right at Souza, which is why he's so worried,' replied Karl.

'Oh well, can't be helped. Its 07:40 now, so I've got a little time to have some food. I'll go join Mes, see how my slave is getting on.'

# 26
# ADMIRAL ZHENG

The *SSS Baochuan,* flagship of the Second Battle Group, was a supercarrier and named in honour of Admiral Zheng's ancient famous namesake. Admiral Zheng was a legend in the Space Fleet in his own right and a credit to his distant ancestor.

Praut took Mes and Karl to the teleport point and been transported to the flagship for the scheduled staff meeting. After rematerialising, Karl continued expounding on the admiral with pride, 'Zheng fought the bureaucrats in WorldGov to a standstill, and eventually got what he'd demanded at the outset…three fully functioning Battle Groups to police the whole galaxy. I'm a great admirer of his.'

'Well bully for you,' Praut said somewhat condescendingly, while being led to the meeting room by Captain Sinclair.

'You wouldn't be so disdainful if we didn't have the Battle Group here right now,' Mes jumped in. 'Thanks to Zheng, we have his Battle Group to deal with this Stimmer. Look what a difference it made on Barnaby.'

'I'm sorry…you're right,' Praut apologised. 'Yeah, I admit, it did make a big difference on Barnaby. I'm just a bit wary of eulogizing too much.'

'When its not warranted, I don't do it,' explained Karl. 'With Zheng, as you'll learn, he earns his admiration.'

'We'll see,' Praut answered cautiously.

Sinclair said, 'Captain Praut, the Admiral is expecting you. He'd like a private word with you before the staff meeting begins.'

Praut raised his eyebrows, puzzled as to why, but left it at that, and simply followed Sinclair.

At the main lift system only Sinclair and Praut continued, while Sinclair's second kept Mes and Karl company.

'Any idea what this is all about?' Praut asked of Sinclair as they stepped out of the lift and walked down a corridor.

'I think the Admiral is of the opinion you have information which your not letting out of your sight. He's always curious about people he has to rely on…wants to meet them face to face.' Sinclair was guarded in what he said about his chief.

Praut sighed, 'In that case I'm as curious as he is… and for the same reasons.'

'Oh, you two will get along just fine, if I'm any judge of character,' Sinclair said with a hint of amusement. 'Here we are, please go in.'

Standing outside the door they'd arrived at was a grim faced marine sergeant. The sergeant saluted Sinclair smartly and slid the door open for Praut.

Inside, sitting at a desk, was a well built elderly man in a crisp white admiral's uniform.

'Ah, Mr Praut,' said the admiral getting up and stretching his hand out in welcome.

'Admiral,' Praut responded by shaking the outstretched hand. It was a firm handshake. 'What can I do for you?'

'Please sit. It is my understanding that this business all began with a number of incidents back in our Solar System…at least the WGS file seems to suggest this. I was wondering if you could fill me in on a number of questions I have.'

'Certainly, admiral. Fire away.'

'All this began with the theft of wormhole technology from a corporation on Mars. Is that correct?'

'It is. The CEO of Darhlburg on Mars asked for my help in retrieving some blueprints stolen from his q-machine. He hired my agency around four weeks ago.'

'That's as I understand it. But how does this Stimmer fit in to all this? And where do the chipped people come from?'

'One of my agencies specialities is an advanced tracer I call a sniffer. When the blueprint thief was teleported off Mars, I sent one of my sniffers after the spacecraft that lifted her, and it took us to a planet called Harmony. There we came across a virtual outfit called Zimmer Inc. On being scrutinised, it hurriedly packed its bags and fled from Harmony into space…again followed by one of my sniffers. I've chased this thing halfway across the galaxy. This brought us to Barnaby, where they shot me out of the sky, only this time the name changed from Zimmer to Stimmer Inc. This is when I first came across this chipped zombie phenomenon. Well you know how that story ended. Now for the current update to this story. A day ago, I went to Lowry and managed to nab an admirable chap called Dr Adam Rubin off the planet. Curiously, he'd managed to avoid getting chipped. He informs me that with few exceptions, all the people on Lowry have a biochip in their heads…but this time the outfit calls itself Rimmer Inc., and according to him, he thinks that they come from the nearby planet called Fourex. If and when we clear Lowry of biochips, I suspect we may have to deal with the same problem on this Fourex planet. Now since Fourex is the last inhabited planet in this sector of the galaxy, I am going to presume that it will be the origin of our biochip plague.'

Zheng sat quietly and listened attentively to Praut's story. 'And you still have no idea who this Rimmer is or their purpose in producing these zombies?' he asked.

'I think we're close to finding out, when we clear Lowry. I think the info will be there…on the planet, in their computers. At least I hope it will be. On Barnaby, they took their computer with them. On Lowry, I think they'd settled in and felt safe, so it'll be in the q-machines…and I've got just the fellow to retrieve the info.'

'Mr Praut, I believe you have set my mind at rest, and for that I thank you. Have you any questions for me?'

'Yes admiral. I understand Commissioner Souza is with you?'

'Yes, he insisted on coming. I didn't invite him to our little meeting for fear he'd try to influence my judgement with regards to you. He's somewhat wary of you, and I didn't want to prejudge you. I prefer to make up my own mind.'

'Why has the commissioner taken against me so?'

'He's of the opinion you're a loose cannon. He can't control you and give you orders the way he usually does with his minions, which means you're *out* of *his* control. You're a civilian and beyond his jurisdiction. Commissioner Souza is used to giving orders that are automatically obeyed. That's his bureaucratic mindset…and you just don't fit in. Hence the loose cannon.'

'Oh? Is that all? I thought it was something I said that upset him.'

'No, I don't think so. To him, you're simply not under his control, and he's not happy with that. Anyway, I'm glad we had this little chat. I must say, you sound crisp and coherent…and I'm afraid I must disagree with Commissioner Souza's assessment of you. Now, if that's all, shall we go and join the others in the meeting?'

'By all means admiral, you lead the way.'

The main meeting room was two rooms away and as they entered, the room stood to attention, with the exception of Souza. He sat glaring with perplexity at seeing the admiral enter with Praut. Praut was pleased to see Rubin standing next to Mes and Karl in the front. Next to them, Barkin was chatting with Helmut and Mykola, while

Sinclair watched them. Sinclair seemed to be keeping an eye on all the non Fleet people from Barnaby.

'Right gentlemen, please be seated. Commissioner,' the admiral acknowledged Souza's presence with a curt nod. 'I've just been getting a briefing on the background to our current situation. Most of you already know what my intentions are, but for the benefit of those not in the loop, let me lay it out. I can't emphasise this enough…we are dealing with an unknown foe. My WGS contacts inform me, they are fairly certain that our foe is an alien entity.'

There was an audible gasp in the room.

The admiral continued, 'Their assertion is based on the technology they've come across so far. They are quite certain the crystal technology they've found in the missiles used on Callisto, and sent in to take out Mr Praut on Earth, is non human. My tech people have examined the biochips being used and have concluded that it is far in advance of what humans have managed so far. Its not the chip so much, as the sophisticated construction of the chip from biological materials. They've corroborated the WGS conclusion of its alien origin. I asked them to keep their conclusions quiet, but now I've no reason for maintaining the secrecy.

'So far humans haven't come across any alien life forms in this galaxy, so we have no paradigm to work from, however, it would seem that these aliens are not being too friendly, what with missile strikes in our own Solar System, and turning humans into zombies with this biochip. So I have to conclude that this first contact is not going to be a peace mission. In our turn, we have to show them that this sort of behaviour isn't going to win them any friends. Mr Praut here, had concluded that it might be a human breakthrough in new technology, probably on a planet near here called Fourex, and I earnestly hope he proves to be right…but I'm going to go on the basis that we're dealing with an alien entity, and be more cautious as a result. It's the worst case scenario principle.

‘So as to the plan of action; I propose to park my Battle Group in orbit round Lowry, and to disable all the satellites round the planet. We’ll concentrate our big guns on the central admin tower in Stretford. The *SSS Baochuan* and the *SSS Dolgoruky* with the cryogenic stasis cubicles will park over Stretford’s admin centre, while disabling the anti-teleport sweep. Then we’ll proceed with de-chipping the population as fast as we can. We’ll start with the people in Stretford’s admin centre and work outwards. There’s around a million people in the capital and my people estimate it’ll take about five hours to de-chip that many. The *Dolgoruky* has some ten thousand cryogenic stasis cubicles on board accompanied by their technicians from Barnaby. The *SSS Intrepid* hospital ship will be standing by to take the confused de-chipped people.’

On the holo screen in front of the admiral figures began to appear:

Three minutes per person
1,000,000 people
10,000 cryogenic stasis cubicles
3,000,000 minutes ÷ 10,000 = 300 minutes = 5 hours

‘As you can see, this’ll take some time. We finish with de-chipping Stretford and then move onto Pendlebury and Salford. The whole operation will take us at least twenty hours if all goes well. Captain Sinclair informs me this Stimmer-Rimmer entity tried to board his ship last night and that they’ve managed to change their signature to avoid our sensors. I have my tech people working on this problem as I speak. In light of what I’ve told you, I am making it a priority to catch this Rimmer ship. We need to get a lot more info on this alien lot if we’re to be effective. To that purpose, I would like Dr Rubin, Mr Praut, my second, and Commander Wesley to stay behind after this briefing. We won’t go in on Lowry until we’re certain our sensors can image this Rimmer ship. I can't have a repeat of what happened on Barnaby. This time there won't be any escape. I want the Rimmer ship caught…or barring that…put out of action. Right gentlemen, dismissed.'

The meeting broke up and the admiral went and had a quite word with Souza, probably trying to unruffle his feathers.

After he'd finished with the commissioner, the admiral led the way into a smaller room next door.

'Please, make yourselves comfortable,' Zheng invited his quests. 'Wesley, put some drinks on the table,' he ordered his commander. 'Dr Rubin, Mr Praut, this is Vice Admiral Bennett, my second in command. He'll be in charge of the *SSS Dolgoruky*. Commander Wesley has taken it upon himself to become our alien expert.'

Praut and Rubin both nodded at the vice admiral and sat next to each other round the table.

'What did you think of the briefing?' Praut asked Rubin in hushed tones.

'Strange to have your own conclusions confirmed by an admiral.'

'You mean regarding the aliens?'

'I do. I'd pretty much come to the same deduction myself, mainly because of the biochips.'

'I wonder what he wants with us?'

'We're just about to find out.'

'Dr Rubin, Mr Praut,' the admiral began, 'I asked you to stay behind because I need your help. I want you to give me an idea of what I might expect from an alien entity. For a start, I only have a q-machine simulation of what to expect.'

'That's more than I have,' replied Praut. 'Have you got a visual?'

'Henry, put the visual on the screen,' Zheng asked his commander.

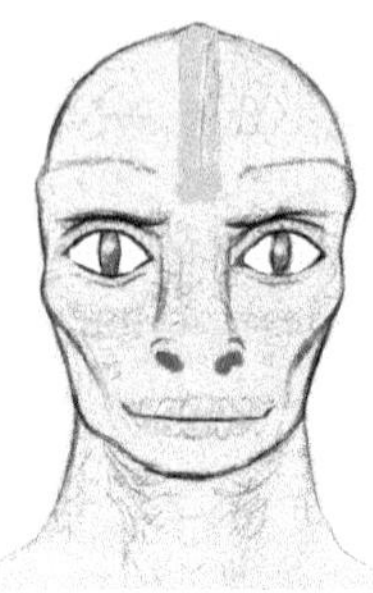

'Ah, our friend the evolved Troodon,' exclaimed Rubin.

'You're familiar with this sketch?' asked the admiral in surprise.

'Who wouldn't be. It's the stock sketch of an alien every time one is asked for.'

'Please explain.'

'Had the K-T extinction not taken place on Earth 65 million years ago, its what the most intelligent of the dinosaurs would have probably evolved into.'

'And is it wrong?'

'Not exactly wrong, but kitsch. Spindly fingers and a bulbous, bald head with large, almond-shaped eyes. It falls right into Protagoras' bias, "Man is the measure of all things." The probability of intelligent life evolving somewhere else in the universe has always been rated as high, yet the odds of it being humanoid, is blurred by subjectivity. We can't get above our own thinking. It's a heuristic bias stemming from the point of view of the thinker.'

'So how do we get round this conundrum?'

'For a civilization similar to ours, and there goes the bias again, to develop a technological culture, it would seem in addition to intelligence, an alien species would need the equivalent of opposable-thumb hands, something analogous to our eyesight, some structure that can be utilized for communication, and a brain equivalent that is capable of developing some kind of language. These senses need to be there to enable it to get on top of its environment. But the statement I just made is full of subjectivity.

'Lets face it, an alien may have an unimaginable chemistry, incredible shapes, sizes, colours, indescribable appendages and inconceivable opinions. We can't insist it follows the particular route that guided human evolution. Without knowing an alien's ecology, the environment in which it evolved, its futile to speculate on its appearance or intelligence capabilities. There could be many alternate evolutionary pathways, each unlikely, but the sum of the number of theoretical pathways to intelligence may nevertheless be quite substantial.'

'I should have brought you in at the outset. It would seem that my producing any kind of guesswork as what to expect is pointless.'

'Not exactly pointless, but not to be used as definitive. Its essential we keep an open mind. Do not expect….' Rubin left it hanging there.

The admiral sighed, 'I'm just a simple voyager through space. But if I am to meet a foe in battle, I need to have some perspective of my foe. Even if that perspective is kitsch and littered with subjectivism.'

Praut had been listening to the interchange between Rubin and the admiral, and finally offered his own view on the matter. 'Admiral, don't be too despondent as to what this image has thrown up,' Praut threw his hand at the holo image of the proposed alien. 'Throughout our long history we've only ever had a subjective notion of what an alien might look like. Because you haven't got a paradigm, I'm convinced it won't slow you down. Tenacity and resolution are the watchwords of the space navy, and its clear we are here to protect the human race from a pernicious foe. Surely that will do?'

'Yes, you're right…it *will* do. *Nos Vos Protegant Per Galaxy.* We Protect You Throughout The Galaxy, is our space navy's motto, and by my ancestors, that's what I intend to do.'

*

Later that morning, back on the *Faust*, Karl informed Praut that Clay was working with the ship's sensors, trying to update them to the new settings sent over from Zheng's tech people.

'He's been at it for over an hour now, cursing and fiddling with the dammed thing. He's grumbling that they're too sensitive and will pick up too much background interference.'

'If that's what Zheng's tech boys have come up with, there's no point arguing with it,' concluded Praut. 'We need to catch this Rimmer ship.'

'Oh, and we've been ordered to stand by to get under way in the next half hour,' Karl told him.

'About time,' Mes added. 'People are getting restless, and itching to get under way…me being one of them.'

'And me,' chimed in Fanny and Olga in unison. Both had been standing in the doorway listening to Praut.

'The *Baochuan's* captain has asked the *Faust* the *Humboldt* and the *Catz* to stay close to it…to stay within its protective envelope,' Mes informed Praut.

'But that means sitting above Stretford for five hours while they clear the place of biochips,' complained Praut.

'Not necessarily,' Karl told him. 'It'll take five hours to clear all of Stretford, but only about and hour or less to clear the administrative tower.'

'Where's that bloody genius? Never around when I want him.' Praut complained.

Just then Clay reappeared back on the bridge. 'Who's taking my name in vain?'

'I was,' Praut told him. 'I want you to be ready to go down into Stretford's tower and take their q-computers apart. We're looking for anything unusual. Anything alien, anything that looks like its non-human-new-tech. You know what I mean?'

'Yes Dil, I know what you mean. I was listening in on the meeting earlier. I heard all that lot about aliens.'

'Were you now? Nothing's safe from you…you scamp.'

'Aw Dil, you'd only complain if I didn't…you know you would.'

'Fixed the sensors?'

'Now I have.'

Both men laughed at each other's gripes. Clay was right, Praut did encourage Clay to circumvent every convention. He never knew where it might lead. A few times in the past it had led to a crucial breakthrough in a complex case.

# 27
# LOWRY

When the order finally came, the whole Battle Group moved across the parsec boundary and headed for Lowry. Disabling the many satellites surrounding the planet didn't take long, although some were constructed to fight back robotically, and closing down the planet wide anti-teleport sweep was achieved quickly by Zheng's tech people. The sweep radiated outwards from Stretford's tower and up into the satellite system.

Initially, resistance came in the form of high energy weapons secreted in strategic bunkers peppered round Stratford, and later, the other two cities. Drones, maser, laser cannon fire filled the skies. Myriads of missiles were fired from the ground, but the Battle Group's shielding held and there were no casualties. The resistance was fierce and short, lasting a half an hour at the most. The various sources of Lowry's defences were quickly suppressed by the Battle Group's overwhelming fire power.

While the rest of the Battle Group ensured that nothing flew in Lowry's sky, the two huge ships, *Baochuan* and the *Dolgoruky*, parked themselves above Stretford's administrative tower and began the laborious process of teleporting and de-chipping thousands of people, ten thousand at a time. Just above the two large ships, the hospital ship *Intrepid,* hovered in a stationary position. It scooped up the confused de-chipped masses coming out of *Dolgoruky's* cryogenic stasis cubicles. Then it teleported them back down to the outskirts of Stretford. There, they were left to mill around until the whole planet was de-chipped.

'Can't they move any faster? We've been sitting above this tower for over two hours now,' Praut complained to Mes.

The *Faust*, *Humboldt,* the *Catz* and the *Lazarev*, were waiting for clearance to land in the vast plaza in front of the massive admin tower.

'Here it comes…' Karl exclaimed.

'*What*?' said a startled Praut.

'The clearance to land,' Karl reminded him.

'About bloody time. Right, take her down. Mes, Mes, are you listening?'

'Aye aye Captain,' Mes replied with a grin.

'Karl, I want you to go with Clay and keep an eye on him. Make sure he doesn't get into any trouble…and keep me up to date on anything he discovers.'

Karl gave a mock salute in response.

Mes brought the *Faust* down to the ground, settling between the *Catz* and the *Lazarev*. The *Humboldt* parked itself on the other side of the *Catz*.

'You're staying with the ship,' Praut told Mes. 'Keep your ear on the Battle Group's comm lines. Dr Rubin, you're with us.'

When the ship's gangways were opened, the emergent invaders were met with an eerie silence. Toting his laser rifle, Karl led Clay down the gangway, followed by Praut and Rubin. Sinclair's marines were already on the ground and fanning out, heading for the tower entrance.

'Dammed weird, no people anywhere,' Karl threw over his shoulder at Clay.

'They've all been teleported, Karl, you know that,' Clay stated the obvious.

'Yeah, I know; still its strange with all this silence.'

'So why are we carrying these weapons?'

'Just in case. What if there's some the teleport missed?'

'Naw, not possible!'

'Clay, we're dealing with the unknown here. Don't get duped by your mindset. If we're dealing with aliens; anything's possible.'

Clay looked dubious and screwed up his face in disbelief.

Praut joined them. 'Hold on you two, enough chatter. Let Sinclair's marines go through the admin centre first, let them check it out. When they've cleared it, head for the q-machines. According to Adam, they're down in the basement two floors down. You know what you have to do. Find any clues as to who this Rimmer is.' Then Praut spotted Barkin emerging from the *Catz*. '*Max*, over here.'

Sinclair led a large squad of his space marines through the tower's entrance and they spread-out throughout the ground floor. Sinclair's job was to secure the admin tower.

'Hi Dil, how's it going?' Barkin sauntered over, followed by a cluster of his toughs, all toting laser rifles. Barkin had proclaimed he would provide protection for Praut's people. 'Hi Adam,' Barkin said to Rubin.

'So far so good. Clay's itching to get at the computers,' Rubin replied.

Praut said to Barkin, 'Can you detail four of your men to follow them and watch their backs?'

'No prob.' Barkin pointed to four of his men. 'Am I coming with you?' he asked Praut.

'Seems an idea,' Praut told him. 'Once we get the all clear from Sinclair, what say we take a gentle stroll through the building. I'm looking for anything out of the ordinary… anything alien looking. Know what I mean?'

'No, but I'll keep my eyes peeled.'

'No sign of Rimmer?'

Barkin shook his head. 'Buggers seem to have disappeared.'

Praut nodded at Rubin, 'Dr Rubin here, can give us a tour. He should know this tower inside out.'

A little while later, Praut put his hand up, 'I'm getting the all clear from Sinclair in my earpiece. Let's go.'

Barkin and his men were the first through the tower's sliding doors. Praut was followed by Rubin, Karl and Clay, then came Helmut and Mykola with about ten others, all toting laser rifles, forming a protective cluster round Fanny and Olga. The rest of Praut's people followed them into the admin centre. They had no idea what to expect.

Praut began giving orders, 'Fanny, Olga, find the admin offices and sift through any e-documentation you can find. Helmut and Mykola, take your people and go help them. Keep me informed. Clay head for the machines down below. Keep in touch.'

Barkin waited until Praut had finished and then followed Rubin to a large holo console interrogation screen.

Rubin said, 'Building plan,' in a clear crisp voice.

A plan of the admin centre appeared in front of them, hanging there in the air.

Barkin followed this up with, 'Armoury.'

Silence, no change to the holo screen.

'I said *armoury*,' Barkin said a little louder.

Still no change on the screen.

'Let me try,' Praut offered. 'Locate Governor's office.'

The holo screen stayed stubbornly fixed on the building plan.

Rubin said, 'Its frozen.'

'Well so much for that. Seems we're not gonna get any help from that direction,' Barkin said in disgust.

Rubin suggested, 'Let's head for the top floor. That's where the brass usually hide…then we can work our way downwards.'

'Those look like the elevators over there,' Barkin pointed at translucent tubes in the middle of the hall. 'The building can't be much different from our central dome in Ventura.'

Rubin verified this and led the way to the lifts.

Barkin had some twenty men with him and they split into two groups, taking two lifts to the top floor.

Praut was the first out of the lift, and abruptly stopped, forcing Rubin to walk into his back. On the top floor landing they discovered a shambles, as if someone had hurriedly tried to destroy all of the equipment. Various e-pads were strewn along the corridor and the landing, mostly crushed underfoot. Slide doors were left open, tables and chairs overturned. Smashed consoles and many holo consoles put beyond use. Every piece of e-equipment had been wrecked.

'*Karl*, *Karl*, can you hear me?' Praut shouted into his throat mike.

'Yes Dil, loud and clear. What's up?'

'You down in the computer room?'

'Yes we are. Clay's just getting to grips with the machine. He's had to reboot them as the power had been cut. Thanks to Sinclair, the power's back on.'

'Thank goodness for that. I'm up on the top landing and all the e-equipment's been smashed up. I was worried they'd done the same to the q-machines.'

'No, we're okay. Don't know what we'll find yet, but Clay's working on it.'

Rubin had been listening in on the exchange. 'Tell them to look out for booby traps,' he advised Praut.

Barkin added, 'We found quiet a few on our q-machine in Ventura, before we whisked it away to the sub.'

'Clay can deal with them. Its not the first time people have tried to mess with him. I'd trust Clay with any q-machine. I've yet to come across anybody as good as Clay when it comes to computers. Its no idle boast.'

Barkin shrugged, 'Just thought I'd mention it.'

'So what do you think was the point of all this carnage up here?' Praut asked Rubin.

'Looks like a tantrum to me.'

'Tantrum eh? Never thought of that. Could it be?'

'At the moment that's what it looks like to me as well,' Barkin seemed to agree with Rubin. 'There's no sense to it.'

Again Praut spoke into his throat mike, 'Fanny, you found anything interesting?'

'Hi Dil,' came back Fanny's voice. 'There's a lot of wreckage where I'm at. Someone's tried to destroy all of the equipment,' she complained.

'Same up here. We're on the top floor,' he informed her. 'Do the best you can. See if you can find any plans. Check all the optical drives. Liaise with Clay on the q-machines. He'll be able to retrieve the info.'

'Will do. Out.'

'Surely, everything's on the q-machines?' queried Barkin. 'All the info you're supposedly looking for.'

The group was walking cautiously down the corridors looking into every room.

'Max, You're right of course,' agreed Praut, 'but I'm just making sure we don't miss anything. I want to go through this tower with a fine tooth comb. Because we're not dealing with an ordinary entity, they may have habits we could overlook.'

Rubin added, 'Remember the biochip…what if their storage drives are biological, and when threatened, they're simply eaten or decompose?'

'Now that's a thought. Where did that come from?' Praut asked.

'Just trying to do some lateral thinking,' Rubin answered.

'Biological computers? Is that possible?' The thought had just struck Praut.

'Of course its possible,' replied Rubin. 'In fact its old hat. Using DNA as a means of storing info has been around for ages. Welcome aboard the lateral bandwagon.' Rubin looked bemused at Praut, then continued, 'But using entangled photons is quicker, hence quantum computers. We're down to the subatomic level, which is a good step below the biological. With q-machines, everything happens at light speed, and with entanglements, its parallel. The result is almost instantaneously, even with the most complex matrix or simulation you can come up with.'

'You're as bad as Claymore,' grunted Praut.

Just then Praut heard from Clay in his earpiece.

'Dil, you there?'

'Yes, Clay, go ahead. Found something?'

'I'll say I have. You need to come down here and have a look.'

'Right, I'm coming down. Be there in a jiff.' Praut turned to Barkin, 'Look Max, Clay's found something on his q-machines that he wants me to look at. Can I leave you up here to go through the rest of the tower. Dr Rubin, I'd like you with me. You might be able to explain what Clay's found. After all, it is your planet.'

Praut and Rubin headed back to the lifts and descended into the bowels of the admin centre to where Karl was waiting for them.

'Hi Dil,' said Karl and led them down a corridor. 'This way. What we've found is outrageous. Zheng and Souza will have to see this as well.'

Praut's senses pricked up. He thought, maybe they've finally found a breakthrough in this whole sorry business. 'Well, you've tweaked my interest…I hope it warrants it.' Praut was still sceptical.

'You'll see for yourself. If it doesn't blow your mind, I don't know what will.'

At the end of the corridor was a blank wall. 'Now what? Where are you leading us?'

'It's a holo blank wall. Just keep going through it. They've tried to disguise the entrance into the computer room.'

'Have they now?' Praut was getting curious.

Karl led them through the holo blank wall, into where Clay was manipulating a holo image of what looked like some kind of laboratory.

'Hi Clay, what've you got for me?' Praut walked over to where Clay was, with Rubin in tow.

'Have a look at this,' Clay pointed to the holo image of lab plans. 'This is really awesome. Oh by the way, I've found Darhlburg's missing wormhole blueprints.'

Praut did a double take. 'You've what? Darhlburg's blueprints? Where are they?'

Clay pointed at a small cube lying on the console. 'Yeah, but that's not what I called you down here for. This is far more worrisome,' and Clay pointed again at the holo image of the lab.

Praut was torn between having just accomplished his Agency's initial task, and this holo image Clay kept pointing at. 'Okay, so fill me in. What am I supposed to be looking at?' He was wondering over to the small cube lying on the console.

Rubin was scrutinising the image closely with astonishment on his face. 'The blackguards,' he kept repeating. 'The disgusting blackguards.' Then Rubin came and grabbed Praut's wrist and pulled him to the holo image. 'Have a look at this.'

'Will someone please tell me what I'm supposed to be looking at?' Praut snarled at the image.

'This is the biggest danger I've yet come across to the human race,' Rubin said in disgust. 'It's an advanced genetic processing lab with an industrial production line. From the accompanying documents, its aim seems to be to boost the ordinary human genome with physical and mental capabilities, but to sublimate their leadership genes to that of obedience to authority to the point of subservience. What it tells me is, they can't be all that confident in the long term effect of their current biochip.'

'What the shit?' exclaimed Praut.

'Whoever designed this lab is trying to harness the human race as a subservient species to their interests, what ever *they* may be. Remember this is my field. More to the point, there's systems and subsystems here that I've never come across. This wasn't designed by humans…but it was designed to be used by humans…probably biochipped people. Hence I'm able to make most of it out.' Rubin stood there looking at it, shaking his head.

'But we've outlawed most of this kind of gene manipulation for centuries,' Praut said.

'I know,' Rubin replied, scrolling through more of the image plans. 'And here's the reason why. It also looks to me like this is only the beginning. Their next phase,' he continued to scroll through the image, 'involves human cloning…and on a massive scale. If we hadn't come along, within a month at the utmost, they would have had this clone production line working and would have mass produced human clones.'

'But…but, that's illegal. We've outlawed it,' Praut repeated, almost speechless.

Rubin continued, 'Listen to this. They've redesigned the human genome to act more as an android, rather than an independent thinking species. This would have been mass produced and then sent to our other planets. I'm sorry, I'm having a hard time taking this in.' Rubin turned his head away in disgust.

Karl and Clay had been listening to the interchange between Praut and Rubin.

'Androids?' Karl put in. 'If they produced those, they'd remove the very spark of individuality that produces both the criminal and the genius,' and he looked pointedly at Clay. 'We'd loose everything that makes us human; we'd loose the human spirit and end up being mere machines. This has got to be stopped. Now this Rimmer's got me *really* riled.'

'This is no mere Rimmer any more,' Rubin told him. 'This is clear evidence we're dealing with an alien entity… and a malignant one to *us* at that.'

Praut intervened, 'Clay, can you download this onto a cube and send the content up to Zheng's ship. I want them to have a close look at this. Mark it for the urgent attention of Zheng and Souza.' To Rubin he added, 'Any idea where this lab is situated?'

'I think it's on the outskirts of Pendlebury on the western coast.'

'Clay, can you add that info to Zheng's cube,' Praut told him, 'and my recommendation that the facility be found and utterly obliterated, as a priority.'

'It beggars belief that one supposedly sentient species would want to do that to another sentient species,' Rubin lamented. 'I mean, androids are a mere human racial memory of slavery, and that of serfs to the now defunct and disgraced aristocracy. These supposedly pseudo intelligent automatons were once popular in Science Fiction as antagonist who inevitably go rogue in the story. Surely, no human would want to vie with an intelligent machine. Why would we want to produce a robot except to use it as a surrogate slave. The idea that humans would produce autonomously intelligent machines is asking for trouble. Why create a headache for yourself?

'A machine is a machine and should stay a machine. It has no business being designed to be more intelligent than a human. The now ancient and obsolete Turing Test came out of a warped mind, one with little or no self esteem of its own humanity. The same sort of warped thinking had rapacious so-called fortune telling futurologists speculating that machines would become so intelligent that they would ultimately take over from humanity...and that would be the end of humanity. These dead-end futurologists made predictions that stemmed from the thinking of a suicidal mind. These doom merchants in reality hate humanity and yearn for its demise. These spurious futurologists even gave a date when humanity would be overtaken by machines… some time around 2099. The date came and went, and humanity totally ignored their idiotic sensation seeking predictions. How self destructive and deprecatory can some self indulgent people be?

‘You don’t need an android machine to clean your house, or perform any sort of task. You design the house to self clean, and design the job to self-perform, independently, but not with legs so it moves around. Autonomous androids and robots are a bad fantasy of a lazy mind…good for story telling, but not much else….’

Praut was looking strangely at Rubin. ‘What’s set that tirade off?’

Rubin stopped in mid sentence, ‘Oh, its part and parcel of my obsession with chip implants…and this biochip menace that I’ve been struggling with for the past year. Chip implants, androids, robots, meddling with the human genome…they’re all part and parcel of the same thing, really. People can’t seem to stop fiddling with our human makeup. Evolution’s done a good job, and it took it millions of years to accomplish us. We come up with a new scientific toy and we can’t help trying it out…without thinking of the consequences. We now instil morality and ethics right from the beginning, but still some people try to circumvent their upbringing.’

Praut relaxed and smiled at Rubin, ‘Adam, count your blessing that’s the case. It’s what makes us human.’

# 28
# RIMMER INC.

'Fanny, did you send the e-parcel off as I asked you to?' Praut forked another piece of bass into his mouth.

'Yes, Dil, just as you asked me to. Darhlburg's blueprints are winging their way back to Mars, courtesy of Zheng's comm people…with your message attached...and the Agency's final invoice for the job.'

'Addressed to Van Rag Yang...CEO?'

'Yes, honest.'

'Oh, and make sure you get an acknowledgement they've received it...thanks.'

'But Dil, we still don't know why this stupid lot stole the blueprint in the first place.' Fanny didn't like hanging questions. 'They've tried to wipe the wormhole info from the gq-net and wasted their time on stealing this blueprint. To what purpose?'

Praut smiled at her, 'Good point. I need to get to the bottom of this, just so I can dot the *i's* and cross the *t's*. I can't leave it without knowing the full answer. Things like that haunt one's dreams if they're left unanswered and turn into nightmares.'

They were sat in the crowded executive diner near the top floor of Stretford's admin tower. Clay had got the q-machines linked back to the food replicators in the diner and all of Sinclair's people were eating there, having first put the place in order. Barkin's people were sat with Praut's people and the whole mess were hungrily scoffing all their favourite meals.

They'd spent most of the morning watching Clay turning up various bits of information. Some confirming the alien origin of their antagonists, although there was no indication as to where they originally came from. What had become clear though, was that Rimmer had come to Lowry from the nearby planet, Fourex. That was all logged. So whatever the humans did on Lowry, would have to be repeated yet again on Fourex, if possible. Clay had stayed with the q-machines and was still working on them, having declined Praut's offer of food.

'Max, after this meal break, we'll go and see how Zheng is doing, shall we?' Praut said to Barkin. 'Zheng should be well under way in clearing Pendlebury. Then there's only Salford to do.'

'That Rimmer lot will be shitting bricks by now. I wonder what they'll come up with as their final shot?' Praut noted Barkin's turn of phrase had always been colourful.

'They behave more like sneak thieves, these aliens. If that's the case they'll go quietly,' offered Mes.

'What about the attacks the other night?' queried Helmut.

'Well, there's that of course,' answered Mes weakly.

'I don't think we've seen the last of these things,' Karl put in. 'They're both sneaky and pushy, which is only to be expected when playing for such high stakes.'

'What high stakes,' asked Olga innocently.

'The whole galaxy and the human race,' Rubin pointed out to her.

'Oh that,' was her only response.

Praut took the opportunity to tease Olga, 'The whole human race and the galaxy at stake and she says, *oh that.*'

'Dil, leave her be,' Fanny intervened. 'Can't you see she's a bit sad.'

'What's she got to be sad about?' demanded Praut.

'You know she always gets sad when we finish one of our jobs. The missing Darhlburg blueprint's been found and retrieved, and is on its way back to its owners. What the Agency contracted to do, is finished.'

‘What? And you think I’m just going to pack up and go back home?’ Praut screwed up his face. ‘Weren’t you listening to the bit about *humanity* and the *galaxy* being under threat? About me dotting the *i’s* and crossing the *t’s*.’

‘You mean we’re going to follow this to the end?’ she asked.

‘You can always go back home if you want to, but I’m staying. I want my revenge for the deaths of Edel, Tilmore and Harry. This isn’t over until I get my pound of flesh.’

‘You’re a bit blood thirsty,’ Barkin observed, while listening to the exchange.

‘And I suppose you’d just let it go at that if three close friends of yours were murdered by this scum?’

Barkin grimaced at the accusation. ‘No, of course not. I’d do what your planning to do. And while we’re at it, people close to me have been murdered, and I’m coming with you. I want *my* revenge.’

‘Now this question has arisen; anybody who wants to pull out and go home is at liberty to do so. Fanny’s right, the job’s finished.’ Praut looked around at his people. ‘I won’t hold it against you. You can use Helmut’s shuttle and head back to the Solar System. You don’t have to tell me now, but let me know within the next two hours.’

Nobody said anything for a few moments, then Karl said, ‘Me and Mes have talked this over and we’re staying till the end. This thing’s to big to leave like this. Just thought I’d let you know Dil. You’ll need combat people.’

Suddenly, all of Praut’s people were wanting to talk all at once. All were insisting on going on to the bitter end, come what may. Nobody was going home and leaving Praut to go on alone. They wouldn’t think of it. They also wanted some payback for Edel, Til, and Harry.

Praut looked solemn, ‘Thanks guys. I knew I could count on you.’

Sinclair’s voice came over Praut’s earphone, interrupting Praut’s gratitude. ‘Captain Praut, I thought I’d inform you, I'm just getting info over my comm of a battle brewing over Pendlebury.' Sinclair was only sitting four table down from Praut.

'Has it anything to do with the lab info I gave the admiral a short while ago?'

'Everything to do with it. As soon as the Battle Group's sensors located the huge lab, entrenched robot defences opened up on the Battle Group. The admiral's used an EM pulse weapon, a high powered, deep burrowing, microwave missile to knock out the lab's electronics. Don't know how it went…it was the last I heard, only a minute ago. I was under the impression you were heading down there?'

'That was my intention. What do you advise?'

'Hold back for half an hour, see how this thing develops.'

'Agreed!'

'By the way, why would you want to go to Pendlebury? There's nothing there.'

'I'm real curious about this lab we uncovered. Then there is Rimmer Inc. They haven't shown themselves yet, but I'm pretty certain they will, especially as the noose tightens.'

'What? You want to have a go at them?'

'I've got a score to settle with them. They're not going to get away that easy with killing my people. All my lot feel the same about this. This is payback time.'

'Why not sit back and relax. Let the big boys in the Battle Group settle your score for you. The admiral's ship is better equipped to handle this Rimmer than your shuttle.'

'Oh I may hide behind the admiral's ship, but me and mine need to see the Rimmer ship burn.'

'Suit yourself…but go careful.'

'I promise.'

Praut waited for the half hour to pass then said, 'Listen up. I'm intending to go and have a look at this lab, and hopefully watch it been obliterated, but I also suspect Rimmer is about to show its teeth.'

'I thought it did that with the lab battle,' Barkin interposed.

'No Max, that was just a sideshow. I'm guessing that the real battle will be when the Rimmer ship tries to escape from this planet back to Fourex. Zheng has made it clear he won't permit this Rimmer ship to escape him twice.'

'So you think the real battle is yet to come,' Barkin asked.

'I do. I know Mes and Karl are still eager to have a go at Rimmer, but this could be more dangerous than before. I'm going to order Helmut to stay here in the capital with his ship. Anybody silly enough to go with me is welcome, but know the risk.'

Praut rose to go, and all his people rose with him. That Barkin would go with him was a given.

'Clay still fiddling with his machines in the basement?' Praut asked Karl.

'As far as I know,' Karl replied. 'Can't pull him away from the bloody thing. He's completely engrossed.'

'Good, leave him there. Helmut,' Praut turned to his team leader. 'Have one of your people keep an eye on him. Olga and Fanny are staying with you.'

'I'll keep an eye on Clay,' Helmut affirmed. 'I'll check on him from time to time.'

Fanny and Olga looked at each other, not certain if they'd heard right.

'Don't you want us with you?' asked Fanny.

'Not this time Fanny. You and Olga I want safe with Helmut. No arguments.'

'Okay,' is all Fanny said. She pulled Olga to the side and joined Helmut.

'Max, you taking your ship, or coming in mine?'

‘I’d better bring mine along just in case. Two are better than one in this type of venture. One of us gets in trouble, the other can do the rescuing.’

Down in the tower’s lobby, Praut cast one last look at the enormous interior before exiting. Out in the plaza, a large number of people were milling around, looking lost.

‘Must be the de-chipped people coming back into the centre from the outskirts of the city,’ Rubin offered.

‘Why’d they let them roam free,’ Praut asked.

‘What are you going to do, lock them all up?’ Barking asked in surprise. ‘The biochip has been removed and they have to pull themselves together and get on with their lives.’

‘I suppose your right,’ shrugged Praut. ‘seems a bit chaotic just to leave them to roam around like this, that’s all.’

‘We haven’t abandoned them, just like that, as you put it,’ Barkin defended. ‘Once the whole de-chipping process is finished, our cryogenic stasis cubicles technicians will turn their hand to giving support to those that need it the most, as they’ve done on Barnaby. Some seem to pull themselves together relatively quickly, others take longer to get back into the swing of things. It’s those that the technicians concentrate on. Counselling services and other help is what they provide, but first comes the de-chipping. According to Zheng’s schedule, everything ought to be over by tomorrow, then the technicians are free to help the confused people.’

‘Enough of this. Let’s get under way,’ and Praut led his people to the *Faust* entrance gangway.

Helmut and his group went towards the *Humboldt*.

Barkin set off with his rogues to the waiting *Catz*.

Once in the air, both ships set off towards the west. After a short while, Karl reported an incoming comm from Zheng’s supercarrier.

‘Dil,’ Karl called out, ‘I’ve just got a warning from Zheng’s people that all ships are to stay clear of the

Pendlebury area. Three unknown spaceship have arrived from the south and are attempting to engage the *Baochuan* and the *Dolgoruky.*'

'*There...*what did I say?' Praut cried out. 'I told you Rimmer wasn't going to let it go so easily.'

'Shall I slow?' asked Mes.

'No! Maintain course and speed,' ordered Praut.

'Didn't you hear what I just said?' asked Karl. 'We're being ordered not to go near Pendlebury.'

'I heard you,' growled Praut. 'Now you hear me. We're heading in for the kill. I may not be able to down the Rimmer ship myself, but I'm going to watch Zheng take it down. Mes, do you think you can keep us safe? Can you outmanoeuvre the Rimmer ships?'

'I can try,' asserted Mes. 'If your sure you want to do this...then I'm game. If we're gonna take a risk, we might as well make it full-size.'

'There's a woman after my own heart,' smiled Praut.

'Let's get this straight,' said Mes mischievously. 'I'm *not* after your heart. 'I've got plans of my own.'

'Dammed, rejected once again. Lucky in war but not in love,' bemoaned Praut, broad grin on his face.

'Barkin on the comm,' Karl advised. 'Wants to know what you intend to do? Must've had the same warning from Zheng.'

'Tell him to follow my lead...or he can turn back. His choice.' Praut had become serious.

A little way further on, the two space shuttles came onto a bizarre scene. Over the city of Pendlebury hung two massive battleships enveloped in a shimmering combined protective forcefield, being fired down on by three strange looking ships hovering above the battleships. The laser come maser beams were ferocious.

'What's Zheng doing?' Praut demanded of Mes. 'Why's he not firing back?' he was gazing at the external visual screen.

'Looks like he's trying to drain their power,' Karl replied. 'The two battleships have enormous power reserves, and he estimates his attackers are less fortunate. It's a poker play. As soon as Rimmer stops firing, Zheng will open up…and Rimmer knows this. I don't think Rimmer can afford to stop firing, yet….' Karl left the sentence hanging.

Praut watched the screen for a full five minutes before the three Rimmer ships suddenly stopped firing. It was a poignant moment. Silence and tension hung suspended in the air above Pendlebury. The Rimmer ships began to move away, powering up, about to flee, when Zheng's ship opened up with its massive firepower, closely followed by the *Dolgoruky*. The fire power from Zheng's ship pierced one of the Rimmer ship's forcefield. The Rimmer shields were weakened as a result of the power drain. Next moment it exploded and began to fall, then it dropped like a stone, down onto Pendlebury in a fireball. The ship hit one building, knocking it sideways into another building, and then ricocheted off into another building, completely destroying it. The smouldering wreckage of the spaceship intermingled with the destroyed building was strewn all over the area.

Praut watched edgily as the *Dolgoruky's* massive firepower pierced another of the Rimmer ship's weakened forcefields. It also began to break up and dropped onto Pendlebury in a flaring fireball. This time the wreckage landed on a road in between two rows of buildings.

'Now for the last bastard,' snarled Praut through clenched teeth. 'Get him.'

Both the *Baochuan's* and the *Dolgoruky's* immense firepower was finally turned on the last Rimmer ship and it all but disintegrated in mid air, such was the huge force concentrated against it. Small pieces of the last Rimmer ship landed all over the place in Pendlebury, but caused little damage, the pieces were so small.

'That was utter madness. It was sheer suicide going up against the battleship and the supercarrier,' Mes said, shaking her head as she watched the finale of the short battle.

'Wasn't it just,' Praut said with great satisfaction. Then he asked Mes, 'You catch that on the holovid?'

'That's automatic Dil,' Karl informed him. 'Of course its on the holovid. You want to watch it again?'

'I might, just to cheer me up.'

'Grisly,' mumbled Karl. 'Most grisly.'

'Put me through to Max on the *Catz*,' Praut ordered Karl.

'Hi Dil, what a show? Heh?' A hearty voice came over the connection when Karl got through. 'Don't see that every day.' Barkin was just as hyped up as Praut.

'Was it worth the trip?' Praut asked Barkin.

'Front row seats…and then some. Loved every moment of it. That's what I call payback. All I could think of as I watched the ships go down, was all my friends that died when we tried to get into Barnaby's dome in the underground tunnels.' Barkin's voice became all solemn. 'I had great satisfaction watching that, but I can't say I'm happy. That Rimmer lot brought this on themselves.'

'Yeah, and there's Fourex to come,' Praut added. 'Unless those Rimmer ships were automated, a lot of lives were lost today. It's made it easier to live now that my people have been revenged…but yes, you're right, its not a happy moment. I feel a bit ashamed at my blood lust.'

'Oh hell Dil, you're only human,' Barkin said over the comm line. 'It's a normal reaction when people close to you are killed…wanting revenge.'

'So I'm told. Still seems like I'm gratifying the remnant of the savage in me.'

Karl called out, 'Got an urgent comm from Zheng's ship. Putting it on speaker.'

'Hallo, hallo, this is Admiral Zheng. Is that Captain Praut?'

'Yes admiral. Congratulations on your victory.'

'Did you, or did you not, receive an order to stay away from this area? Answer me!'

'Sorry admiral, that was my fault,' intervened Karl. 'I received the order but I didn't pass it on to Captain Praut.'

'Whom am talking to?'

'Second Officer Karl Wolfe, sir. I'm in charge of communications.'

'Would you mind explaining why you didn't pass on the comm to your captain?'

'Sir, I knew how important it was for Captain Praut to see your victory over the Rimmer ships…so I withheld the comm from him. I take full responsibility for my actions.'

Praut was staring in amazement at Karl taking the blame for what he'd done. He was gently shaking his head.

Mes stared at Karl with disbelief, and admiration.

'My apologies Captain Praut. I'll leave the disciplining of your Second Officer to you. However, it does seem a little strange to me that Captain Barkin's communication officer and yours, both withheld my prohibition order from their captains. It almost smacks of collusion. Since I have no proof of any wrong doing, I'm forced to accept both explanations. I'm telling you now, I wouldn't like to see a repeat of such a coincidence in the future. Zheng out.'

'I don't think he believed me,' Karl voiced after a moment of silence.

'What prompted you to do such a silly thing?' Praut asked.

'Just thought it would save an awkward situation,' answered Karl.

Praut went over and shook Karl by the hand. 'Karl, you are one rare human being, and I doubly welcome you aboard this Agency.'

Mes looked on, pleased at having such a loyal friend.

'Now, what was it the admiral said about Barkin coming up with the same excuse?' Praut now wore a semi puzzled expression. 'Karl get me Max. Make sure the comm is secure.'

'Hi Dil, what's up?' Barkin's voice seemed guarded.

'Max, you heard from the admiral?'

There was a moment of silence.

'Yeah, why?'

'You rogue, you came up with the same excuse Karl did, and it's made the admiral suspicious.'

Another moment of silence.

'What excuse is that?'

'Your comm officer took the blame for not passing on the *keep clear* order….and so did our Karl.'

There was loud guffawing over the comm link.

'Well bless me. Must be telepathy…put it down to all this comm work.' More loud guffawing was heard in the background.

'Well, it seems to have worked. But the admiral warned me not to repeat this type of thing.'

'Repeat? Never happened the first time, did it? Give my regards to Karl for his initiative,' Barking said, still chuckling. 'See you later. Out!'

Praut stood there, head cocked to one side, somewhat bemused by what had just occurred. 'Close call, heh?'

'Did they clear Pendlebury of its inhabitants,' asked Mes, still concerned for possible casualties.

'They had time enough,' Karl answered. 'Should have been just about through when the Rimmer lot arrived, if you count the hours they were here.'

'So the buildings were empty…the ones destroyed by that Rimmer ship?'

'Must've been. Don't let it worry you Mes, I don't think there was anyone in them.'

Mes gently nodded, 'Not really worried, just don't like to see the innocent suffer.'

Praut finally made a decision, 'Mes, get us out of here, back to Stretford. I've seen enough.'

'What about the lab you wanted to see?' Karl asked.

'Nah, that was just an excuse to watch Rimmer go down. We need to go back and have a meeting of all our people. We got to decide where we go from here. Zheng's Battle Group will go on to Fourex…do we tag along, or do we pull out and go home?'

'Shall I inform Max of what we're doing,' asked Karl.

'Good point. He'll need to be included in our meeting,' Praut agreed. 'Yes, tell him, and suggest he follows us back to the capital.'

# 29
# WORMHOLE COORDINATES

Back in Stretford, Praut's Agency meeting was a subdued affair. The gathering of some twenty six people was held in the Exec canteen on the top floor of Stretford's tower. Nominally, the Praut Agency had fulfilled its contract with Darhlburg and people should have been congratulated, and that should have been that. But Praut had his teeth into Rimmer and wanted to know who they were, where they came from, and what was behind their theft of the wormhole technology. More to the point, he wanted to know why three of his people had been killed.

Praut was backed by Barkin, who insisted he was going to continue the hunt with or without Praut. 'I have to get to the bottom of where this biochip business comes from…and to put an end to it once and for all. Those are my orders. They've attacked my home planet and I'm not going to let them off that easily. What if they come back in a few months time and it starts all over again? If we don't root them out from their base, they'll be a persistent menace and nobody will rest easy. My orders from Governor Catz is to destroy Stimmer. The least I can do is follow Zheng's Battle Group to Fourex.'

Praut listened politely and then put it to a vote. Helmut and his team, together with Mykola and his team, were for going home. Praut's team, egged on by Mes and Karl, insisted on going on with Praut and Barkin.

Praut made an attempt to justify his decision with, 'I really can't rest until I track down the people who built that missile that killed Edel and Til. Especially if it turns out they're not human, as seems to be likely from what Clay has turned up on Stretford's q-machines.'

'Dil, I'll go back and look after the Agency while you finish this thing,' offered Helmut. 'Me and Mykola will keep the Agency ticking over until you return.'

'Thanks Helmut. Sorry to load this on you. The sooner you get started, the sooner you'll be home.'

'We'll leave tonight.'

* * *

The next day, Stretford was getting back to some kind of semblance of normality. People were beginning to return to whatever they were doing before Rimmer came on the scene. Space Marines and fleet people were everywhere, helping the population to cope. A small minority of the population had been hospitalised on the *SSS Intrepid* because they couldn't cope without the biochip. Their neurotransmitter levels had been compromised causing a variety of psychological disorders. Those levels had to be stabilised by the neurology staff before they could be released. Both Pendlebury and Salford were clear of biochips, but each was some five hours behind in their transition to normality.

'You heard from the admiral?' Mes asked Praut while going over the control console of the *Faust* with an antistatic huffer.

'I put in a request to join the Battle Group on their journey to Fourex, but I've heard nothing so far.'

Rubin was still with them and listening in. He said, 'I'm only guessing, but the admiral is probably weighing up the pros and cons of letting you tag along.'

'Because I disobeyed his orders to stay clear of Pendlebury?'

'I should imagine,' shrugged Rubin.

Praut shook his head, 'Can't be helped…had to be there.'

'He'll end up thinking like Souza,' Mes said.

'What? That I'm a loose cannon?'

A slight nod of Mes' head.

'Where's Karl got to?'

'He's down in the basement checking on Clay.' Just then a ping announced the arrival of a message. 'Here it is Dil,' declared Mes. 'The admiral requests you go and see him at your earliest convenience.'

'Oh well, we'll soon know the worst. I'd hate to see Max go on alone without me.'

Rubin said, 'Oh the admiral will probably chew you out but he'll take you along in the end. I'm sure of it.'

'What about you, Adam?' Praut asked Rubin. 'What are you going to do? Go back to your lab here in the capital?'

'Well, as a matter of fact, I was hoping to tag along with you to Fourex…if you'll let me.'

Praut looked surprised. 'Your welcome to come along, but…why?'

Rubin looked relieved at the invitation. 'Aliens. It looks like you've actually rooted out some real aliens…and I'm overwhelmed with curiosity of what they look like, and all the rest. I've been speculating on aliens for a long time now, and here's a chance to get close to the real thing. Call it scientific curiosity. I'll try not to get in the way.'

* * *

A spaceferry from the *Baochuan* took Praut back to the supercarrier, now returned to orbit around Lowry with its companion ship the *Dolgoruky*. Half the Battle Group was sitting on the ground helping the people of Lowry get back to normal, while the other half of the Battle Group was in orbit on guard against further attacks.

The spaceferry docked with the *Baochuan* and Praut was surprised to see Commander Wesley at the airlock.

'Captain Praut, the admiral is waiting. Please come this way.'

Up a lift and down a series of corridors, they eventually arrived at a door guarded by two burly marines.

Wesley knocked on the door and heard, 'Come in.' The door parted sideways.

Zheng was sitting behind a desk, talking into his throat mike. He motioned both Wesley and Praut towards him and pointed at two chairs.

Wesley was surprised to be asked to stay, but sat down, as did Praut.

'Now, Mr Praut,' began Zheng, having concluded his throat mike business. 'I'm afraid you've lived up to Commissioner Souza's expectations with that Pendlebury stunt of yours,' said Zheng, a grim look on his face.

Praut sat impassive. No point in squirming at this point.

'I've received your request to join the Fourex expedition...but frankly, if you can't follow a simple order to stay away from a battle zone, then you would simply be putting yourself and my people at risk. There's a good reason why I gave that order…you must see that. When there's heavy laser and maser cannon fire in progress, the targets must be clear. Any confusion in a battle zone and people may hesitate…and that costs lives. I know all about your Second Officer taking the blame…and he's to be commended for his loyalty, but that little trick is as old as war itself.'

Praut sat and took it. He was beginning to get annoyed at the ticking off, but he'd do the same if the shoe was on the other foot.

'Now Mr Praut, if I agree to let you tag along with me, can I rely on you to follow my orders?' Zheng sat and waited for Praut's answer.

'Admiral, I feel like a school kid that's just been caught sending rude messages on my e-pad. I apologise for entering the restricted battle zone and assure you that in future, I will follow your orders to the letter.' Praut thought that should do it.

'Good, that's settled then,' Zheng said resolutely; then added, 'But let me make it clear, that should you go back on your word, I will have Commander Wesley here, escort your ship back to the Solar System in person.' Almost as an afterthought he added, 'Tomorrow, I'm holding a planning meeting on our Fourex action; you and Barkin are both invited. I'll let you know the time later. Thank you for your attention.'

Praut understood it to be a dismissal. Wesley stayed in his chair while Praut got up and went out through the slide door. He was both angry and ashamed after the dressing down he'd just received. The problem was, he deserved it, and he was aware of that single salient fact. Being his own boss for such a long time had made him reluctant to take orders from anybody. Once upon a time, as a serving senior police detective, he'd taken orders without hesitation. But now, he frankly didn't need to, but here was *the* situation where he wasn't in charge, and yes, there was a chain of command. With Pendlebury, he'd merely done what he'd always done…pleased himself. The result, he'd just experienced, and he didn't like it. He had two choices. He could abandon the expedition and return home in a huff, or he could swallow his pride and accept the chain of command. If Zheng gave an order…he would have to obey it to the letter no matter what he thought of the order. It was a simple choice—and he chose the latter. His curiosity won the day.

Back on the *Faust*, still parked at the northern end of Stretford's huge plaza, Praut was quiet, and most of his people guessed what had occurred. All he told them was, the next day there was to be a planning meeting for what was to happen on Fourex. Karl was to keep an eye out for a message from Zheng giving the time of the meeting. The *Faust* ought to be ready to depart the following day.

'By the way Dil,' Karl said, now back at his comm station, 'Clay thinks he's found a clue as to why this Rimmer was destroying wormhole technology.'

Praut's ears pricked up. 'Go on.'

'The info was in a file marked *Ultra Secret*, *Umber eyes only*, whoever Umber is. It was squirrelled away on a data cube hidden in the Governor's office at the top of the tower. There was a compartment in the wall camouflaged by a holo image hiding the screened off area. It was found by Sinclair's boys in their detailed search of the office. They showed it to me, and I gave it to Clay to decipher. He had a hard time decrypting the code. He's never seen anything like it…the code I mean. Clay says it must be alien origin. Anyway, the cube had special 3D galactic coordinates on the outer reaches of the Fourex Solar System. Clay reckons they're wormhole coordinates. He's suggesting they're jump off and arrival coordinates in our galaxy for somewhere outside our galaxy.'

'Who've you told so far?' Praut wanted to know.

'Nobody. I've only just heard from Clay,' said Karl.

'Tell Clay to keep it under his hat,' Praut told him, 'and that goes for you and Mes. I'll inform the admiral of this at the meeting. Where's Fanny and Olga?'

'I think Olga's in her cabin,' said Karl. 'She's fiddling with one of her sniffers. Fanny's in the tower somewhere. Why?'

'Get in touch with Fanny, ask her to come back. I've a job for her.'

'I'll do that right now.' Karl began talking into his throat mike.

'Mes, get Clay to finish up down in the basement. Anything of interest, tell Clay to pop it on a data cube and bring it with him. We're taking off in an hour or so. I'm taking the *Faust* up into orbit near to the *Baochuan.*'

'Max? Max, you there?' Praut was speaking into his throat mike.

'Yes Dil. What's up?' came the reply.

'Can you come over? I need an urgent word with you. We've found something.'

Barkin and Praut were seated in Praut's cabin on the *Faust*.

'Clay thinks he's found some alien wormhole galactic coordinates near the Fourex planet. Keep this under your hat, but if it turns out to be true, it would give a nasty explanation to all that's been happening recently. My wormhole thefts, the alien technology and the biochips. All of it makes a lot more sense if aliens are using wormholes to jump in and out of our galaxy.'

Barkin was suddenly alert and very attentive. 'But why thieve your wormhole stuff in the first place? Don't get that.' Barkin answered.

'Don't you see Max, our wormholes don't work properly *yet,* so if they can prevent our scientists from perfecting them, we can't possibly follow the aliens back to where they come from. They're covering their backs, so to speak.'

'Sorry Dil. I was being a bit dense.'

'They can come and go as they please, but if anything goes wrong, all they have to do is jump out of our galaxy, and we can't follow. That way we don't know who they are or where they came from.'

'So what are you going to do?'

'I've put Fanny on to it. She's to get in touch with Helmut, who's on his way back to Earth on the *Humboldt.* I want him to chase up the two groups working on stabilising the wormhole technology. Helmut's still in comm range and Fanny is in touch with him as we speak.'

‘Wasn’t your Agency working for one of those groups?’

‘Yeah, Van Rag Yang at Darhlburg Industries. We’ve sent his stolen blueprint back to him. Now Helmut is to try and hurry him up. Him and Randoline Walcott at Singularity Inc. We need them to put in some overtime and get the finished product ready real soon. I think Walcott might be almost there, at least that’s what she told me. I’m going to try and get the admiral to push her a little bit. I’ve a sneaky suspicion we’ll need it for Fourex.’

* * *

The next day before the main planning meeting, Praut sat opposite the admiral, explaining Clay’s latest discovery on Stretford’s q-machines.

‘Admiral, what my computer expert has uncovered are 3D galactic coordinates on the outer reaches of the Fourex Solar System. They were heavily encrypted but he’s broken the cipher, and it would indicate that it allows these aliens to jump in and out of our galaxy at will. They can come and go as they please, and if anything goes wrong, all they have to do is jump out of our galaxy, and we can’t follow. That’s because we haven’t got a functioning wormhole at the moment.’

The admiral sat and listened attentively showing no sign of emotion whatsoever. He was likely an excellent poker player.

‘From my information, Randoline Walcott at Singularity Inc. is the most likeliest to stabilise our wormhole, and she’s close to doing so. I would urge you to encourage WorldGov to give her a hand.’

‘Well Mr Praut, you are full of surprises. One moment you nearly wreck one of my battles, yet the next, you’re providing without doubt, the most crucial know how on our enemy to date. I have to ask you. How reliable is this info?’

'I would stake my life on the facts provided by my computer expert. Actually, in the past, I've done just that.'

'Now let me tell you what we've been up to. Our people back in WGS have already extrapolated that wormhole technology is crucial to what we're doing here. A couple of days ago before we set off for Lowry, I advised WorldGov to make it a priority that the two outfits, on Mars and Callisto, be given full Government backing and financing. I've been informed that Singularity Inc. is almost ready to test its stabilised wormhole. The little push WorldGov gave them was all that was needed. I'm hoping that once when we're positioned round Fourex, we may have a working wormhole, despite all the attempts to sabotage the enterprise.'

It was Praut's turn to look surprised by this turn of events.

'Don't look so shocked Mr Praut. WorldGov has been hard at work on all the info its gathered. Computer simulations have shown that the wormhole was crucial to the outcome of this business. The rest you will hear in the meeting that's just about to take place.' The admiral rose and stepped towards the sliding door, which parted, into the next room.

Praut followed the admiral into the large salon, where a number of senior fleet officers were gathered. Commissioner Souza sat at the head table, looking self important. Souza motioned Praut towards him. 'Mr Praut, I've nominated Dr Rubin to be appointed interim Governor of Lowry. What do you think? Is that a good idea.'

'Commissioner, that is an excellent choice. I commend you for your wisdom.' Praut then went and sat in the front row in between Rubin and Barkin in a large salon on the *Baochuan.* The admiral took the rostrum and Souza brought the meeting to order by using his mallet.

'Gentleman,' the admiral began after clearing his throat, 'I've just had some interesting new information from the Praut Agency…and I must commend Mr Praut and his people for this crucial intelligence. First, I will announce that yesterday I sent for reinforcements. The First and Third Battle Groups should arrive in two days time. I'm proposing to wait for their arrival. It has now been fully confirmed that we are in fact dealing with aliens hostile to the human race. From what we've discovered on this expedition, I cannot call missile attacks, biochips, and that astonishing lab we uncovered near Pendlebury, as being in any way friendly to us. Again, I have Mr Praut to thank for the lab's location.

'My forensic people have been sifting through the lab's debris and the overall picture they've put together is so outrageous towards humans, that I'm intending to bring the full might of Earth's resources against these aliens. Hence the reinforcements. Our action against this enemy must succeed. The future of the human race depends on it. After millions of years of evolution, the human race cannot end up as slaves to these aliens. As we speak, the Solar System back home, is being mobilised to support our enterprise. A Fourth Battle Group is being put together as a matter of priority. We must prevail.

'Now for the new intel Mr Praut has provided. It would seem that the aliens are jumping in and out of our galaxy via wormholes. We don't know yet from where. Mr Praut has provided me with 3D galactic wormhole coordinates on the outer reaches of the Fourex Solar System. I'm proposing that when we move in on Fourex, that Admiral Formby's Third Battle Group, with the *SSS Liaoning* in the lead, establishes a firewall perimeter round those coordinates and ensures that nothing comes in or leaves via that remote wormhole mouth.

'The First and Second Battle Groups will encircle Fourex and we'll try to do what we did on Lowry. The worst case scenario is, we aren't going to be allowed to de-chip the population and we'll end up in an almighty battle. I fear this scenario. Because this is the last base the aliens have in our galaxy, they'll fight tooth and nail to hold on to it. The detailed tactics will be worked out by each Battle Group commander. Nominally, the *Baochuan* will be the flag ship of the whole fleet. Any questions.'

That their ship was to be the flag ship went down well with all the assembled officers. The information that they were embarked on a historic battle which they had to win at all cost, went down less favourably. The responsibility made the officers nervous.

Barkin raised his hand. 'Admiral, aren't remote wormhole coordinates usually mobile?'

'Good point Captain Barkin. At this point in time, I'm assuming they are fixed. Why? You have to ask the question, why put galactic coordinates into the computer at all if they're mobile and the mouth changes with every jump? Why secrete them in such heavy encryption? For reasons I cannot yet fathom, bearing in mind all the above, I'm pressed to assume the coordinates are fixed. Clearly it would be foolish not to be on the lookout for other remote wormhole arrival points, and that will be part of the details to be worked out by Admiral Formby. We'll know more when our own wormhole experts arrive. Any other questions?'

Barkin again, 'Any idea when that's gonna be sir?'

'Only a rough estimate. Likely to be a week from now,' Zheng told him. 'Now if there's no more questions, I'll ask Commissioner Souza to adjourn this meeting. One last announcement before you go; I'd like to thank the Praut Agency and Mr Praut for the invaluable intel he's provided to date. I'm sure that WorldGov will see fit to reward him when this is all over. Thank you.'

# 30
# SSS LAZAREV TRAGEDY

The Second Battle Group was parked in orbit round Lowry waiting for the other two Battle Groups to arrive. Lowry was being left to get back on to its own two feet, albeit with a lot of fleet support personnel still helping them. Getting a planet back to how it was before its people were turned into robots, was proving more difficult than expected.

The day following the planning meeting was a drag, and the waiting was getting on people's nerves.

'You've got a gemail,' Karl informed Praut as the Agency boss stood looking at a holographic image of the Fourex planetary system. He noted Fourex was the fourth planet of a seven planet Solar System with a hot sun.

'Who from,' Praut asked absentmindedly, still staring at the Fourex image hanging in the air.

'Its signed Randoline.'

'What's it say?' The signature got Praut's attention.

'Just one word...*Thanks*.'

'What? That's it? *Thanks*.' Praut stood there on the bridge, in a thoughtful mood. He understood the message and assumed this one word was for all the help she was now getting from WorldGov.

'Right Karl, send her a one word reply.'

'And the word is?' Karl's eyes narrowed.

'*When*?' Praut told him.

'That it? Just *when*?'

Praut pointed his finger at Karl, 'Careful mien Herr, you're in danger of getting your nose dirty.'

'You mean I'm sticking it in where its not wanted, heh?'

'You've read that right. So I'm going to leave you guessing.'

'That's a bit unfair.'

'Unfair! Unfair! When you were born, did you hear anybody say life's going to be fair? No! Then assume its isn't.'

'You're a hard task master *boss*,' said Karl, screwing up his face in mock resignation.

Just then Fanny entered the bridge. 'Dil, a little update on my progress with the wormhole companies.'

'Shoot.'

'Darhlburg is being non-committal. Won't say where they are in their development, or when they'll be ready.'

Praut scowled, 'They're stalling. Probably means we can't expect anything from them. What about Singularity?'

'Much more promising. They won't give a date but the PA to the CEO says they're almost ready to show. One more test and they hope to be able to demonstrate a live jump.'

'That's more like it. Thanks Fanny…good job. Put a short message together to that effect and send it to the admiral.'

'Will do.'

'Olga still fiddling with her sniffers?'

'I think so,' said Fanny.

'And Clay? He still trying to untangle the stuff he downloaded from the q-machine?'

'He's been at it all night,' Karl told Praut. 'A lot of it's encrypted.'

'What time are we expecting the other two Battle Groups tomorrow?' Praut asked Mes. 'Any idea?'

'Late in the day, as far as I can make out,' Karl intervened. 'I had a comm chat with the *Baochuan*, and the guy I was talking to suggested it was likely to be sometime late in the afternoon.'

Over the tannoy came a loud e-ping, and then, '*Alert*, *alert*, this is Vice Admiral Bennett on the *Dolgoruky,* there's an unidentified spaceship attempting to leave the planet's atmosphere. The nearest Destroyers are ordered to intercept and detain. This is a priority order. Acknowledge.'

'Listen to that! How come they missed that one?' Praut wanted to know.

'Must've been hiding somewhere deep,' Mes speculated. 'Probably at the bottom of the ocean.'

'Sneaky blighter,' mouthed Karl.

'Can we go after it?' Mes asked Praut.

'Better not. I gave my word to the admiral we'd behave,' Praut told her.

'Ah, to hell. All this waiting and now we can't even have some fun,' she bemoaned. She was bored hanging around doing nothing.

'We'd only get in the way,' Praut tried to calm her. 'And if they loose the rogue ship, they'd only blame us.'

Mes looked disappointed, but then bucked up and said, 'Game of chess?' she offered Karl.

'Set the board up then,' he answered.

A holographic image of the spatial Raumschach 3D five tier board appeared between the two players, with all the pieces in their places.

'You were white the last time, so I'll start this time,' Karl insisted.

'Karl, while your playing your game, keep an eye out on the comms for any progress in that Rimmer ship chase,' Praut asked.

'Will do boss,' came the response.

'Rubin still in his cabin?' Praut asked Fanny, who was just about to leave the bridge.

'As far as I know,' she replied.

Praut followed Fanny off the bridge. Fanny trudged off to her quarters and Praut knocked on Rubin's door.

'Come,' came from inside.

Praut slid the door open. 'Hi Adam. Give any more thought to Souza's offer?'

'I can't see myself as a Governor somehow. I'm a lab rat. Always have been. I thrive in a lab, but admin work would just bore and frustrate me. I told Souza I'd think about it, but to tell the truth, I've already decided to turn it down. I still want to join you on the Fourex expedition. I couldn't if I were made Governor. I know it sounds selfish of me, but I'm no good at this admin stuff. They'll find someone else.' Rubin sat half dejected, torn between the kudos of the offer and his distaste for admin work.

'Well, if that's your decision, then I'll support it. As I said before, you're welcome to join us to Fourex. So what are you doing now?'

'Dil, I'm trying to get an idea of what to expect when we come across these aliens. I'm analysing all the data Clay has come up with. It's proving to be difficult. We have so little to go on.'

'It would be nice if we had a holo image to go on, but from their attitude to the human race to date, frankly I don't care what they look like. I'm happy to fry them as they are...whatever their shape or makeup. I've lost three people to them. Barkin has lost a lot more. Lowry's in a mess thanks to them, and I'd hate to think of what they've done to Fourex. Then there's the three and a half thousand killed on Callisto. I'm with Zheng…go in with maximum force and wipe them out, before they do that to us.'

'Still, it's a pity it's come to this,' said Rubin.

'Pity or no pity, this is the reality of the situation. Go with what we have.'

'Yes, you're right. They have been belligerent towards us. We do need to do everything we can to survive.

In the final analysis, its what drives us humans...curiosity and survival.'

'Over Praut's earphone came, 'Dil, can you hear me?'

'That you Karl?' he answered.

'Dil, you'll want to hear this. The airwaves have gone haywire. The comm chatter suggests trouble.'

'Excuse me Adam, Karl is calling me to the bridge,' and Praut hurried out of the cabin.

'Ah, Dil, listen to this,' Karl switched the comm traffic to the tannoy system as Praut came onto the bridge.

From the tannoy came a voice, 'Stand down *Lazarev*, you're getting too close. Let the *Richelieu* take the lead. Captain Sinclair, did you hear me?'

Clay appeared on the bridge just ahead of Fanny and Olga. The noise of the tannoy had drawn them out of their quarters.

Another voice intervened, 'Captain Sinclair, this is Vice Admiral Bennett, I order you to veer off. Let the destroyer *Richelieu* take on the enemy.'

Another voice took over, 'What is the man doing? The enemy is likely to…..'

There came a lot of crackling over the tannoy, then what seemed a loud burst of noise.

'That's an explosion,' Karl informed Praut. 'Something's gone up. I'd recognise that anywhere.'

Again a voice over the tannoy, 'Oh no! I told him not to get too close, didn't I? What was he thinking of? Is the *Richelieu* okay?'

Another voice took over, 'Damn the man.' It sounded like Vice Admiral Bennett. 'Both gone you say?' He must've been talking to one of his officers on the *Dolgoruky*.

Then the tannoy system went quiet.

'What's your guess as to what's just happened?' Praut asked Karl.

Karl looked at Mes, and she shook her head. 'From my reading of what I've just heard,' Karl took a deep breath, 'the *Lazarev's* just blown up. No idea why Sinclair did what he did. Must've had his reasons. Maybe the Rimmer ship aimed itself at him? Maybe he was trying to save another ship…this *Richelieu?* Anyway, the Rimmer ship and the *Lazarev* have both exploded. That's my assumption.'

'You mean Sinclair's gone?' Praut found it hard to grasp. 'But the *Lazarev* was a battle cruiser. How could a Rimmer ship take out a battle cruiser?'

Mes said softly, 'Bennett was trying to warn him not to get too close. He must've guessed what that Rimmer had in mind.'

Praut's people became quiet for a moment on the bridge of the *Faust*. Each person trying to remember Captain Sinclair in their own way. They'd travelled together from Barnaby and knew him to be a quiet efficient officer. Polite but firm.

'These so-called aliens are piling up our hate onto themselves!' Praut merely voiced what the whole crew felt.

After this tragic incident, those not on duty, returned to their cabins in a subdued mood. Nobody felt like saying or doing anything. The rest of the afternoon disappeared while Karl listened to the comm traffic regarding Sinclair. A careful search and watch ensued for any other Rimmer remnants.

* * *

The next day, Mes informed Praut, as he arrived onto the bridge, that they'd all been invited to a memorial service for the *Lazarev* and its crew. It was to be held in a couple of hours on the *Baochuan.* Everyone put on their mourning finery for the sad occasion. Praut wore his white captain's uniform. Mes and Karl their first and second officer whites. Fanny and Olga wore black as did Clay and Rubin.

As they materialised on the *Baochuan*, the *Faust* crew were met by Commander Wesley. 'Captain Praut, Vice Admiral Bennett would like a quick word with you before the service begins.'

Praut was surprised, but followed Wesley to a small room off the main corridor.

'Captain Praut,' began Bennett in a hushed tone. 'I wonder if I might ask you to say a few words at the service. I'm told that Captain Sinclair had a high regard for you, as did his crew.'

That was another revelation to Praut. Sinclair was always correct with him, but they hadn't spent much time together. He really didn't know him that well. What could he say. 'Only a few words?' Praut asked.

'Yes, just a short oration. It seems that Sinclair had the opinion that as he was in uniform, he had to be here, but you as a civilian had a choice…and you chose to be here. That's what he admired.'

'Well, that's not quite right is it?' Praut protested. 'I have a job to do. I have a contract to be here, civilian or no civilian. I'm just as obligated as he was. Yes I could walk away, but that would have ruined my reputation.'

'We're well aware of your contract with Darhlburg, Mr Praut.'

That was another bombshell. What the hell? Did they have him bugged?

'Don't look so shocked Mr Praut. WGS would be a poor sort of agency if it didn't know in detail what you were up to. When you wondered off to Barnaby following your sniffer, WGS was fully aware of what you were doing. It was in their interest to allow you to pursue that lead…doing a little poking around, almost on their behalf.'

'You make it sound as if I were working for them,' Praut objected.

'Don't get offended; we're all on the same side, that's what I'm trying to say to you. Often you can go places and do things, where WGS would be forced to hang back. But they did have continuous reports regarding your doings. In the end it was the reports of what was happening to you that gave them the impetus to act. Its why we're here at all. Anyway, can I rely on you for the oration?'

'Well…if you think it appropriate, I'd feel privileged.' Praut decided that Bennett was right; they were on the same side.

'Thank you. Now, shall we go and join the others?'

In the huge missile room of the *Baochuan*, a large number of fleet officers were gathered. Praut and his crew stood to the left of the front line, next to Barkin and some of his cleaned up ruffians, who were outfitted in spanking new sky-blue uniforms. At the front stood WorldGov Foreign Affairs Commissioner Souza with Admiral Zheng, the Commander of the Second Battle Group, with his second in command, Vice Admiral Bennett, at his side. All three looked very solemn. The service was led by the Chief Moral Guardian of the Battle Group, who stood by the outsized missile shaped ceremonial wreath, ready to slide it into the external firing chute.

'We are gathered here today on this sad occasion,' intoned the Chief Moral Guardian, 'to remember the lives lost yesterday on the battle cruiser *SSS Lazarev*. I will hand over to Admiral Zheng who would like to say a few words in their memory.'

Zheng gently cleared his throat and began, 'Captain Sinclair and his crew sacrificed their lives to save the crew of the destroyer *SSS Richelieu*, which was about to be rammed by the enemy ship. In doing so, they gave their own lives in the best tradition of the Space Fleet. May his memory live a long time.' Zheng then gave way to Vice Admiral Bennett to say a few words.

Bennett spoke for a short time, recounting Sinclair's Space Fleet record and his many decorations. Then it was Praut's turn.

Praut looked serious, and began slowly, 'I was more of an acquaintance of Captain Sinclair, than his close friend. We travelled from Barnaby together and I found him to be a fair and just officer…always looking out for the interests of the Space Fleet. I wish I had known him better…but it was still a privilege to have known him at all. I'm truly sad that he is no longer with us. I would, however, like to straighten out one inaccuracy.

'The other day at a meeting, Admiral Zheng gave me and my Agency the cachet of having discovered the galactic coordinates of the enemy's wormhole. That is not quite correct; it was Captain Sinclair who uncovered the hiding place of the data cube containing the coordinates when he scrupulously searched the offices of the pseudo Governor running Lowry for the Rimmer lot. I'm simply giving credit where credit is due. It's only through Captain Sinclair's diligence that we have those coordinates. All my people did was decipher the data cube.' Praut noted that a flicker of amazed pride hovered over Vice Admiral Bennett's face but there was no change on poker faced Admiral Zheng's face. Commissioner Souza seemed to smile ever so slightly at Praut's acknowledgement of Sinclair's credit for discovering the wormhole coordinates.

Praut stood back and the Chief Moral Guardian came forward to stand by the long wreath. He nodded, and the wreath was loaded into a missile tube, followed by a *whoosh*, which shot the wreath out into deep space. The service ended there.

At the reception following the service, as Praut and his crew passed Souza, the commissioner held him back by tapping his elbow. 'That was a kind thing you did for Captain Sinclair…giving him the credit for those wormhole figures. On behalf of WorldGov, I thank you, and commend you for your action. You do keep surprising me with your unpredictable behaviour.'

‘Why thank you Commissioner,’ Praut replied, tongue in cheek. ‘I shall do my utmost to continue to surprise you in the future.’

Souza raised his eyebrows and allowed Praut to carry on trying to catch up with his people, who’d continued to head for Barkin and his crew on the other side of the room.

# 31
# REINFORCEMENTS

Back on the *Faust,* following the simple service for Captain Sinclair, people were pensively waiting the whole afternoon for the arrival of the two Battle Groups. They were due any moment and would triple the number of spaceships parked around Lowry. Then the real work would begin. The expectancy was causing a ripple of excitement in every ship in orbit round Lowry.

Praut had ensconced himself in Rubin's cabin and was whiling away the hours in discussion with him. Praut was trying to explain a disturbing thought which occurred to him: 'When I was talking of Sinclair at the service earlier, it suddenly struck me…what the hell was I doing here on the other side of the galaxy? This whole thing began with a simple ordinary contract to retrieve a wormhole blueprint—and now look at it—all of Earth's fleets are involved. There's aliens implicated, and the future of the whole of the human race is at stake. How the hell did it get so big?'

'You're making a classical mistake Dil. You're only looking at it from your own subjective,' offered Rubin. 'With or with out you, the aliens were on Fourex, Lowry, and Barnaby…and spreading. You and your people got sucked into this…it didn't grow from your involvement.'

'Trust a bloody scientist to bring objectivity into my simple introspection,' smiled Praut. 'But I suppose you're right. I'm really just an onlooker. However, you'll agree…the thing is big; probably the biggest thing me and my agency have ever been involved in. It's almost scary, if it wasn't for the massive forces about to gather here today.'

'I almost feel sorry for those poor aliens,' Rubin said moodily.

'*What*? How do you do that Adam? How do you manage to compartmentalise your mind in such a bizarre manner? Sorry for a life form that has no respect for other life forms? That kills and enslaves humans? That's tried to enslave you and turn you into a robot? You can't be serious?' Praut just couldn't understand Rubin's thinking.

'Dil, try to understand,' Rubin made an attempt to explain. 'For a long time, for hundreds of years, ever since mankind went into space, we've sought out aliens. Sought out other life forms to show we weren't the only intelligent life form in this galaxy. The more thoughtful people even assumed that prior to a warp drive, the Solar System might be in quarantine by the more intelligent aliens who didn't want such a raw and destructive life form as humans amongst them until we'd calmed down. Now we've found this alien…and it turns out to be profoundly antagonistic to our own kind. It's just such a huge disappointment. Can you understand that?'

'Put like that, yes I can. But that doesn't change how I feel towards these aliens,' Praut said in a tone filled with disgust. 'I've lost three good people to this life form…and I want my revenge. Now, can *you* understand *that*?'

Rubin shrugged in resignation. 'Yes Dil, I can understand that. And if the forces gathering here today are anything to go by, you'll have your revenge quite soon.'

They'd been bantering back and forth like that for some time and it was getting late.

'*Dil*,' suddenly came through Praut's earphone. 'Dil, can you hear me…its Karl. The two Battle Groups have just come out of hyperspace. Come and have a look. Its mind boggling…the number of ships out there.'

'Adam, the reinforcements have arrived. You coming?' Praut got up and was already through the sliding door.

Rubin was hard on his heals.

'Well?' Praut asked Karl as he entered the bridge.

'Come and see for yourself on the external screen. It's a magnificent sight.'

Praut walked casually to Karl's station and looked at the external viewing screen. 'Do you know who's out there…I mean the details,' Praut asked in a subdued tone.

'Any combat pilot can reel off the numbers in their sleep. Admiral Murat's First Battle Group with the supercarrier *SSS Bolivar* as the flagship, and seventy one of the finest ships ever built. Mes, care to do the rest?'

'Sure,' she answered blithely. 'Admiral Formby's Third Battle Group with the supercarrier *SSS Liaoning* as the flagship and fifty four ships. Making a total of a hundred and twenty five ships just arrived.'

'And with Zheng's ships,' Karl took over again, 'that makes a hundred and eighty eight ship all together.' Then Karl stopped himself. 'Sorry, a hundred and eighty seven. We lost one yesterday. Still, Rimmer and the aliens…say your prayers.'

'You should already know by now, *the* cardinal rule of combat,' Praut pointed a finger at Karl.

Karl stared back puzzled, 'And what's that?'

'Never underestimate your enemy…I'm sure you've heard that before.'

'What? You think the aliens can match our firepower?' Karl said incredulously.

'I think Dil is right,' Mes intervened. 'If we want to win, we'll need to go with caution, especially considering what's at stake.'

Karl's enthusiasm crumbled. 'Ah come on,' he said defensively. 'A hundred and eighty seven spaceships for goodness sake. They can't match that surely?'

'All I'm saying is, we must win this battle or we're done for as a race. So let's make sure.' Praut was being serious. 'Go in with maximum force, I agree, but be prepared for the most ferocious fight we humans have ever been in. Take note of their technology Karl. The funny missiles we came across with the strange crystals…that personal force-field suit Barkin lifted from them. The difficulty you had knocking the Rimmer ships out of the sky over Barnaby. It all suggests a technically advanced race. We underestimate them at our peril.'

Karl stopped and was looking at Praut, almost as if he were seeing him for the first time. 'You know, I'm a fool. You're right of course. I just got carried away looking at all those ships out there. What you're saying is just good sense. I'll keep it in mind. Thanks for reminding me.'

'What are friends for,' shrugged Praut.

Rubin soon lost interest and went back to his cabin.

Fanny and Clay had come onto the bridge in the middle of the discussion, and now Fanny said to Praut, 'Hang on Dil. What if the aliens simply back off and disappear? What if when we get to Fourex, all we find is a planet full of chipped people…but no aliens?'

'Then that would be the worst scenario I can imagine. It would mean a constant threat hanging over the heads of all mankind. We have to finish with this, or we're in big trouble. We can't have a hostile alien threat simply going on forever. At the moment we have their galactic wormhole arrival coordinates, but if that becomes useless, then they could pop up anywhere in our galaxy. This time they did a furtive attack at the rim of our galaxy, but the next time it could be near our Solar System. If the biochip is introduced the way Adam suspects it is, then what's to stop a bottom to top creep along the chain of command, say in WorldGov, right to the top. That would be a catastrophe for humans. No, we need to use the advantage we have at the moment to finish this once and for all. I don't care how we stop them; talking or wiping them out, but stop them we must. But Fanny, now you can see why I value your presence so much.

No one else brought up this last scenario…of them vanishing.'

That last compliment from Praut tickled Fanny's self-respect. She arched her neck and her red coiffure went up a notch.

Clay relieved Karl from the comm station and began his usual fiddling with the receiver screen, trying to hack into and overhear the privileged info he was not supposed to hear. His hands sped across the touch screen until he found something. 'Dil…Dil…eh, just getting something over the earphones, the admirals are setting up a planning meeting for tomorrow morning.'

'Yeah right, okay,' Praut was half listening.

'Do you want me to keep you up to date?' Clay asked.

'Yeah, okay,' Praut said half heartedly, deep in his own thoughts.

'Penny for them,' Fanny said to Praut.

'Eh? Oh, sorry, I was just thinking over what you said,' Praut replied.

'What? About the aliens disappearing?'

'Yes…and what we could do to stop it if that happened. Frankly I can't see a solution. It's a nightmare scenario; a classic gorilla warfare scenario. The enemy appearing, doing some damage, and then disappearing.' Praut was still scratching his chin in thought.

'There must be a solution to such a conundrum,' suggested Fanny.

'We'd have to find a way of working out the wormhole origin from their current wormhole exit coordinates. It's something for Walcott to work out…it's way beyond my poor brain.'

'You mean the Singularity people?'

'Yes. She's the expert on wormholes. If we found the origin of the alien home world…that would be the end of their game. Anyway, its getting late and we should turn in.'

Praut shouted to Mes, 'Mes, I'll take over in the pilot's chair, you get some sleep. Karl knows when to spell me?'

'He does. I reminded him before he left. Goodnight boss.' Mes yawned and headed for her cabin.

Fanny disappeared, leaving Praut and Clay the only ones on the bridge, with Clay on the comm station.

* * *

It was late morning before everyone was awake at the same time. The ship's three watch system was strictly enforced by Praut, as was usual on all ships. Mes was ensconced in her pilot's seat and Olga was on the comm station. Praut and the others were having a late breakfast in the lounge-come-dining room.

Praut looked around the large comfortable room and thought that at last he had a *Faust* worthy of his Agency. Catz had insisted he take full legal possession of the spaceship, to the point that he'd handed Praut the registration papers himself. Catz had presented Praut with the ship's log book bound in real reindeer hide leather. Armaments had been upgraded and the engines modified to give maximum warp speed. Catz had even installed a small q-machine borrowed from Zheng's Battle Group. That's what Catz thought Praut had been worth to him in the battle for Barnaby.

True, the WGS was already taking an interest in Laudo and his thugs, but it wasn't until Praut asked for a Commission to be sent, that WGS had woken up. Laudo's invasion of the nightclub meeting was the last straw and the two WGS officers pushed hard for the Commission to be sent. But if Zheng were to be believed, then WGS and WorldGov had been monitoring Barnaby closely and Praut's Commission request was the final impetus to send in Souza and the troops. No matter how it had come about, the latest *Faust* was a vast improvement on the old *Faust*.

Praut sat at the head of the table with his introspections and watched his people stuff themselves with their favourite breakfast food from the ship's replicator. Rubin sat to his left, and was thoughtfully toying with his food.

'Are we going to the admiral's meeting?' inquired Clay, who was sitting to Praut's right.

'Heh? What?' Praut came out of his revelry. 'No Clay. We've not been invited. Its purely a military meeting. No civilians.'

'Oh!' Clay looked disappointed. 'Do you want me to hack into the room's cameras?'

'No, definitely not. If they catch you we'll be barred from going to Fourex, period. You're to leave the hacking alone for the moment…you hear me?'

'Yeah, I hear you,' Clay mumbled. He wanted something to do and was getting bored.

Rubin smiled at Clay's antics and leaned closer to Praut. 'Find something for him to do,' he whispered into Praut's left ear.

Praut thought for a moment, then said, 'Clay, I want you to go away and draw me an alien.'

'Huh? Aw…you're pulling my leg.' Clay couldn't believe what was being asked of him.

'No, I mean it,' Praut said as seriously as he could. 'Try to remember all the stuff you've pulled off the q-machine about aliens…then from all that, make me a guess drawing, a drawing of what you think the alien might look like. Can you do that for me? It might help us if we ever have to meet one.'

Clay saw that his boss was being sincere. 'Well, if you think it'll help…sure I can try to stick something together. It'll only be a speculation though.'

'It's all I want. I'm going to ask everyone to do the same. Then we'll have a vote as to who's image is the most realistic, and they get a surprise prize.'

Everyone at the table was suddenly listening.

'Yes, I'm being quite serious,' Praut said to all those present. 'You heard what I just said to Clay…that goes for all of you, including you, Adam, and the two people standing watch right now.'

Rubin chuckled out loud. 'Well, why not. Get everyone at it.'

'By the way,' Praut told them, 'I'm gonna have a go as well…so you'll have some competition. I want you to try and produce the best possible image you can manage. Let your imagination rip. The only qualifier I insist on is…it must be your own original work. No copying. Oh, and I'll want to know the reason why you drew it as you did. So work out a reasoning for the drawing. You know, gravity, atmosphere, evolution, and so on…and don't forget, this alien is intelligent and scientifically advanced.'

Praut got up and went to tell Mes and Olga what he'd arranged. He came back and found Fanny, Karl, Clay and Adam all looking at each other, trying to size up who would be the most difficult competition. Inevitably all eyes ended up on Rubin.

'There now, you've started something that's going to be hard to stop,' Rubin told Praut.

'It'll keep people busy until we move off to Fourex.'

'Dil,' came over his earphones from Olga. 'Dil, I've just had a message from the flagship. They want us to be ready to move off. Do I acknowledge?'

'I'm coming.' Praut hurried out onto the bridge. 'Anything more?'

'It seems we're to follow Earth's fleet to within one parsec of Fourex,' Mes told him.

'One parsec would put us within easy reach of Fourex,' Praut said dubiously.

'It's still 3.26 light-years away from our destination,' Olga informed him.

'With current technology, I've a feeling it's a little close for comfort,' answered Praut.

'You're not serious?' asked Olga.

'We're dealing with an unknown enemy,' Praut reminded her. 'A technically advanced enemy at that. I'd of preferred a kiloparsec as a distance…more at arms length.'

'Well, we'll soon see who's right…the admirals or you,' muttered Mes.

'It'll take us the best part of a day and a half to get within a parsec of that planet,' Praut told them. 'Plenty of time to do some drawings. Anyway, acknowledge that we're ready to move,' he said to Olga.

'You still gonna ask people to do those alien drawings?' Olga asked in surprise.

'Of course! I want to see what we come up with… especially Adam. I want us to get familiar with the concept of aliens…to the point of contempt. We will probably have to kill them. So…get to know your enemy.'

'Dil, I can assure you,' Mes said with some venom, 'I don't *need* to get to know this enemy to kill them. I thought I'd proved that over Barnaby.'

'You mean in the flying sub?' Praut remembered. 'Well, yes you're right…but you and Karl are the exception.'

'More coming in from the flagship,' Olga told him. 'We're to be ready for warp within half an hour.'

'Are we ready?' he asked Mes.

'We're ready,' she replied.

'Good. Let's get everybody in their places then.'

'Attention everybody,' Mes put over the ship's tannoy system. 'Warp in half an hour. All personnel to their stations.'

All seven crew members filled the bridge. Clay relieved Olga from the comm station and began doing something on his e-pad. The others settled into their acceleration seats and waited for the countdown. The half hour passed quickly for some, like the pilots, who were busy inputting the one parsec galactic exit coordinates into the navcomp. Time went slowly for others, like Olga and Fanny, who sat and waited for the ship to make a move. They waited and waited, but no order to warp came from the flagship.

'Dil,' Mes tried to get Praut's attention, 'Clay's hacked into the inter-flagship comm traffic. I'm hearing something about the fleet being scanned by three unknown spaceships just at the limit of our sensor range.'

'Can you put it on the speakers?' asked Praut.

From the speakers came a commanding tone: 'I want five destroyers to check the hostiles out. Scramble the Falcon Squadrons.' It sounded like Admiral Zheng's voice.

'Yes sir. I'm sending the message to Admiral Formby right now. The hostiles are on his outer edge. Falcons scrambled sir.' Sounded like one of Zheng's officers complying.

'Hold the warp order till we see what Formby reports.' Zheng again.

'Yes sir.'

Over the next half hour, there followed a lot of mundane comm traffic from the Group's speakers. The comms were reporting Falcon fighters probing the hostiles.

Then came, '*What? Again?* How did that happen? Did we get the culprits? *No!* What do you mean ***no***? I want a full report on what happened. Better still, ask Admiral Formby I'd like to see him on my flagship…right away.' Zheng's voice was edgy with anger. 'We lost a destroyer and they got away? Is that what you're telling me?'

'That's what it looks like sir.' One of Zheng's officers reported edgily.

'Switch that off,' ordered Praut. The speakers went dead. 'Mes, did I hear that right? Did we just loose another destroyer to that Rimmer lot?'

'That's what it sounded like Dil,' she told him.

‘Why are we still here? Why hasn’t Zheng ordered a pursuit?’

‘He wants to know exactly what happened and why,’ Karl told Praut.

‘Zheng’s being cautious,’ Mes intervened. ‘Remember what you said about us not knowing this enemy. Who’d of thought they’d come back? Maybe they want us to chase them into an ambush.’

‘Damn, I’m just getting impatient to be off,’ Praut admitted. ‘Mind you, Zheng’s right to be cautious. That’s two ships the admiral’s lost in as many days. This can’t go on. We’ve got to start taking scalps as well, or we’ll loose it.’

‘No Dil, we can’t loose the war,’ burst out Clay from his comm station. ‘We just can’t.’ He was looking quite worried.

‘It’s alright,’ Karl patted Clay on the shoulder to calm him. ‘We’ll win, I promise you.’

The waiting dragged on for another two hours while Zheng and Formby mulled over what had gone wrong. Finally the long awaited warp signal came and Mes informed Praut they’d been ordered into hyperspace.

# 32
# A PARSEC TOO FAR

When the fleet came out of hyperspace, the klaxon on the *Faust* blared repeatedly, two long hoots and one short one. The noise was unbearably loud.

'What's going on?' Praut demanded of Mes.

'The signal's coming from the flagship. I read it to mean stay in position and do not move.'

Following the klaxon, the tannoy system announced, 'Action stations. With immediate effect, each ship is to come to a complete halt. Do not move…I repeat, no ship is to move…no manoeuvring at all. We've come out into a huge minefield. You can't see them because they're camouflaged, but we're in the middle of a massive minefield. Wait for the Scooper ships to do their work.'

'*Bloody aliens*,' shouted Clay in frustration tinged with a little fear.

'How the hell….?' Fanny burst out and left the sentence hanging.

Praut sat there shaking his head, unwilling to believe the situation. 'What did I say yesterday? Never underestimate the enemy…eh?'

'How do they know we're in a minefield?' asked Rubin.

'Adam, *we* may not be able to see them or detect them,' Mes informed him, 'but those flagships have equipment I've only dreamt of. If they say we're in a minefield, you'd better believe it.'

'And what the devil is a Scooper ship?' Rubin persisted.

'You'll see, be patient,' Mes advised.

‘So now what?’ Praut wanted to know. ‘What happens next?’

Almost in answer to his question, over the tannoy from the flagship came: ‘Attention. Stay exactly where you are. The Scooper ships have been deployed and are working as fast as they can. Stay alert for the *All Clear*. Out.’

‘There you go,’ said Karl. ‘First they’ll have to de-cloak the mines and let the Scooper ships scoop them up. That should clear a path through the lot.’ Karl looked furtive. ‘Alternately they could produce a fireworks display and blow their way through it,’ Karl informed Rubin, tongue in cheek.

Mes was shaking her head and looking sideways at Karl with a smile, ‘I’ve a feeling if we try blowing our way through, we’ll set the lot off…and that won’t be too good for Adam here.’

‘Ever the optimist,’ remarked Olga, with a skewed smile of apprehension.

‘What I want to know is, how the hell did they manage it? How did they know we’d come out of hyperspace just here?’ demanded Praut of nobody.

‘Those three spaceships they chased earlier must’ve been eavesdropping on the flagship’s comms. It’s the only thing that makes any sense,’ suggested Clay.

‘You should know, you and your hacking,’ said Olga sarcastically.

‘Aw, give us a break Olga,’ complained Clay.

‘So what’s this Scooper ship business,’ Praut asked Mes.

‘The scooper ship was first developed by the Space Navy on their q-machines in their simulated space battle scenarios,’ Mes explained. ‘It’s a spaceship with a bubble for a bridge, attached onto the outer shell of an oval shaped ship. The nose opens like a mouth and tractor beam snatches the mine in as fast as it can…into a powerfully shielded anti-matter chamber, hence the shape of the ship. There, the mine explodes, but because of the anti-matter, there's hardly a shudder. Those mines that aren't scooped up, are teleported into the anti-matter chamber by the three flagships. The Scoop ships were initially invented to deal with the worst kind of nuclear weapon.'

'How big are they?' Praut asked.

'Come and see for yourself. Dil, come and look at this,' Karl called out.

Praut walked over to the external screen and looked over Karl's shoulder, 'What am I looking at?'

'The weirdest spaceship you've ever seen,' Karl informed him. 'There, its just coming into view.'

A huge bulging space vessel, shaped like a bulbous old fashioned artillery shell, filled the screen. Its nose was gaping like a whale's mouth and it began scooping up….nothing.

'Karl, I thought you said they would first de-cloak the mines,' observed Praut.

'Seems I was wrong,' Karl replied blithely. 'Seems they don't need to. They can detect them as they are. What does it matter Dil, as long as they scoop the buggers up and destroy them.'

Praut tilted his head slightly, 'Fair enough. How many Scooper ships do we have?'

'Four with our Battle Group, and three each with the other two Battle Groups,' Karl reported. 'Ten altogether. Won't take too long…scooping and teleporting the mines. Mind you, it depends on how big the minefield is.'

'Well, lets settle down and do some drawing. You know what I mean…e-pads out. Looks like we'll be here for a short while,' Praut urged.

There was a collective sigh from almost everybody, except Rubin. He disappeared into his cabin only too willingly. This had Clay smirking at Olga over his eagerness.

'*Faust*, hallo, is that the *Faust*?' came over the tannoy.

Mes switched it to her earphones and replied, 'Yes this is the *Faust*. What's up?'

Something was said into her earphones and she replied, 'We're not drifting, I can assure you of that. We've been perfectly stationary as ordered.'

More from the outside source.

'No, we have not moved. Your instruments are at fault. We haven't moved since we arrived.'

The earphones again.

'Yes of course I've checked. Fine, I'll check again.'

'What was that all about?' Praut inquired.

'Ah, the flagship is accusing us of drifting towards the Scooper ship that's near us.'

'And have we?' Praut asked.

'Just a bit…but not by much.'

'By how much exactly?'

'A few meters. I took my eyes off the instruments for a moment, that's all.'

'Why didn't the autopilot take over and keep us in position?'

'I switched the autopilot off.'

'That was a silly move. Stay awake or hand over to someone else.'

'Yes boss.' Mes felt chastised and resented it, but she knew Praut was right. The silliest accidents always happen with the slightest inattention. Letting the ship drift like that in a minefield was careless. Even the flagship spotted it.

Over the next hour, the Scooper ships cleared a pathway through the minefield wide enough for the whole fleet to manoeuvre its way gingerly out of the minefield into clear space. Although in the process, one of Admiral Murat's First Battle Group stealth Corvettes, normally used for reconnaissance work, steered closer to a mine than it should have, nudging it. The resulting explosion damaged its integrity shielding, and the admiral was forced to send it back to Barnaby for repairs at the New Knossos ship yards. The *All Clear* sounded over *Faust's* klaxon a short while later.

'Is that it?' Praut asked of Mes.

'Unless there's more loose mines floating about the flagships haven't picked up…yes. That's it,' Mes informed him.

'I'll bet the captain of the Corvette is in for a tongue lashing,' Clay mused.

'He was lucky it wasn't worse. Considering what we've just been through, I'd say we came off pretty lightly,' Karl said in response.

'Remember this,' Praut told them, looking at each of his crew in turn. 'It looks like the aliens are pretty tricky in their tactics. Keep your wits about you at all times. There's a lot at stake.'

Mes, as the First Officer, took it upon herself to answer for all the crew, crisply saying, 'Aye aye captain.'

No sooner had the fleet settled, then half an hour later, the alarm sounded over the tannoy. '*Battle stations, battle stations*. All shields up. Scramble the Falcon Squadrons. Frigates and Corvettes to engage. We have a three pronged attack being launched on the outer perimeter.'

'*Damn them,*' Praut shouted. 'What a nerve. Mes, what's that about Falcon Squadrons?'

Karl intervened, 'They're the space fighters held on the supercarriers. Each flagship is a supercarrier. There's thousands of them on the three flagships. The Frigates and Corvettes are our outer defences; these are picket ships known as the outer screen, and the fighter spacecraft are our probes for breaking through the enemies defences. Me and Mes were combat pilots in those little beauties, the Falcon 227B. I wouldn't mind having a go right now on one of them.'

‘Steady there. I need you here, not out there,’ Praut advised him.

‘Yeah, I know, still…..’ Karl looked nostalgic.

‘So what do you think is happening right now?’ Praut asked Karl. ‘Take a guess…try to picture it.’

‘Frigates and Corvettes, backed by Destroyers are engaging the attackers, supported by the flagship’s Falcon squadrons,’ Karl surmised. ‘If you get Clay to hack into the flagship’s comms, you’ll get it straight from the horses mouth.’

‘Clay….’ Praut didn’t need to say anymore.

A short while later, from the tannoy system came, ‘What do you mean they’ve vanished. Have you done a thorough sweep?’ It sounded like Vice Admiral Bennett was having a problem with what he’d been told.

Praut looked quizzically at Karl, then at Mes.

Mes responded, ‘If I were the enemy, I’d be thinking of hit and run tactics. This Fleet is a big son-of-a-bitch to take on in a frontal assault. So I’d be looking at guerilla actions where I’d pop up here and there with hit and run tactics. I’m sure the admiral has already worked that out.’

‘So we don’t know where they’ll strike next? Is that what your saying?’ Praut asked in an unhappy voice.

‘Afraid so, boss. I think that’s what we just heard over the tannoy system,’ Mes told Praut.

‘I’m sure the flagship’s q-machines will sort things out,’ offered Clay.

Praut stared at Clay, wondering what he had in mind. ‘Explain yourself,’ Praut demanded.

Clay cleared his throat, ‘Predictive algorithms have come a long way since they were first invented in the dim and distant past. Most q-machines now self generate the most complex and elegant algorithms to simulate an opponents behaviour. In fact, the beauty is they’re almost 99% accurate in their predictions. That is a huge improvement on the current batch of hoax futurologists who use stone age methods and predict below 50%-50%. All an analogue simulation model needs is a complex algorithm that simulates a target system representing any alien guerilla action as an analysable system. The current alien action provides the quantum computer with the raw data, and from that, the machine should be able to predict when and where the next alien guerilla attack will take place. I wouldn't be at all surprised if the admiral hadn't expected to come out in that minefield.'

'Oh come on now. That would mean he's putting us in danger deliberately,' Praut protested.

'Not at all,' defended Clay. 'I *mean* what I just said. Half the trick is going along with what the enemy expects of you. It lulls your opponent into a sense of complacency. Look at our casualties. Barring that silly Corvette—we haven't sustained any casualties. I assume the algorithm has been fed with *all* the alien data to date. That gives us a powerful model. And if the enemy is using a similar modelling process, which I assume it is, we simply follow what the enemy predicts, and then at a crucial moment we do the unexpected. The human genius of it is knowing when the crucial moment comes. That's Zheng's job. That crucial moment is likely to be the war clincher. If the admiral follows this line of thought, which I expect he will, it puts the aliens into deep doodo.'

Praut almost had his mouth open. 'Predictive algorithms? Analogue models? What the.... What if the aliens have q-machines as well and they do the same with their algorithms and bloody models and outsmart our q-machines? Where are we then?'

'Then it's the better machine that wins, but do they have a Zheng? And will they abandon the model at the crucial moment and do the unexpected?' smiled Clay.

Praut's eyes narrowed. 'This is a dangerous game. Are you sure the admiral is following your script?' Praut asked in consternation.

'If he's not, then he's in the wrong job,' answered Clay.

'I hope you're right…or we're for it. So now we wait until the machines fight it out?' asked Praut.

'Not at all,' intervened Karl. 'We go on as before, on to Fourex as planned. We strap in and wait for the order to warp. At least that's what I expect the admiral to decide. In the mean time, we will all have to keep a weary eye out for alien attacks. The battle continues until the war is over.'

'Thank goodness for small mercies. I thought we were going to sit here and wait for the machines to fight it out.' The last was said with a heavy tinge of irony by Praut.

'Hang on Dil,' Mes said suddenly. 'I've got a message coming in from the flagship. They say they're sending us an escort.'

'Heh? Escort? Why?' Praut wanted to know.

Over the tannoy system came a voice, 'Hallo, is that the civilian ship *Faust*? This is Captain Kono of the Fourth Carrier Space Wing. We'll be your escort until we reach Fourex.'

Praut looked to Karl to explain what was happening.

Karl shrugged and said by way of explanation, 'A Carrier Space Wing usually has nine squadrons. Its heavy duty protection from my point of view. What do you think Mes.'

'I'd agree. Someone thinks we're vulnerable.' Mes addressed Clay, 'Clay, could this be anything to do with those algorithms and computer predictions you just spoke of?'

'Most definitely,' Clay agreed. 'Its just the type of thing I might of expected.'

Holding her hand up, Mes said, 'I've got Barkin's voice on my earphones. Dil, want me to put it on the tannoy?'

'Yes, go ahead.'

'Dil, you see what I see? All the space fighters out there just for us two?' Barkin was chuckling into the mike.

'Hi Max, where've you been. All this going on and not a peep out of you. Keeping your head down, eh?' Praut was in a teasing mood.

'Yeah, yeah. What about this Captain Kono. He been in touch with you yet? He's been bending my ear.' The *Faust* crew heard the laughter coming from the *Catz* over the tannoy.

'Yeah, just introduced himself a minute ago,' answered Praut. 'Know what's going on?'

'No idea,' came the response from Barkin. 'I was just getting in touch, hoping *you* could shed some light on the subject. We heard the attack warning from the flagship… then this Kono guy turns up with his mates. Why do we need an escort?'

'Max, calm down before you give yourself a heart attack,' advise Praut. 'I've just had Clay give me an earful of algorithms and behavioural models, all to do with his computers simulating the alien attacks. He's guessing that the escort has something to do with the predictions the computers have thrown out.'

'*Thrown out* is right. The bloody machines are getting into astrology now, are they? Predictions? Futurology? Give us a break.' The background laughter got louder over the tannoy.

'If the admiral didn't take it seriously, he wouldn't have sent the escort,' Praut threw back at Barkin. 'Think on that while your tickling your funny bone.'

'Aw come on Dil,' Barkin teased, 'you got to admit, when machines start predicting nursemaids for us, even your funny bone ought to start rattling. Never heard so much balderdash in a long time. Me and my lads need nursemaids like we needed those biochips.'

'Have it your own way Max, but when the shit starts flying you might be grateful there's a few nursemaids between you and the aliens. Come over for a meal later. We'll have another of these chin wags,' Praut invited.

'Thanks, I'll do that. See you later, out.'

'I'm half tempted to agree with Max regarding the escort,' Karl announced when the comm went quiet.

'And I'm taking this totally seriously, in spite of Max and his chortling,' Praut told Karl. 'What Clay told us is too credible in the circumstances…especially the battle of the computers. Remember on Earth, the current battle being waged between the conglomerate's various q-machines? Is this any different?' Praut stared at Karl.

'Put like that, I suppose not. Okay, I'll go along with the script.'

Over the tannoy was heard, 'This is Captain Kono. Enemy has just popped out of hyperspace near us. Prepare for immediate warp to Fourex.'

'Mes, get with it. *Get us out of here*,' Praut yelled.

'*Bloody aliens*,' shouted Clay again in sheer frustration.

# 33
# FOUREX SYSTEM

The *Faust* came out of hyperspace on the edge of the Fourex Solar System with its klaxon bleeping out the electronic general alarm to battle stations. The dark vacuum of space was brightly lit up with laser and maser canon fire criss-crossing everywhere. They'd emerged into the midst of a full blown battle.

The Fourex System had two gas giants and five other planets, only one of which was inhabited. The Fourex Sun was class F, yellow white with a stronger luminosity but its gravitational pull was only slightly greater than our own sun. The inhabitants of Fourex were on the fourth planet from their sun.

'*Shields up*!' yelled Praut, but he didn't need to say anything. Mes was already way ahead of him.

Praut mouthed, 'From the frying pan into the fire.'

'Heh?' asked Mes, wondering what Praut was saying.

'We've warped out of one nasty situation into *this* bloody fire-fight,' he said more loudly. 'Look at the fireworks going on out there.'

'I'm looking, I'm looking. What do you expect to happen in a war situation? Flower power?' Mes was busy with her shields and weaponry. Karl, as the co-pilot, was doing the same. Karl had found some targets and was letting loose with everything the *Faust* had got in her armoury. Clay was hooked into the comm system, searching for news. Rubin was still in his cabin, wisely keeping his head down. Fanny and Olga were still securely strapped into their seats.

Over the tannoy blared a voice, 'Captain Kono here, *Faust*, stay as you are, we'll stay with you as long as we can to protect you.'

'CSW, thanks. Keep us appraised. Roger and out,' Mes said crisply in reply.

'Is that the rest of the fleet?' asked Praut, staring over Karl's shoulder at the external viewing screen.

The screen was filled with the fleet's spaceships, vessels of varying sizes all seemingly firing at targets into the middle of the Fourex Solar System where Praut supposed a large number of alien spaceships were also gathered…and the firing was being returned with interest. Only the powerful energy shields surrounding each vessel prevented the fleet's ships from being blown to pieces.

'I'm picking something up over the speaker,' Clay announced. 'The inter-flagship chatter is saying that most of the enemy spaceships are robotic. They sense that the inner ring of defenders close to Fourex itself may have life on board, but the ones that are hammering us are robots.'

'Why the dirty villainous scum,' burst out Mes. 'Can't even get the satisfaction of blasting a few aliens to bits.'

'Robots?' spat out Karl. 'If I ever get my hands on one of those alien bastards, I'll tear its limbs off with my bear hands…if it has any.'

'Why don't I send in one of my sniffers to monitor the aliens?' asked Olga, from where she sat.

'The point of the exercise being….?' asked Praut.

'You'll know which ship to target. Which ship has an alien on board rather than a robot,' answered Olga somewhat smugly.

'Can you do that?' Praut wanted to know.

'I might be able to. Clay?' Olga turned her attention on Clay. 'Have you got *anything* at all that's alien from all that computer searching on Lowry?'

Clay sat and thought for a moment. 'I might have… but it may be only one word.'

'Anything will do. I need to programme something into the sniffer to search for. What is it?'

'*Umber*. Even then, I'm not sure what it is,' replied Clay. 'It's not a human word, that's all I know. I found it in connection with the wormhole coordinates.'

'Well? Shall I have a go?' Olga asked Praut. 'Your decision.'

'Go for it. We got nothing to loose, and a lot to gain. If I can let the admiral know which ship has a definite alien on board, he can target it. Take it out…and who knows. It might change the dynamics of this battle.'

'That's assuming he doesn't know already,' added Karl.

'Trust you to spoil a good idea,' Praut smiled at Karl. 'Go for it Olga. Let's do our special bit in this mayhem,' Praut encouraged.

Olga unstrapped herself and rushed off to load a sniffer into the external tube. She soon returned to one of the ships consoles and began programming in the instructions the sniffer was to follow. She rechecked the instruction set, and then pressed the go button and sent the sniffer on its way.

'Is that it?' Praut asked, when Olga sat back looking satisfied.

'That's it. We'll soon know if Clay's got it right,' she was staring at the monitor, tracking the sniffer on its way.

'Let's hope nobody thinks to shoot it down,' Fanny told her.

'What? Oh no, I didn't think of that,' Olga suddenly felt a pang of fright for her baby.

'We're in the middle of a battle zone. Somebody might wonder what it is and take a pop shot at it,' Fanny said.

'Clay,' Praut said quickly, 'get on the blower to the flagship and tell them not to shoot at the sniffer. It's there to help them.'

'Right Dil, will do.' Clay talked into his throat mike for a while, then said, 'They've told me, if it's hit it'll be by accident, not by intention. They've programmed the auto-cannons and warned the gunners that it's a friendly.'

'Thanks Clay, you're a pet,' Olga heaved a sigh of relief.

The tannoy suddenly burst into life, 'Hallo *Faust*! Captain Kono here, I'm being pulled off by the flagship to deal with a problem, but I'm leaving one squadron for your defence. I've told the *Catz* as well. See you soon, out.'

'We should be okay, eh?' Praut asked Mes, slightly worried by the turn of events. He peered at the external screen, looking for a threat. All he could see were flashes and laser beams streaking across the vacuum of space. A couple of space fighters came into view, firing their lasers at an unseen object...then letting off a couple of missiles.

'No sweat,' she replied. 'Look at Karl, he's as happy as a kid in clover. He's doing what he likes best…blasting away at the enemy. He won't let anything near us.'

Indeed, Karl was firing both laser and maser cannons at targets only he could see.

A sudden shudder ran through the ship.

'Hey, we got a hit there,' Mes remarked in surprise. 'Karl, did you get him?'

'Yeah, I got him. Bugger got closer than he should of. But he got one of our fighters.'

Praut watched as the screen lit up with an explosion near the *Faust,* and another explosion a good distance into the Solar System. 'Was that our fighter?' he asked Karl.

'The one close to us was…and the other distant one was the enemy. I got him good. Sent a maser shot up his chute. One bugger less.' Mes had been right, Karl was in his element.

Another shudder went through the ship, closely followed by two more.

'Are they targeting us?' asked Praut.

'Someone is,' Karl replied. 'I think it's a couple of enemy ships. They must think we're an easy quarry. I'm gonna teach them they're wrong.'

'Don't go overboard. Make sure you don't over expose us.' Praut was worried for his crew.

'Dil, this is one case where Karl *needs* to go overboard,' Mes corrected him, 'otherwise we end up as a sitting duck. The more he piles it on, the more likely the enemy will think twice about chasing us and look for an easier victim.'

'Sorry, I was just thinking of your safety. Go ahead and do what you need to do. Don't mind me. Mes, you take charge during the battle. You've got far more qualification than I have.' Praut was about to leave the bridge.

Mes put her hand up, 'Dil, you're still the captain. I need you here on the bridge. I'll do the battle, but you keep an eye out for the other stuff. Deal?'

'Deal!' Praut sat down and relaxed.

Another shudder hit the ship.

'How's the shields holding up?' Praut asked Mes, jumping to his feet.

'Eighty five percent,' she responded. 'Still good.'

'Keep me posted.'

'Wilco.'

Two hits in quick succession nearly knocked Praut off his feet.

'Clay, can you get Max on the comm?'

'I'll try.'

'I want to see if he's getting the same hammering we are.'

'Sorry Dil, I'm getting too much interference. I think the aliens are jamming our comms.'

‘They can’t do that surely? Are they blocking the flagship as well?’

‘Hang on, I’ll check.’ After a short while Clay reported, ‘No, I’m receiving the flagship’s comms. Here’s the latest. Looks like Admiral Formby’s Third Battle Group is having a hard time securing the exit coordinates on that alien wormhole. The other two Battle Groups are having more success. Admiral Murat’s First Battle Group has flanked the aliens and is coming in on the fourth planet from the outer rim of our galaxy. It seems the aliens didn’t expect that, and Zheng’s Group is hammering them from this side. It sounds like its tough going but we’re making headway. That’s what’s coming through on the comms Dil.’

‘I’ve got a lock on one of the ships…well my sniffer has. What’re we gonna do about it?’ asked Olga.

‘Karl, any chance you can get a bead on that ship. Olga, show Karl which ship the sniffer says got the alien on board,’ Praut told him.

Olga rushed over to Karl and gave him the 3D coordinates of the enemy ship.

Karl let off a quick succession of barrages in that direction.

In response, another jolt shook the ship, followed by another two in quick succession.

‘Shields are at seventy three percent Dil,’ Mes reported.

‘Mes, get us out of here before the shields are compromised,’ ordered Praut.

‘*Right boss*,’ she yelled back. ‘I’m heading for cover behind that planet.’

‘Yeah, right, get going,’ said Praut. ‘Which planet?’

‘It’s the sixth planet of the system…unoccupied.’

‘Go ahead.’

‘We’ll loose sight of the sniffer if we go behind the planet,’ complained Olga.

‘Take you choice, get blown to bits or loose sight of your sniffer?’ Praut peered at Olga.

She gave in, ‘Oh all right, go ahead.’

A bit of manoeuvring and then, ‘Well hallo, what’s this?’

‘What’ve you found?’ Praut asked.

Mes said chuckling, ‘It’s the *Catz*. It’s hiding there already. They beat us to it. Smart move I must say.’

On the tannoy came, ‘Hallo *Faust*, this is Squadron Leader Bellamy. Our fighters will leave you now you’ve found a safe spot. We’ll head into the battle. Good luck. Out!’

‘Thanks squadron leader…and good hunting to you,’ Mes responded.

‘Clay, can you put us through to Max?’ Praut requested.

‘Yeah Dil, the planet is blocking the alien jamming.’

‘Hi Dil you old rascal. It’ll cost you to park in my parking space.’ Barkin was laughing as were some of his crew in the background.

‘Trust you to find a cosy spot in the middle of a battle,’ responded Praut. ‘As for the cost, we’ve been paying it already, out in the open. A bunch of those aliens have been targeting us. How about you?’

‘That’s why we got out of there,’ chuckled Barkin. ‘Same thing happened...power got a bit low. Got a bit hot, so we high-tailed it out of there for the moment. Let the big boys take care of the baddies.’

‘You still in good shape?’

‘Yeah, no damage. Left before our shields gave way.’

‘Same here,’ Praut reported. ‘Clay’s been listening on the comms, he tells me Formby’s having some trouble but Murat is clouting them from the other side of us. Came on them from behind. Zheng’s hitting them hard from this side.’

'While we're hiding behind this planet?' Suddenly Barkin's laughter stopped. 'Now you've made me feel like a real bastard.'

'Oh come on Max, we don't really have the clout to do a lot of damage.'

'Yeah, but hiding is bad for my morale. What say we creep round the other side of this planet and see if we can find an alien or two?'

Praut looked at Olga, then at Mes. 'What'd you think? Shall we chance it?'

'If both our ships stay in formation, we might be able to use our combined fire power like one of the big boys,' Mes told him. 'Let's go for it!'

Praut said, 'Olga, once we're out from behind this planet, tell me what your sniffer is doing.'

'Right Dil,' answered Olga.

Both the *Faust* and the *Catz* nosed their way out carefully from the sheltered side of the planet to the sunny side. There instantly followed a number of hits from the enemy. Both vessels then let rip at the source with their own cannons, piling it on until the power units began to complain. Karl was as intense as Praut had ever seen him, concentrating on hammering the enemy.

'Whoa there Karl, stop for a moment,' Mes shouted into his right ear. Let the power packs regenerate. We can't sustain this level of fire…we're not a battleship. I'm heading back behind the planet until we regain full power.' She spoke into her throat mike for a moment to let the *Catz* know her intentions.

'Aw Mes, those fusion power packs go on forever. Let me keep going,' griped Karl at being taken out of the battle.

The *Faust* broke off and sneaked back to the dark side, to take cover behind the sixth planet.

'Don't worry Karl, as soon as the packs recharge, we're going right back in and you can resume blasting away,' Mes consoled him.

'Yes Karl, take a breather while you can. Don't worry, Mes'll have you back at them in a short while,' Praut added his weight behind Mes.

Grudgingly, Karl got out of the co-pilots seat and went to get a drink from the replicator.

'Get me one while you're out there,' Praut shouted to the disappearing Karl.

'And me,' added Mes.

'Well,' Praut turned to Olga. 'Did you see what was happening with your sniffer while we were our there?'

'It's latched onto one of those ships near Fourex and is following its every move,' she replied.

Praut seemed pleased, 'Good, keep it up. If your hunch is right, it's a ship with an alien on board. Get Clay to send the info to the flagship. Let them know the sniffer coordinates and the coordinates of the ship its tracking. Tell them how important it is that they concentrate some serious fire-power on that ship.'

'Right Dil, I'm on it.' Olga went to talk with Clay.

'The *Catz* is just coming into our parking orbit,' Mes informed Praut.

'Must've a better fusion power pack than ours. Anyway, its good we're both still shipshape,' he replied.

Karl came back with the drinks and handed Mes hers and then Praut's.

'So we wait here to recharge and then….' Praut stared hard at Mes while sipping his tea.

She didn't feel at all intimidated by the stare, simply took a sip of her drink and said, 'Back out into the affray… what else? Mind you, I've got one idea in my thoughts.'

'Want to share it with me?'

'Going after the ship Olga's sniffer is tracking. I mean both us and the *Catz*.'

'Not without clearing it with the flagship,' Praut told her. 'I made a solemn promise not to do anything like that without asking permission from Zheng. I'm sticking to that. We go chasing after that alien without permission, and Zheng promised to nail my carcass to the nose of this ship… and lets face it, I'd look silly nailed to the nose of this ship, don't you think?'

'Oh I don't know. I've been thinking we needed some kind of mascot out there,' Mes said mischievously.

'That will do. Clay, get through to the *Baochuan* and tell them what we have in mind. Ask them if they have anything against us going after the alien vessel. Tell them it would be us and the *Catz*. And another thing, hack into the comms and find out what's happening out there…how the battle's going.'

# 34
# CHASING THE ALIEN

'You could've knocked me down with a feather when the flagship gave us permission to go after the alien vessel,' said Praut, still somewhat flabbergasted by Zheng's decision.

'Barkin didn't sound too happy when we told him what we had in mind,' Mes responded in a querying tone.

'Oh he was just grouchy cos it was our idea,' suggested Fanny. 'You know Max likes to be in control.'

'You realise we're going right into the middle of this shit?' offered Karl.

'I thought you were keen to have a go at the aliens,' asked Mes.

'Oh I am, just thought it easier whacking them from a distance. We were in a good spot near that planet. Don't like being out in the open in a battle.'

'Never mind, I'll look after you while you keep whacking them with those cannons,' smiled Mes.

'So if I end up in pieces, I'll know who to blame for it will I?' Karl laughed at Mes.

'Don't worry, I'll collect the pieces and send them back home, I promise.'

'Hell, now I feel a lot better,' Karl sat back in his seat smiling.

Praut broke up the banter with a serious question, 'Clay, what's coming through on your hacking? How's the battle going?'

'Admiral Formby's Battle Group has secured the wormhole site,' Clay told Praut. 'At least that's what he reports to the *Baochuan*. Admiral Murat is tearing the alien defences apart in the rear and is trying to reach Fourex itself. But Admiral Zheng is bogged down on this side of the system. It seems the aliens have concentrated their main effort against his Battle Group. He's taking a hammering. Formby is sending some of his ships to help Zheng.'

'That means we're going out into the worst of it. How's the power packs?' Praut asked Mes.

'Fully charged. We're ready for them.'

'And Olga, have you still got a good bead on your sniffer. Know exactly which ship we're chasing?'

'I'm watching it all the time. You can't see it from this distance but its hugging the left side of Fourex.'

'So we're gonna have to charge through the main battle area to get to it?'

'Not necessarily,' intervened Mes.

'You got a better idea?'

'Instead of going through the middle, we could go round in a quarter circle and come in on Fourex from the western sector. The battle isn't half as bad in that direction. We'll have to go outwards as if we're leaving, then do the quarter circle. That ought to confuse them.'

'Good, go for it. Make it happen.'

Mes talked to the *Catz* via her throat mike, letting them know what she was up to, then she engaged the impulse engines and made to retreat out of the Fourex system altogether, heading outwards.

'Hallo,' came over the tannoy system, 'this Captain Kono. Compliments of the admiral, our entire wing has been ordered to accompany you on your mission. Is that okay by you?'

'Welcome,' Mes answered. 'You're a sight for sore eyes.' She looked at Praut for him to approve her words.

He nodded and smiled.

'Yes, you're most welcome. You're aware of what we're after?'

From the tannoy, 'Yes, I've been briefed on the target. Say what you need us to do, and we'll try to carry it out. Over and out.'

Karl had a big grin on his face and he did a thumbs up sign with his hands.

Near the outer edge at the Fourex System's heliopause, Mes swung the *Faust* to the right, closely followed by the *Catz* and Captain Kono's Carrier Space Wing, pursuing the quarter circle till she reached the extreme western point of Fourex. Another right turn and both vessels with their space fighter support, headed directly for the fourth planet of that solar system.

'I've just understood why the admiral gave us the go ahead for this mission,' Praut said to Mes, while she was busy concentrating on her piloting and looking out for the enemy.

'Why?' she asked despite herself.

'Cos we're a flanking manoeuvre and it helps Zheng in his battle plan. Anything that distracts the enemy from his Battle Group, he'll approve. That's why he let us have the Carrier Wing.'

'Yeah, okay, good.' Mes was coming to a point where she needed all her piloting skills. She only half heard what Praut had said.

As the little group closed in on their prey, Karl saw one of the space fighters explode, then a number of shudders hit the *Faust*.

'*We've been spotted*,' shouted Mes. 'Karl, let them have it.'

'Right,' and Karl began targeting the nearest alien ships with laser and maser fire. He loosed a number of missiles off at a couple of other targets.

'The big one, behind this lot in front of us, is the one we're after,' Mes said to Karl. 'See if you can hit it.'

'No prob.' He turned his attention and his fire to go through the front line of ships, letting the *Catz* and Kono's fighters deal with the ships directly in front of them.

'Captain Kono, can you hear me?' Mes said into her throat mike.

'Hallo *Faust,* coming through fine. What can I do for you?' came back over the tannoy.

'Can you take care of the ships directly in front of us. We're after the big bastard hiding at the back.'

'Wilco, out,' and the tannoy went dead.

Two more jolts ran through the *Faust* as the enemy targeted them.

'How are the shields?' demanded Praut.

'Holding,' replied Mes. 'They're fine.'

'What about your sniffer Olga. Still tracking the big ship hiding back there?' Praut asked.

'Yes it is. Seems to be firmly rooted on it. Remember it's only got one alien word in its programming…*Umber*. My little baby has clamped itself onto that ship. It must mean there's an alien *Umber* on board, whatever that means,' Olga replied.

'Olga, its time you recalled your sniffer or it'll be destroyed in the battle,' advised Praut.

'Oh, yeah, good idea. I'll do it right now.' She hurriedly began giving instructions into her throat mike to retrieve her beloved sniffer.

'We're almost through,' Karl announced. 'The fighter wing has cleared a way through. They've taken out some five ships. Me and the *Catz* have mangled three. We're almost clear. I don't like the look of that big sod waiting for us. It looks mean from where I'm sitting.'

'That's our target. If you don't like it, you can get out right now and walk back to Lowry,' Praut said just a little testily.

Karl shouted back over his firing, 'What, and leave you guys with all the fun…not on your life. I'm staying to the bitter end.'

Out of nowhere, a Battleship and three Destroyers appeared to their left.

The tannoy burst into life, 'Hallo *Faust*, Commodore Lansing on the Battleship *Yorktown* at your service. Compliments of Admiral Murat. Need any help from our little group?'

'Do we? I'm real glad to hear from you,' enthused Mes. 'We're after that big enemy vessel sitting back near Fourex. We think there's an alien on board. Can you target it?'

'We'll give it a good try, over and out.' The tannoy went dead.

With the added firepower, there ensued a massive barrage of laser, maser, and missile fire onto the alien vessel. To everyone's amazement, the enemy ship's shields held and it sustain little or no damage.

'Oh come on, give you bastard,' shouted Karl in frustration.

The sustained overwhelming fire power finally began to impact on their target, and the enemy's shields began to buckle bit by significant bit. It took some time and a lot of hammering but the enemy shields ultimately gave, and then the continuing barrage made holes in the alien vessel. Too late, it made a futile attempt to get away. The damaged ship's engines fired, and failed. A small lifeboat shot out from the dying enemy vessel, heading down to Fourex. Then its own weaponry ceased, and it lay dead in space.

A cheer went up on the bridge of the *Faust*. Karl tried to get up to do a little dance of victory but Mes' flaying arms prevented him. Clay kept on repeating, '*Yeah, yeah, yeah….*' Fanny sat smiling, and Praut had a grim smile of satisfaction on his face.

A few moments went by and then the tannoy burst into life, 'Hallo *Faust, Yorktown* here. Is that what you had in mind?'

Mes said into her throat mike, 'Something like that. A big thanks from Captain Praut and all of the crew of the *Faust* for your timely appearance and help. I'm sure the *Catz* will support our sentiments. Our regards to Commodore Lansing.'

Back came, 'Pleasure to be of service. Now we have new orders to rejoin our Group to engage the enemy and help Admiral Zheng. He's still in the thick of it. *Yorktown*, over and out.'

'Good hunting,' Mes returned. The tannoy went dead.

Karl watched the big battleship and three destroyers depart on his external view screen, heading into the rear of the enemy still fiercely fighting Zheng's Battle Group.

Praut came to look over Karl's shoulders at the view screen. He seemed to be staring at the dead alien vessel. 'Clay, Fanny, Karl, and where's Adam? I want to go and have a closer look at that alien ship over there. Mes, can you get us closer to it?'

'Sure, no prob,' Mes replied. 'You leaving me here all alone?' she asked.

'Sorry, as the First Officer, someone has to mind the store. We won't be long. I want to see if we can pick up some more info on where these aliens came from. Keep a sharp eye out for any hostiles,' Praut told her.

'I will,' she replied.

'I'll need Clay to go through their computers.' Praut eyed Clay, 'Clay, go and get Adam out of his cabin.'

'Right boss,' Clay went to fetch Rubin.

'Adam is the alien expert here, so I want him with me. See if he can make any sense of all this,' Praut swept his arm out in the presumed general direction of the dead alien vessel.

‘You wanted me?’ Rubin asked as he came onto the bridge.

‘Yeah, suit up Adam, we’re going out to visit the alien vessel out there. I’m sure you’d want to come along.’

‘Absolutely! Wouldn’t miss this for anything,’ Rubin enthused.

‘Can I come along,’ asked Olga, ‘or have you forgotten me?’

‘Sorry Olga, yes I did forget. Yeah, come along. Go get suited up.’

The little troop of five headed for *Faust’s* airlock.

‘Karl, can you shoot a connecting line across to the alien vessel?’ asked Praut. ‘Preferably near one of the holes in the ship. It’ll save us having to look for their airlock.’

‘Yeah, easy,’ Karl replied. ‘Wait till we open our airlock, then I’ll shoot a guided rocket tether over there. It’ll clamp onto the skin near the hole and we’ll pull it taut. We then clip our suit’s roller motor onto the tether and we’ll be over there in a jiffy.’

‘When we get over there, we stay in our suits no matter what. And look our for booby traps,’ Praut warned his crew. ‘Oh, and no wondering off on your own. We stay together.’

The *Faust* airlock was opened and Karl shot his tether across. It sailed over to a hole blasted by a laser cannon near where Karl thought the alien vessel’s bridge might be. After that he pressed a button on this side of the tether and a motor pulled the tether tight. The alien vessel was in a bad way with holes everywhere in its dark yellow outer skin.

Karl volunteered to go first, so he attached his suit’s roller motor onto the taut tether and the motor engaged, sailing him over the fifty meter gap to the alien vessel.

When he stopped, he said into his throat mike, ‘It’s okay. Come on over. It’s quite safe.’

Fanny went next, followed by Clay, then Olga and finally Praut. Karl had got inside the neat hole made by the high powered laser cannon and waited to pull the rest of his crew mates inside. One by one, he pulled them all into the hole, until they stood there wobbly on the deck, looking at the bright yellow colours all around them. The place looked and felt strange, if only because of the different hues of yellow surrounding them.

‘Check your suit’s grav meter,’ Praut told Karl.

‘One half g,’ Karl replied.

‘Yes, I thought my grav meter was on the blink when I saw that. Adam, make a note, the aliens are from a planet with half of earth’s gravity.’

‘Already noted Dil,’ Rubin replied.

‘Keep your wits about you, all of you. Get your zappers out and set it to *kill*. There may be aliens still left alive. Can’t rely on them all being dead,’ warned Praut.

The helmets near him nodded their compliance and each suited hand held a zapper ready for action.

‘Karl, see if you can find the bridge of this tub.’ Praut indicated the way Karl might look.

Karl led the way through the curiously coloured but charred hangar, to a half ajar door towards the innards of the vessel. He pulled at it and it opened fully into a wide corridor. All five members of the expedition wobbled down the corridor in the lighter gravity until they came to a cross section. Karl took the circular pathway opposite leading upwards. No steps, just a smooth pathway going upwards to the next floor. They came out into a large circular room with a myriad of electronic machinery surrounding the walls. A narrow part of the wall above the e-machinery was filled with brown coloured glass or similar, giving a stunning view into outer space. The group stood and stared at the flashes and cannon fire going on further out in the distance, where they’d originally been, where they presumed Zheng was battling for supremacy over the alien fleet.

‘Clay, have a look around. See if you can spot any computers,’ ordered Praut.

'Right Dil,' Clay went to look around the machinery.

'The rest of you, go and have a careful look around the whole room. Make sure there's no aliens on this deck… dead or alive. I say again…be careful.' Praut didn't like the scene; it was much too quiet for his liking. Where were the crew of this huge ship?

Rubin wondered off to look at some machinery standing in the middle of the room.

'Dil, I think I've found something,' Clay reported via his throat mike, waving his hand from the other side of the room.

Praut spoke into his throat mike, 'Hang on, I'll be with you in a mo.' Praut glided over the deck to where Clay was already fiddling with a touch screen.

'Looks a bit like one of the touch screens I spotted in the basement on Lowry. I think it's a way in to a q-machine.'

'Well, get on with it,' Praut admonished. 'We haven't got all day. We need to hurry. I'm gonna have another look around. If you find anything, download it. Clay, download as much as you can and we'll sort it out back on the *Faust*.'

'*Watch out!*' shouted Olga's voice in Praut's earphone.

Fanny's voice gave a stifled scream over the same earphones. At the same time a laser flash lit up the room. A shot had been fired on the other side of the room from Praut.

Then a return zapper flash being fired in the direction where the laser shot had come from. Two more zapper shots were fired in the same direction and one more laser shot was fired from the circular entranceway to the room.

'*Anybody hit?*' shouted Praut at his people.

'Fanny's down,' cried Olga. 'I think its serious.'

Praut bounded across the room to where Fanny was supposed to be. He saw Olga standing above the figure of Fanny, horror on her helmeted face. Praut noted part of him was aware of Karl pursuing the alien who'd fired the shot.

In another part of Praut, horror and sadness was spreading into every nook and cranny of his being.

Fanny lay on the deck with a hole the size of a fist where her liver should have been. For a split second, Praut just stood there rooted in shock. Stunned, but only for a split second, then he shouted to Olga, 'Wrap a couple of suit patches back and front to stop the air from leaking out of her suit entirely. *Quickly! Quickly!*'

Olga moved fast to carry out his instructions. Praut pulled a patch from his own emergency aid-pocket and handed it to Olga. Both he and Olga ensured the leaks were stemmed. Praut wrapped sealing tape round Fanny's midriff over the patches. Rubin arrived at a run and stood watching, pain on his face, for what seemed to him, Fanny's demise.

'We're gonna have to move fast. We've got to get her back to cryogenic stasis cubicle on board the *Faust* as fast as possible, within the next ten to fifteen minutes before brain death sets in.'

'Right,' said Olga.

'Agreed,' added Rubin, suddenly realising he'd been wrong.

'Karl, Clay,' Praut shouted into his throat mike. 'Fanny's hurt bad. Drop everything, come and give us a hand. We need to get her back to the *Faust* quickly.'

When Karl arrived and saw the mess, he stamped his foot in anger. 'Got the bastard, though.'

Clay came at a run, just managing to stop in the difficult low gravity.

'Now you lot, quick, grab a limb each and we'll take her back to the *Faust*. If we get her into the cryogenic cubicle within the next ten minutes, before brain death sets in, we can get her to the hospital ship and they'll be able to fix her up.'

Karl had his zapper out all the way to the hull but no more aliens appeared. Getting Fanny across to the *Faust* proved to be relatively easy in the weightless conditions, and then the crew rushed her into one of the ten cryogenic stasis cubicles Praut had installed for his Lowry snatch trip.

Once Fanny was safely in the cryogenic cubicle, Praut stood back and looked at the frozen figure with her flaming red hair and sadly shook his head. 'I hope she'll be alright, I really do. I'm not sure what I'd do if I lost another of my people. This whole thing is a total nightmare. Poor sweet Fanny.'

'She'll be alright. Just need to get her to the hospital ship now,' soothed Olga, holding Praut's hand.

Clay and Karl stood to the back, on either side of Praut, both looking dejected. Rubin stood in the doorway, leaving Praut's people to console their boss.

Praut shook his head again and went to see Mes on the bridge.

'How is she?' Mes asked.

'How do you think?' Praut said sadly. 'She's frozen. Vital signs seem okay. I came to ask you to get in touch with the hospital ship, what's its name?'

'The *SSS Intrepid*. You might want to wait till the battle is over if Fanny's stable,' Mes advised. 'The *Intrepid* will be overloaded with casualties right now…that's assuming its in one piece. With aliens, you never know… they might have targeted it.'

'Zheng would not put it into the battle area. She's probably somewhere at the edge of this system. Try and locate her for me, there's a sweet. Oh, and see if there's any news of how the battle's going.'

Normally, Mes would have taken offence at being referred to as a *sweet*, but not this time. She could see Praut was shaken to the core. Fanny was his personal assistant and been with him from the start.

'I'll locate the *Intrepid* Dil,' Mes told him. 'Don't worry, if Fanny's stable she'll be okay. 'Go have a drink and try to calm down.'

Praut saw she meant well and did as she advised. He found Clay and Karl sitting in the lounge-come-dining room, both quietly talking in whispers.

'What are you two up to?' Praut inquired, trying to brighten himself up.

'Before you called me to help you, I'd done like you said. I downloaded quite a bit of stuff from the alien computer. I need to get to work on it,' Clay told him. 'There might be some important stuff on it.'

'Clay, go to work. If you need more computing power, you might try one of the flagships.'

# 35
# SINGULARITY INC.

The battle for Fourex was over, but the sense of victory was muted by the number of Earth vessels lost. In the absence of Clay, Karl had began exploring the hacking game to keep himself occupied. From the comms he was able to tell Praut that the fleets losses were being reported to the flagship as thirty nine, and a substantial number were listed as badly damaged.

One of the major factors in the fleet's victory was when Admiral Formby's Third Battle Group, while guarding the wormhole coordinates, employed a massive nuclear device to close down the newly opened wormhole, just as the enemy attempted to reinforce their battle fleet by bringing through fresh spaceships.

Zheng had sustained the worst casualties; twenty seven ships. Admiral Murat's timely reinforcements had saved his bacon. It had been a titanic struggle because the enemy had expected the Earth fleet to come from the direction Zheng was coming from and had put their heaviest defences there. What galled the people on the flagship most of all was that half of the enemy they faced were unmanned robot ships. The other ninety percent were chipped humans; only ten percent were actually alien ships.

'Have you been through to the *Intrepid*?' asked Praut from his captain's chair. 'What's the news on Fanny?'

Karl answered, 'The news is good. They've patched up the liver, growing another liver using the residual cells. The implanted liver is doing well. Fanny's awake and says there's hardly a scar where she was hit. Modern medicine heh?' Karl was on the comms while Olga sat in his co-pilot's chair.

'Thank our lucky stars we had those cryogenic cubicles installed,' said Praut.

'By the way, Fanny says thank you, and see you soon,' added Karl. 'The other news from the comms is, the Fourth Battle Group is due to arrive tomorrow. We're getting reinforcements.'

'Any idea who's the admiral in charge of it?' asked Praut.

'Nobody's mentioned a name yet,' replied Karl.

'Now that Fanny's going to be okay, we seem to have got off fairly light in this battle. Hope our luck holds,' Mes told Praut.

'What do you mean?' asked Olga. 'Aren't we finished yet?'

'Afraid not,' Praut told her with a smile, trying to soften the news. 'We still haven't stemmed the alien invasion. At the moment, we don't know where they came from and when they'll try again.'

'Oh double damn!' Olga responded to the news. 'I thought this bloody shambles was over. So what next?'

'Next, we need to discover where these perishers are from and go pay them a return visit,' Praut said seriously. 'We've got to convince them to stay out of our galaxy. From what we've just been through, that's not going to be easy. They know our address but we don't know theirs. We have to change that.'

'Yeah, that's fine, but what's the next move,' asked Mes. 'How we gonna find their address?'

'My money's on Clay,' Praut replied. 'I'm hoping he's downloaded something useful from that alien ship. 'Fanny's near death mustn't be in vain.'

'You think he'll find their home world from all that gumpf he's trawling through right now?' Mes said with a hint of scepticism.

'He'd better, or I'll send him back to that bloody alien ship and have him try again until he succeeds,' Praut said with some relish.

'Where is Clay? I lost track of him after we teleported Fanny to the hospital ship,' Olga asked.

'He's teleported himself to the flagship. He's chasing computing power. They've got the best q-machines.'

As if on queue, 'Hallo *Faust*, this is the flagship,' the tannoy announced. 'We have a message for you from Admiral Zheng.'

'Go ahead *Baochuan*,' Karl told them.

'First, congratulations on your victory over the alien vessel. Secondly, I'm to tell you that Randoline Walcott is due to arrive tomorrow with the Fourth Battle Group. She'd like to have a chat with you. And thirdly, it's a question; are you intending to stay on with us for the next phase of the operation?'

Karl looked to Praut to supply him with the answer.

Praut nodded, 'Tell them yes, we intend to see this through to the end.'

'Yes *Baochuan*,' said Karl. 'Captain Praut says we intend to stay to the bitter end. Thanks for the congrats and the Walcott info. Out.'

'What day is it?' Praut asked suddenly. 'I've completely lost track of time.'

'Dil, the battle's been raging for the last two days,' Olga informed him. 'Nobody's slept while this was going on. How could they?'

'Yeah, but what time is it? Is it morning or is it night? Let's have a look at the clock.' Then Praut thought to take a glance at his own watch. It said 10:00 Earth time.

'Is it really? In that case, I assume we're back on the three shift system,' asked Karl. 'Who's going to bed first?'

'Can I suggest we leave only one person on watch for now,' said Mes. 'We don't have the manpower to do a proper three watch system…and I'm volunteering for the first watch.'

'Good idea,' Praut agreed, heaving himself out of the captain's chair and heading for the exit. Karl and Olga followed him. 'Where's Adam? In his cabin?'

Karl nodded in answer to Praut's question, then disappeared into his own cabin.

Praut slid his cabin door open and looked at his bunk. Not bothering to undress, he flopped down on the bunk as he was, and slept the sleep of the exhausted.

* * *

The next morning when Praut came onto the bridge, he found Karl in the pilot's seat, quietly humming to himself.

'There's a message for you from the *Tornarsuk*,' Karl announced brightly.

'The what?'

'The *Tornarsuk*. It's the Singularity vessel that came in with the Fourth Battle Group this morning. The message is signed by somebody called Randoline.'

'Ah, now why didn't you say so. It's the wormhole woman from Callisto. Now I remember, Singularity's dome is based in the Tornarsuk crater on Callisto. So, she's come in her own vessel has she?'

'And it's a big bugger. You should see it. It's lying out there beside us. It's taken up most of my screen,' Karl complained. 'Why'd she have to park it so close?'

'Well let's have a look.' Praut came and peered at the external screen over Karl's shoulder. He saw a large spaceship, more like one of Zheng's destroyers, sporting a large red S surrounded by a blue ellipse painted on the ship's hull. 'Well I am impressed,' Praut declared. 'WorldGov *have* splashed out some credits on her after all.

Last time we met, she was complaining of the cost of her project.'

'Shall I read the message?'

'Yes please.' Praut waited.

Karl read, '*Suggest we meet. Need to discuss wormhole target.*'

'Her coming here must mean she's got a working wormhole. Can't think of any other reason she'd come along with a Battle Group.'

'Want me to set up a time with this woman?' Karl asked.

Praut looked at his watch, 'Damn, it's almost lunch time. Should have woken me earlier.'

'Mes told me to let you sleep,' Karl replied.

'Ask Ms Walcott if two o'clock would suite her?'

'Right, will do. Oh, and Clay says he's found something you'll be pleased with.'

'Where's Clay?' asked Praut.

'He's in his cabin. Dil, he's really been overworking it. I caught something about the alien home before he turned in. He was bushed.'

'I hope that means what I think it means.'

'*I thought I heard your dulcet tones*,' a familiar woman's voice shouted from the lounge-come-dining room next door.

'*Fanny!*' shouted Praut, as he recognised the voice. He rushed next door to find Fanny sitting at the table sipping a drink. 'Should you be up so soon?'

'Oh don't fuss so. I had to bludgeon the quack to let me go. She kept wanting to do more tests on me. I can't stand hospitals, so I insisted she sign me off.' Fanny seemed a little paler than before, but otherwise her green eyes twinkled with mischief. She looked remarkably normal, considering. She shook her head, sending her red hair swirling and said, 'You should see your face. Honest, I'm not a ghost. I'm fine…a bit stiff that's all.'

Praut sat down opposite her and looked hard into her eyes. 'You're going to take it easy young lady, and that's an order from the boss.'

Fanny smiled at him warmly, 'It seems I have your quick thinking to thank for being here at all. A few more minutes and poof, no more poor Fanny. Look,' she lifted her jumper to show Praut where they'd fixed her up.

'But there's nothing to see,' Praut said in surprise.

'Of course not. They did a good job,' she laughed.

Indeed, Praut looked closer and saw just ordinary skin where the fist sized hole had been; there wasn't even a tiny scar to show she'd been badly injured. 'It was the cryogenic cubicles that saved you, really. Lucky we had them installed. It argues for having one on board every vessel.' He was getting embarrassed.

'Don't try to get out of it…you saved my life…admit it,' she said almost timidly. 'Anyway, thank you…boss. No, I mean it Dil. I'm indebted to you beyond the point where I can repay you.'

'There now, that's enough of that. I did what any sensible person would have done. I value your contribution more than you think. Just thank you for being here Fanny, and I mean that.'

She stretched out her hand and gently placed it over his, then squeezed it.

Praut returned the squeeze, then sat in embarrassed silence for a second before quickly saying, 'I've just had Randoline Walcott on to me, asking me to meet her. Want to come along…are you strong enough?'

Fanny retrieved her hand and said, 'Yes, I'm strong enough. Just try and stop me.'

Praut smiled at her feistiness, 'Don't worry, it's just a short jump across to the ship parked next door. From the size of her ship, I assume she's got teleport facilities.'

'Is that the ship Karl's been raving on about?' Fanny asked.

'I assume so. He complained to me about its size just now,' said Praut.

'When do we go?'

'Shortly…in about an hour. Need to do something?'

'Change the hue of my face. I need to put some colour back in my cheeks. I look like death warmed up,' Fanny patted her cheeks as proof.

'You look fine…but if you must.' Praut tried to stay out of women's cosmetics advice. It was a no-win situation.

'Won't be a tick,' and Fanny left to go to her cabin to adjust her makeup.

Clay popped his head round the corner of the doorway.

'Just the man I wanted to talk to,' voiced Praut. 'Come and explain what's been happening.'

'Can I get drink first?' Clay asked.

'Sure, get me one while your there.'

Clay came back and plonked two glasses on the table. 'I got some good news.'

'Well, let's hear it.'

'I think I've found where the aliens come from.'

'That's what I was hoping you were going to tell me. Right, let's have it.'

'It took me a lot of decrypting on the big q-machines, but the stuff I downloaded from that alien ship had home coordinates. We know what the exit coordinates looks like from my earlier work, so when I came across a similar one, but different, I decided to check it out. You'll never believe where they come from.' Clay didn't mean to create suspense. It was just his way of explaining.

'Well come on man, spit it out before I loose more hair,' Praut exclaimed in exasperation.

'Andromeda. At least that's where the galactic coordinates seem to come from. I think I'm right, but someone's going to have to recheck what I did. I haven't told anybody yet, not before I told you.'

‘But that’s our neighbouring galaxy. Clay, have I told you recently, you’re a genius. Andromeda, heh? It may explain why they chose to visit us.’ Praut sat back thinking. Then he said, ‘We’re going to have to take it to the admiral as soon as I finish with Ms Walcott. We got to get his people to check your work.’

A good half hour went by before Fanny reappeared. What she had done to her face made her look like the Fanny of old. The pale features had been replaced by rosy cheeks.

‘What about the physical side? You sure your up to this?’ Praut asked getting to his feet, still concerned at her early return.

‘*Fanny!*’ exclaimed Clay as she walked in. ‘You’re okay. I’m so glad to see you. I was real worried.’

‘Yeah I’m fine Clay. Good to see you too.’

‘Come on Fanny, we need to get going. Its almost time.’

Back on the bridge Praut looked at Karl and said, ‘Why didn’t you tell me Fanny was back? I nearly had a heart attack when I heard her voice.’

‘Sorry Dil, it slipped my mind. Want me to open a channel to the *Tornarsuk*?’

‘Yeah, ask them if they can teleport two people from here to their ship.’

‘*Tornarsuk,*’ Karl said into his throat mike, ‘two to teleport across to you; ready? Captain Praut and the woman standing next to him. Have you got them?’

‘Roger,’ came over the tannoy.

Next, Praut and Fanny dematerialised and rematerialised on the deck of the *Tornarsuk.*

Randoline Walcott was standing there as a welcoming committee.

‘Mr Praut, how nice to see you again. I see you got my message.’

Praut shook Walcott’s hand and said, ‘May I present my personal assistant, Fanny Fester.’

'So nice to meet you,' said Walcott, hand still outstretched.

Fanny shook the proffered hand.

'Now, I need to have a word with you. Admiral Karpov had some good words to say about you on the journey out.'

'Did he now, and who's Admiral Karpov?'

'Why he's the admiral in charge of the Fourth Battle Group. He's on the battleship *SSS Vishal.*'

'Am I right in assuming you have a working wormhole?' Praut changed the subject while they walked along a corridor.

Walcott lowered her voice, 'Well, yes we have. We've finally ironed out all the bugs and *our* wormhole doesn't squelch people.' She came to a room and slid the door open. 'We can talk in here. Make yourselves comfortable. I'll get someone to pour some drinks.'

All three sat round a round table in comfortable contour seats.

'So why didn't you use it to come out here. It would have been much quicker, surely?'

'You mean the wormhole? The admiral didn't want to advertise the fact that we've got a working wormhole. Neither did WorldGov. I think Admiral Zheng had something to do with that advice.'

'Hmm! Cagey but smart,' admitted Praut. 'It'll give them one hell of a shock when we appear at their home world.'

'Any idea where that is yet?'

Praut screwed up his face, looked at Fanny, then smiled, 'As a matter of fact, we do have an address. I was leaving here immediately after my meeting with you to tell the admiral where we think it is. I was given the info just before I teleported to you.'

'Care to tell me?'

A steward in a white coat came in bearing a glass of green tea each, for Praut and Fanny, and a glass of Russian tea with lemon for Walcott. He left as discreetly as he'd entered.

'This info still needs to be double checked, but my computer expert thinks it's next door…in Andromeda. We had their exit coordinates for here in our galaxy, and now we think we've discovered their galactic entrance coordinates from where they left to come here.'

'Andromeda? Huh? That could be a problem,' Walcott said, taking a sip of her tea. 'I've been working on the assumption that we're jumping inside this galaxy…but if you've got verifiable coordinates for another place….' She left the sentence hanging.

'I hope this isn't going to be a problem,' Praut asked, taking a sip from his own glass.

'I'm not sure yet. I've brought all the equipment I'll need, with me. I've got seven q-machines on this ship…and sufficient power to open a wormhole, but I'm going to have to run a few simulations with this Andromeda thing.'

'So that's why the ship is this big?'

Fanny was carefully sipping her tea having said nothing to contribute to the conversation. She seemed to be contented.

'It has to be, if we're opening wormholes,' Walcott replied. 'There's a huge power requirement. I've got four large fusion reactors on board each capable of generating forty gigawatt of power. That's a combined 1.6 terawatts of power. We're using exotic matter from scalar quantum field fluctuations to create the 100 km wormhole and we need the same exotic matter to keep the wormhole open.'

'Are you now? During the battle we had problems with recharging our power packs. We could have done with some of your power then.'

'Was it bad, the battle I mean? Somebody said you took quite a few casualties.'

‘We lost thirty nine ships and an equal number were damaged. We badly need the ships from the Fourth Battle Group simply as replacements. As for our meeting, I assume I’ve given you all you wanted to know?’

‘Yes Mr Praut, you have…and more. I need to get on with the simulations right now.’

‘You’ve just arrived from Earth, and we’ve been away for almost three weeks now. What’s happening at home?’

‘Oh well, I can spare a few minutes to tell you. WorldGov has gone into a tizz. All private production has come to a halt in the whole Solar System. All replicators and those massive printers are now producing only war material. They’re churning out warship after warship. When we left, they were well on their way to putting together the Fifth Battle Group, and I was told on the qt, they’ve got another five Battle Groups to be built in the pipeline. Now there’s a need for them, they’ve gone building crazy. Then there’s the galaxy wide campaign that’s been launched to inform people of the existence of hostile aliens bearing biochips, turning people into robots. All the inhabited planets are being made aware of how the biochips are implanted. A pat on the back and boom, you’re a robot. They’ve been told to avoid such contact…to be careful who they allow to touch them. Everything’s in turmoil back on Earth. You’re better off here.’

‘Sounds like we’re missing all the fun,’ said Fanny. ‘As for being better off here, you should see the state of the hospital ship. I’ve just come from there and it’s full of casualties. Give me the green fields of Earth anytime.’

Praut patted Fanny on the arm, and said to Walcott, ‘We’d better go and see the admiral now. He needs to be told what we’ve found.’

# 36
# OUR WORMHOLE

Admiral Zheng looked serious. ‘Andromeda you say? How reliable is your information?’

‘Came from the same source sir, that gave you the wormhole exit coordinates that Admiral Formby was guarding. Those proved reliable didn’t’ they?’

‘Yes they did. Well I’ll get my experts to recheck you man’s work, but we’ll go with these coordinates as if they’re the real thing. It’s that little computer expert you have with you, isn’t it?’

‘Guilty. He’s not just an expert admiral, he’s a genius. Without him, we’d still be floundering. We now know exactly where the aliens are…and we have to assume there’s more than one planet inhabited by them in the Andromeda galaxy. I only hope these coordinates are for their home world.’

‘So do I. Even then, we don’t know how many there are. I need more ships….I….’ Zheng was unusually speechless for a split second. ‘We need more ships,’ he said angrily, ‘if we’re going to pursue the aliens to their home world. Ideally I’d like a thousand spaceships….big ones.’

‘I’m told by Singularity’s CEO that WorldGov is readying five more Battle Groups.’

‘That’s supposed to be classified. Oh what the hell. I suppose you’re on our side.’

‘Haven’t I proved to be so far?’ Praut asked.

‘It was that alien vessel, wasn’t it…where you got the information?’

Praut nodded his agreement.

‘I knew I was right to let you go after it.’

'You let me go after it so as to take the pressure off of you. I was another flanking movement.' Praut stared at the admiral to see if he would deny it.

Zheng smiled ever so slightly, 'Yes, I admit it. I was getting hammered, so when you offered to flank the enemy, how could I resist?'

'Lucky for us, Commodore Lansing turned up with his battleship or we would have been in trouble.'

'Luck had nothing to do with it. I sent Lansing to help you for the same reason I sent you. No use having a flanking manoeuvre that doesn't have the fire power to make it work.'

Praut's estimation of the admiral rose a notch on that news.

Zheng asked, 'Did you get a look at the aliens? What are they like?'

'One of my people says he killed one. I'll get him to have a word with Dr Rubin and see if they can't come up with a sketch. As soon as they do, I'll let you have it. What I can tell you is, their planet has only half the gravity of Earth. Don't know if that's of any use to you. We got that from their ship.'

'It all helps to build a picture. We'll add that to the simulator, see what it comes up with. By the way, I've sent an expert team under Commander Wesley, over to the alien wreck to see what we can learn. If we find anything useful, I'll let you have a look at it. See what your Dr Rubin can make of it. I assume he's still with you?'

'Yes he is, and thanks. That it then?'

'Thanks for coming and giving me some good news. If I get the go ahead to go to Andromeda, do you want to tag along?'

Praut's face looked grim, 'To the bitter end. I nearly lost another of my people to the aliens recently. I want to see them dealt with…properly.'

'Right, pop up to the teleporter and they'll see you back to your ship. Take care.'

Back on the bridge of his own ship, Praut noticed Mes had taken over from Karl, and Clay was back on the comms station.

'What's the traffic saying?' Praut asked Clay, knowing he'd hacked into the flagship comms.

'How'd you know I'm listening to the flagship?' protested Clay.

'Because you've got ears?' Praut teased. 'Does a cat groom? Does a dog like bones? The nature of the beast will out.'

'Aw Dil, I'm not a beast. Anyway, the comms are mostly to do with the arrival of the Fourth Battle Group. They're wondering if they should keep the Group intact or use the new ships to replace the casualties. Admiral Karpov's people are resisting that idea. They're saying that replacement for the casualties are on the way using a wormhole.'

'*Whoa there*…did you just say wormhole? You sure they mentioned a *wormhole*?' asked Praut.

'That was a few minutes ago. It was the *Vishal* that mentioned it.'

'*Of all the cretinous things to do*,' Praut exploded. 'If the aliens are listening to our comms, the way you are, then the cat's our of the bag. They'll know we have a working wormhole. Remember, that's the original reason we got involved, them trying to prevent us from perfecting a working wormhole. Do those stupid people on the *Vishal* know what they're saying on an open line?' Praut was getting really angry.

'I assume they think in the aftermath of the battle, there's no aliens left,' Clay surmised.

'They'd be wrong,' exclaimed Praut. 'If you can hack the comms, so can they. Get in touch with the *Baochuan,* use encryption. Message for Admiral Zheng. *Apropos our earlier conversation, comm people on the* Vishal *are referring to using a wormhole to bring your replacements in, on an open comm line. No encryption. I don't think the aliens are going to be surprised when we appear at their planet*. Signed Praut. Send it.'

Clay was shocked that his boss was turning squealer, but he sent the message as requested. Praut was the boss after all. 'I've sent it. No response.'

'There won't be for a while until the info is verified. Then I expect heads to roll. They haven't used the wormhole up to now so that we could surprise the aliens when we first use it…popping out of nowhere on their doorstep. Now some jerk with a loose mouth has scotched that bombshell.'

'You sure the aliens are listening to our comms?' Clay asked, just to be sure there was substance to Praut's suspicions.

'We're at war…and intelligence is half the battle. You're listening to the comms just for the fun of it, for something to do, but the aliens would be stupid not to do the same. Think about it...use your head.'

'Put like that, it makes sense,' Clay admitted.

'Remember the minefield? You were surprised we came out of hyperspace smack into the middle of that minefield. Remember what I said then…that it was probably the three alien ships the Frigates chased? They were probably listening in on our comms. It's even more crucial now for aliens to listen in on us. They've just lost a big battle. What are we going to do next? Wouldn't you want to know?' Praut spread his arms as if what he said was self evident.

'Yeah, sorry. I'm not using my bonce,' Clay said apologetically. 'I suppose we should use encryption all the time in our comms. Why don't we?'

'Laziness. So far humans haven't had an enemy to contend with, not until these aliens came along. So we got lax and lazy. Now we're at war, we're playing catch-up. I would guess Zheng will issue an order to the effect that all comms are to be encrypted, now the danger has been pointed out to him.'

'Its gonna spoil my fun if he does that,' Clay said grouchily.

'You'll find a way round it, I'm sure you will.'

'Hey Dil, if I find a way round it, won't the aliens do the same?'

'Blast you and your over-active brain. So now, I want you to find a way round it so we can show the admiral how not to do it. Will you do that for me.'

'Sure Dil, no prob.'

Praut stood shaking his head in consternation at the turn of events. One moment they had a secret shocker of a wormhole to hit the enemy with, then the bombshell disappears due to unsecured comm chatter. Its like finding they had a spy in their camp.

To top it, the klaxon began bleeping the alarm and the tannoy announced, '*Battle stations, battle stations*. This is the flagship. This is no drill. Enemy wormhole has appeared on the edge of the system. Incoming fire expected.'

'Right everybody, look alive,' shouted Praut. 'Get strapped in and get the cannons ready.'

Karl rushed to the bridge from his cabin, as did Olga and Rubin.

'Karl, get on the cannon. Enemy incoming. Where's Fanny,' Praut wanted to know the whereabouts of all his people.

'She's in her cabin with sleep plugs,' Mes told him. 'She probably hasn't heard a thing.'

'Fine, let her sleep. She's been through enough. I'll keep an eye on her,' Praut said.

'Which direction?' asked Karl.

'Western part of this system,' Mes informed him.

'That's in our vicinity,' Karl replied.

The tannoy burst into life, 'Max here. You ready to do some alien bashing?'

'Tell him to take the lead,' Praut said to Clay.

Clay replied, 'Yes *Catz*, we're ready. You lead and we'll follow.'

Again the tannoy system came to life, 'This is the *Liaoning,* we're close by. Stay behind us. Make no moves. We'll deal with this. I've a present to deliver to the invader. Stand by for a big nuke explosion.'

'Shit, their gonna do it again,' exclaimed Praut.

'Do what?' asked Olga.

'Admiral Formby is going to try to collapse the alien wormhole with a massive nuclear missile,' Mes explained. 'That's what they did with the other alien wormhole on the other side of Fourex when the aliens tried to bring in reinforcements.'

A few moments went by and then the *Faust* shook from the aftershock wave that hit from the wormhole imploding. Unbeknown to those on the *Faust*, the huge missile had a yield of 60 Megatons, a massive nuke by any standards. The megatons were needed to cause the wormhole to implode.

'Are the shields up?' Asked Praut of Mes.

'Yes, they are,' she answered.

'And will they shield us from the nuke radiation?' he asked, worried for his crew.

'I think so. Wait, I'll check….yes they will, the figures are holding, but only just. Any closer and it might have given us a problem,' she said with a measure of worry in her voice.

'That's a relief,' Praut said putting a smile on his face, but with some effort. He really did think they were too close.

A shudder ran through the ship, followed by another.

'There's an alien loose somewhere out there,' Karl told them. 'We're taking hits.'

'See if you can get a bead on where those shots came from,' Praut told Mes.

'I'm trying to, but the power signature from the vessel next to us, is distorting our sensors,' Mes replied with frustration. 'What is that ship? Why's it parked so close to us?'

Karl intervened, 'It's the wormhole ship, from that Singularity woman, you know. You were asleep when they came in with the Fourth Battle Group.'

'Mes, get us away from it, now,' ordered Praut.

Mes engaged the impulse engines and moved the *Faust* a distance from the *Tornarsuk.*

'The supercarrier *Liaoning* with its Destroyer escort has gone after the aliens,' reported Mes.

A flash lit up the external viewing screen and Karl went wild.

'Did you see that? One of the destroyers smashed an alien vessel...blew it to bits,' enthused Karl. 'When the wormhole disappeared, those alien ships got stranded here...nowhere to go. Hey wham, there goes another one.'

'How could we see it? You're hogging the external screen,' complained Rubin from where he sat, strapped into his seat.

'Yeah, I suppose I am. But you *should* have seen it. Two aliens gone. It was glorious...a real pow...pow,' Karl continued to enthuse.

'Dil, there's a message coming through from the flagship,' Clay informed Praut.

'When it's all in, read it back to me,' Praut told him.

'Wait, its encrypted. I'll have to run my algorithm before I can read it to you.' A moment went by, then Clay read, '*Note taken re previous message, thanks for the heads up. General Order issued to the Fleet for all comm traffic to be encrypted as of now. Better late than never. Still, it's a pity the cats our of the bag.* Signed Zheng.'

‘Just had a thought which you might not like,’ Rubin informed Praut.

‘Don’t like the sound of this. Let’s have it then,’ Praut stared at Rubin.

‘I’ve just heard we’ve got a wormhole ship next to us, or we did have, am I right?’

‘Yes Adam, go on.’

‘That assumes we’re going to chase the aliens back to where they come from, am I right again?’

‘Keep going.’

‘Well we’ve just watched one of our battleships whack a wormhole, haven’t we…with a nuke? So…what’s to stop the aliens doing the same to our wormhole when we open it near their home world?’ Rubin stared back at Praut.

‘Shit…eh, nothing at all…I suppose. Surely the admiral’s thought of this?’ Praut asked worriedly.

‘I’d check if I were you. If we can close a wormhole, then the aliens must be able to do the same to us.’ Rubin just shrugged his shoulders.

The rest of the crew looked at Rubin as if *he* were the spy in their midst.

Rubin noticed the enmity, ‘I just thought I’d bring this up before we left for wherever the aliens live, that’s all.’

‘And rightly so,’ Praut jumped to Rubin’s rescue. ‘Weird nobody here thought of such an important thing. I’m sure the admiral’s got this covered. But….’

‘But you need to make sure don’t you?’ Rubin added.

‘Yes. Listen up all of you,’ Praut announced, ‘I’m giving a special vote of thanks to Adam for raising the issue. Thanks Adam. Keep that up. We need to cover all our bases.’

That lifted the minor tension the crew formed against Rubin. All of them gave a thumbs up sign to Rubin, indicating their appreciation for him raising the problem.

‘Right Clay, send a message to the *Tornarsuk,*’ Praut instructed him. ‘For Ms Walcott: *You must have seen the way the battleship destroyed the alien wormhole just now. Expect your wormhole to be treated in the same way. How are you going to stop the aliens closing your wormhole? Any ideas?* Signed Praut.'

'Right Dil, I'll encrypt this and send it,' Clay replied.

'Good. Next message to Admiral Zheng: *The* Liaoning *just nuked an alien wormhole—how do we stop the aliens doing the same to our wormhole?* Signed Praut.'

'Okay, I'll send this as soon as I get an acknowledgement from the *Tornarsuk*,' Clay informed him, then began to encrypt the second message.

Praut smiled encouragingly at Rubin. 'See what you've caused…and humanity as a whole may yet thank you for that bit of tangential thinking. Between you and Clay, we've got a two man Think Tank all of our own.'

Rubin unstrapped himself from his seat, 'The alien danger is over for the moment?' He posed it as a question.

'Yes, for the moment. We can step down from battle stations.'

'Then I'll retire back to my cabin, if I may,' Rubin asked.

'By all means,' responded Praut.

*

For the whole of the afternoon there was a measure of quiet on the *Faust* as people settled back into their normal routine. The only break came when Barkin called Praut to put in a tongue-in-cheek complaint that the battleship *Liaoning* had stolen his fun by taking on the aliens alone. Praut told him to be patient as the next phase of this war would give Barkin more than his share of so called *fun*… maybe enough *fun* to last him a lifetime. At the end of all this, Barkin would be yearning for the quiet life on Barnaby rather that moaning about the loss of *fun*.

Near the evening, although there was only the on board clock to tell them that it was the evening, Karl shouted into his throat mike to alert all the crew, 'There's a wormhole just opened on the edge of the system to the south of Fourex.'

Praut left his cabin and rushed onto the bridge followed closely by Mes and Clay.

'That's the direction where Zheng's ships are located, isn't it?' Praut asked.

'Yes,' replied Mes. 'He must know the wormhole's opened in his area. We should be hearing a call to battle stations any second now.'

Stubbornly the tannoy remained quiet. Then it burst into life, 'Now hear this, this is the *Baochuan*, please remain calm. The wormhole just opened up in our area is one of ours. Our reinforcements and replacements have just arrived.'

Hearing this, the three people on the bridge of the *Faust* began to cheer…mainly as a release of their built up tension. They were expecting another battle, and instead it turned into a celebration.

'A working wormhole,' exclaimed Praut in delight and wonder. 'Finally that bloody woman has proved as good as her word…she's done it.'

'Send a message to the *Tornarsuk*,' Praut told Clay. '*Congratulations, we've just witnessed the proof of your hard work. Well done*. Signed Praut.'

# 37
# CLEANING UP FOUREX

Fourex, being on the outer rim of the galaxy, had attracted those immigrants that were eager to remove themselves as far away from central government influence as they could. BelAir, the capital of Fourex, was a chaotic city, much in keeping with the inhabitants lifestyle. Buildings were built in a higgledy-piggledy manner with no eye to the aesthetics of planning. It had the visage of one of those ancient Earth towns that had grown organically as more people arrived and put up new dwellings.

The inhabitants were the scam artists, the criminally minded, those running from the tax authorities, or any authority at all. In ancient times the planet would have been called a tax haven where corporate entities could find ways of establishing attractive offshore shell subsidiaries. Most business enterprises on Fourex were of a shady and shoddy nature more suitable for smuggling and making fake goods, copies of well known brands. It was a boast that on Fourex the best known brands were available at a tenth of the market price. What they didn't tell you was, you got what you paid for.

Soon after the battle was finished, the flagship announced that the First and Second Battle Groups were getting ready to de-chip the population of Fourex now the aliens had been sent packing. This would likely take at least twenty four hours, since the population of Fourex was twice the population of Lowry. After cleaning up Fourex, there would be a strategic planning meeting regarding their looming trip to Andromeda. Praut, Rubin and Clay were invited.

On hearing the news, Karl exclaimed, 'About time we dealt with Fourex. Poor buggers must've been slaves for a long time. I wonder how long the aliens have been in occupation here?'

'Barnaby was being done for about a year, so Lowry probably took another year. Sounds like they've been under their thumb for about three years,' Praut speculated in answer to Karl's question.

'So how come WorldGov didn't do anything about it until we got involved in Barnaby?' asked Clay from the comm station.

'Bureaucratic sluggishness, obviously,' put in Fanny from her seat. 'The bigger they are, the slower they move. It goes with the territory.'

'Mind you, look where we are now they *have* moved,' said Karl with the space fleet in mind.

'And we still have no idea what these aliens look like, do we?' Mes asked, staring at Karl.

'Karl, what about this alien you said you killed,' Praut asked. 'Did you sort anything out with Adam? Have we got a sketch of one?'

'So-so. A spindly type. I didn't get a look a it. I got a shot off at it, but I didn't see the body. I must've killed it since it didn't appear again,' Karl tried to excuse himself.

'Ah, that's no good. I thought you saw the body. Seems like we're going to have to wait until Commander Wesley reports back to the admiral. He's been sent by the admiral to scour the alien ship for clues,' Praut informed them.

'What are we going to do while they clear Fourex?' Mes asked.

'What about the sketches I asked all of you to do? Anybody finished yet?' Praut looked around, still pursuing the alien image, but was met with stony silence. 'I see,' he lamented. 'You're all too shy to show me your work, is that it?' More silence.

'Adam's got this spindly drawing of a thin skeletal creature with an elongated head,' Karl offered again.

'Is that what *you* saw?' Praut wanted to pin down an image.

'Well sort of, but as I said, I didn't get a good look at it.' Karl was genuinely apologetic. 'All I saw was a yellow space suit, admittedly a bit lanky, but about average human height, disappearing through a doorway. I'm fairly certain I hit it with my laser. I'm sorry, that's the best I can do. Maybe this Wesley fellow can come up with a better image.'

'I hate not knowing what my enemy looks like,' bemoaned Mes. 'You can tell a lot from how somebody looks.'

'Clay, have you broken the encryption of the comms yet?'

'Just working on it Dil. Our encryptions are pretty good. Takes a lot of computing power to try and break them. We don't have it…not for this heavy encryption they're using. But I do have a message coming from the *Tornarsuk.*'

'Well? What does it say?'

'I'm just running the algorithm. Here it is: *Appreciate the congrats. The* Bolguard *just came through. We can now generate two wormholes.* Signed Randoline.'

'Heh? What....two wormholes? *Bolguard*?' Praut stood scratching his head. 'Bolguard's Walcott's original name. I have to assume the *Bolguard* is another wormhole ship…and if it is…we can appear in two places near the alien planet. It's got great implications...heh?'

Rubin appeared on the bridge, yawning.

'Are we making too much noise for you?' Karl asked light-heartedly.

'Eh? Oh no, I just thought I'd see what was happening out here,' Rubin replied, rubbing his eyes.

'Now you're here Adam,' Praut intervened. 'Maybe you could fill us in on what Fourex is really like. After all, they're your next door neighbours.'

'You want to know what Fourex is like, eh?' Rubin suddenly said with some venom. 'It's a *cesspit* of a planet. It's the name of a condom not a planet. If it wasn't for the aliens, I'd leave it to rot in its own garbage. The scum of the galaxy has ended up here on the outer rim running from the law. Full of hucksters, criminals, and flimflam artists. The former Governor of Fourex was a con artist, notorious for making false accusations against rivals, arresting them, and making the people he didn't like disappear.'

A voice from behind Rubin said, 'I can name you another planet in the same cesspit.' Fanny came up behind Rubin, looking fresh and lively, having just got herself a drink.

'And which planet is this?' Rubin enquired, not convinced.

'Harmony. You ever hear of it?' she asked.

'Ah yes, and I admit you're right,' acknowledged Rubin. 'We've colonised over four hundred planets to date and some were done in such a hurry that they attracted some unsavoury characters eager to leave Earth's jurisdiction.'

'If Fourex is such a dump, why bother de-chipping the people. Leave them as they are,' Clay put in callously.

'We can't just leave people with biochips in them... makes us as bad as the aliens,' insisted Praut. 'And its morally and ethically unacceptable.'

'BelAir, Fourex's capital, has a notoriety unmatched by any other capital,' Rubin continued. 'There *were* a number of big players there with the muscle to keep others at bay, corporations using the place as a tax haven. Now we have a chance, this cesspit needs cleaning up.'

'Wasn't it you Clay, who asked earlier why WorldGov didn't do anything about it until now?' Praut reminded Clay.

Clay screwed up his brow trying to remember, then nodded absent mindedly.

'WorldGov tends to let these kinds of planets collapse under their own corruption; then it comes and picks up the pieces and puts it right,' Praut explained. 'If Fourex is as bad as Adam says it was, then WorldGov would have been supplied with fraudulent reports as to its health, would have been left to get on with its own cesspit until it collapsed. Likely any WorldGov agents sent on a fact-finding mission would have disappeared without trace.'

'Message coming through from the flagship,' Clay announced.

'Decrypt it and read it to me,' Praut told him.

Clay ran his decryption algorithm and read: '*About to dechip Fourex. When we've finished with the capital BelAir, maybe you'd like to come down and let your computer genius trawl through the admin's computers. He seems to be able to find things we miss.* Signed Zheng.' Clay sat quietly trying not to blush.

'There Clay, you're getting a reputation,' Praut said smiling in his direction. 'Don't look so embarrassed, you deserve the praise.'

'Should we tell Barkin?' Mes asked.

'Yeah, good idea. Put him in the loop. I wouldn't mind having him by my side if Fourex is as bad as Adam says.'

Rubin retreated back into his cabin saying, 'Well if you don't need me, I'll get on with some of my work.'

Four hours went by before they were given permission to land on Fourex.

'There's a dome down there, in the middle of open ground,' Mes informed Praut, as she brought the ship down to BelAir. 'I'm going to park in the open just a little away from the main entrance.'

'Fine. Let's sit inside and wait for Barkin's ship to land,' Praut told his crew. 'I want some of his roughnecks with me when we go inside that dome.'

As on Lowry, the de-chipped population of BelAir had been teleported to the outskirts of the city and left to mill around until the whole planet had been de-chipped.

Zheng had moved operations onto the next large city, Sundown, and was now busy taking the alien biochip out of those inhabitants.

'Here comes the *Catz*,' Mes told Praut.

Barkin's ship landed with a roar, and then cut its engines. The doors slid open and the ramp came down. Two cagey figures came down the incline holding laser rifles at the ready. They slowly meandered towards the dome entrance, peering at it cautiously. Barkin followed them down the ramp but hung back, and ten more of his roughnecks followed him.

Praut watched on the *Faust's* external screen and smiled, 'Ever the wary one,' he exclaimed to Mes. Into his throat mike he said, 'Max you old scoundrel, good to see you. Still looking for a fight, eh?'

'And you're still hiding inside your ship, I see. Don't be shy, come out and join us. Don't worry, I'll protect you.' Praut heard Barkin chuckling into his throat mike.

The *Faust's* doors opened and Praut came out, fully dressed in a spacesuit. 'Don't trust these aliens. I'm staying inside this protection until we've looked around a bit.'

Barkin's roughneck's on hearing this, began openly laughing at Praut's precaution.

Barkin said, 'Zheng's people have been through this lot. If there was a problem they'd have warned us, don't you think?'

'That's assuming they found the threat,' Praut insisted.

'What threat? Come on Dil, your being a bit timid. Its not like you. What do you know I don't?' Barkin demanded with another chuckle.

Praut pointed at Barkin's two men that had come out of the ship first. They were a little way off near the dome entrance. They seemed to be furiously scratching at all exposed parts of their body. Then they both unexpectedly dropped their laser rifles and began frantically swatting the air.

'*Quick, close the doors*,' Praut shouted into his throat mike at his ship.

It dawned on Barkin that his two people were in trouble and he edged backwards towards his own ramp, pushing those behind him backwards, shouting, 'Get back in the ship, hurry.'

'*Its coming from the dome*,' Praut shouted at Barkin via his throat mike. He watched, safely ensconced in his spacesuit, as Barkin's people hurried back up the ramp and speedily slammed the door closed. He watched the two roughnecks turn bright red and the skin on their hands and faces began to disappear, eaten off by some unseen bug. They finally fell to the ground and writhed about in agony in pools of liquid from their own bodies.

Praut turned in horror and rushed back to the safety of the *Faust*. 'Karl, make sure you don't open the inner door until you've checked and vented the airlock,' he ordered Karl, who had been readying to come out next. 'I think we've got some kind of nanopest out here. Disinfect the airlock, make sure non of the little buggers get inside our ship.'

'Right Dil! I'll sift our airlock clean before I open the inner door…let the scrubbers do their work thoroughly.'

Over Praut's earphones came Barkin's angry voice, 'What the fuck was that? I've just lost two good men.'

'I'm guessing that it's some kind of nanobug left behind by the aliens. From what I observed, it attacks the skin and dissolves the flesh. Max, I had no idea beforehand these things were there. I swear to you. I wore the spacesuit out of precaution. The aliens are tricky and I thought better safe than sorry. My sympathies for the loss of your men. No one should die like that.'

Once back inside, Praut was pacing about angrily. 'Clay, get in touch with the flagship and tell them what's happened. Tell them there's an alien nanopest of some sorts in the atmosphere. Ask them what they can do about it.'

A little later after Clay had sent the message, there came reply; 'Dil, the flagship says their too busy at the moment. Their hands are full. There's a battle going on around some place called Sundown. They've found two new underground labs protected by a huge number of robot guardians. They suggest we inform Admiral Formby's Third Battle Group and ask them to take care of it.'

'Thanks Clay. Can you get in touch with Formby on the *Liaoning* and tell them the problem. Ask them if there's any way they can get some counter nanobots to neutralise the one's in the air. Tell them we think they're coming from the central dome. Ask them to send out a general warning regarding the nanopests, just in case there's more planet wide. Get an acknowledgement.'

After some time went by, the tannoy suddenly burst into life, 'Hallo *Faust,* this is the *Liaoning,* please switch to the secure channel.'

Praut's eyebrows went up, 'Aha, seems they're learning.'

Clay responded by doing so, and then said, 'Secure channel engaged. Go ahead *Liaoning*.'

Again from the tannoy, 'Message received and understood. We've been expecting something like this. The *Bolguard* is coming to your rescue. She a bit too big to put down in the space available, so she'll hover above you. She has the resources and the answer to your problem. *Liaoning* out.'

Fifteen minutes later the tannoy came to life, 'Hallo *Faust*, this is Captain Lombardi on the *Bolguard*.'

'Well bless my soul, hallo again Captain Lombardi,' Praut enthused. To Clay he asked, 'Are we still on a secure channel?'

Clay nodded.

'Mr Praut I presume?' Lombardi asked. 'I hear you need our help?'

'It seems so. I see they gave you the *Bolguard*, and well deserved, I'm sure. As for the help; did the *Liaoning* explain the problem?' Praut asked.

'Indeed it did,' replied Lombardi. 'We have the computing power and the replicators. I assume you need us to produce some nanobots to neutralise the bots that attacked your men?'

'That would be appreciated. I'm sure we'd all be grateful for your help. We think the pests are coming from the dome below you.'

'No problem. Give us an hour and we'll have a billion attacking engulfing nanobots ready for your pests. *Bolguard* out.'

'You know this Captain Lombardi?' Karl asked Praut in a surprised tone.

Mes answered for Praut, 'We both met him on the way to Callisto. We were in his vicinity to answer his *Mayday*.'

Karl didn't quite understand the explanation so he just shrugged his shoulders.

'Well, what do you know? We rescue Lombardi, and now he's come to rescue us. Life is cyclical, I'm sure of it,' Praut said to Mes, smiling at his own wit.

'You may be right Dil,' Mes responded, 'but the thinking sounds more like astrology to me, rather than logic.'

'Spoil sport!' returned Praut. 'Anyway, while we're waiting, why not get some food inside us. It must be about time for a break. I'll take Fanny and Karl with me and then they can spell Mes and Clay. By the way, where's Olga?'

'She must be in her cabin,' suggested Fanny.

'Ask her if she wants to join us for some food.'

Fanny went to fetch Olga, while Praut and Karl went into the lounge-come-diner and began programming their meals on the replicator.

Fanny came back alone saying, 'Olga doesn't want any food. She's not feeling too well.'

'What's up with her,' a concerned Praut asked.

'Oh its nothing serious…it's a woman's thing…you know,' replied Fanny, programming the replicator with her own meal.

'Oh, yeah. As long as she's okay. I'll pop in later to see if she wants anything,' Praut said, not entirely convinced Olga was okay.

Once both shifts had eaten, Clay announced that the *Bolguard* was on the line.

'Put it on the tannoy,' ordered Praut.

'Hallo *Faust.* Captain Lombardi here, we're ready to go. You say the locus of the pests came from the dome?'

'That's right,' Praut replied.

'We'll send our nanobot cloud to circle the dome at 20 meters diminishing inwards,' announced Lombardi. 'They're programmed to engulf and dismantle any pests they come across. I'm sending a second cloud into the atmosphere to search for any pests up there.'

'We need to get into the dome,' Praut told Lombardi. 'Keep me posted as to your progress.'

Another hour went by before they heard from the outside world. The tannoy came to life, 'Hallo *Faust*, this is the *Tornarsuk.* We have some news from the fleet for you. We're hovering close to our sister ship the *Bolguard.* The bad news is that the nanopests have attacked the de-chipped population of BelAir that's milling around the outskirts of the city. It's a sinister development and may put the whole of Fourex's population in danger if this isn't contained. The nanopests have made a bit of a mess of the inhabitants, presumably because they're no longer chipped.'

'Whom am I talking to,' asked Praut, since he obviously wasn't talking to Walcott.

'This is Captain Fenshaw. The fleet has informed us that the battle around Sundown has taken a turn for the worse. We've been ordered to stay well away from the area. Small nanodrones from the alien labs are attacking the supercarriers. Its turning into a nano battle with Zheng sending in nanobots to wipe out the nanodrones. We've been sent here to bolster the *Tornarsuk's* efforts. We've been told by the flagship to look out for femtobots.'

'Femtobots? What the hell are femtobots?' Praut wanted to know.

'They're a lot smaller than nanobots. Nano, then pico, and then femto. You can imagine the problem. We're here to produce picobots to deal with the femtobots. The *Bolguard* will deal with the nano, and we'll deal with the femto. Admiral Zheng is assuming the worst. We may have to abandon this planet if we can't contain these femtopests.'

'What about this area? Are we safe here?'

'For the moment, but not out in the open. Captain Lombardi tells me you wanted to get into the dome. I'm afraid that's probably out. The aliens are creating a nasty situation with their robots. It's best if you and your sister ship lift off and join us up here.'

'Clay, get through to the *Catz* and tell Barkin what you've just heard. Tell him we're abandoning the dome because of the nanopests. Get him to lift off and join us near the *Tornarsuk.*' Praut was worrying over the fate of Fourex's population. 'And Clay, how's the hacking coming along?'

'I'm nearly there. I've written an algorithm that decrypts the encryptions, only its still too slow. There's a minute's time lag before the translation come through and

I'm trying to straighten it out…be surprised how long a minute is in this game.'

'Well it's getting urgent, what with all this new stuff going on. I want to know what the flagship is saying, where we stand with these pesky robots. What are they doing with the population? There's millions of people at stake.' Praut couldn't believe Zheng would simply abandon Fourex and its population as Fenshaw implied.

'Dil, I've just registered two massive explosions on my instruments, just about where that other city Sundown is located,' Mes reported to Praut.

'Any idea what kind of explosions?' Praut came and stood over Karl's shoulder looking at the external viewing screen, although there was nothing to be seen.

'Small nukes,' she replied. 'I think it might have been those two robot labs near Sundown.'

'So Zheng is using nukes, is he? That's a bad turn in events. Means he's been forced to use them. Damn these bloody aliens. Why couldn't they have stayed in their own galaxy?' Praut said with venom.

# 38
# MILLIONS DEAD

Admiral Zheng moved all five Battle Groups to the edge of the Fourex Solar System in anticipation of the grand strategy meeting on the flagship called by the Admiral of the Fleet. The meeting was to discuss how to best deal with the aliens when they got to Andromeda, in the light of their current experiences. Fourex hadn't gone all that well.

At the meeting, the five admirals sat at the head of the table presided over by the fleet commander. Missing from the table was Commissioner Souza, who had stayed on Lowry as interim Governor.

At the outset, Vice Admiral Bennett stood to make a short announcement. 'Gentlemen and ladies, I'm pleased to announce that WorldGov has just officially confirmed the appointment of Admiral Zheng as Admiral of this Fleet and commander of our mission to Andromeda.'

The floor burst into rapturous applause while those round the table gave Zheng a polite clap as their plaudits.

Zheng rose to his feet, 'Thank you, I appreciate all of your sentiments, but…we have work to do. I called this meeting to inform our friends of what we, the military, have decide to do at our closed planning session. We have with us civilians and they've been a valuable asset to us so it's only fair they should know of our plans. We would like to share what we've learnt of the enemy…and what we propose to pursue as the winning strategy for this senseless war.'

There was a murmur of approval from the room at the positive implications of Zheng's words.

‘Since the arrival of the Fifth Battle Group late last night,’ and Zheng acknowledged the new face at the table with a slight bow, ‘A hearty welcome to Admiral Schumann on the *SSS Europa,* we now, in my assessment, have sufficient vessels in the fleet to head for the enemy’s front yard. It’s time we took the fight to the enemy’s home world. Before we leave, Admiral Schumann informs me that the Sixth Battle Group is almost ready to join us. I propose to leave the Sixth Battle Group to defend our own galaxy when we go to Andromeda.

‘Once more I must congratulate Mr Praut and his Agency for giving us vital information, such as the galactic coordinates of the enemy’s home planet. He has at his disposal an exceptional young computer genius who has provided us with this information. I also welcome in our midst the CEO of Singularity, Ms Walcott, and her two captains, who have provided us with the means to get to Andromeda by completing the construction of a viable and stable wormhole. I also acknowledge the presence of Captain Barkin and his men from Barnaby, the planet that woke us up to this alien menace. Thank you all for your presence and invaluable assistance.

‘Next, I sent Commander Wesley to sift through the debris of an alien ship we disabled. He’s come back with vital information on the enemy. I hand over to Commander Wesley for the next part of this presentation.’

From the far end of the table, a tall Wesley rose to his feet. ‘Thank you admiral. It was due to Captain Praut’s action that the enemy vessel was disabled and I bow to him and his crew’s valour. Incidentally, that damaged ship was their alien wormhole opener, so that’s one less to contend with. What we’ve discovered from that vessel is that the alien comes from a planet with half of earth’s gravity. It is a spindly intelligent creature about two meters tall, with a thin skeletal structure. It’s bipedal but with a balancing rear appendage and has two upper body appendages with seven fine digital manipulators. It's bifocal with over large hearing on either side of the head. Hardly any sense of smell due to the environment it lives in, which is misty and high in $CO_2$ levels, well beyond our capabilities to breath. Its skin is photosensitive and contains Xanthophyll, a yellow pigment, hence all the yellow colours on their spaceship. From what we've been able to discern by going through their vessel; they have a hive culture with a single leader at the apex. We have come to the conclusion that due to their hive mentality, they may not see the biochipping of humans in the same abhorrent way we do.'

Rubin was agog with what he was hearing, as was the rest of the large room. Praut and his group were sitting at the front next to Barkin, then Randoline Walcott and her two captains.

Wesley continued, 'The aliens are linked into a hive mentality and placing biochips into humans merely links the humans into their hive. It might even be seen as an honour for those humans to be linked into their hive. We need to be careful as to our anthropomorphic judgemental attitude towards the alien's intentions. However, we do need to explain to the aliens that what they did was contrary to our benefit and cannot be tolerated by humans. That would be my reason for going to the alien's home world. To talk to them and force them to back off from their one-sided approach to us.'

'Thank you commander, that has been most illuminating. I believe you have a picture of the alien to show us,' Zheng encouraged Wesley, while giving him a severe look for overstepping his remit.

At the press of a button, a full size holopic of the alien appeared on the top table. There was a collective gasp from the entire audience. Finally, there it was, their enemy was revealed to them.

'Thank you commander,' Zheng intervened as the holopic disappeared. 'Now we can see with whom we are dealing with. As for the commander's idea of talking and explaining ourselves to the aliens…that will be dependent on the alien's reaction to our appearing on their doorstep. I propose to go there with overwhelming force, and let *that* do my talking for me. If they ask to parley, then I'm prepared to listen, but my instructions from WorldGov are clear…to stop the alien invasion of our galaxy at all cost.

'We are now in a position to open two wormholes in the enemy's Solar System. I must say, the ease with which we have closed the enemy's wormholes had me worried, but a solution has been worked out which should prevent this from happening to us. My tactical advisers have proposed we send in a wormhole guardian force to protect our open wormholes. Two reduced Battle Groups will carry out this initiative; we think they will be sufficient for the purpose. The rest of the fleet will target the enemy wherever they are.

'Another precautionary measure will be to take only one Singularity ship with us, and leave the other here with the Sixth Battle Group. Should the worst case scenario prevail, this ship will create an escape wormhole for us so there'll be a route back to our galaxy. Thanks to our comm-gauge wormholes, we will have almost instantaneous communications between Andromeda and the Singularity ship left behind. Remember, we're not going there to wipe the aliens out, but to discourage them from coming here to enslave our human population. However I achieve that, by talking or waging war, that's my remit. Anybody have any questions?' Zheng sat down.

Praut rose to his feet and said, 'Yes admiral, I have a point of information to ask. What has happened on Fourex? What happened to the final outcome of the nano conflict, and what's happened to the population of Fourex?'

Zheng replied, 'Since Admiral Formby was in charge of tidying up our operations on Fourex, I'll let him answer the question.'

Formby didn't get up but spoke from his seat, 'It's been a bit of a disaster for the population. The good news is, we've eliminated the femtobots and the nanopests from the planet, using similar counter measures. We eventually had to use nukes to destroy the four labs we discovered and we've carefully mapped the planet from space to ensure we didn't miss any. We used picobots to contain the femtobots and nanobots to kill the nanopests…both supplied for us by the Singularity ships.' Formby nodded an acknowledgement at Walcott. 'However, half the remaining population of Fourex are complete basket cases—they've been under the biochip far too long, almost three years. They're currently on the four hospital ships, being taken care of. They'll be sent back to Earth for further treatment. Of the remaining fifty percent, thirty percent were killed, I mean literally taken to pieces by the nanopests, before we could manage to contain them. The planet is now clear of a threat, but only a fraction of the population has survived intact. We've positioned a large number of advisers planetside to help them recover, but this is a complete disaster zone at the moment.'

'Thank you admiral for that information,' Praut sat down, seemingly satisfied with the explanation.

'If that's all, I'll close the meeting,' Vice Admiral Bennett told them. 'Any further queries can go through the proper channels.'

As they were leaving the hall Praut's shoulder were hunched in concern.

'What's up,' Fanny asked Praut as she walked by his side.

'All those millions gone, just like that. I saw Max's people being taken to bits by those nanopests and it really is no way to go. Now they tell us millions went the same way. I just find it mind-blowing, that's all.'

‘Yes I noticed you were a little upset in the room,’ Mes added her voice to the conversation. ‘I’m sorry for them, but war is like that. It’s always been like that.’

‘I’m a sleuth not a warrior,’ Praut said gloomily to them both. ‘I search out and discover things…like…like where Darhlburg’s blueprint vanished to. That was a success. Darhlburg can’t complain that we didn’t do our job. But this mass murder business isn’t for me. Yeah, we loose some and we win some, and I try to get even one way or another…but millions? No, that’s not for me. Peculiar thing is, I’m still feeling vengeful for Edel, Til, and Harry. I still want my pound of flesh from the aliens for them. How weird is that?’

‘It’s not weird at all,’ Fanny told him. ‘It’s what makes us human. We’re full of pathos and contradictions. Unlike the minds of the aliens, humans have complex individual emotions, such as the ones your feeling right now. We’re social, but individuals at the same time. I can’t imagine a hive alien feeling sorry for the death of so many of its fellow beings.’

‘Dil, you old dog, what’s up? You’re shoulders are sagging as if you’re feeling sorry for yourself,’ walking up behind him, Barkin clapped Praut on his left shoulder.

‘I was just saying, all those millions…dead.’

‘You mean on Fourex?’

‘Where else?’

‘Yeah, well, that’s life…and oh, death eh?’

‘Does nothing phase you, Max?’

‘Can’t afford it Dil. Life’s too short. Lost a good many friends to these aliens back home. Lost another two…well you saw it for yourself. Can’t mope about. Got to get on with things, like getting my hands on a few aliens on their own planet. Roll on Andromeda…we’re coming to *get youooo!*’

Praut smiled, shrugged his shoulders and said, 'Thanks Max…you're a tonic. Just what I needed.' Praut turned the smile into a huge grin.

Both men then began laughing in earnest and playfully punching each other on the arm.

'They're letting off steam, venting their tensions,' Karl said, as a way of explaining this rough behaviour to the others.

Fanny, at first seemed shocked by it, but then relaxed. Mes shook her head at the boys antics, having witnessed this many times in her combat days. Clay was laughing from the side lines...enjoying it.

Both men calmed down as they saw Randoline Walcott approach them with her two captains.

'Mr Praut,' she began, 'I had the impression earlier you were concerned at what happened on Fourex, but from what I've just seen, it seems I was wrong.'

'Does my tomfoolery preclude my concern?' Praut asked somewhat severely.

'Well no, I just thought….' and she hesitated.

'Forgive me, Ms Walcott. I agree the horseplay is somewhat immature, but it's shifted the melancholy to the side. My friend here, Max Barkin,' Praut indicated to Barkin with his hand, 'has just put some of my qualms into perspective. I'm sure you have your own way of dealing with the occasional patches of darkness.'

Walcott nodded at Barkin, 'Put like that, then yes I do have my own way. What I really came over for, was to ask you if you'd care to come over to the *Tornarsuk* for dinner tonight…and of course, your invited Mr Barkin? I'd like to talk a few things over with you. Maybe you could bring your computer wizard with you.'

While they were chatting, the group were walking down the corridor towards the teleporter room. Mes was talking to Lombardi and introduced Barkin to the two Singularity captains.

‘About six tonight?’ Praut asked Walcott.

‘Fine, we’ll be waiting,’ and with that Walcott marched off, followed closely by Lombardi and Fenshaw, into the teleport station.

‘Well, what did you think of her,’ Praut asked Barkin.

‘Don’t really know,’ he replied cagily. ‘Pushy and driven, I’d say…but don’t quote me.’

‘What? With that rough lot you brought along with you…I wouldn’t dare,’ smiled Praut.

‘They’re for the aliens, not you,’ returned Barkin. ‘And they’re pussycats really.’

‘I believe you.’

‘Would I lie to you?’ Barkin dared Praut to contradict him with a glitter in his eyes and a broad grin.

With that, the group followed Walcott’s people into the teleporter room.

Back on the *Faust*, Praut voiced his thoughts out loud, ‘I wonder what Walcott wants? Must be something to do with computers, especially if she asked Clay to come along as well.’

‘Why not wait and find out instead of speculating?’ Mes suggested.

‘Always stay ahead if you can—that’s been a useful motto of mine, and its held me in good stead. Anyway, you’re probably right. Well Adam, what did you make of the meeting?’ Praut asked Rubin.

‘Hang on, let me show you something first,’ and Rubin went to his cabin and brought back his e-pad. ‘Have a look at this,’ Rubin held the e-pad out to Praut.

On it was a sketch of what looked like a copy of the alien holopic they’d seen in Wesley’s presentation on the flagship.

‘Well I’ll be blown out into space,’ retorted Praut looking at the sketch in astonishment. ‘You beat them to it…and you didn’t even see their ship. Look people, I told you this guy was bright. Well done. I'm still blown over by it.'

'It's the half earth's gravity that did this,' Rubin tried to explain. 'That was the information that clinched it. I put in green rather than yellow, but then Wesley had an advantage over me, didn't he?'

'I wonder what the rest of the crew has got as their sketches. Mine is nothing like this,' Praut said pointing at the sketch.

The bridge emptied hurriedly as people began to look for something to do. Praut stood chuckling, looking at the sham escapes. 'I'll want to see those sketches you did sooner or later. There's nowhere to hide on this ship.'

Mes was studiously checking her instruments. Clay began fiddling with his algorithm, trying to refine it to decrypt the comms. Olga was heading for her cabin, as was Fanny. Rubin smiled at their antics and slowly sauntered towards his cabin, following Karl off the bridge. Karl had loudly announced his intention of getting a much needed drink.

By the time the evening came, the ship had commenced its usual routine.

'Adam,' Praut spoke into his throat mike. 'I want you with me on this Singularity dinner. 'You've got half an hour to get ready. Formal wear compulsory.'

Praut, Mes, Rubin and Clay stood wearing their formal togs, ready for the teleport to the *Tornarsuk*. 'Clay, you linked my throat mike to their comms as I asked?'

'Yes Dil, just talk into it.'

'Hallo *Tornarsuk*, this is the *Faust*; four ready to teleport to you,' Praut said into his mike.

'*Tornarsuk* to *Faust,*' came the response, 'initiating teleport.'

Lombardi was waiting with Barkin, to welcome them and escort them to the dining area.

'As you may have guessed, we have a computer problem we'd like your help with,' said Lombardi without any preliminaries. 'They've got it isolated, but can't seem to stop it.'

'I'm sorry? You've got what isolated?' Praut asked a little irritated at the turn of event. He was hoping to have a little relaxation before getting down to business. He smiled quickly at Barkin to say hallo.

'One of our q-machines is infested with some kind of infection…they've disconnected it from the other machines but…' Lombardi just realised he'd overstepped the proprieties of his welcoming duty. 'I'm sorry, I should leave this problem to the technicians. Ms Walcott is waiting to receive you.'

Clay's ears pricked up at the mention of a q-machine and Praut saw he was twitching to get at the computer.

Lombardi led them down to the dining room, but just before they went in, Praut suggested Lombardi take Clay to where the problem computer was.

'He's going to be impossible until he has a go at it. I'll explain to Ms Walcott where you've gone,' said Praut.

'Thank you Mr Praut. That would be a good solution.' Lombardi and Clay wondered off further along the corridor.

'Almost didn't make it,' said Barkin. 'Last minute problem. Would have been a pity to miss you cuddling with your lady friend.'

Praut gave Barkin a severe look, then burst into a chuckle. 'Keep it up, just keep it up. There'll be blood spilt before the evening's out.'

The door slid open onto a large room. On one side there were a number of contour couches and chairs. In one of them sat Randoline Walcott sipping a drink. She rose as Praut, Barkin, Mes, and Rubin entered.

'Welcome Mr Praut, Mr Barkin, and Ms Monat.' She raised her eyebrows at Rubin.

'Let me introduce Dr Adam Rubin of Lowry to you,' said Praut. 'Adam is our alien expert. Ms Walcott, the CEO in charge of the wormhole project,' Praut explained. 'By the way, Captain Lombardi's taken my computer specialist off with him to sort out your problem. He asked me to tell you.'

Walcott looked suitably embarrassed at this information. 'I was hoping he'd do this after we've all had dinner.'

'When Clay heard there was a computer problem, I couldn't hold him back. He'll be along shortly. I shouldn't think its going to take him too long to sort it out.'

Walcott shook her head in disbelief, 'No I'm afraid its quite serious. We've been at it for a whole day.'

'You don't know Clay. I've never come across anyone like him,' said Praut. 'He's a real genius when it comes to computers.'

Walcott had a real waiter take their drinks order then continued. 'Let me tell you what happened. One of my scientists, against explicit standing orders, connected his e-pad to one of the q-machines. Next thing we know, it began chewing up data. First emergency move was to isolate this machine from the other six.' Walcott waved her hand at the seats, inviting them to sit. 'The scientist's e-pad must've been connected to gq-net and got infected that way. Mind you, he must've been targeted; it wasn't by chance.'

'We're in a war situation; we're all targeted. It would be stupid of the aliens not to do so if they could,' intervened Mes.

'Yes I suppose you're right. I mean that's why my machines are not connected to the net so that no outside intervention is possible.'

The drinks came and were handed around.

'Well, here's to Andromeda,' Walcott proposed the toast.

Praut, Barkin, Mes, and Rubin raised their glasses, '*Andromeda*,' they all responded.

‘Is your wormhole able to reach another galaxy?’ asked Barkin, settling comfortably in his seat.

‘We had a few sequence reiteration problems, but they’ve been successfully sorted,’ Walcott replied. ‘As long as we have good 3D galactic coordinates to aim for, it should all work out fine.’

‘And that was down to Clay, I ought to tell you,’ Praut pointed out. ‘I couldn’t have done half of what we’ve achieved without him. It was Clay who found the coordinates on the alien vessel.’

‘This Clay, is he the small brown haired young man I’ve seen with you?’ Walcott inquired.

Praut nodded, ‘That’s him.’

‘What has me intrigued,’ Rubin asked Walcott, ‘is how you’re going to open two wormholes from one set of galactic coordinates?’

‘That’s not really a problem. We have one set of 3D coordinates and then drift the second set a decimal of a degree to whichever way we need to, south, west, east or north, and…there you are,’ answered Walcott.

‘So you’re changing the original coordinates by a decimal of a degree?’

‘That’s it.’

An electronic bell sounded calling them to the long dining table nearby. They all rose, and at the same time the door slid open, and Clay came in, looking mightily pleased with himself.

‘Clay,’ called out Praut. ‘Don’t tell me you’ve sorted the glitch out already?’

‘Yeah, wasn’t a big deal. It was that bloody grabworm we had a run-in with back in the office. Banged in my killer programme and poof…gone.’

Walcott’s brow furrowed in disbelief. She slowly shook her head, but kept walking towards her seat at the head of the table.

Praut looked at her meaningfully. The look said, *I told you so.*

'So Mr Clay, we're clean?' Walcott asked as she sat down, still not quite able to believe the speed with which this young man had accomplished the task, a task her people had struggled with a whole day.

'Yes Ma'am. Your computer's clean,' Clay said in a satisfied tone. 'Gosh, I'm hungry.'

'Would you like anything special to eat?' Walcott asked. 'We have roast venison for the main meal.'

'Oh that's good, I like that,' enthused Clay.

The whole table laughed gently and good naturedly.

# 39
# ANDROMEDA

'Andromeda is named after the Chained Maiden of ancient Greek mythology. She was chained to a rock as a sacrifice to a monster, but saved from death by her future husband, Perseus.'

Rubin had been asked by Praut to give the crew an idea of where they were going and so he put together a small presentation in the dining-room-come-lounge.

'The Andromeda Galaxy,' Rubin continued, 'shown on the astral charts as M31, is approximately 780 kpc away from the Milky Way. That's around 2.5 million light-years as the crow flies,' Rubin smiled at his own wit. He was back in his element, in front of a class giving a short lecture. 'Constellation Andromeda has a bright yellowish wormhole nucleus, similar to our galaxy. It has dark winding dustlanes, and bluish spiral arms and star clusters, which frankly, pretty much describes the Milky Way as well.'

'Sounds more like a travelogue,' came a heckled comment from the back of the room.

'Quiet there Clay,' Praut admonished on Rubin's behalf. 'Or I'll make you get out and walk there.'

'The exercise would do him good,' intervened Karl.

'Karl,' Praut looked severely at the co-pilot, encouraging him to be quiet as well.

'That's our destination,' Rubin pointed at a holopic of the galaxy on the table in front of him. 'Somewhere in there is where our alien enemy comes from. What we still don't know is how long they've been around, and how many planets they've colonised in Andromeda. We don't even know if the coordinates we have, come out near their home world, or near a militarised planetary war base. These questions I leave to the military. I assume they've catered for such surprises. What we do know, is the alien comes from a planet with half of earth's gravity. It's a gangly intelligent creature about two meters tall, with a thin skeletal structure. It's bipedal but with a balancing rear limb and has two upper body limbs with seven digit-like fingers. I'm quoting from Commander Wesley's speech. It's bifocal with over large hearing and hardly any sense of smell. The environment it lives in is high in $CO_2$ levels, well beyond human ability to breath. Its skin is photosensitive and contains Xanthophyll, a yellow pigment. And from Wesley's assumption, they have a hive culture with a single leader at the top. Any questions?'

'Is that it?' asked Olga, ever obliging.

'What? You want *more*?' Rubin asked in affected alarm. 'Dil only hired me for a taster. If you want more you'll have to pay the normal student rates.'

Olga looked puzzled. She thought Rubin was being serious.

'He's having you on,' Fanny told her. 'He's getting as bad as Dil, with his sardonic twists.'

'Oh!' said Olga smiling again. 'A person can't even come out to a lecture without getting their leg pulled.'

'Be glad I'm not a alien, or I'd pull it off and have a quick nibble on it,' laughed Rubin.

'How'd you know they're not vegetarians?' returned Fanny, coming to Olga's aid.

'Clay, get on the comms and find out what's happening out there,' Praut ordered, trying to subdue the unruly outburst.

'Yes Dil,' Clay rushed off back to the bridge.

When Praut came onto the bridge, holding a glass of green tea, he looked at Clay. 'Well? Any news yet?'

'Something seems to be happening,' said Karl from his co-pilot's seat. '*Hey*, a wormhole mouth just opened up…there's ships coming through. Hey Dil, come and have a look at this.'

Praut came to stand and look over Karl's shoulder, staring at the external viewing screen.

'Must be the Sixth Battle Group coming through,' he suggested to Karl. 'If it is, then we're close to leaving for Andromeda. Zheng's been waiting for this lot to come through before setting off.'

'Anything on the comms,' Karl asked Clay.

The tension on the bridge increased as the crew realised they might be close to leaving for Andromeda. The jump into another galaxy was felt with trepidation by everyone; it was the unknown element that set their adrenaline pumps racing.

'I'm just getting something,' Clay announced. 'The whole fleet's been put on maximum alert. The flagship is calling for the Singularity ships to be ready to open their wormholes.'

'Clay, have you cracked the encryptions?' Praut asked all of a sudden.

Clay was quiet for a moment, then said, 'Yes Dil. I found the problem just before Adam's presentation. This is the first time I've had a chance to try it out.'

'Have you informed the flagship of your hack?'

'Not yet.'

'Do so *before* we go down the wormhole. They've got to know its possible, otherwise the aliens will do the same and put us at a disadvantage.'

'Yes Dil. I'll do it now.' Clay began to concoct an encrypted message to the flagship regarding his method. He seemed to do it reluctantly, always a bit selfish in giving away his secrets.

Praut held up his hand, 'Right, listen up everybody. Are you ready for this Andromeda trip? No second thoughts?'

A deathly silence met his question.

‘This is your last chance to back out of this.’ Praut stared at his people. ‘It could be more dangerous than anything we’ve ever done before. No one will think any the less of you if you decide not to go.’

No one spoke up or even acknowledged Praut’s statement. Its as if he hadn’t said anything.

‘Dil, I’ve got an acknowledgement from the flagship regarding the encryption,’ Clay told him. ‘They say thanks, and much appreciated. I think they’re going to try and change the encryption…then I’ll have to start all over again.’ It sounded more like a complaint than a message.

‘Don’t grumble, you know you enjoy these challenges,’ cajoled Praut.

‘Hang on Dil, there’s a general order coming through,’ Clay listened intently for a moment, then said, ‘Its come. We’re to be ready to go through the wormhole in half an hour. The order is from the flagship.’

‘So, this is it. We’re leaving our galaxy for the first time in human history,’ Praut announced loudly. ‘Columbus, Gagarin, Laufenberg, eat your hearts out. Karl, keep a sharp lookout on the external screen for the wormhole.’

‘Laufenberg?’ Olga looked puzzled.

‘Come on? Which school did you go to?’ Karl chided her from across the bridge. ‘Captain of the *SSS Voyager III*. The first manned ship to leave the Solar System.’

‘Oh, that Laufenberg,’ said Olga, with a touch of embarrassment.

The tannoy suddenly burst into life, ‘Hallo *Faust*, this is the *Tornarsuk*, keep an eye out on what we’re doing. You’re to follow us through the wormhole. Make sure your sensors are monitoring our whereabouts. We’ve informed the *Catz*; they’re to follow you down the wormhole.’

‘*Tornarsuk*, message acknowledged,’ Clay told the Singularity ship.

‘Dil,’ cried Karl, ‘The wormhole’s opening.’

‘Everybody strap into their seats,’ shouted Mes from the pilots chair. ‘We’re about to go down a wormhole.’

Rubin, Olga and Fanny joined Praut in strapping into their seats.

Moments went by as the rest of the fleet began to split in to two groups.

‘The other wormhole’s opened,’ Karl reported.

Clay said, ‘The *Tornarsuk* is on the move.’

‘I’m on its tail,’ shouted Mes, and she put the *Faust* on the trail of the Singularity ship, following it down into the yawning mouth of the wormhole ten kilometres away.

Vessel after vessel disappeared down the two gaping wormholes, only the *Bolguard* and the Sixth Battle Group remained behind in the Milky Way.

After some time in the mind-bending tunnel, the *Faust* shot out into galactic space, having crossed the intergalactic void to Andromeda, which should have been shrouded in darkness, but was in fact lit up with cannon fire. Laser and maser beams were criss-crossing through the blackness of space, hitting vessels, lighting the shields up. The *Faust* was followed by the *Catz* and a number of other vessels, spewing out of the wormhole into a crowded perilous milieu.

Cannon fire was everywhere; the enemy had been waiting for them in ambush. All of Zheng’s fleet was blasting away at various enemy spaceships infesting this sector of space.

The tannoy on the *Faust* went berserk with a shrill electronic note bleeping its emergency signal. A shudder went through the *Faust*, followed in quick succession by further hits.

‘*How’s the shields holding?*’ Praut shouted at Mes.

‘Fine! That extra reinforcing has done the trick. We’re still at ninety five percent.’

Karl was pumping the cannon button and blasting away at targets only he could see on his screen. ‘The supercarriers are giving them hell. There must be thousands of our fighters out there. I'm having to be careful not to hit any of them.'

'Where are we?' asked Praut. 'Can you see a planet?' The question was directed at either of his two pilots.

'We've come out into clear galactic space. The galactic coordinates were a trap,' replied Mes. 'There's no planet anywhere in sight.'

'The enemy's using some kind of beam to try and close our wormholes,' shouted Karl.

'My sensors indicate the beam is positrons and quark-gluon plasma,' announced Clay. 'The aliens are bombarding the wormholes with positrons and quark-gluon plasma,' Clay repeated. 'They're trying to unbalance the exotic matter used to keep the wormholes open.'

A couple of extra strong shudders went through the hull of the *Faust*.

'What the hell was that?' demanded Praut.

'Nukes going off,' reported Karl. 'Zheng's using nukes on the ships putting out the funny beams. Seems the aliens don't have nukes, so Zheng's using nuke missiles to stop them closing our wormholes.'

'This is getting really dangerous,' spat out Praut. 'Are the nukes having any effect?'

'They're blasting the alien ship to bits. What with the cannon fire and the nuke missiles, the aliens are pulling back,' reported Karl. 'Wait….another wormhole's just opened up behind the alien fleet. The aliens are disappearing down it..... Shit…that's it…they're gone.'

'Is that it?' asked Praut.

'That's it Dil. Coo, its gone quiet out there. All the firing's stopped.' Karl almost sounded wistful. His firing finger was still twitching.

'Hallo *Faust*, *Catz* here,' Barkin's voice came over the tannoy. 'You okay? Any damage?'

'Hi Max, no damage. What about you?'

'We're alright. Just a bit shook up from the concussion waves from those nukes. So where are we? I can't see any planets anywhere. What's going on?' Barkin sounded concerned.

'Good question. It's the same one I'm asking. We'll hear from the flagship shortly. Just have to be patient until they organize themselves.' Praut was trying to sooth and placate.

'Well, glad you're okay Dil, see you soon. Barkin out.'

'I think we've landed into a bit of a mess,' voiced Mes. 'We've lost any element of surprise we may have had. Did you see that, the buggers were waiting for us.'

'Zheng will sort it out,' Praut said without much conviction.

A couple of hours went by with a deathly silence coming from the flagship. The aliens had vanished to where ever they came from, with no further attacks being launched. Mes concluded from observations, they'd come out of the wormhole somewhere in between the two major arms of the Andromeda galaxy, out in clear space.

'Why don't you go and get some drinks while you can,' Praut told his crew.

'I think we're going to have to go back home and try again later,' Clay suggested somewhat despondently.

'Oh, you can't be serious?' complained Rubin, unstrapping from his seat and getting up. 'Not after all that's happened. We can't just go back. We're almost there, just a little more effort and we'll…' He left it hanging not clear what he wanted from this trip. Half of him, the scientist, wanted to befriend the aliens, get to know them—the other half, the human, knew the danger and wanted to help destroy them. The dilemma was confusing his thoughts. He headed for the canteen.

'I'm just getting a message through from the flagship,' Clay announced loudly. He fiddled with his decryption algorithm, then said, 'They've got a new set of galactic coordinates for another wormhole. Because the other wormhole ship is back in our galaxy, we can only open one wormhole here. They want all lightly armed vessels to go through last, and only then for the civilians to follow them. I've acknowledged we received their message,' Clay told Praut.

'Hallo, *Tornarsuk* to Captain Praut, are you receiving us?' a woman's voice came over the tannoy.

'Now what,' griped Clay.

'Praut here,' said Praut into his throat mike. 'Is that Ms Walcott?'

'Yes Mr Praut. It seems Commander Wesley has discovered a new set of 3D galactic wormhole coordinates for us. It may lead to the alien's planet. You've heard the flagship's announcement?'

'Indeed I have. It puzzled me,' Praut replied into his throat mike.

'I thought you should know that our current situation had Zheng stumped until Commander Wesley came up with the answer,' Walcott said into Praut's earphones. 'He'd downloaded all of the data held on that damaged alien space vessel, you know, the one which gave us the current X, Y, and Z coordinates, and then left the q-machine to analyse the rest of the downloaded alien data—all of it in minute detail. The q-machine has just discovered another set of 3D galactic wormhole coordinates. We're hoping this lot will put us at their planet. Zheng is determined to keep going until we find them.'

'You must be close by if I can pick you up on my earphones?' Praut said.

'We came and parked next to you so I could talk with you. I thought you deserved to be informed of what's happening.'

'I appreciate the information. So we're off again? How soon?'

'I'm almost ready to open the wormhole, so stand by.'

'By the way, point of information. Did that alien beam disrupt your wormhole at all? I'm just curious.'

'If they'd managed to sustain it for much longer it might have, but Zheng's nukes stopped them dead.'

'Thanks Ms Walcott. Praut out.'

'What was that all about?' asked Mes.

Nobody other than Praut heard the conversation he'd just had.

'That was Randoline Walcott,' Praut said so everyone could hear. 'It seems Commander Wesley's discovered another set of galactic wormhole coordinates hidden in that data from the alien vessel we knocked out back near Fourex. Walcott thinks they might lead us to the alien's planet. There's only one wormhole ship here, so they're opening a wormhole real soon. Zheng's got his teeth into the aliens and he's determined to get them.'

'What puzzles me is why there were so few alien vessels in the ambush?' Karl speculated.

Praut thought for a second, then proposed, 'Maybe the aliens weren't expecting such a large human flotilla to come a visiting, so although they prepared an ambush, they got bitten and were forced to go for reinforcements.'

'If that's the case, our next encounter may not be so easy,' countered Mes.

'You of all people should know you ought to leave the strategy and tactics to the professionals,' Praut chided her. 'Remember the motto: What you can't control—live with.'

'I'm just saying, next time it might not be so easy, is all,' Mes said in response.

'The wormhole's opened again,' cried Karl from where he sat.

'*Strap in everybody*,' shouted Praut. 'We're on the move again.'

Karl watched as ship after ship queued up to enter the wormhole. Reconnaissance drones were sent down first, followed by thousands of fighters, then they were followed by the five supercarriers. After that came the rest, the battleships, the destroyers, the frigates, corvettes, and then it was their turn. The *Faust* disappeared down the throat of the wormhole with the *Catz* close behind.

They came out as before, into the darkness of space, but with one big difference—they were on the outskirts of a Solar System with planets and a main sequence yellow-white star at its centre.

'Hey look, two gas giants and the fifth planet over there, surrounded by squadrons of alien ships,' Karl announced peering at his external screen. 'Their sun's registering as a main sequence yellow-white star F3V, white in actual colour, somewhat hotter than our sun.'

'Why so quiet?' asked Praut suspiciously.

'They're waiting for us to attack,' suggested Mes, staring hard into space at the alien squadrons.

# 40
# ALIEN PLANET

The quiet didn't last for long. Zheng began to disposition the four Battle Groups, sending them in all four directions round the System's heliopause. He kept his Second Battle Group stationary near the wormhole.

'He's trying to surround them,' Mes informed her listeners.

'Why aren't the aliens attacking?' Praut asked again.

'You know, I think they're hesitating because of our nukes,' Karl suggested as a likely answer. 'I don't think they have them, at least they haven't used any. I think we've got a game-changing weapon.'

'They're on the move…and coming towards us,' Mes informed them. 'Hang on to your hats, I'm moving us out of the way.'

The *Faust* gave a burst of speed which pushed the occupants back into their seats and moved the ship further out, away from the wormhole.

Karl began to fire his cannon, 'There's nine large alien ships closing in on the wormhole.'

'There they go again,' Clay announced. 'They're using their positrons and quark-gluon plasma beam to try and close the wormhole.'

'Brace yourselves…Zheng's gonna whack them with some nukes,' Praut told them, remembering what happened the last time this scenario played out.

'Here we go again,' voiced Rubin, almost parodying Clay.

The nuke shock wave jostled the *Faust* for a short while and then ceased. Olga did a high shriek as the shock wave struck, more from excitement than worry.

'Told you,' Praut said with a thumb up to show he approved Zheng's action.

'That was a dinger,' emitted Fanny.

'The aliens have retreated back to where they were,' said Karl. 'Ah, the other Battle Groups have opened fire. They're piling it on at the enemy around the alien planet. Mes, can't we get in closer. I'm out of effective firing range,' complained Karl.

'Let the big boys have a go, then we'll go in,' retorted Mes.

'There's more ships coming up from the planet,' cried Karl. 'Mes…please…'

'Hold on Karl, Mes is right,' Praut calmed him. 'Be patient, this thing isn't over. You'll get plenty of chances to have a go.'

The tannoy came to life, 'Dil, Max here. Why don't we swing to the right? I've spotted there's less of the buggers over there. We can have a crack at them from that side.'

'Max, you that eager to get into this mess?'

'I've got a score to settle with those bastards. You coming or are you going to sit and watch me do your job?'

'Put like that, you don't leave me much choice,' Praut said into his throat mike.

Karl's face lit up at the prospect of some action.

'Mes, follow the *Catz* wherever it's leading us,' ordered Praut.

'Right Dil,' answered his pilot.

'If the nukes are so effective, why isn't the admiral using more of them?' asked Rubin from his seat. 'We could finish this business once and for all...then we might have some peace.'

‘Nuke missiles need to be used most carefully,’ Mes tried to explain. ‘Karl’s right, they’re a game-changer, but they’re also too powerful to simply blast away with willy-nilly.’

‘*Hang on a sec*,’ barked Karl. ‘There’s more missiles being sent from the supercarriers…from all four directions. I think they’re nukes.’

‘And there’s some missiles coming at us from the aliens,’ Mes informed them.

‘At us or Zheng?’ asked Praut.

‘Well, at Zheng’s ships.’

‘What’s Barkin doing?’

‘He’s moving away from the area, going west.’

‘Follow him. It’ll put us out of harms way.’

Karl was drumming his fingers, getting more frustrated by the minute.

‘I see what the aliens are up to,’ declared Mes. ‘They’re waiting to see our disposition and then they’ll attack.’ She was speculating. ‘Zheng has covered five points of the planet, leaving a sixth as the aliens escape route. Now the enemy know this…in fact here they come.’

Karl concentrated on his screen and his fingers were itching to fire. ‘Mes get me under their belly. Dive down, get me under them.’

Mes complied with her gunner’s request. She dived down underneath the incoming alien squadron. Karl began firing as his auto screen cross hairs matched their targets, pumping out the vitriol from his cannon, up into the alien vessels as they came nearer. In their turn the aliens fired back, giving as good as they got. The *Faust* was being hit time and again, shuddering with every strike.

Olga’s eyes were glazed with excitement. She couldn’t sort out if she was afraid or not. Rubin held his arm rests tightly, nodding his head with every hit on the ship, counting them. Clay was staring hard at Karl, urging him on with his head. Fanny had gotten herself a drink and was sipping it nervously, looking up with every jolt the ship was taking, trying to be nonchalant. Praut held his eyes piercingly on Mes, watching her every manoeuvre intently.

Almost every part of this Solar System was enmeshed in a battle of some sorts. Ships were chasing ships, firing on each other to deadly effect. Other vessels lay dead in space, damaged beyond salvage—both alien and human. The debris of various vessels made it look like a gigantic space junk yard. The big supercarriers were dishing out the harshest punishment to the aliens, but the smaller frigates and corvettes were being hammered.

'Damn them, as quickly as we knock them out, others are coming up from their planet to replace them,' complained Mes.

Karl agreed with Mes' sentiments, 'It's as if the planet down there was a military base with unlimited spaceship stock. We knock 'em out and they bring more up.'

'Karl, less talk and more firing,' ordered Praut.

'Dil, I've just picked up some bad news,' Clay announced. 'The *SSS Europa* has been badly damaged. She's fighting on but it sounds like they're in trouble.'

'That's Admiral Schumman's flagship?' Praut asked Mes.

'Yes,' she responded. 'It's the Fifth Battle Group's supercarrier. That *is* bad news.'

Zheng then gave the order to use more nuke missiles. They were aimed at the alien squadrons surrounding the planet.

'Hey Dil,' Clay called out again. 'I'm just picking it up from the comm traffic. Zheng's sent his nine fighter squadrons to escort a destroyer to deliver a nuke hit on the planet...you know, on the place where those enemy ships are lifting from.'

'Great. That'll get their attention,' proclaimed Karl.

'That's if they get through,' Praut exclaimed.

'I don't think we need *more* of their attention surely,' put in Rubin.

'We do, we do!' contradicted Karl. 'We have to overcome everything they can throw at us…that's the only way to win.'

'Okay, calm down everyone. Let's see what happens,' advised Praut. He went to stand behind Karl to watch the external screen. 'Can you turn this thing towards the planet.'

'Sure, no prob.'

Praut watched the distant fighter squadrons battling it out with the aliens, trying to escort the destroyer through to its destination. Fighter after fighter went up in flashes, but the destroyer eventually fired its nuclear missile at the planet. After travelling through the planet's inner space, then through its stratosphere, and atmosphere, there was a pregnant pause, and then a mushroom cloud expanded until it was clearly seen from space.

'*Boom!*' said Karl as he watched the nuclear cloud expand down on the planet. Then more thoughtfully he added, 'That's a sight I don't want to see too often.'

Praut just stood there peering at the screen, shaking his head. After a while he said, 'They brought this upon themselves.'

As they watched, the firing throughout the battle area seemed to die down—then it stopped altogether. It was a disaster—for the aliens. They had no protection from such a devastating weapon, and had no answer to it.

The tannoy burst into life, 'This is the flagship. Admiral Zheng speaking. We've had a request for a ceasefire from the alien command. I'm ordering all ships to ceasefire as of now. Stay at *Actions Stations*, and stay tuned for further bulletins.'

The people on the deck of the *Faust* were stunned by the news, then a big cheer went up.

Rubin was the first to break into voice. 'He's done it. Good old Zheng!'

'Hold on, its just a ceasefire. Wait until we find out what the aliens want,' cautioned Praut.

'They're suing for peace, surely?' answered Rubin. 'What else could it be?'

'How about playing for time? What about wanting a breather? What about cooking up a devious scheme to undermine our advantage? You've followed the aliens manoeuvres…what do you think?' Praut was scathing in his response to Rubin.

'Oh alright…it could be a trick,' Rubin admitted reluctantly. 'But it could be genuine, couldn't it?'

'What? Like the ambushes and the biochips? Genuine my sainted aunt. I wouldn't trust these aliens as far as I could spit.'

'Let's wait and see,' murmured Rubin as a final remark.

'Look, there's something coming through the alien squadrons,' remarked Karl. 'Looks like a ship…bloody funny looking ship. Never seen anything like it. Looks like three massive bubbles joined together. Its huge.'

Praut peered over Karl's shoulder again. 'I'll bet it's a massive bomb,' Praut told them.

The tannoy came online again to announce, 'This is the flagship. We're being told that the leader of the aliens is on board that bubble ship just coming through their lines. The *Baochuan* is going to meet it. Stay tuned.'

'So's the *Bolivar* and the *Vishal*, look,' Karl declared, pointing to either side of the screen.

'I confirm there's two supercarriers closing in on the alien bubble ship,' agreed Mes.

'What the hell are they up to?' Fanny was trying to see the screen over Praut's shoulder.

'I've a strange feeling I know,' said Praut. He wouldn't elaborate no matter how he was pressed by his people.

As the bubble ship carrying the alien leader cleared its own lines and headed for the *Baochuan*, a missile was fired at the bubble ship by both the *Bolivar* and the *Vishal*.

Karl's mouth opened in shock. 'Hey, they've just fired at the alien leader,' he said. 'The two ships on either side….' he broke off the sentence as the two nuclear missiles exploded and the shock wave rammed the *Faust*.

Rubin jumped out of his seat and came running as the *Faust* settled down. 'Have we just fired on the alien leader?' he demanded.

'Too late Adam. There's no more alien leader left,' said Karl with satisfaction.

'I can't believe what we've just done. He was under a truce. We've violated the truce,' Rubin exclaimed. He simply couldn't understand it. His brain didn't want to take it in.

'The notion of civilised warfare is a human construct and has no place in this battle for survival with an alien,' Praut told Rubin loudly so all could hear. He was staring hard at Rubin. 'This alien has schemed all of our humanity into slavery. There's no room for fair play here. The aliens have never been straight with us since this thing began. We had a chance to destroy their leader and Zheng took it. I, for one, applaud his initiative. I'm proud to be part of his fleet.'

'But…but…' Rubin was left speechless.

The rest of Praut's crew patted Praut on the back to show they were with him all the way.

'Hallo, this is the flagship. I take full responsibility for the order to fire on the alien leader.' It was Zheng's voice. 'If the alien society is a hive society, then removing the head is the most likely way of stopping their war on us. I hope I have just done that.'

'Dil, Max here. See what just happened. Isn't it great. Hear Zheng on the tannoy? Isn't he brilliant?'

'Hi Max,' Praut said into his throat mike. 'Yea, just great. They broke the mould when they made him.' Praut was referring to Zheng.

'*Whoa, something's happening out there*,' shouted Karl, interrupting Praut's contact. 'Oh shit....there's multiple wormholes opening all over the place. One, two, three, four, five…six…seven. Seven wormholes…and there's ships coming through. Alien ships, big ones. Hundreds of them…and more.' A glum look replaced the happy face Karl had just worn a second before.

Praut rushed back to look at the screen. He stood back after staring at their disaster. 'Just when I'd thought we'd won.'

'There's thousands of them coming through,' bemoaned Mes. 'We're lost. There's a few bigger than our supercarriers. We can't take that many on. We're outnumbered ten to one…and there's more appearing as I speak.'

'*What the fuck?*' Max's voice said into Praut's earphone somewhat harshly. 'I don't believe what I'm seeing.' A brief moment of silence was followed by, 'Our goose is cooked, isn't it? The numbers are overwhelming. See you in the next world Dil. There's no way out of this, is there?' The connection went dead.

'Oh no…there's another wormhole opening,' cried Karl. 'Hang on....there's only....ten ships coming out of it.'

'What difference does that make. We're finished,' cried Fanny, clutching at Praut's arm.

'Hallo, this is the flagship again. As you can see, we're utterly outnumbered with this new situation. We're completely surrounded and I've ordered a fight to the last man. Maybe our ferocity in this last battle will deter the aliens from going back to our galaxy and thus help our own people to survive for a while. I'm ordering the use of every nuke we have left. Good luck and remember, we're fighting for the people back home, Zheng out.'

'Send a message to the *Tornarsuk*,' Praut told Clay. 'Thanks for all your help. If you can escape, you should do so now. Tell the people back home what's happened and that the future of humankind is in jeopardy. Tell them to prepare for a final war. Good luck and goodbye, Praut.'

'I assume Zheng's sent a final report to Earth via the comm-gauge wormhole,' asked Rubin.

'Let's assume he has. We'll never know,' answered Praut.

'Wait a mo. That alien armada hasn't opened fire yet,' Karl informed them. 'Why not?'

'Maybe they're waiting for us to surrender,' suggested Fanny.

There was no panic on the *Faust*, but the faces of the crew showed a lot of doom and gloom. They all thought their last moments had come. It was just a matter of waiting till the aliens opened fire—and then that would be that.

More time went by without the aliens opening fire. People looked puzzled and nervous at their stay of execution.

'Hallo, this is the flagship. Admiral Zheng here. We've just had contact from the aliens. The aliens inform us they have a new leader. The new alien leader is from a different planet and a different part of the hive, and was fundamentally at odds with the old leader's war objectives. He is against the old leader's policy of invading the Milky Way. He is asking for full and frank peace treaty negotiations and is waiting for my reply. I thought I should share this information with the fleet. Stand down, but be ready. We may have postponed the battle for a while. Zheng out.'

A huge sigh of temporary relief went through the *Faust*.

'Well, I'll be,' said Mes after hearing the announcement.

'No war...for the moment,' said Karl, half relieved and half disappointed. He'd been mentally preparing to meet his maker.

Olga sat in her seat and wept quietly with the release of tension. Fanny was with her holding her hand. She was almost in tears herself. Clay sat in shock at the turn of events.

Praut began pacing back and forth trying to think. 'Listen folks, we're not out of the woods yet,' he told them. 'Let's hope this works out, but be ready for anything.'

The hours dragged by with no word from the flagship. No vessels moved. All of the spaceships stayed where they were, waiting for a word from their leaders.

Finally the tannoy burst into life, 'Hallo, this is the flagship. Admiral Zheng speaking. I've just concluded my talks with Denat Zuhataum of the Zahuma and we've both decided its time for us to sign an Intergalactic Peace Treaty between the Zahuma and the humans. Our alien foe is called Zahuma. I'm to meet with Umber Aixiy shortly to finalise the signing ceremony. Umber means admiral in their parlance. Tomorrow before we depart for our own galaxy, we will sign the Intergalactic Peace Accord, ending the current conflict between our two races. I have been informed that the aliens, having a *hive* mentality, had assumed the human race wouldn't mind being chipped—it would make them part of the *hive*. We've explained to them that we are not a hive and do mind very much being forcibly chipped. They've apologised and promised to respect our individuality. Please stay where you are for the moment and stay tuned. Zheng out.'

'So, now we know what Umber means,' Clay said with satisfaction.

'Zahuma, eh? Now we have a name for them,' Rubin added.

‘Sheer nonsense that bit about us *not minding being chipped*. Hive my foot,’ Praut spat out. ‘Remember the missiles they fired at us...and the cloning labs we found on Lowry and Fourex? Must take us for fools. Mind you...interesting?’ Praut continued. ‘The old leader wanted war and this new leader wants peace.’

‘What’s so interesting about that?’ asked Rubin.

‘What happens when this new leader is swapped for another leader? Will it also want peace?’

‘Huh, you come out with the dandiest questions don’t you? We’ve just got peace and there you go trying to upset the applecart.’

‘Don’t you think the future of the human race deserves some pointed questions?’ asked Praut.

‘What’s the future of the human race got to do with this present peace?’ Rubin wanted to know. ‘Aren’t you happy with not being killed?’

‘Oh come on Dr Adam, use your brains. All we need for a repeat of this scenario is another ‘*old’* leader.’ Praut emphasised the *old* in such a sarcastic way as to leave no doubt in Rubin’s mind. ‘Who’s to say the next leader of the Zahuma is going to be benign. We can’t take chances with the future of our own race. We must prepare.’

‘What do you have in mind?’ Rubin asked, half expecting the answer he got.

‘When we get back home, the human race *must* begin an all out arms race with these aliens to ensure that humanity has the ability to survive in the long term. It’s the only sensible thing to do.’

# EPILOGUE

Reclining on his hover-loafer, squinting at the midday sun through piercing blue eyes, Praut felt his skin baking beyond wellbeing. His left hand searched for the controls but found another hand already there, fiddling with the controls.

'You beat me to it,' he admitted.

In the corner of his vision, he saw Fanny lying by his side, her flaming red hair delightfully set off by the flimsy green bikini she almost wore.

'It's just a bit too hot, don't you think?' she asked, while turning the holo-sun down a notch or two.

He noted the underbelly of his gondola lightly kissing the water as the airship bobbed gently in the southerly breeze. The blissful South Seas fantasy reconstructed on his holo-deck in his private quarters on the 999th floor of the Europa high-rise in Frankfurt was a dream.

The sea continued to calmly lap at the underbody of the oversized airship while his auto-chef was laying out a table for two in the gondola diner.

'If there's any calls from any Darhlburg executives,' he instructed his auto-sec, 'Tell them I'm out. I don't want to be disturbed.'

'Yes sir,' replied his auto-sec, ever compliant to his every whim.

## END

Other novels by Sasha Garrydeb

# Worlds Beyond Ours

Sasha Garrydeb

In the fourth millennium humans finally invent the warp-drive and set out to explore the Galaxy. The first mission is sent to our nearest star, Alpha Centauri, and the starship returns to a stormy acclaim by earth's population. It then comes as a shock to our planet when aliens visit earth and announce that the Galactic Federation intends to lift its quarantine around the Solar System. Since humans now have warp drive capability, would they like to join the Galactic Federation?

This story brings humanity for the first time into contact with a variety of alien life-forms when Earth's Embassies are sent to other worlds: elfin-like creatures, dinosauroids, insectoids, and many more. As the humans fan out from their home world, they encounter a number of adventures which shape humanity's future for generations to come. Wonders like floating cities in the sky, terraforming other planets and genetic advertising.

The story at the end comes full circle when it culminates in another first contact, but this time from our neighbouring galaxy for this Galactic Federation.

# The Wizard of Kalar

Sasha Garrydeb

On the distant planet of Kálar the two hundred year old life cycle of the Schánda once again menace the idyllic lives of the Bólani, a small tribal village of forest dwellers living in their hollowed Lándo trees.

The schánda stand half a cubit high, have a two hundred year life-cycle and normally live up on the northern edges of the tundra of the planet of Kálar. They are an insect, something like a cross between a spider and a scorpion. The adult form has no poisonous stinger and isn't carnivorous. Then the mating urge mutates the schánda into a massive swarm of ferocious carnivores. It doubles in size, grows the stinger and large claws in its fourth and final moult, then begins its long march from its home-ground in the North of Kálar, south to its mating grounds on the shores of the Golden Sea.

In its path live the small peaceful Bólani tribe who make their homes in living Lándo trees in the forest. Around the same time as the schánda begin their journey, the Bólani's collective unconscious, an imbedded memory of these carnivorous insects, triggers nightmares. They dream of an unstoppable carnivorous procession intent on eating their way to their mating grounds, heading their way.

The Bólani must gather their possessions and flee ahead of the encroaching swarm. They escape south to the shores of the Golden Sea just ahead of the voracious insects. Their long march to the shores of the Golden Sea takes them through a series of adventures with small blood sucking insects, vicious storms, predatory birds, unfriendly villages, lakes of volcanic lava, and desert worms. Only the skill of their apprentice wizard, Morác, saves them from disaster—transforming his powers in the process. Even when they reach the Golden Sea their problems are not at an end.

Imprisoned by a coastal tribe and then buffeted by storms on their flimsy rafts the dynamics of the tribe are changed forever before they finally manage to return to their small forest village back up in the far North.

This is an eco-fantasy tale stretching the imagination beyond the solar system.

# Murder in Hattusas

Sasha Garrydeb

Murder in Hattusas is the 1st Volume of the Hittite Trilogy.

At the close of the Old Kingdom in 1420 BC, the realm of the ancient Hittite Empire is in chaos. Muwatallis, the king has been assassinated in the capital, Hattusas, by the feared Kaska Assassin's Guild. Muwas, the dead king's brother blames the two sons of the previous king, Huzziyas, and he insists he be the one to succeed his brother. The two sons of Huzziyas, Kantuzzili and Himuili, insist the next king be Tudhaliyas, son of Himuili, since rewarding Muwatallis' previous assassination of Huzziyas, is unthinkable. Neither side is prepared to give way, and the scene is set for civil war. Tagrama, the High Priest of the temple of the Storm God Taru, tries to broker a peace, but is up against outright stubbornness.

Muwas then hires Harep, of the same Assassin's Guild, to kill Tudhaliyas. Only Mokhat, the former spiritual adviser to the Assassin's Guild, knows what Harep looks like, and he is determined to stop all the damnable assassinations. He's had enough of the Guild's murdering ways.

Muwas calls upon his Mittani allies, the Mittani King Saustatar, who sends his son Artatama with an army to Muwas' aid. The Kizzuwatna King Shunashura changes allegiance and abandons the Mittani in favour of Kantuzzili's faction, sending an army to help Tudhaliyas.

The Pharaoh Amenhotep II threatens to invade Mittani unless they pull their army out of Hatti. Saustatar refuses.

When Tudhaliyas meets Nikal, he falls for this daughter of the Kizzuwatna king. They announce their engagement. Harep, the hired assassin, makes a number of attempts on Tudhaliyas' life, but is foiled. The major Battle of the Wide Plateau settles the civil war but in the mean time, Harap manages to kidnap Nikal.

The protagonist, Mokhat, is in search of himself after his sordid ministrations to a bunch of murderers. It is a bronze-age thriller, which includes a romp through the Hittite landscape, a civil war, and chariots in battle. This is a tale of love and adventure set in the most fascinating recently discovered culture of the ancient world.

A must for all fans of the Hittite civilisation.

# Madduwatta's Rebellion

Sasha Garrydeb

This is the second volume of the Hittite Trilogy.

It has been three years since the Battle of the Wide Plateau put Tudhaliyas on the throne in the Hittite Empire, yet instead of feeling secure, he feels menaced. His chief spy, Satipilli, has vanished, and trouble is brewing in the west, possibly from Ahhiyawa. The Mittani are threatening Isuwa on the eastern border, seeking revenge for their humiliation in the civil war. All this requires reliable intelligence reports. Tudhaliyas is forced to turn to the unknown faces of Mokhat and Palaiyas and asks them to go to the west, to Millawanda, and discover what has happened to Satipilli, the chief spy of the Hittites.

On their journey, they are followed and someone keeps trying to kill them; with each failure, their attempts become more desperate. The assassins follow Mokhat and Palaiyas but are finally dissuaded; then they suddenly reappear in Khemet (Egypt). Somebody doesn't want them to complete their mission.

At the close of the Old Kingdom in 1417 BC, Madduwatta, the Governor of Lukka, a nominal vassal of Tudhaliyas, has plans of his own. How is he implicated in all this? He has his eyes on Arzawa. He badly needs friends, and will ally himself with anyone prepared to help him achieve his goal. But who has stirred him up? Who has gone to all these lengths to create a rebellion for the Hittites?

Meanwhile, Ahhiyawa is in the grip of a Civil War, with two brothers fighting it out for the throne in Millawanda. The outcome of the conflict will impact on their neighbours, Arzawa, the Hittites, and the Governor of Lukka.

Palaiyas, a Prince of Tiryns, decides to go home to make peace with his father, the king. While in Tiryns, he's abducted by his uncle, Elektryon, the king of Mycenae, and brought to account for his desertion; then forced to complete his tour of duty on Keftiu (Crete). Mokhat follows him and rescues him. After Khemet (Egypt), Ugarit, and Lukka, they finally discover the truth. Mokhat falls in love in this romp through the ancient Med, all in a search for Satipilli.

# Mittani Kidnapping

Sasha Garrydeb

This is the third volume of the Hittite Trilogy.

Ammuna, a disaffected senior Hittite General has had enough of the Hittite King's interference in his career and has sold himself to the Mittani Crown Prince Artatama for golden shekels. Worse, he's kidnapped King Tudhaliyas' 6 year old daughter, Princess Asmunikal, for those golden shekels.

It is now six years since the Battle of the Wide Plateau put Tudhaliyas on the throne (Vol 1—*Murder in Hattusas*), in the realm of the ancient Hittite Empire, and three years since Madduwatta's Rebellion was dismantled by Tudhaliyas, (Vol 2—*Madduwatta's Rebellion*), both times with Mokhat's help.

In this third volume of the Hittite trilogy, the reader is invited to participate in a seventeen-day pursuit from Hattusas to Nineveh, in a romp through the landscape of ancient Mesopotamia, when Mokhat's *special forces* chase rogue General Ammuna and his gang of mercenaries into the heart of Assyria, trying to rescue the kidnapped daughter of grief stricken King Tudhaliyas and his consort, Queen Nikal.

Tudhaliyas invades Mittani to force Artatama to release his daughter. The Kizzuwatna army is on the march, in support of the Hittite King, as is the Pharaoh, both allied to Hattusas by binding treaties. Cities allied to the Mittani come under attack one by one. There are catastrophic consequences for Artatama's father, King Saustatar of Mittani when a Hittite army appears on his doorstep. Has Artatama overstretched himself? Has his ambition become his downfall? Will the *special forces* rescue the princess?

www.ingramcontent.com/pod-product-compliance
Lightning Source LLC
LaVergne TN
LVHW020517100826
845148LV00010B/1258